THE DEMON AND THE FOX

Book Two of The Calatians

by Tim Susman

Argyll Productions
Dallas, Texas

The Demon and the Fox
Production copyright Argyll Productions © 2018

Copyright © Tim Susman 2018

Cover and interior artwork © Laura Garabedian 2018
http://www.FairyTalesWithTails.com

Published by Argyll Productions
Dallas, Texas
www.argyllproductions.com

ISBN 978-1-61450-426-9

First Edition Trade Paperback July 2018

CONTENTS

For Ned
Who has always been there

CHAPTER 1: THE CALYX

If you're going to search the ruins," Master Odden said, "you'll have to summon a demon."

Kip Penfold, the stout master's apprentice as of one week before, sat up straighter in the chair in Odden's office, his long bushy tail curling around one of the chair legs. "I can do it," he said.

Behind him in a copper brazier, a large lizard-like creature moved restlessly. Covered in black scales around which the bright red-gold of its nature showed in cracks, it radiated heat and an acrid smell of phosphorus that battled the autumn chill and smell of leaves that crept in through the shutters. Kip's position in front of the desk, between the brazier and the shutters, meant that his large triangular ears were warm and his fingertips cold. He preferred that, to be honest; the fox-Calatian's ears were most often cold this time of year, so it was pleasant to have them warmed. And he enjoyed sitting in Odden's office for two reasons. The first was that he almost always learned something new about sorcery when he sat before the broad oak desk. The second was that he had decided that one day, when he was a master sorcerer (when), he would have an office very like this, packed with old books and scrolls and knowledge, with a phosphorus elemental and a window that looked out from Prince George's College of Sorcery down Founder's Hill to the town of New Cambridge. And his friends Emily,

Malcolm, and Coppy would have nearby offices. Perhaps the outer buildings destroyed in the mysterious attack some six months before would be rebuilt by then, but Kip still loved the ancient White Tower, even with its cold stone, even living as he did currently in its damp, mold-infested basement.

Master Odden reached behind him to the large bookshelf and found a large tome by feel without taking his attention from Kip. "Wouldn't be teaching you if I thought you couldn't," he said, bringing it to his desk and flipping pages to the fourth in a dozen thin leather bookmarks. "In the interest of not having three or four demons floating wildly about, you're going to watch me do the spell first."

Kip's large ears flattened down from their upright position. "What could an unbound demon do?" he asked. "I mean, are there limits on their powers?"

"Demons can apply their will to bend reality as they see fit," Odden recited absently, his finger moving down the page. "First order demons like Burkle have little power to do anything more than what Burkle does: clean floors, move desks. They could be a nuisance if unbound but more likely would return home quickly. Second order are more powerful and can affect people, though rarely permanently. Third order are used in war. It was a third-order demon that froze Napoleon's commanders at Waterloo."

He paused at that, and Kip nodded, trying to see the words on the page, but the writing was tiny and the contrast not strong enough for his eyes to make out. "I've seen the re-creation, sir."

"Many of the wars of the last hundred years have been strategic application of third-order demons and fights between them. Third order demons have particular affinities, so not all of them would be able to freeze fifty soldiers, or burn an entire town. Ah, here we are."

Odden's finger stopped at a name, which he copied with his other hand onto a scroll and slid across the table. "Pronounce that."

Kip took the paper and held it to the lamp. "Nikolon?"

"Knee," Odden said. "Nee-koh-lahn."

Kip tried again, and this time Odden gave a quick nod of approval. Kip returned the paper to the desk. "Isn't there a fourth order of demons?"

"Mm, yes." Odden closed the book. "But it takes an enormous amount of power and discipline to bind one even for a handful of minutes." He stood. "We suspect it was a fourth order demon that destroyed the college."

Kip stood hurriedly, clasping his paws together. He wanted to ask what that would look like, the fury of the most powerful order of demons unleashed on four simple brick buildings and a hundred sorcerers and apprentices. He had only heard the noise of it, rolling down the hill on a warm spring night like thunder, and now the crushed and broken buildings were hidden below wood and canvas tents to all eyes save for demons.

As Odden replaced the first book and took down a second, Kip asked, "Are the names of the fourth-order demons also in that book?"

"They are, which is why this book is not in the library but remains under my care."

"What about when you're not here?"

"The book is well protected." The sorcerer opened the second book to the summoning and binding spells, on facing pages, and turned it toward Kip.

"But—"

"It is not your concern." Odden's large, pale hand gestured toward the tome, "The summoning of demons is. Now, recite the spells."

The first spell bore enough similarities to the elemental summoning spell that Kip had found it easy to memorize. Rather than asking any of the other questions clamoring in his mind, he asked, "Sir, why does it take more power to summon demons than elementals?"

"Hm, yes." Odden leaned back and gazed past Kip to the brazier. "Elementals wish to move around. They are simple spirits—you will have noticed—who grow bored as easily in their home sphere as they do here. Reaching out to them, you provide a conduit for them to go somewhere interesting. Demons are spirits of a different sphere, and understand very well what a summons from a sorcerer means: binding and work."

The phosphorus elemental in the brazier, who had introduced itself to Kip as Benny, now peered over the lip of the brazier with curious, ember-bright eyes. "Who's got home spheres?" he demanded in a high-pitched crackle. "We got a Flower, that's all."

Kip turned to smile at Benny. "The Flower's at the center of the sphere," he said. "You just can't see the edges because you never go far enough from it."

"Why would we?" Benny shifted, making a clanking noise in the brazier.

Odden tapped the book. "Penfold, focus on the lesson."

So Kip recited the spell again, slowly and then faster, and then they moved on to the binding spell. "This is the more difficult and important of the two," Odden said. "An unbound demon can inflict any kind of pain on a sorcerer, from a minor itching curse to a lifelong affliction. They usually stop short of killing, but they have left sorcerers and other people so crippled that they choose death soon after."

"Why wouldn't they kill us?" Kip asked.

"We do not know. Our bound demons, when asked why they will not kill sorcerers, say only that they have not been ordered to, and unbound demons are not inclined to answer questions. Now attend; this is the most important thing: simply because you have summoned a demon does not mean you can bind it. The binding more than the summoning requires a calyx to enhance the sorcerer's power. Therefore you will use only the names of demons researched by previous sorcerers, whose power is known. Summoning an unknown demon puts you at great risk, and unless you become a demon researcher, you should never resort to that."

Kip nodded, his eyes drifting up to the tome with all the bookmarks in it. "Where do the names come from?"

"Old manuscripts, from the Greeks and Romans and Carthaginians, and some older than that even. If you care to study the history of demons, Florian will allow you access to the library's books on the subject. Now, the binding spell."

After another hour of recitation of both spells, Odden got to his feet. "Very well, you are at least as prepared as I was for my first lesson. Go to the cupboard there and bring out the items you will find on the top shelf."

The tall, narrow cupboard stood as high as Odden; the taller fox reached the top shelf with ease. "Careful," the sorcerer said as Kip's paw found a pewter goblet and then the handle of a narrow silver knife. His fur prickled as he lifted the weight of the knife and drew its blade out into the light. Perhaps, he thought desperately, it was only symbolic.

He turned with them in his paws to see his master stopped, one hand on the handle of his office door. He huffed out a breath. "There are, er, preparations that must be done."

"All right." It took a moment for Kip to realize what he meant, and by the time the door was opening onto the outer room of Odden's office, Kip knew what he was going to see.

On one of the beds sat a Calatian, a short dormouse in a linen tunic and trousers. Kip knew him, but not well: Jacob Thomas, whose son Matthew was two years younger than Kip and now worked the Thomas family farm. Behind him stood Master Patris, the school's headmaster, arms folded under his thick white beard. "We're ready," Odden said.

Staring at his feet, Jacob rose and shuffled past Odden and then Kip into the room. Patris followed him at a slow pace, closing the door behind them. As Jacob made his way to the chair Kip had been sitting in, the headmaster pushed him to one side and took the chair.

Odden said, "Stay there, Penfold."

Kip hadn't moved, still leaning against the desk. He set down the goblet and knife for Odden to pick up and curled his tail around his legs as his master took them to the other side of the desk where Jacob stood. His father, who had been a calyx for all of Kip's life, had never told him what happened in that private ritual between sorcerer and Calatian. All Kip knew, vaguely, was that more powerful magics required the participation of a Calatian, of any species. He had also never been told that the headmaster had to attend calyx rituals, but as Patris's eyes didn't leave Kip, he suspected he knew the explanation for that.

Jacob remained still, staring down at his feet, his tail limp. Odden set the pewter goblet on the desk, keeping the knife in his hand. Kip knew that his father had survived many calyx rituals without being killed, but something primal in him wanted to leap across the desk and knock the knife away. He kept seeing the knife plunge into Jacob's neck, no matter how strongly he told himself that Odden wasn't going to do that. To control his anxiety, he turned aside, and there met the eyes of Patris, expectant, even hungry for his reaction.

This, oddly, helped. Turning aside had been a weakness and Patris had seen it, and Kip hated that. His desire to confound Patris flooded him, more immediate than his fear for Jacob; it allowed him to turn back and watch the ritual with the confidence that Odden would not stab Jacob. Indeed, the sorcerer turned the knife so the edge rather than the point faced the dormouse. The silver blade held Kip's eyes as Odden seized the dormouse's paw and with a series of quick scrapes exposed the skin on the bend in his left elbow. Jacob took the goblet in his right paw, held it under the bare spot, and then turned his head to his left.

Odden, with his back to Kip, turned the dormouse's arm and then pushed the point of the silver knife into the skin.

Blood pushed past the knife and dripped down into the cup. Jacob's eyes squeezed closed but Kip's remained open. He forced himself to remain outwardly calm even as the sharp tang of blood reached his nose through the haze of phosphorus, aware of Patris's scrutiny. "You must be careful," Odden said in a toneless voice. "This is where the vein is closest to the skin, but push too deeply and you may pierce the artery. If blood gushes rather than trickles, press the wound closed and call Master Splint immediately."

Numb, Kip nodded, though his attention was on the vessel that was gathering the blood. Just because it was a goblet didn't mean it was for drinking. Maybe they had to hold it, to touch cloth or fingers to it.

After a time, Jacob lifted his head to the sorcerer. Odden shook his head. "A little more this time," he said.

An eternity later, it seemed to Kip, Odden wiped the knife clean with a stained cloth and then, as Jacob placed the goblet on the corner of the sorcerer's desk, dropped the cloth onto the dormouse's wound. Jacob pressed his fingers there and waited.

"That's enough for now," Odden said. "Thank you, Thomas."

The dormouse stood, still holding the cloth to his arm. Kip waited for Patris to get up, to leave, but when the headmaster remained still, the fox strode to the door and opened it. Jacob walked through without a word of acknowledgment, his thin tail dragging on the ground behind him.

At the thunk of the door closing, Odden cleared his throat. "Your father never told you."

Kip shook his head. Keeping his tail and ears calm was taking all his energy; he felt he couldn't spare any to speak. Patris had turned, rested an arm over the back of the chair so he could watch the fox, and Kip was determined not to give him anything he was hoping for.

"That's good. That's what we instruct. But you never know when families choose to, ah, you know, parents feel they must warn their children."

Kip swallowed against the lump in his throat. The smell of blood refused to dispel in the still air of the office. "No."

"The magic that made Calatians," Odden slipped again into a recitation, "remains in their blood. Though it does not allow them to access magic any more easily..." Here he touched a finger to the goblet and interrupted himself, with a look at Patris. "Hm."

"I don't..." Kip cleared his throat. "I don't know any other Calatians besides Coppy who can cast magic."

"No. And Lutris is not as proficient as you are." The master lifted his hand. "The blood of the Calatians does help a sorcerer focus and reach more magical energy when ingested."

Of course it was ingested. He tried desperately not to picture his father bleeding into a mug.

"The effects last only for a short time. A swallow is sufficient to summon a demon of the first order, and that's all we will be working with now."

We? Patris's presence felt even more sinister now. He was going to watch Kip drink Calatian blood.

Odden's hand rested on the pewter mug. "We will recite the spell several times until you are confident in it. I will drink and cast the spell first. You will attend, then you will drink and cast the spell with the name I give you. Is that clear?"

"But—"

Odden opened his mouth, but Patris spoke first. "Penfold, if you will not follow your master's most basic instructions, we can bring an end to this relationship."

By expelling him from the college, of course; Patris's meaning was clear. Kip swallowed. "Yes, sir."

Patris nodded back to Odden as though he'd rendered the other sorcerer a service, and Kip's master spoke again. "There is much you do not know or understand." He picked up the goblet of blood and moved to the empty dais in the center of his office. The movement brought a fresh wave of the smell to Kip's nose, but he managed not to flinch. "I shall speak the spells slowly so you may follow along," Odden said. "Binding first and then the summoning."

When he'd summoned the phosphorus elementals, Kip had only spoken the summoning spell because he hadn't been sure it would work, and had had to hurriedly bind his elemental before it set the whole basement ablaze. He focused on that memory as Odden took his first drink. When he set the goblet down on the desk, red smears remained around his lips.

Kip breathed a little easier when the sorcerer wiped his face with a cloth. He perked his ears, trying to ignore the smell and Patris's presence as Odden walked around the desk to the work area. The fox came to stand beside his master as the sorcerer recited the binding spell and tied it to the summoning.

When he finished the summoning spell, the air in front of his hands shimmered and a strong tingle like peppermint oil assailed Kip's nostrils. The fox had learned to associate that sensation with the presence of a demon, but had only told his friends at the school that he possessed this ability. Fortunately Odden didn't notice the fox's nose wrinkling, his attention fixed on the summoned demon, who materialized as a stout young man with pale skin and coal-black curly hair, thick enough almost to make him modest despite his lack of clothes. Between his legs, though, a scaly green serpent emerged from the thatch of hair and looked about the room with glossy black eyes.

"Clothe yourself so as to conceal your form from chest to knees, Eichann," Odden said, bored, and a moment later the serpent and much of the demon's body vanished beneath a dirty white toga wrapped around his waist and over one shoulder. The demon's expression didn't change.

"You must always command demons very precisely, Penfold." Patris turned his chair to face the demon.

Odden frowned, half-turning toward the headmaster before he stopped himself. "Yes. Had I simply ordered Eichann to clothe himself, he might have donned a single sock, or a cap."

"Yes, sir." Kip kept his voice low, hoping that Odden would hear and perhaps Patris might not. He knew this about demons, because when Kip had tried to gain admission to apply to the college, the demon guarding the gates had also been maddeningly precise in his interpretation of his orders.

"I only wish to please," Eichann said in a thick Celtic brogue.

"Of course you do. You also hope that this pathetic display will cause me to lose concentration and thereby unbind you. Penfold, would you care to dismiss him?"

The demon's eyes lit up as he took in the fox. "Oh, no calyx this, eh?"

"And don't speak to demons, except to order them," Patris said from his chair. "It can provide no benefit."

"Don't cast such aspersions on my conversation," Eichann said.

"Quiet, Eichann," Odden ordered, and the demon stopped talking.

"But..." Kip stopped himself, remembering his master's previous objection, but this time Odden did not interrupt him. "Sir, the time I learned to summon elementals, I talked to them to gain an understanding of what their home looked like. I've talked to Burkle—a little—and from your text I have an idea of what to reach for, but if I might ask Eichann a question?"

"As Patris has said, asking questions of demons is rarely fruitful. They perceive truth subjectively, so ordering them to tell only the truth restricts them only to telling the truth as they see it, which can be anything. I have heard demons claim that our world is but a dream in the mind of the greatest of demons, I have heard them play on a sorcerer's sympathy by claiming to be pained by the binding and even that they were once human, I have heard them claim that, ahem, inappropriate physical contact with a demon's corporeal form can grant you the demon's powers, and so on."

At this last one, Odden looked away from Kip. The fox suspected that perhaps Odden had directly experienced the disproof of that one, but did not feel inclined to ask. "No other sorcerer has learned sorcery in the way I have," he said. "So perhaps none has asked the questions I would like to. Can it hurt to try?"

"It can waste all of our time." Patris spoke up with a sneer.

Odden, if he heard, ignored the headmaster. "Suit yourself. Eichann, you will answer the questions of Penfold as fully and truthfully as you can."

The demon's face took on a slightly mocking cast as he turned to Kip, attentive. Kip faced him and said, "How does your home smell?"

"Home?" Eichann said. "I have no home, and therefore it has the smell of absence, of nonexistence, of void."

"The place where you are summoned from." Kip kept his composure. "What does it smell like?"

"Ah, well, everyone smells differently, do they not? You with your fox's nose may smell the memory of pine where I smell only the dog lying on the wooden bench."

"What does it smell like to you, then?" Kip asked.

"To me? To me it smells like magic and decay, the thick power in corruption and rot. Magic swirls like a tide around us and each demon has his individual scent of power, the greatest of maelstroms and the least of eddies. Imagine the smell of a boneyard if each corpse contained within seeped magic to the surface rather than putrefaction."

Patris made a noise of exasperation. Odden raised a hand. "Enough." To Kip, he said, "You see what I mean about talking to demons. Smell of magic, indeed. Please banish him now."

"Indeed," Kip murmured. As he gathered magic and the familiar purple glow rose around his paws to match the power in him, he stopped before speaking the spell. "Do I not need…enhancement?" He kept his muzzle level with Odden's black hair, ignoring the smell in his nose and the gleam of pewter.

"You shouldn't, for Eichann. But if you find your power insufficient, we can try again with the calyx."

No. He would be sufficient. He raised his paws and recited the banishment spell he'd learned, focusing the power of the words on the demon in front of him as he spoke its name.

Magic crackled through his fur, left him in the form of the spell, and then Eichann vanished, taking with him the tingle in Kip's nostrils.

Odden's hand stroked his beard. "Well done," he said, though quietly and with a reservation that raised Kip's hackles. Hadn't he cast the spell perfectly the first time? "Now you try a summoning."

The pewter goblet sat on the desk like a demon itself, one Kip could not banish with a spell. "Sir," he said, "since I was able to—"

"Drink, Penfold," Odden ordered. "All of what remains."

He had to walk past Patris to pick up the goblet, and the white-maned headmaster's eyes never left him. His paw shook slightly as he grasped it; he hoped the headmaster hadn't seen that. Kip steeled himself, faced Odden, and raised the blood to his lips.

He held his breath so the smell wouldn't overwhelm him, but the warmth and taste were nearly as bad. It wasn't that the taste was objectionable; it was that the blood tasted like raw meat but with a sharp bitterness to it that Kip could only associate with the person it had come from. He gagged, but forced himself to swallow.

"Now," his master said, handing him a cloth, "you should feel stronger when gathering magic. Prepare the binding spell and then summon Nikolon."

Kip wiped his muzzle. Ignoring his stomach, which threatened to revolt, he focused on his feet on the stone floor, one step and then another back toward Master Odden and the work area, putting Patris at his back, though not out of his mind. One deep breath, two, and then he stood next to his master and pulled magic into his paws again.

The process did not feel much different than it had before, though perhaps it was easier to gather magic. This time was nothing like the rush of magic he'd gotten the first time he'd touched the walls of the White Tower, when he'd heard a voice in his head say *Fox?* and had levitated himself in a panic to get rid of the magic. There was a stronger urge to cast a spell now than he was used to, but not much stronger; that was the main difference he felt.

"Your magic looks stronger." Odden gestured to the purple glow around Kip's paws, brighter than before. "Cast the spell."

The words of the binding spell were the same he'd learned before, and the feeling of it was the same as the one he'd used to bind the phosphorus elemental. He created the spell, an empty cage, and then he spoke the words of the summoning. As he spoke, he called to his memory the image of a boneyard and imagined himself standing there with the sharp peppermint sting in his nostrils stronger than he'd ever felt it in real life. Imaginary Kip reached down into the soil and said the name: "Nikolon."

The air in the office shimmered; the tingle burst into Kip's nostrils again with the appearance of an olive-skinned slender woman, as naked as Eichann had been, but without any monstrous substitutions in her anatomy. When she saw Kip, her eyes widened, and in a moment her form changed to that of a naked female fox-Calatian, her breasts flattening, russet and white fur sprouting all over her body, a bushy tail growing from just over her buttocks, and her Roman features replaced with the narrow muzzle, black ears, and slit-pupiled yellow eyes of a fox. "What a surprise," she purred.

Behind them, Patris made a choked noise. "Hold the binding, Penfold," Odden said. The master's eyes had widened. "Well done."

"I've got it." Nikolon—wasn't that a male name?—struggled at the binding magically even as her fingers explored the furred curves of her body, but Kip's will and power kept her in place easily.

"They let you cast magic now?" Nikolon took a step toward Kip. "The world is changing."

"Stop," he ordered her, and she froze every muscle, those yellow eyes still fixed on his.

"That is a good command to use," Odden said, just as Nikolon took another step. "However, you did not specify for how long to stop."

"Do not come closer than two feet from me," Kip said, and then quickly added, "and do not move farther than five feet from me."

Nikolon stopped outside the two-foot boundary and rested a black paw on her white midriff, teasing the fingers through the fur there. "This form is rather delightful," she said. "I can see what you like about it."

"I was born with it," Kip said.

"But," Nikolon continued, "it must get dreadfully warm. And dirty." Small hairs drifted from her fingers to the ground, but vanished before they could touch the stone.

"The usual command," Odden murmured. "Even though you mean to dismiss her immediately."

Kip nodded and recited. "Make no move save on my order; speak no word save on my order; exert no power save on my order."

Nikolon straightened and composed herself, perfectly attentive.

"Excellent," Odden said, and though Kip appreciated the praise, he felt ill. Here was a demon, yes, but in the form of a Calatian, bound to do his bidding, summoned with the blood he could still taste on his tongue. *It's not a living creature*, he told himself, and yet the commanded obedience still rankled with him. The thought crossed his mind that this was what humans felt like, and he shook his head to dismiss it. Even slaves could not be commanded so completely, and Calatians were not slaves.

So he gathered magic again and spoke the dismissal spell, and just as Eichann had done, Nikolon vanished, taking with her the sharp smell of demons.

"Very good, Penfold," Odden said.

"You're not to summon any demons save on the order of a master." Patris had stood, Kip could tell from the elevation of his voice.

"I was getting to that, Patris." Kip's master took a breath. "You will of course use this spell only under my supervision or order."

"Yes, sir," Kip said.

"Then I think that is enough for today."

Kip hoped that Patris would remain behind when he left Odden's office, but the headmaster followed him out. "You seemed remarkably untroubled by the ritual," the sorcerer said once they were out in the hallway. "Did your father really tell you nothing about it in the nineteen years up to now?"

"Nothing," Kip said. "I swear it."

Patris remained uncomfortably close to Kip in the narrow hallway. He smelled of laundry soap and sweat, of suppressed fear. "You understand the necessity of it?"

"Yes, sir."

"You understand that your apprenticeship was made over my objection and continues to exist on my sufferance that you abide strictly and completely by the rules of the College?"

"As I expect all apprentices must, yes, sir," Kip said.

"Good." Patris strode ahead and Kip let him gain distance. At the stairs, though, the headmaster turned. "And do not forget that you, too, have now participated in the ritual."

He stomped up the stairs with a determined tread. Kip leaned against the wall for a moment and then hurried down, the taste of Jacob's blood still coppery in his mouth and nose.

CHAPTER 2: THE FIGHT

Kip's indecision over whether to tell his friends about the calyx ritual lasted all of four minutes once they were again all together in the basement. "They drink the blood of Calatians!" he said, pacing back and forth through the old papers and dusty stone floor.

Coppy, the otter-Calatian who'd also become an apprentice, didn't react with the horror Kip had hoped. "I thought it might be something like that," he said.

"You never said. We talked about it for months!"

"I know." Coppy rested a paw on Kip's arm. "Didn't want to upset you. People do horrible things to Calatians in London and I heard summat about blood when I was a cub there."

Kip's tail lashed back and forth. "I wish you'd told me."

"I couldn't." Coppy squeezed his forearm. "It was your dad. If he wouldn't tell you, 'twasn't my place."

"You don't have to protect me all the time," Kip said.

The otter lifted his paw and rubbed at his whiskers. "But I really didn't know for sure. Why start trouble with rumours?"

"Now we know, though." Emily Carswell, a young woman in her early twenties, sat outside a cleared half-circle against one wall, in which a phosphorus elemental waited. She picked up a sheet of old paper, crumpled it, and tossed it to the lizard. "It's revolting. I won't drink blood."

"If you want to summon a demon, you will," Kip said. "Or if you want to perform any other strong magic."

"That's ridiculous," Emily said. "Calyxes weren't even around for three of the Great Feats. So how were they cast?"

"You can't cast a Great Feat every time you want to summon a demon." Leaning against the door to the basement, Malcolm O'Brien folded his arms and smiled. The Irishman's black hair hung into his green eyes, but he made no effort to brush it away. "Might as well bring down a barn to kill a mouse, my da used to say."

"Tch." Emily held out her hands to the glowing lizard. "There's got to be a way."

"Aye, and all the sorcerers simply prefer to bind themselves to Calatians, drinking blood to do magic. Much easier than this other way."

"They'd never had a woman or Calatian sorcerer, either," Emily said. "It's an age of new things." She turned to Kip. "You didn't have to drink any of the blood, did you?"

Kip flattened his ears and stared fixedly at Neddy, the phosphorus elemental. "Oh, Kip," Emily said.

"Sure, and what would you do?" Malcolm asked. "If your master orders you to?"

"Patris was there." Kip lowered his voice. "He made it clear—again—that if there's something I don't wish to do, I need only tell him and he'll be all too pleased to end my association with the College."

Emily tried to recover from her earlier scolding tone. "Isn't he supposed to be having lessons with Adamson?"

"Oh." Coppy adopted a snooty voice. "I'm certain Master Adamson can teach himself quite well, thank you."

They all chuckled, the tension broken, and Kip smiled gratefully at the otter. "How was your lesson with Windsor?"

Coppy's broad, whiskered muzzle turned up to his. "Well," he said, "I didn't have to drink any blood, so I suppose it was better than yours that way. Not in any others though."

"I thought he'd be easier on you now you're his apprentice," Malcolm said.

"Hah." Emily tossed her head. "You don't know him at all."

"Not as well as you," Malcolm agreed. "Aye, if these masters weren't teaching us sorcery, it'd hardly be worth doing these lessons at all."

"So, Kip." Emily pointedly gave him her full attention. "What are you going to do?"

Coppy, too, shifted on the floor, and Kip felt the weight of the otter's stare. "I…I have to become a sorcerer, right? That's the only way I'll be able to change anything. Get more Calatians admitted, find an alternative to calyxes…"

"Ha." Malcolm raised an eyebrow. "Next to that, mucker, finding out who destroyed the college will be easy."

"One thing at a time." Kip returned Malcolm's smile with a little difficulty. He'd drunk enough water to kill the taste of blood in his mouth, but the memory was more difficult to dispel.

"Who was it?" Coppy asked.

"Jacob Thomas. The dormouse."

"Oh, aye." Coppy rubbed his whiskers thoughtfully.

"One of your friends in town, or less so?" Emily asked.

Kip shook his head. "I don't know that he cared what I was doing. I didn't even know he was a calyx until today."

Malcolm uncrossed his arms and stepped forward into the basement. "Didn't think you'd many friends left in town."

"He's still betrothed," Emily reminded him.

"Oh, aye, but that's not quite friendship, is it?" Malcolm grinned at Kip. "Good job she wasn't the calyx, eh?"

Kip shuddered. "She's too young, and I don't know any calyxes who were women."

"There was Bridget Markham," Coppy said.

"Oh?"

The otter nodded. "Your father mentioned her once. And there were some back home in London as well. Not common, but not unknown."

"Then I'm glad it wasn't her as well." Kip sighed. "That might have ended the engagement permanently."

"What are you meant to do with a demon, then?" Malcolm sat on the other side of Kip from Coppy and Emily, and Kip lowered himself to the ground as well, curling his tail over his leg so it wouldn't rest on the dusty paper.

"Investigate the ruins. The Masters have already looked for any elemental traces left behind, but Master Odden wants me to send a demon down there and search more thoroughly for any clue. He thinks it was demons and not elementals anyway."

"Demons wouldn't leave traces, would they?"

Kip shrugged, and Emily replied, "That's what he's going to find out."

"Sounds like grim work," Malcolm said as Coppy rested a paw on Kip's.

"It's all right." Kip sighed.

In the ensuing silence, Emily cleared her throat. "Kip, Coppy, I've got news as well. I don't think it'll make up for your day, but…my old teacher from Boston sent me a letter today."

"There was mail?"

She nodded quickly and held up a piece of folded paper. "Nothing for you. Sorry. But Master Hobstone said that he and some other sorcerers have been meeting with the independence movement."

"The rebels, you mean."

Her expression soured. "It sounds dirty when you say it that way."

Kip shared a look with Malcolm. "They're hoping to rebel against the Empire, aren't they?"

"They'd like to achieve independence by peaceful means."

"Which is why they're recruiting sorcerers?"

Emily read from the paper. "'We sincerely hope that we may enact a peaceful separation from our Mother Country, to lay claim to the rights that should be ours as native-born citizens of the American colonies, but should London resist, we must needs be prepared for a battle.'"

"They'll get a battle." Kip rested a paw on Coppy's arm as the otter opened his spell book and silently recited spells.

"I don't see how you can admire John Adams and not have at least a small amount of interest in independence." Emily set the paper down. "They want to begin a new country here."

"What do they want with me?" Kip asked, to forestall an argument.

"Master Hobstone asks if I would talk to any of the new apprentices, 'but most especially either of the two excellent Calatians.'"

"Why us?" Coppy didn't look up.

"He doesn't say."

Kip exhaled. "Patris has already warned me about talking to the rebels."

"Independence movement."

"He doesn't care what I *call* them." The fox shoved a pile of paper across the half-circle boundary on the floor, and Neddy leapt on it, incinerating the entire thing in a blast of heat. "If he thinks I'm going to rebel against the Empire, he'll expel me faster than Neddy took care of that paper."

Emily tossed her head so that her shoulder-length brown hair flared out before settling down again. "It won't hurt you to simply talk to them. Either of you."

"Aye," Malcolm said. "I'm certain Master Windsor will be much more forgiving than Patris."

Coppy flinched at the name. "I'd rather not," he said, and returned to his spell studies.

"Why are you so interested in them?" Kip asked Emily, squeezing Coppy's arm.

She fluttered the paper in her hand, then set it down next to her spell book. "Because Master Hobstone took me seriously. He taught me enough to get admitted here and I owe him at least the courtesy of passing along his request."

"And now you've asked me and Coppy," Kip said.

Emily opened her spell book and stared down at it as though she were reading, but after a few minutes she said, "If you really want to find a new way, you've got to step off the path eventually." Nobody answered, but Kip folded his paws in his lap, thinking about Jacob Thomas.

"It might not be so bad," Coppy whispered to him that night, as they lay side by side on their bedrolls. "Talking to the independence people, I mean. Maybe we could learn sorcery somewhere else."

"Here and London are where the best sorcerers are," Kip replied, paws laced behind his head as he stared up at the ceiling. There was enough light from Neddy's glow in the dim basement for his eyes to pick out patterns in the stone, and after months of sleeping here, he knew them well. "The ones in Boston are the ones rejected by the colleges. What are they going to teach us?"

Coppy hesitated. "Magic without calyxes? Like Emily said?"

The word brought back the coppery taste to Kip's mouth and the desire to go find his father and ask why he hadn't shared that knowledge with Kip. He forced both down. "If they don't have calyxes, they can't summon demons, and if they can't summon demons, they'll lose any war they start with the Empire." Odden's book, page after page of powerful demon names, danced before his eyes. "And if sorcerers didn't need calyxes, what would happen to New Cambridge?"

"People wouldn't…" Coppy paused. "It's not just the sorcerers they fear."

"No," Kip said.

"The Church says we're people."

"And Farley Broadside, good churchgoer, has taken note of that?"

Coppy's large chest rose and fell. "The world's not made of Farleys."

"No, but they live in it."

"I suppose." Coppy turned onto his side, away from Kip. "I'd like to believe there's more good people than bad."

"Me too," Kip said.

"As long as the good people stay together, we'll do okay."

"I have to stay in this college." Kip clenched his fists and stared up at the ceiling, lit with flickers of Neddy's light. "Whatever it takes. When I'm a full sorcerer, then I can worry about the rest of it."

"I understand why you can't talk to them," the otter said softly. "But if Patris were not here, if there were no risk, would you want to? For the chance to create something that's never before been seen?"

It was difficult to imagine the College without Patris. Kip spoke after several seconds of considering his words. "Perhaps."

"Didn't you say you wanted to perform a Great Feat? Maybe it doesn't have to be a magical one."

The otter's positive assurance eased the pressure in Kip's chest. It was a good thought, and he stored it away for a future time when he might make use of it. "Thanks," Kip said, and reached out to clasp Coppy's paw.

For a moment they lay in silence, until the otter spoke again. "Did you summon a demon?"

Kip lay and stared up for the length of time it took him to trace one line from the relative brightness over the phosphorus elemental to where it met the wall on the other side. "Yes."

"Good," Coppy said.

Searching the ruins would take time, so over the next few days Kip had to practice not only summoning and binding, but holding demons for long periods of time. Master Odden had him keep a demon bound while studying history books, and then while casting easy physical magic spells, and then while casting spells that required more concentration.

Through all of this, he maintained the binding on Neddy, but that drew very little of his energy and none of his focus. Unlike the phosphorus elemental, Nikolon fought whenever Kip cast a spell, at the times his magic reserve was weakest, and once managed to break the fox's binding. Kip was ready, though, and even as Master Odden was casting his spell, Kip cast it as well and re-bound the demon.

"It's important you know what it feels like when a demon escapes the binding," Odden said as Kip picked the prickly burrs out of his fur that the demon had cast there, "and you will not be summoning dangerous demons for quite a while yet."

It was fortunate that Patris had given up supervising Kip's lessons after that first one, or Kip was sure the headmaster would have had much more to say about Kip making the exact mistake every apprentice (so Odden told him) made in the course of this learning. Additionally, each of the lessons began with the uncomfortable calyx ritual, but without Patris in the room Kip found it easier to endure. For his own peace of mind, he tried to drink less and less of the calyx's blood every time, to see whether there was a point at which he would no longer be able to summon a demon. If there was, he did not find it in those two weeks that concluded the first month of his apprenticeship.

At dinner in the outdoors dining tent, Kip and his friends talked about the work they'd been doing in the afternoons with their masters. Emily's master, Argent, had been focusing strongly on her translocational magic, and by the end of the first month felt that perhaps in as little as another week she would be ready to transport herself. "It's all in the memory of the place," she said. "I'm very excited to go home to Boston and show off to Mother."

"I don't see why you couldn't summon elementals." Kip cut a piece of the cheese they'd been provided and paired it with a hunk of bread. "It's mostly a matter of knowing the place they come from."

"But it's not a real place," she pointed out. "How am I supposed to know how I feel there?"

"You imagine it." He ate the bread and cheese and then tapped his nose. "Smell works for me."

"Far better than for the rest of us." Malcolm sat beside Kip and across from Coppy. "Master Vendis says I'm not to try summoning anything until Easter at the earliest."

"You're too good at locking doors and keeping things out," Kip said. "What about you, Coppy? You haven't said a word about your work with Windsor."

The otter chewed his apple thoughtfully. "It's all physical work, you know. Same thing we did all last year. I'll be doing it until I get it right, I suppose." He put the apple down. "So sometime next year perhaps."

"You'll get it before then." Kip smiled. "You're smart enough. But you should ask him about summoning water elementals, or doing water alchemy."

"I miss the water." Coppy said. "But if I can't keep five rocks in the air at once, how am I supposed to focus on water elementals or water alchemy?"

"I can summon fire elementals and demons, but I can't translocate," Kip said. "Malcolm can't do either but he's getting really good at blocking magic. Look, now that we can practice without supervision, let's just all look at our books and see if anything appeals to you."

"We tried that before." But the otter's objection was quiet and Emily spoke over it quickly.

"That sounds like a marvelous idea," she said. "And if nothing calls to you, then we'll pick a spell you want to know and you'll start learning it."

Coppy nodded and then turned toward the back of the tent, where Farley Broadside and Victor Adamson sat around their table. Since the Selection where over half the students had been sent to the road crews, the military, or simply dropped from the school for lack of talent, the dining tent had become even more set in its seating pattern. In the other back corner, away from Farley and Adamson, sat Jacob Quarrel and Matthew Chesterton, the only other two apprentices. Though the tent seemed quiet, Kip and his friends knew that a fight was always one or two provocations away, and often the fox's acute hearing let him eavesdrop on Farley's plans to start one, giving him and his friends an edge.

This evening, the stout bully and the slender blond boy sat with heads down, paying little attention to Kip and his friends. Still, Coppy gave Kip a questioning look, so the fox focused his ears in that direction.

"They're not talking about us." He kept his voice low. "They're talking about Adamson's research."

"That's good." Malcolm shot the back table a scornful look. "Maybe he can gather his research if he can't gather any magic."

"What's he researching?" Emily asked.

"Can't tell." Kip flicked his ears. "He's talking about a book he read that had a spell in it he wants to try."

"If he does find a way to cast magic," Malcolm said in a lower, more serious voice, "look out."

"He already has a way to cast magic." Kip squared his shoulders and lowered his brow, chewing with his muzzle open in an imitation of Farley.

The motion caught the stout boy's attention. He looked up and squinted at them. "Hey," he called. "If the lady wants a kiss, she can ask me herself."

Malcolm barked a laugh and Coppy's paws tightened into fists, but Emily sliced a piece of bread calmly. "If he's waiting for that, he'll be an old man before he's done waiting."

"Kip's summoning demons," Coppy called over to the table. "Did you know that?"

Kip reached across the table to grab Coppy's paw as Farley's eyes narrowed. "What are you doing?" he hissed.

The otter wrested his paw away. "I want him to know what we can do so he'll leave us alone."

"That won't work!" Kip cried, but Farley was already standing.

"Demons, huh? Something worse than what he already looks like?"

"Something powerful enough to take care of you."

Overhead, three ravens looked down at them, but Kip knew not to expect any help from them. The masters had made it clear that fighting each other was one of the ways students learned magic; even Patris rarely punished Kip for his role in the fights, unless Farley or Adamson came off noticeably worst. Even now, his nose tingled at the presence of some invisible demon in the dining tent, but it was only there to control the fight, not prevent it.

And Farley was surely heading for another fight now. His expression darkened and flushed, and his voice lowered. "I'm learning some things too," he said.

Kip couldn't see Victor Adamson's expression, but the boy's head was bowed and he ran fingers through his short blond hair. If Farley was learning something, it was more likely from Victor than from any master. "Coppy," he growled, "leave him alone."

Coppy looked back stubbornly, but then Malcolm joined the conversation, calling across to Farley, "Like how to wash? Would make class a great deal more pleasant for all of us."

"Har har," Farley said. "When I do learn, I'll teach the animals there. There's a stink in here alright, but it ain't me." Adamson must have murmured something to him, because Farley added, "They started it! I won't let 'em talk to me like that."

"Maybe Kip's demon can give you a proper bath," Malcolm said pleasantly. "And do something about that language of yours at the same time. It's a fright, it is. No wonder you've no friends left."

"I've got friends."

"Oh, aye, Adamson there? I'm guessing you're as good a friend to him as that knife he's holding."

"Charming," Emily muttered under her breath.

"Probably true, though," Kip whispered to her.

"Don't care what power he has," Farley called. "Or what you all do together in that basement at night. I can take care of him any time I like."

At that, he stood, and Kip and his friends tensed. Coppy slid off his bench and got to his feet. "And I can take care of you anytime. Done it before."

Victor put a hand on Farley's wrist; Farley shook it off. Quarrel and Chesterton sat frozen, staring at the rest of the students, and Kip knew Farley was trying to figure out if he was gathering magic. Intending to show that he wasn't, he raised his paws.

That simple gesture ended the tense silence, but not in the way Kip had hoped. Farley ducked, his hands glowing lime green. Coppy's paws glowed turquoise and Malcolm's orange, but the otter struck first, pushing Farley's table hard and knocking him back a few steps.

"Not so easy without Carmichael around, is it?" Malcolm taunted, but even before he'd finished the sentence, Kip's muzzle was forced shut and his arms pinned to his sides. He recognized it as the physical immobilization Farley had used on Coppy the previous month, but knowing what was paralyzing him didn't help him counter it.

By this time, Emily too was gathering magic, though keeping her arms under the table so that the glow wasn't visible. Malcolm and Coppy's attention was fully trained on Farley, and even Emily had turned, so none of them noticed Kip's plight. Coppy hadn't bothered to gather magic again; he crossed the dining tent with four steps, shoving the table aside as he yelled, "Don't cast it. Don't cast it!" at Farley.

Only then did Emily turn to see that Kip had remained immobile. "Wait," she cried, but Coppy had already landed on Farley, grappling with him. The otter's thick musculature made him more than a match for even Farley, and with the boy focused on his spell, Coppy was able to knock him down and land at least two punches before Farley threw him aside.

And then Kip was lifted and flung toward the opening of the tent, outside into the bitter cold air. As horrible as immobilization had been, being moved around against his will was a hundred times worse. And Coppy had endured this for half an hour or more, being floated about in the air helplessly before Kip had finally appeared so that Farley could slam the otter into the stone walls of the Tower.

He wasn't slowing down. The tent receded before him, and the memory of Coppy only fixed in his mind what Farley intended to do to him. Did the school's demons know that a fox-Calatian's bones were light, far more fragile than an otter's or even a human's? Would they stop him before—

His back and shoulders slammed into hard stone, and distantly he heard a series of cracks. There was a moment of shock, and then as he toppled forward, pain exploded through his upper body. He fell, the air cold through his fur as the ground rose to meet him, and he squeezed his eyes shut through tears of agony.

CHAPTER 3: DEPENDENCE

He woke to a dull ache in an unfamiliar bed, softer than his bedroll and higher off the ground, with a rough cotton sheet over him and his head propped up on some rounded surface. He ached from his neck to his lower back and also along one side of his jaw, but a few cautious movements reassured him that his shoulders and back were whole, if bruised. He was able to lift his head enough to see a small stone room with a narrow shuttered window, but not enough to see if there were chairs or other furniture around him.

The first smell he caught was a light smell of blood, but he couldn't be sure it wasn't his own. With his next breath he caught a trace of the scent of the healer, Master Splint, and then he understood what had happened. No other beds in the room were occupied, so his friends must have not sustained serious harm. But Coppy…Coppy had physically attacked Farley, something he'd only done twice before, both times down in New Cambridge, both times when Farley had thought to attack the two of them in some place without witnesses. Here he'd done it in full view of the other students and the ravens, and although Kip could sympathize with Coppy's feelings and the need for revenge after his humiliation, he wished his friend had had a little more restraint. It said something about Farley's nature, though, that he was the only one who'd driven Coppy to violence.

If Coppy were expelled, what would Kip do? He lay and thought about that. Before their Selection, he would have said that he'd follow Coppy away from the school. Coppy hadn't wanted that then and wouldn't want it now. His chest did tighten at the thought of life without his closest friend, the emptiness of the basement at night. Malcolm and Emily were good friends, but he and Coppy had shared happy times like the Feast of Calatus and difficult times like, well, anything involving Farley. Coppy knew his parents, had lived with them, understood Kip's feeling of betrayal at their departure. He knew what it meant to be a Calatian in this world.

Secondarily, anyone who thought Calatians had no business learning sorcery would only have him left to worry about, and there were enough people on that list—Farley, Patris, other masters, perhaps even Victor, though his motivations were difficult to fathom—that Kip felt exhausted at the mere thought of having to watch out for all of them.

(Here he wondered briefly whether Patris hoped Farley might actually kill him. The black mark to the college would be the major deterrent to that, he felt, and yet he couldn't be entirely sure of it.)

The book he'd discovered in the basement, Peter Cadno's journal, might help, if only he could figure out why nobody seemed to notice him while he was holding it. He could keep it on his person all the time, setting it aside only for their classes and for his lessons with Odden. Malcolm and Emily might wonder why he didn't take meals with them anymore, but their meals would be quieter, safer affairs.

But he would hate to live like a fugitive in his school, hiding like an animal, running under cover from one place to another. There were enemies, yes, but there were also people willing to fight for him even if Coppy were gone: Emily and Malcolm; Masters Odden, Argent, and Windsor at least. And his father.

Lessons and his friends had kept him from thinking much about his father since the calyx ritual, but now Kip's thoughts turned to him. He'd received only one letter from his parents since they'd moved to Georgia to live near the rebuilding of Prince Philip's College of Sorcery, and that had been a warm if short note letting him know that they missed him, they hoped his studies were going well, and they'd found a house to live in. He had hoped that there would be correspondence between the surviving school and the rebuilding one into which his father could sneak some letters, but either that was not the case or his father had nothing more to tell him.

Nothing about what it meant to be a calyx, to come and bleed for the power of sorcerers whenever they needed a demon or a more powerful spell. Nothing about the life Kip would have to lead as a sorcerer, drinking the blood of his people. He tossed in the bed, wanting as he had so many times in the last two weeks to call out to his father to ask why he hadn't at least warned Kip.

But he knew what the answer would be: the sorcerers had instructed him not to. And furthermore, would that knowledge have made Kip hesitate in his studies? Knowing what he would have to go through, would he have limited the magic he sought? Even now he recalled the small increase in power—but barely noticeable compared to the surge he'd felt the first time he'd touched the Tower walls, which he suspected had been the work of the spirit of Peter Cadno entombed in its stone.

The power from whatever resided in the walls hadn't come to him again, and might never, so how useful really was it? If Peter was protecting the White Tower from within its stones, he had remained silent since that first surprised outburst at Kip's touch.

If Kip could access that power, though…he could summon demons, and what things might he be able to do with fire? Fire would gain him power and status for sure; only two or three other sorcerers in the Empire specialized in fire. If he became accomplished with it, even Patris might one day grudgingly acknowledge his value.

And yet…Odden had challenged him to hold fire in his paw for ten seconds, and Kip had not yet figured out that simple trick. He could keep a fire going for maybe four seconds before his skin began to burn.

Rubbing the pads on his fingers against the pad on the heel of his palm, he felt only smooth skin, not the roughness of the burn he'd grown accustomed to. Master Splint had healed his paws as well, it seemed.

So he lay his paw flat on the bed, palm up, and reached out for magic, to reassure himself that he could still summon fire. If he'd been quicker, if he'd pulled fire into the dining tent, maybe Farley would have stopped. Maybe Coppy wouldn't be in danger of expulsion. Maybe Kip wouldn't be lying in a room behind the healer's quarters.

His paws remained dark. The magic he was used to finding so easily was gone.

He fought down panic. He was tired; that was all. He closed his eyes, focused, and reached out again.

The world remained cold and dark.

Kip breathed faster, but tried to keep his focus as he fell back to the earliest incantation he remembered, a chant to help the sorcerer focus while gathering magic. He'd been preoccupied with Coppy's fate and the calyxes; he hadn't been focusing. He recited the chant, emptied his mind, reached out.

Still nothing.

Then this was his punishment, rendered at last by Patris: magic had been taken from him. He would have to leave the school because he could no longer work even a simple spell, and he hadn't Victor's money to make up for that. He would return to New Cambridge, perhaps work on a farm, and maybe one day he would come up to the college again, not to learn magic, not to feel the thrill of magic in him and the joy of altering the world around him, but to sit in a chair and bleed into a cup so that others might cast spells.

No. No, no. He half-fell out of his bed and found himself with his nose to the floor. The movement shot pain through his aching muscles, but he barely felt it. He pressed his paws flat to the stone, turned his face to the side so his muzzle could lay against it, and reached into the stone as he would reach into the earth for magic, but this time with words: *Peter, you helped me before, please, please, help me now, don't let them do this to me, don't let them take this away from me, please,* please.

The stone remained cold and dark as the earth. Kip gathered his will and was about to make another plea when a barrier somewhere broke and magic flooded into him.

He collapsed to the floor and sobbed, holding the bright violet glow of his paws by his eyes and drinking in the flickering, familiar light as though it were the water of a cold spring on a summer day. Weak with relief, he called into being a fire on the floor in front of him and poured his magic into it, keeping it close enough to warm him but far enough not to burn. Its light and heat fed back into him, and his muscles loosened, his tail uncurling to lie flat on the floor.

Thank you, he whispered in his mind.

It is my pleasure.

Was it the same voice that had cried a startled, *Fox?* into his head months ago? It was hard to tell because the word had been so short and so long ago, but what else could it be? And now there was a presence like a demon or elemental hovering on the edge of his awareness, but none of the tingling in his nose that accompanied a demon.

Peter?

A long pause. *Yes.*

Afraid of breaking his connection with the stone, Kip lay flat with his paws still pressed down. Questions burst in his head, but the foremost one came out first. *Are you a fox?*

I was.

Now <ansmæk>?

Yes. My spirit remains in the stone. Lord Primus's greatest feat.

I thought you said you created the spell. In your journal.

I may have. It has been hundreds of years. He called it his spell. The voice grew somewhat more distant. *Nobody had done anything like it before. And yet we have spirits. Why might that spirit not be sundered from the body and bound to another? He feared the Spanish might set demons against the Tower now that the power of my blood was becoming known.* Another pause. *Our blood.*

Kip shuddered. *That doesn't mean he can take credit for a spell you made.*

But he was right. The Tower was in danger.

From the Spanish? Kip held his breath. Here could be the solution to the mystery. If Peter knew what force had come against him, Kip could report it; the college could mount a fight against it.

The Spanish at one time, the French at another, even the Iroquois sorcerers, but none of those succeeded in destroying it. None did until this year.

Kip couldn't hold the questions in. *Who did? What destroyed the college?*

A demon. But I believe…I believe it was summoned by someone in the Tower.

In the Tower? This Tower? Where Kip had previously been unable to hold back the questions, now he found himself unable to articulate any. *Do you… Did you… Who was it?*

I do not know. It was not summoned here. But the demon knew how to break defenses, knew the names of all the guarding demons, knew too much to have been sent by an outsider.

You know spiritual magic?

Yes. But I have not seen the knowledge in any mind here, and I dare not probe deeply for fear of revealing my presence.

Is that how the book works? Your journal? Nobody else notices me while I'm reading it.

I can affect minds within the Tower. I still have access to magic.

I remember.

Ah. I am sorry for that. I did not know you were untrained. I felt a kindred spirit and the call to magic…

I'm glad you did, Kip said quickly. *I want to ask you so many things.*

I dare not speak long. I am in danger. The attack failed and the attacker will try again. They know that something prevented the previous attack and they must be seeking me out.

I'm trying to solve it. Where should I look? When Peter didn't answer, Kip pleaded, *Help me keep you safe!*

The remains of the demon's attack lie in the ruins, Peter said. *The sorcerers have not found a clue to the demon's identity but I feel there must be something there. And the attacker will be making preparations for another attack, but I have not noticed any sorcerers leaving the Tower regularly. Perhaps you can—*

His words dropped off and his presence vanished from Kip's mind a moment before the fox's nose tingled with a demon's presence. Kip extinguished his fire quickly, keeping his paws to the floor.

Peter?

No answer came. He rose slowly to his feet as the door opened and Master Splint walked in, rubbing his eyes. "Penfold?"

"Yes, sir."

Splint smoothed down his short red hair with a hand. "What are you doing out of bed? And did you start a fire?"

"Yes, sir." Kip climbed back into the bed. "I'm sorry. For a moment, I couldn't reach any magic, and I thought…I thought maybe I'd hit my head."

"Aye, you did." Splint took two steps toward Kip's bed. "Lost a few teeth and broke your neck, not to mention fracturing your upper back and shoulders. It's a good job I've worked on your father for years or I might not have been able to fix you quite so quickly. But tell me again how you came to summon magic?"

"I…" Kip turned his head. "I panicked. I was so scared. And then I prayed for help and I felt something break and I could feel magic again."

"Hm." Splint paused and then said, "Quetz?"

"Yes, sir."

At the foot of Kip's bed, a feathered serpent appeared hovering in the air, its attention fixed on the healer. "Did Penfold break your binding?" Splint asked it.

Kip held his breath. If he'd given away Peter's presence here so soon after promising to help him, he could have put the Tower in serious jeopardy.

"I cannot say for certain. He struggled against the binding and then it was broken."

"Thank you, Quetz."

The serpent bowed its head and again vanished, though Kip could still sense it nearby. Splint took another step to stand over Kip. "The binding is on this room for patients who might not be in full possession of their faculties. An uncontrolled sorcerer can be quite dangerous. But Quetz's binding is not easily broken; it would take someone practiced in spiritual magic to do so. You say that all you did was pray?"

"Yes, sir."

"Well," Splint said. "I suppose our Lord is as well versed in spiritual magic as any of us. Please do refrain from calling on His assistance for the remainder of your stay here, Penfold." He gave a short laugh, but his expression remained troubled as he left.

The next morning when he returned to the basement, Kip got a fuller account of what had happened. Coppy hugged Kip tightly enough to make all his bruises hurt again, but he didn't mind. "I didn't even notice," the otter said. "I'm so sorry!"

"None of us saw," Malcolm said.

"But I made Farley lose control of the spell." Coppy stepped back. "And then you fell and just lay there."

Emily gave Kip a gentler hug. "It looked rather bad," she said. "But Master Splint appeared very quickly and a demon did pull Coppy off Farley."

"Reckon the ravens called him," Malcolm said. "Splint, not the demon."

"The demon was there all along." Kip flexed his shoulders and winced at the sore muscles. "It lets us fight until something bad happens."

"What if Farley'd killed you?" Coppy went from mournful to furious in a heartbeat. "How would it have reversed that?"

"I'm tough to kill." Kip managed a smile. "But I haven't been hit that badly in years."

"I tried to catch you before you hit the ground." Coppy gestured with his arms out. "But I only got outside in time to see you hit the Tower and then…"

"We all froze," Malcolm said. "Except Em."

"What did you do?"

Emily scowled. "Translocated Farley to the ceiling of the Great Hall. He caught himself before he hit the floor." She kicked at a pile of paper, raising a cloud of dust. "I thought Malcolm would've caught you."

"Oi," Malcolm said. "Any of us could and none of us did, and what's more, the fox stands before us almost as good as new, so there's no need to point fingers about."

"I don't blame any of you. It was Farley who threw me around." He reached out to Coppy's shoulder. "It was horrible. I don't know how you bore it for as long as you did."

"Had no choice." Coppy sniffed. "But you rescued me."

"Look." Malcolm stepped forward. "Haven't I just been saying there's no need to harp on about who rescued whom? We're all safe and sound and the next thing is to decide what's to be done about Farley."

"He's not being expelled, I expect," Kip said. "But Coppy, you're not either?"

The otter shook his head. "We've none of us been disciplined."

"Rules may be different for apprentices." Malcolm tapped his cheek. "Fights happen. If it's only broken bones, Splint can mend those."

"If not the bruises." Kip pressed on his shoulder and winced again.

"Oh, don't touch it, then." Emily pulled his paw away.

"Not to mention," Coppy said, "if Patris expels me, he'd have to expel Farley, because you were hurt worst. Then he'd lose all that money Adamson's father is giving him for Farley's tuition."

"I don't expect Patris feels he would have to do any such thing." Kip flicked his tail. "But Malcolm's right; let's look forward, not back. What can we do?"

"We're going to practice catching people," Malcolm said. "We decided."

"Who's going to get tossed around?" Kip looked around at the three of them.

"We're going to make a rag doll and stuff it with paper." Emily kicked at the pile again, and again a cloud of dust rose.

Malcolm waved his hand in front of his face and stepped back. "Stop doing that, will you?"

"Ey," called Neddy from his clear-burnt half-circle. "When you're done, can I have the doll stuffed with paper?"

They had time to practice after dinner, but there was little room in the practice tent to throw a rag doll far enough that it was a challenge to catch it. Kip had the idea of levitating to the roof and practicing their magic there, and there they had plenty of space. The drawback was that night had already fallen and the wind hissed around at them unblocked by any buildings, but it wasn't too strong, and Kip lit fires to keep them warm while they practiced.

"You should learn to manipulate air," Malcolm grumbled as Coppy swept the layer of snow aside so it wouldn't melt under the flames.

"Master Argent told me about air elementals," Emily said. "They're quite nervous and you can call them and bind them, but asking them anything is a different matter. They speak a strange language and they won't talk to you unless they trust you."

"How do you get one to trust you if you can't talk to them?" Coppy wanted to know.

Emily leaned back close to the flames. "I've no idea. He didn't tell me. I'm not sure he knows."

"I'm pleased the phosphorus elementals are so amenable," Malcolm said. "Or maybe they just like our fire-fox here."

"They seem good-tempered with everyone." Kip leaned against the cold stone of the crenellations, sheltered from the wind. "But fire is like that too. It will live happily wherever you set it. Air is everywhere but wind comes and goes according to its own will."

"What about water?" Malcolm asked, directing his question at Coppy as he set their rag doll up against the wall. "Seems very agreeable as well."

"Don't know. Kip's met a water elemental but I haven't."

"Only briefly," Kip said. "It seemed curious but it had to create words in a fabric, so we didn't talk much."

Malcolm nodded and gathered magic, then lifted the doll from the roof about a foot. "Everyone ready?"

"We're not meant to be ready; that's the point," Emily said.

"Fair enough." Malcolm grinned and launched the doll into the air at an angle so that if they didn't catch it, it would fly off the edge of the roof on the other side.

Emily and Coppy both gathered magic quickly, and the doll's flight came to a stop while it was still in view. "Well done," Kip said.

Malcolm elbowed him. "You're not going to try?"

"He's holding the fires," Emily said. "Kip! Must you do that now?"

Kip had lit a fire in his paw again but now extinguished it. He'd thought perhaps the cold night air would help, but it hadn't. "He's right, I should try as well. The fires take very little attention."

"Let's make it a contest, you and me." Malcolm cracked his knuckles. "I'll try to sweep it to that side of the roof." He pointed to the left. "You try to swat it the other way. See who's fastest, eh?"

"All right." The fox laughed. "Let's go."

Malcolm won the first round, sending the dummy halfway to the left before Kip's spell took hold. Then Emily and Coppy wanted to play the same way, and they took turns in pairs trying to be first to hit the flying dummy while one of the others launched it unexpectedly.

Emily and Malcolm's cheeks bloomed with a bright red flush a half hour later, when by their unofficial count Malcolm was ahead, with Coppy not too far behind. "What's that at the gate?" Emily asked, distracting Malcolm during a round against Kip so that the dummy flew over the roof, falling to the ground directly in view of the seven-man group being led back to the Tower by a white-maned sorcerer who could only be Patris.

Coppy reached out, arms glowing turquoise, but Patris shot an arm in the air and the dummy stopped where it was. A moment later, a black dot took off from his shoulder, spreading wings and making its way up to the roof.

"Uh oh," Malcolm said. "We're for it now."

Panic flared in Kip, froze his feet to the stone. He couldn't even extinguish his fires before the raven landed on one of the parapets near them and surveyed them all. Before any of them spoke, it croaked, "What is the meaning of this?"

"We were practicing," Malcolm said quickly.

Kip sagged in relief that the raven hadn't said, "You're expelled." He braced himself against the parapet, even though it was covered in snow, and leaned over. Patris was leading the group of men toward the Tower entrance again, hurrying against the cold.

"Practicing what? Humiliating me in front of Mr. Adams and Mr. Bayard?"

"John Adams is here?" Kip hurried to look over the roof at the men disappearing around the corner of the Tower.

"John Quincy Adams," the raven said, "and he is here to see…"

His terror at crossing Patris already forgotten, Kip called magic to himself and climbed over the parapet, dropping down the side of the wall as he cast his levitation spell. The last of the men had disappeared from view by the time Kip's feet touched the cold stone of the path. He hurried after them, but Emily alit in front of him with her hands out.

"Kip, you can't just break in on a meeting with Adams and Patris."

"I wasn't going to." He heard two more people land behind him and reached out to the fires on the roof, promising them more life later as he extinguished them. "I just want to tell him I admire his father's writing."

"You know why he's here, right?" The wind blew Emily's hair back from her face; she turned to avoid taking the brunt of it on her nose.

"No?" Kip walked toward the Tower entrance. "Come on, at least let's get inside."

She fell in alongside him, Malcolm and Coppy hurrying up behind. "He's here to talk about independence," she said in a low voice.

Kip folded his ears back against the wind. "How do you know?"

They reached the doors, firmly closed as if nobody had passed through them all day. Kip reached for the doors but they swung open before he could touch them. Nobody held them on the other side, but as they hurried through, Malcolm gestured the doors shut behind them with hands that glowed orange.

"I know," Emily said, hurrying toward the fireplace and the phosphorus elementals crowded there, "because Master Hobstone told me that he'd be coming to talk to the sorcerers here."

"About independence?" Kip distracted himself from the sinking of his heart by greeting the lizards as they crowded up to the edge of their boundary. There were a few new ones, but he remembered everyone's names.

Emily waited patiently for the chaos of greetings to subside. "Yes," she said in a low voice, though the Great Hall was empty. "They want independence through peaceful means."

He'd so wanted to at least meet the son of the great writer who'd defended Calatians in print so many times. But if John Quincy Adams espoused the cause of independence, Kip couldn't risk talking to him. "Then why come ask the sorcerers for help?"

"I mean…if the Empire doesn't want to let the Colonies go peacefully…" Emily frowned. "Master Hobstone explained it better. It isn't about fighting; it's about being ready in case the Empire starts fighting."

"And making sure the Empire doesn't have these sorcerers if they want to fight." Malcolm spoke up.

Emily opened her mouth to retort, and then her expression calmed and she said, "Yes, I suppose that as well."

"So do you want to join them?" Kip asked.

She held her hands out to the fire and stared into it. As if emboldened by her attention, the elementals answered Kip's question.

"Why not join up?"

"Independence ain't so important."

"Oh, like you'd know."

"When we aren't here, we're independent, right?"

Kip held up a paw to them. "Shh, give us a moment, fellows."

"I don't know." Emily turned from the fire. "What do you all think?"

Coppy looked at Kip while Malcolm spoke up. "Sure, independence would be a fine thing, but Mother London won't let go her revenue-producing children without a fight, and we've got to be ready. This whole idea of going peacefully is nothing more than a front, I'd wager my ma's front teeth on it."

"I don't think we need to fight." Emily saw where Coppy's attention was. "Kip? I know you're worried about Patris. Forget about him for a moment. What do *you* think?"

"I don't know." He didn't want to start an argument here, now.

Emily leaned in. "Your John Adams favors independence."

"He's talking in theories and possibilities."

"The way he does about the Calatians?" she asked sharply.

Kip looked away and set his jaw. What little he'd read of John Adams' arguments in favor of independence had always inspired him, but so had the arguments about the treatment of Calatians, and now in order to pursue the latter, he felt he was bound to ignore the former.

Malcolm spoke up, either to ease the tension or to fill the silence. "We've a few in New York along the same lines. General Hamilton's the most outspoken. Though to be fair, Hamilton's outspoken about pretty much everything."

Emily cleared her throat. "Adams's cousin was executed forty years ago, along with the other 'traitors' then, and he still talks about it. Mentions things like, 'a cause worth dying for' without saying what he means, but if you know about poor Samuel, you know what he's talking about." She rubbed her hands together. "So we should go talk to him."

Kip looked back toward the staircase. "About what?"

"About independence." She cocked her head. "To find out what they plan. We're powerful now, Kip. We can make a difference. Even if we leave the school, the things we know—we could turn the tide of battles."

"You think so?" He gestured to the outside of the Tower. "We're four apprentices, barely apprentices. You know how many apprentices there are in London? How many Masters?"

"The right person at the right time can make a difference. Would London send all their sorcerers over here, if it came to that?"

"You should know," Kip said, "how easy it is for sorcerers to travel."

"What? Oh, this." Emily gestured with a hand. "Master Argent says that the most skilled translocational sorcerers can take two other people with them, and there are maybe a dozen of those. We have to go to places we've been before, or places where someone we know very well is currently. You can't just tell a sorcerer, 'go to Fort Duquesne' and have him translocate an entire battalion there."

"No, but he could take one calyx and summon a demon."

"There are sorcerers who specialize in military strategy, too," Malcolm put in. "Should there be a war, I'm sure they've thought of all the ways one might use sorcery in battles. In fact, they're probably chafing at the bit for a war. Imagine making all those lovely plans and never having the chance to use them."

"There's always a war sooner or later," Coppy said.

"There doesn't have to be." Emily stretched her feet out. "The movement has a number of excellent lawyers and politicians."

"Is there a movement to stay with the Empire?" Kip asked.

"Tch." Emily glared. "Our entire society is a movement to stay with the Empire."

Kip's ears flattened. Emily lowered her voice. "At least you should be aware of both sides, shouldn't you?"

Coppy, at his side, stayed quiet. "Maybe," Kip said. "But Patris is already angry at us today, and going out of my way to talk to a representative of the independence movement could hardly make my situation here any better."

"Forget about Patris!" Emily turned to Malcolm for support, but he only shrugged.

"I would love to, but I can't. I'm supposed to be searching the ruins." Kip raised a paw. "If you see Mr. Adams, do tell him how much his father's writing has meant to me."

CHAPTER 4: AFTERMATH

The idea of joining the independence movement still gnawed at him as he strode out of the Tower into the chilly wind. The sun had nearly set by this point and the wind had picked up, cutting through Kip's fur. He folded his ears down and hurried toward the nearest practice tent—not the one near the gates that Adamson had set fire to, but one more intact.

He hated that he'd used Patris's fear as an excuse for his own insecurity, but Patris did control their fates. What if Mr. John Quincy Adams convinced the headmaster that independence was a right and just cause? It would remove the burden from Kip of making the choice: if Patris went along with it, so would he. If he and Emily and Coppy and Malcolm joined the independence movement without Patris's support, if they were considered useful enough with their current skills—who would continue their education? The few sorcerers who would join them in defecting from the Empire? Spain? France? The Dutch and Portuguese had small colleges, enough sorcery to hold off the larger European powers; the Turks and Slavs and Russians had sorcery as well but Kip spoke no language they would know, and of course Japan and China and others in that part of the world about which he knew even less. But the acknowledged world powers in the realm of sorcery were England, Spain, and France, now in that order. And Kip wanted to learn from the best. He wanted to be part of the best.

A small fire brought light and heat to the dark practice tent. Kip set aside his worries as best he could, because he needed a clear mind to summon the demon. He recited the words of the summoning in his head to make sure he had them right, and then realized that he had no calyx.

Did he really need one, though? He hadn't felt a great increase in power, and Nikolon had not given him much struggle at all. Master Odden seemed to think that Kip did need a calyx's blood, so perhaps it was safest to continue to use it.

The thought crossed his mind that he might ask Coppy for his help, but Kip rejected that thought almost immediately. He would never ask that of Coppy, never. He sighed and put out the fire. He would not be searching the ruins tonight.

But as he left the practice tent, the body of the Tower rose before him. He stopped to look at its ancient stone. There was another Calatian near him, one he'd forgotten, one who had willingly lent him power in the past.

He curled his tail around his body and hurried through the darkness to the wall of the Tower. Turning his back to the wind, he set his paws to the cold stone. *Peter? I need some extra power. Just enough to summon a small demon.*

No response. The spirit was scared and shy; Kip tried again, remembering the feeling of reaching out and finding the presence at the edge of his awareness. *I don't need to talk to you. But if you're there…*

Still nothing. Kip inhaled. *If you don't help me, I'll have to go draw blood from another Calatian.*

No words came to his head, but power burst inside him as it had that first day he'd touched the Tower. This time he controlled it more easily, had time to breathe a soft "Thank you" before stepping away from the wall.

He checked to make sure he was alone outside, as unlikely as it was that anyone without fur would venture out into the lowering temperatures and frigid breeze. The grounds were still as far as he could see, and though his eyes wouldn't make out fine detail at a distance, they were quite good at spotting movement.

And then a flash of white caught his eye, eighty or so yards away in the orchard. Probably Forrest moving about again. How did he survive living outside in this weather? Kip made a mental note to go visit him and see if he needed blankets or food.

For now, though, he had power and a task before him. Back inside the practice tent, sheltered from the wind, he spread his paws, glowing violet with the power in him, and began the spell.

Nikolon appeared again as a sleek, naked vixen, as tall as Kip but more slender. "I do so enjoy this form," she purred, sliding paws down her sides and giving him a hopeful look. "Eventually I will find the type that appeals best to your tastes."

Alone, without Odden beside him, Kip hesitated. Demons could have corporeal form, and it would be at least two years, probably three, before his betrothed could stand before him like this. Certainly the more he thought about it, the more his body approved of the idea. What would it hurt? Out here in the practice tent, nobody would ever have to know.

But he had to maintain focus. If he let the binding slip, who knew what Nikolon might do to him? He took a deep breath. "You will become incorporeal and descend below this tent, into the ruins of the building there."

She bowed. "As you command, master."

"And you will relay to me what you can see and smell there, and will follow my instructions as you search."

It was unsettling to watch her talk. Her ears didn't behave normally; they remained upright all the time. And her tail hung like a piece of cloth from her back unless she remembered to wave it around, when it animated briefly before falling back against her legs. "As you command, master," she said again.

"Now go." The feeling of ordering another person about did not sit well with him, even if it was a demon that only looked like a person. He was certain that watching through her eyes as she explored the ruins of a building where some fifty people had died was not going to improve his evening.

Nikolon's form vanished, but the telltale sharpness in Kip's nose remained, diminishing only slightly over the next few seconds. And then more sights and smells crowded into his perception, overlaid on what his own eyes and nose told him. He closed his eyes to focus better on what the demon was sending.

The first sight he saw was a jumble of broken bricks and pieces of something black. Only when Nikolon approached one of the black things and sent him the faint smell of tar did he recognize them as shingles from the roof of the building.

"Lower," he said aloud, and Nikolon must have heard him, because she descended through the rubble. Wooden beams, broken wooden laths, and pieces of lime plaster dominated as the demon made her way through the buildings.

"What should I look for in the ruins?" Kip asked.

Master Odden had walked him out to the tents while the sun was out and the weather not too cold, not because Kip didn't know where the ruined buildings were, but because it was a nice day and he wanted to walk around. That was what he'd said; Kip suspected that there might be other reasons: Patris still upset over his previous day's Selection and that of Coppy, or perhaps Kip's perfumed scent in Odden's close office. If he didn't wear the perfume, his natural musk was strong enough to be objectionable to some people, but there were also people who didn't like excessive scent of any kind. Odden had never complained, but Kip had been asked to "take a walk outside" enough times in his childhood to consider his perfumes a possible reason whenever that happened. It was on his mind now too because his store wasn't going to be replenished, with his father and mother gone to Georgia, unless he went and bought more perfumes from Boston.

"The Masters have cleared all the spell books and spell items," Odden said, stroking one hand along the canvas of the tent, its shadow deep black against the canvas. "We have found a great quantity of burned wood, but little or no burned flesh. I believe that your affinity to fire may help you discover some clue that the rest of us overlooked."

"Like what?"

Odden shook his head. "All we know is that some kind of magic was worked here, of course. Fire was involved, but was it the primary attack or a secondary effect? Most of us feel it was primary, but we have no direct evidence of that. If we could identify the type of attack, we could narrow down the list of demons who might be responsible, and with some luck might be able to summon a few of them. They might be made to tell us who had previously summoned them, though questioning demons is never a sure proposition. Or we could definitively say it is a demon not on our lists, which would probably point to the Spanish as the attackers."

"How will I know what kind of fire was used?"

"You won't, not at first. But once you've investigated, we can send to London for Master Cott to come take a look at what you've found."

Kip's pulse quickened. "The fire sorcerer? He would come here?"

"Aye." Odden brushed the canvas again and looked at the ground below which the rubble of the building rested. "He has already asked to meet you. There are not many fire sorcerers in the empire, you know."

"I know," the fox said.

Now he searched through the sights and smells Nikolon sent him for anything that reminded him of fire. Once they'd passed the roof, the signs came thick and fast: wood burned black, great quantities of ash, burned cloth and furniture still in its original shape but now made of charcoal. Some spans of charcoal looked so fragile that Kip winced as the demon's sight came up to and passed through them, but not a speck of ash was disturbed by the spirit.

Worse, the feeling of desolation grew with every second. Burned and broken walls, furniture, clothing—there a piece of paper half-consumed with a drawing on it, but the drawing was nothing important as far as Kip could see, so he didn't instruct Nikolon to wait or go back. At one point Nikolon passed through a jewelry box, open and empty. Which one of the masters had taken the jewelry, Kip wondered? Or had it been emptied before the attack or during it? Was the demon one that had a taste for gold and silver, perhaps?

"Wait," he said aloud.

Nikolon stopped. The view in front of her was clearly the remains of a bed, crumpled and scorched, and on it was a small pile of ash. Some smell came through the ash to him, a faint trace that set him thinking about the hunger of fires and stirred the desire to call a fire to life in the practice tent. "Sift through the ash," he said. "Show me anything unusual."

I cannot say what is usual, Nikolon replied, but obliged him by diving her perspective into the ash.

Kip shook his head, expecting a cloud of soot in his nose, but of course he caught only the thick smell of the ash, and then Nikolon's perspective stopped and the demon's voice came to him, flatter than her normal affect. *This is unusual.*

In her view was a small bead, perhaps half an inch across, made of some kind of opalescent glass with flickers of red and gold. "What is it?" Kip asked.

It is demon-made.

"But what *is* it?"

It is…glass.

Kip examined it further. "All right. Bring it up here now."

Nikolon didn't answer, but the bead remained in her sight as she navigated through debris and back through the roof. And then the bead worked its way through a gap between boards and rolled to Kip's knees. "Thank you. Resume the search."

He picked up the bead and rolled it between two fingers as Nikolon's sight and smells overlaid his again. The glass, smooth and cool to his touch, held no blemishes or marks that he could find. It became too distracting to look at it while also focusing on Nikolon's explorations, so Kip set the bead back on the ground to investigate later.

The next stretch of time—half an hour? An hour?—passed in a similar haze of torn and ruined clothing, broken furniture, charcoal and ash, and nothing that stood out as unusual to him. He did come across more of the glass beads, often in the same general location as beds, and a horrible thought came to him after the fifth of these. "Nikolon, could these beads be the remains of people?"

Nikolon hesitated. *Anything is possible.*

"Do you think they are the remains of people?"

A longer hesitation. And then: *Yes.*

Kip swallowed. He pressed fingers to his eyes. "Can you search for a small glass bottle, the length of my finger? If there is a label still on it, it would read 'Rosewater and Amber.'"

"Here," Kip said, pushing the small bottle into Saul's hand. "Can't have you smelling worse than all the other apprentices."

The tall boy laughed and slung an arm around Kip's shoulders. "Always lookin' out for me. Don't worry, though, when I get a calyx you know I'll send for you."

Kip's tail vibrated with excitement. To get to see the college from the inside, with one of his closest friends... "I don't know if my father wants me to be a calyx, but I know I'd be a good one." He'd almost told Saul then about the spellbook his father had brought home only a month before, about how he'd already learned to reach out to the magic in the earth and call it to him and how he thought he saw a violet glow dance around his paws when he did. But his father had impressed upon him that if the sorcerers found out, they would take the book away and maybe worse.

If Saul were a Calatian, Kip would have trusted him with the secret. But if he were a Calatian, he would not be enrolling in the college to foster his magical ability.

"I can't wait," was all Kip said. "Come and tell me about the magic you're learning when you can."

"Oh, I'll do more than tell you." Saul grinned. "You're the smartest Calatian I know."

At the time, Kip had been so excited to hear that; later, he had mentioned the remark to his father and had been upset that his father hadn't been happy for him. But later, when Saul had enrolled at the college, his father had explained to him the difference between "smartest Calatian" and "smartest person," and though Kip still cherished his friendship with Saul, it took on a different cast from that point on.

But still, language and semantics aside, Saul had promised that Kip would be allowed to come to the college and see the grounds.

Nikolon moved in a blur of motion that made Kip queasy, but he could not shut his eyes to it. *Here*, the demon said, but the bottle that swam into view was not the right one.

"No," Kip said. "Keep looking."

Two more times Nikolon stopped, and neither time was it the right one. *I have finished searching these ruins*, she said.

"Did you find more of these glass beads?" The one she'd brought up lay on the wood. Kip didn't want to touch it anymore.

Yes. Many of them. Do you wish them brought up?

"No." Then he thought that it might be good to give them a consecrated burial, but the enormity of that task overwhelmed him. "Not yet. Go search the ruins under the dining tent."

He didn't know exactly where Saul had been housed. His friend had never made it to Selection; that was to be in late May, Kip thought. A week or two away when the attack had killed all of the current and aspiring apprentices.

Or...nearly all. Forrest, the apprentice who'd survived, had never spoken coherently about anything, let alone what he'd witnessed that night. Studying spiritual magic was said to be dangerous to one's sanity, but it was just as likely that the devastation and loss of all of his friends had been too much for him.

Nikolon's sight moved through dense earth, the smell refreshingly healthy, and then back into rubble and ash. Kip tuned out the blur again until Nikolon said, *I have found it*, and he found himself looking at a small glass bottle that he recognized instantly from his father's shop. The label had been only partly burned, enough that he could still read "Rosew" and "Penfol" in his father's precise script.

He wanted desperately in that moment to talk to his father, and then he remembered the experience of the calyx and what his father had gone through, and his fists clenched again.

Master?

"Is there one of those glass beads nearby?"

A quick scan through ash and then a glimmer. *Yes.*

"Bring the bead and the bottle both here, please."

Again, Nikolon obeyed without comment. There was more disruption; the larger bottle did not pass as easily through debris and earth, and Nikolon was obliged to sear a hole in one of the wooden planks over the ruins to get it out.

This caused a bit of a stir as people were eating in the dining tent, but Kip only saw the scene through Nikolon's eyes and he had not asked the demon to transmit sound, so he got the smells of cold roasted chicken and fresh bread, and the sight of people jumping back from the floating bottle, and then the bottle was out and into the night air, and then it was inside his tent.

"Thank you, Nikolon. Stop showing me what you see and smell."

His double vision and smell vanished as the bottle and bead dropped neatly into his paw. Very carefully, he pried the cap from the bottle, releasing a powerful burst of rose and amber scent, and dropped the bead into it. He exhaled when the cap was firmly back on the bottle.

Nikolon did not reappear, but Kip knew she was still present from the feel of his binding in addition to the peppermint tingle in his nose. He kept the bottle in one paw as he spoke. "Nikolon? Have you seen anything like this effect before? Humans reduced to..." He held the bottle up, trying not to remember that it contained all that was left of his friend.

No.

"Do you know anything about what demon might have done this?"

No.

"You did react to finding it, though. Can you explain why?"

The naked vixen shimmered into view, but merely sat cross-legged in front of Kip, as a comrade rather than a would-be seductress. "It was unexpected and unusual."

"Even to a demon? You said you couldn't judge what was usual." When Nikolon didn't say anything, Kip realized he hadn't asked a question or given an order. "Please explain what you mean by 'unusual.'"

"We have not seen all things. We exist in a dimension that has little to do with the real world and now find it confining. Still, it is troubling when…" The vixen fixed Kip with a gaze. "When the unreality of our world finds its way into this one."

"All right. Thank you." The light strain of holding the binding reminded him that he'd never held a demon this long. He could have held the binding for much longer, if the strain only grew at this rate, but he had been thinking about calyxes, and the demon's Calatian form provoked further thoughts. "How long may you be bound in this world before it becomes intolerable?"

The vixen gazed at him fixedly with her strange stiff ears. "Anything may be tolerated for any length of time. A greater time exacts a greater price."

Kip sighed. "How long before the price is too great?"

"Who can say what is too great?"

"For you?"

"I have not yet experienced that point." Nikolon kept her expression neutral.

"I see. I hope that if that point arrives while you are under my binding, you will inform me."

"If you order me to do so, master, I surely will."

Kip shook his head. Perhaps Master Odden had been right about the usefulness of talking to demons. "I will call you again when I have need of you." He took a breath, wrapped his paw around the glass bottle, and spoke the banishment words.

The vixen bowed her head as she disappeared. Kip kept looking through the empty space and then brought the bottle to his nose and eyes. The bead inside glowed very faintly with the remnants of fire magic, not enough to pull Kip to cast a spell, but like a scent that was <yora>, over a year old, one that he had to put his nose right up to to get.

This, then, was perhaps all that was left of his friend. He had mourned Saul's death months ago, but the tragedy had remained hidden below earth and rubble and tents, and he'd lost sight of it with the urgency of his studies. Now he wrapped one paw warmly around the bottle, picked up the loose bead, and left the practice tent.

Kip wasn't hungry, so rather than join his friends in the dining tent, he returned to the basement. He tucked both beads under one corner of his bedroll, gave Neddy some paper, and then paced back and forth, thinking about the demon's discovery. Talking to someone who'd seen the attack might not shed any new light on what kind of fire had been used, but he wanted badly to hear about it.

Staring at Neddy's tracery of glowing skin, Kip couldn't stop thinking about what the fire that had reduced people to glass beads had looked like. Had the fire struck everyone in a flash? Had it spread like lightning in a streak or popped from one room to the other? The ruins had been the cold ashes of a fireplace that showed him nothing about what the fire had been like when it was alive.

Of course he would tell Odden about the beads, and Odden would know what the sorcerers who had survived the attack had seen. Kip had likely heard all of their stories already, so he doubted anyone would have more insight. But there had been another survivor, hadn't there?

Forrest kept to himself, and the few times he'd spoken he'd seemed to be a few drops short of a full bottle. If approached and asked directly, gently, about the night in question, maybe with a specific question about fire, he might be forthcoming. At least he'd be more satisfying than a demon to talk to. And perhaps Kip could get a riddle to pore over with Emily and Coppy and Malcolm. Or at least Coppy, if Emily were still going on about independence.

Kip had an excellent excuse to see the apprentice, too: As far as any of them knew, Forrest lived in the orchard, and a human sleeping out in this cold would not be having a good time of it. Why had they never thought of him before when the nights had dropped to below frost levels and the wind cut across Founders' Hill like a frigid waterfall?

The wind had actually died down by the time Kip was halfway to the orchard. He brought his ears up, thanking God for small favors. Then he hesitated, wondering if he should get food from the dining tent, but he was already too far, and Forrest had survived this long somehow; he clearly didn't need help.

As the fox approached the orchard, he scanned the frost-limned grass and leafless trees for any signs of life, but whatever movement he'd seen before was not repeated. He would have to search for Forrest by scent—difficult in the breezeless cold air—and sight, which became clearer as he drew closer. His eyes might not be good at distance, but the light of the stars was enough to illuminate the world for him twenty or thirty yards away.

Ears and nose alert, he crunched through snow and frozen grass off the path. As he drew closer to the trees, he caught the scent of Forrest's rank body odor, but could not see the apprentice himself until he had one paw on a cold tree trunk.

Forrest lay curled on the ground in his dirty white robe, his face gaunt and as pale as the snow he rested on. Kip hurried to his side and knelt beside him. The apprentice's dirty blond hair lay in streaks across his face, one stirred faintly by his breath. To the touch of Kip's rough pads, his skin felt cold and rigid as the tree trunk, though it did warm the air for a claw's breadth around him. If Kip's fingers were skin, perhaps he'd be able to discern further traces of life or tell whether Forrest was near death or simply in a kind of hibernation.

But the black spots on his ears could not be a good sign, and the young man didn't respond to pressure on his shoulders or to being shaken. Kip rocked back on his heels and considered. He could take Forrest into the Tower, but perhaps it would be better to warm him right here, and Kip had the means to do it.

Away from the trees, he cleared a space and then called a fire into being there. He wasn't confident in his ability to bind it to a small area, but with concentration he could keep it from growing. The key was to keep it away from Forrest's robes…

A high-pitched scream cut the air at the same time as the dirty white robes flapped and the still form sprang to life, leaping on the fire. In a panic, Kip pulled the fire back as the smell of burning cloth filled the air, and soon they were plunged into the relative darkness of a starlit night.

But the screaming continued and now Forrest leapt up to flail with his fists at Kip's shoulders. "No fire! No fire! The trees!"

"Hey!" The blows didn't hurt, but Kip fell back under the passion of the man's cries. "I had it under control! You need to get warm!"

"*No fire!*"

Kip trapped both wrists in his paws. "That fire wouldn't hurt you!"

Only then did he notice a soft brown light over the pale white hands he held. He released them. "Wait—"

He stood among the trees alone on a humid night, late spring or early summer. The quarter-moon lit the night, but not as brightly as Kip would expect, even though the sky was cloudless. The smells of grass and apple flowers surrounded him, but again, muted. And yet the outlines of the four buildings surrounding the Tower stood out crisply against the starry sky, as did the faint lines that marked the gates in the distance. High in the dark walls of the Tower, light glimmered in a single window and then went out. Warmth flickered inside the buildings that he thought at first was fire, but no; the windows were dark. What was he sensing, then? Not scent; the only scents on the night air were of grass

and trees and flowers, dull and muted as though he had a cold. Or—

He was seeing through someone else's eyes, smelling through their nose. He hadn't noticed it until he'd noticed the differences in what he could see and smell.

And hear. In his ear whispered a voice, but when he turned there was nobody there. The voice was in an alien language, high and whistling, but Kip understood what it was asking. "I felt I should be with the trees," he replied with Forrest's voice. "They need me."

He placed one hand against the nearest tree trunk as the voice spoke again. "You may stay as long as you wish," he replied.

The normality of Forrest's voice unsettled Kip more than the dulled senses. He tried to ask, "Who are you?" but he could not affect what he was perceiving. This was a memory, he knew, and he knew what night it was, and that filled him with excitement and dread.

"Someone else is awake, or was." Forrest's arm pointed up at the Tower. Seeing his own hand, white and furless, jolted Kip, but the memory did not falter. "Was that Master Jaeger's window?" The reedy voice spoke again. Forrest nodded. "I shall ask him tomorrow."

And then the hair on the back of his neck stood up. A tide of magical energy like an undertow pulled him toward the buildings. One arm was not enough to brace him against the tree; he hugged it with both and watched the College. "Something's wrong," he said, his voice higher with alarm, but the reedy voice did not answer. "Go tell—"

Fire burst from each of the four surrounding buildings, bright reddish flames shooting from each window and door, and a deep, rumbling roar filled the air. Panic surrounded Kip, not just his own but also emanating from the tree he held and the others around it. He held on to the tree desperately as it cried out with a deep, resonating thrum inside him, and he made a keening noise himself. In the four buildings, the flickers of warmth he'd felt earlier vanished all at once, leaving cold emptiness in the wake of the bright gouts of flame.

And as soon as the lives had been extinguished, the fire died down. With a rumble like thunder, each of the four buildings slowly collapsed inward under its own weight. Clouds of dust and ash rose in the air, and even with a human's nose Kip could smell it.

Sparks skittered up the walls of the Tower but died before getting very far. There, the warmth of life persisted, and he clung to that even as he wept against the tree. "Why didn't I get them all outside?" he cried. "I could have saved them!"

The trees joined his lament and he turned his grief to comfort. "You're still here, my trees, my dearest. I'll save you," he promised. "I'll never let the fire get you. Never."

Kip lay on the ground and stared, dazed, up at the stars. His ears ached with cold and his nose felt like ice, but his heart raced as though he'd just been running from Farley for hours. However he'd fallen, he didn't remember it at all. But he could see in the starlit night, and he could smell Forrest and the distant dinner as well as the trees and earth. He was himself again.

He'd heard the attack from down the hill, a place that now felt as remote as London from the fire and carnage that Forrest had witnessed. The terror he'd felt paled next to the wrenching the memory had left inside him from the loss of life, the devastating fire and the terror of the trees and whatever demon—demon?—had been gibbering in Forrest's ear. Nikolon had been sobered by the remnants of the attack; perhaps any demon witnessing it would have been equally terrified.

Slowly he pushed his elbows under him and sat up, reaching to rub life back into his ears. Forrest lay in the same position he had before. Kip had no idea how the young man could survive out here in the cold, but there was not much he could do to help.

After a moment's reflection, he stripped off his tunic and draped it over Forrest's form. "Sorry," he said, but Forrest didn't stir.

He barely noticed the absence of his tunic now that the evening wind had died down, but he hurried his steps back to the Tower, feeling a lack of more than physical warmth. At the door of the Tower, he caught the scent of several unfamiliar men on the outside of the door; they must have left while he was in the orchard.

The low murmur of voices came from behind the great doors, and when he opened them he recognized Patris's deep growl along with a less familiar voice. He hesitated, but they might have seen the doors open already, and anyway he didn't want to hide out in the cold until they went away. Perhaps if he had Emily's translocation ability he would one day be able to jump to the basement without encountering anyone, but for now he had to brave Patris.

The two sorcerers stopped speaking when Kip stepped through the door, both Patris and Master Warrington, a sorcerer Malcolm had talked about as specializing in defensive magic but who had declined to take him on as an apprentice.

Patris bore his usual expression of distaste. "There you are," he said, and Kip's hackles went up. If the headmaster had been looking for him, that was no good sign. "Back late from dinner? What happened to your shirt?"

"I left it with Forrest." Kip saw no reason to lie. "He's sleeping out there in the orchard."

"In this weather?" Warrington exclaimed.

"I tried to warm him with a fire, but he did not take well to that."

"Of course he wouldn't." Patris spoke as though Kip were a cub who'd tried to burn down his own house. "He loves the trees. How would you think he would feel about fire?"

Kip bristled, as much because Patris was assuming he was stupid as because Patris was at least partially right, even though he'd been controlling the fire and it would never have harmed the trees. "I thought he was dying. I would have brought him back here, but..." He trailed off. He still could have fetched Forrest, but having been lifted and moved against his will, he didn't want to subject anyone else to that, even for good reasons.

"He's survived out there this long," Patris said. "If he's happy, he's welcome to stay."

"But surely," Warrington began.

Patris held up a hand. "Go talk to Jaeger if you're worried. Forrest is his responsibility." Kip walked past the fireplace toward the basement, but Patris took two steps in his direction and said, "A moment, Penfold."

Kip curled his tail against his leg and turned. "Yes, sir?"

The old sorcerer's lip curled. "Mr. Adams was desirous of speaking to you. I promised I would relay that message to you, and now I have."

"Thank you, sir."

"And let me add one of my own."

Here it came. Kip stopped himself from protesting his disinterest in the independence movement and let Patris lecture him for several minutes on his duty to the College and the Empire. "Yes, sir," he said when Patris had finished.

The sorcerer squinted at him. "Is that all you have to say?"

"What else should I say, sir?"

Patris straightened the collar of his robe and then brushed imaginary dust from it. "Why was Mr. Adams interested in speaking to you? Have you been in communication with him?"

"I have not. Did you not ask him that yourself, sir?"

The old sorcerer scowled. "I have more important things to worry about."

Kip inferred that he had asked and had not received a satisfactory answer, and he liked Mr. Adams a little bit more. "I'm sorry I'm unable to shed any light on his request. I assure you I have no interest in acting against the College or the Empire."

"Go on with you." Patris dismissed him with a wave and turned back to Warrington.

Kip watched the two of them mount the stairs, and then allowed himself a smile as he hurried down to the basement.

At the base of the stairs, in the dank shadows, the door wouldn't open. The smell of Neddy came strongly through the door, obscuring any other scents, but Malcolm's magic was as distinctive as the Irishman's scent. Kip rapped sharply. "Hey," he called. "It's me."

A moment later, Malcolm opened the door. "Sorry! Was teaching Coppy to lock the door."

"Coppy did that?" Kip smiled at the beaming otter, who'd stood and tucked his spell book under one arm so he could hug the fox. "Excellently done."

"Malcolm says there's ways to let certain people through the locks always," Coppy said, "but even he can't do that yet."

"Working on it, though." Malcolm scratched his head. "Where were you at dinner? We missed you."

Emily sat with her spellbook open on her knees and had not got up to greet Kip, nor did she make any indication that she agreed with Malcolm. The fox took a seat near the edge of Neddy's circle and crumpled a paper. "I was searching the ruins," he said. "And then..." He tossed the paper to Neddy and watched the fire consume it. Not reddish like the fire that had destroyed the school, but a purer, cleaner fire, with white at the core of the yellow.

Malcolm cleared his throat. "And then?"

Emily was at least looking up now, and Coppy set aside his spellbook. Kip took a breath. "I went to see Forrest. I saw him moving around the orchard and I thought...I thought he might be cold."

Briefly, he told them what had happened, and saw the opportunity to use Forrest's memory to impart Peter's information. "The light at the top of the Tower went out right before the attack," he said. "So it was someone in the Tower coordinating the attack."

"Really?" Emily sniffed. "Seems a large conclusion to jump to."

"It makes sense to me," Coppy said. "Who else was awake just before the attack? Who's on that floor?"

They turned to Malcolm, who'd been on more of the upper floors than any of the rest of them. "Which was it, Kip? Six or seven?"

Kip shook his head. "Don't know. Seven is where that big meeting room is, but there might be another small room there. Six is more likely, I suppose."

"Jaeger's on six," Malcolm said. "I'm not sure who else is. Most everyone we know is on two through four."

"Who don't we know? Barrett, Sharpe, Brown, Campbell, Waldo..."

"I'd like it to be Sharpe." Kip sighed.

"He was the one who spoke against us getting in?" Coppy asked, and Kip nodded.

"The others are mostly absorbed in their own research." Malcolm sat amid the paper. "Which could as easily be 'how to destroy the college' as anything else, I fancy."

The room fell silent, and then Emily looked up from her book and met Kip's eyes. "Was it horrible?" she asked softly.

Kip walked over to his bedroll and picked up the loose glass bead. Rolling it between two fingers, he held it up. "I think...I think the demon consumed all the people and left only these pieces of glass behind."

Emily gasped, then stood and approached Kip. Coppy and Malcolm, too, came forward. None of them seemed inclined to touch the glass, but when Kip held it out in his paw, they all leaned in to look.

"Hard to see in this light," Malcolm said,

"I can give you four seconds." He called magic into his paws.

"Don't," Coppy said, but Kip had already conjured a flame onto his other paw, holding it close for the length of time he could stand it.

"I'll have to learn eventually," he said to Coppy's drooping whiskers. "Master Odden said ten seconds."

"Maybe once you've burned all the skin off your paw," the otter said.

"That's all that's left of a person?" Emily was still staring at the glass bead. "Does it feel…?"

Kip offered the bead to her, and after a moment's hesitation, she took it. "It doesn't feel like anything," he said. "I think it gets warmer when it's near a fire, but that could be…"

"We get warmer when we're near a fire as well." Malcolm leaned over to look at the glass bead in Emily's fingers.

"Yes." Kip held his paw out and Emily dropped the bead into it. He rolled it between his fingers, trying not to think of where it had come from. "There were hundreds of them. In Forrest's memory, I—he felt them all die."

"What kind of monster could do that?" Coppy asked, eyes wide. "Could kill all those people with a thought?"

Emily looked up at the ceiling. "One that is out there right now trying to figure out how to do it to the rest of us."

When Kip and Coppy lay down to sleep, Kip took the bottle out from under his bedroll and looked at the glass bead inside it. "You never met Saul," he said softly to Coppy.

The otter's eyes gleamed in the darkness. He shook his head slowly.

"He was my friend. He wasn't the best, but he was a human and he was my friend."

"He didn't protect you from Farley, though."

"No, no. He couldn't, not all the time." Kip tucked the bottle away. "He didn't deserve to die that way. None of them did."

"Seems like it was quick, though. He wouldn't have suffered." After a long silence, Coppy said, "And if the attack hadn't happened, we wouldn't be here. Not that that makes it right, but…some small good came out of it. You don't think Saul would've wanted his death to help you out if it could?"

"I don't know," Kip said. "I hope so."

CHAPTER 5: SPIRITUAL HOLDS

Master Odden was quite interested in the glass bead. "I would like Master Cott to examine this," he said. "This does not match the abilities or proclivities of any demon known to me, and I am the most well-versed in the names of demons in this college. We could talk to Florian perhaps…"

"I would be happy to take it to Master Cott." Kip seized on his chance.

"You have only been studying here for a month." Odden stroked his beard, looking amused. "And yet, it might be profitable. I will wait a week or so before making the request on your behalf, as Patris is in high dudgeon after Mr. Adams' visit yesterday."

"He is not a fan of the independence movement," Kip said. "That's all right. Neither am I. I hoped that going to London might accomplish both removing me from his immediate presence and convincing him of my devotion to the Empire."

"Mm." Odden examined the glass bead again and then set it in a small drawer in the front of his desk. "It may be difficult to convince Patris, but see that you do nothing to confirm his suspicions."

And with that routine unfairness, they continued their lesson. Kip worked on bounding his fire, shaping it so that he could control exactly where it burned. But his mind wasn't on his lesson; it was on proving his worth to the Empire with fire magic.

There were few records of great magical fires in history; mostly fire sorcerers became famous for helping armies win wars by burning camps and fields. In the French and Indian war, he recalled, a fire sorcerer had captured Fort Beauséjour. He couldn't recall any stories of fire sorcerers outside of wars, but then, fire was inherently a destructive magic. From the destruction of the war often came new life; the Louisiana territory had come to Britain as a result of its victory in the Napoleonic wars, at least part of which had been thanks to the work of fire sorcery (perhaps Master Cott specifically?). Still. He would have to ask Master Windsor about the role of fire sorcery in history at the next opportunity.

Even though everyone insisted the attack on the college had been a demon, thoughts of fire in war inevitably brought Kip back to the College. Peter's simple statement that someone in the College had planned the attack had thrown Kip's world into turmoil. A month ago he'd assumed he could trust any sorcerer at the college, at least with regards to the mystery of the attack, and now he could trust none.

It had not escaped his attention that Master Odden, self-proclaimed "most well versed" in demon names in New Cambridge, could very well be lying about not recognizing this demon. The architect of the plot would be very interested in any evidence Kip found—perhaps not so eager for someone in London to see it, unless he knew that would yield nothing.

He ended his lesson and returned to the basement to find that Emily was talking to him again. She, Coppy, Malcolm and Kip spent the afternoon practicing what magic they could; Kip cast fires into Neddy's area to the delight of the phosphorus elemental, who jumped into and out of them like a cub playing in mud puddles. They discussed the list of Masters and weighed the pros and cons of each one as potential traitor and mass murderer without coming to any conclusions.

Malcolm made his way up to the sixth floor, but reported that none of the four doors there were marked. He'd tried knocking on one but got no answer, and then a voice had told him to go back to the floors where he was allowed, so he'd hurried down the stairs. "Wish I could smell demons coming like you can, Kip," he said. "Not that that would have helped, but at least I'd not have jumped half out of my skin."

"I suppose," Kip said, "that I can ask Master Jaeger."

Early the next morning, before classes, he walked out of the Tower. More snow had fallen the night before and an inch of it covered the ground, even over the path; whatever magical spirit the masters used to clear the stone had not yet been called upon. Above him, clouds muted the sun's light, but the air was warmer than it often was on clear days, without much of winter's bite in it.

Nobody else was about and no noises save the birds came even to Kip's ears. He did look toward the orchard, but at this distance it vanished in a blur of white, and there was no way he could have seen Forrest unless the apprentice stood and jumped up and down between the trees.

At the wall of the Tower facing the dining tent, he stopped and looked up. The temptation to place his paws to the stone and talk to Peter tugged at him, but Kip resisted; the spirit was nervous enough already without Kip making it worse. So he simply cast the spell that came so easily to him now and lifted himself from the ground, all the way up to the roof.

Snow also lay on the crenellations in the parapet. He brushed a small area clear and sat there, keeping his spell active. "Good morning," he called softly, looking to the left and the right.

As if summoned, a raven wheeled around the corner of the Tower and alit near him. The others had warned him that Jaeger was a spiritual sorcerer and that he might do things to Kip's mind, especially if he were the architect of the attack and he worried Kip was getting close. "I know," Kip had said. "I have an idea."

Now, as the raven croaked a "Good morning," his idea seemed foolish and reckless. What if Jaeger were the one who'd planned it all? Master Windsor had said once that he could summon Jaeger to get information out of Kip's mind, and what if Kip were now delivering that information directly to him? But he forced his tail to still and his ears to stay up, and he smiled at the raven. "I heard you speaking to Forrest last month, when he stopped our fight in the dining tent, and Patris said he's your responsibility. Is he your apprentice?"

The raven gave the coughing laugh of an old man. "He is indeed. Has he been troubling you?"

"Only my conscience." Kip extended a paw in the direction of the orchard. "He sleeps outdoors in the cold of winter. I cannot see how he will survive December, let alone January."

"He is severely troubled," the raven acknowledged. "But he also shares a bond with the trees, and his skin is not as weak as you might think, nor is he without help."

"I thought you would be aware of his situation. I wanted to ask you if there's anything I can do to make it more comfortable. Would he welcome blankets?"

"I believe he would accept them, though he does not believe he needs them."

Kip reached up to rub his ears against his head. "Master Jaeger, may I see you inside? It is rather cold out here."

The raven croaked and then said, "Follow Blacktalon around to the window. Can you translocate yet?"

"No."

"Then reach in through the opening he uses and you should be able to unlatch the entire window. Please enter quickly; you will be in my study and I have but one phosphorus elemental to heat the place."

"Thank you." Kip had hoped to be invited through more traditional means so he could investigate the rest of the floor, but he got to his feet and levitated himself to show that he was ready.

The raven took off and plummeted down, then found an updraft and rose as it approached the corner of the Tower. It banked and disappeared behind the stone. Kip followed, wind searing the edges of his ears and nose with cold.

Blacktalon perched outside a window, and when he saw Kip, he pushed at one pane with his beak. At this distance, it appeared identical to the others, but at the raven's touch it swung open, a space of about a foot square that the bird hopped onto the sill of and then disappeared into. As he drew close to it, Kip saw dimly the study within and a ghostly figure standing in a white robe at the far end of the room. He pushed his arm through the opening and felt about for the latch. It took longer than he would have liked, but presently he found it and pulled the window open toward him.

Once inside, he shut the window and the raven's pane. He stared down at the ground, where in the distance he could see dimly the shapes of the snow-covered trees of the orchard. From here he had even less chance of seeing Forrest, but perhaps if Master Jaeger's eyes were good, he would be able to. Kip turned to face the old sorcerer.

The white puffs of his breath faded as the heat in the room reasserted itself. He stood on the edge of a finely woven Persian carpet with intricate patterns that in the light of the window appeared bright gold and brown, his snow-dusted feet resting on stone in the only space around the carpet that was not occupied by bookshelves. Only a few of the shelves contained books; the rest held sheafs of paper, some bound with dusty ribbons. A brazier containing a phosphorus elemental stood in the very center of the carpet, and adjacent to it stood a perch from which Blacktalon regarded Kip.

"Hello, Mister Penfold." The figure at the far end of the room walked toward him in a queer halting motion, stopping to hold out a piece of meat to the raven, which it gobbled down quickly. "It is pleasant to meet in person."

"Yes," Kip extended a paw, then withdrew it when Jaeger did not extend his hand.

"I apologize for the frequent use of Blacktalon as an intermediary. He is an excellent companion but somewhat, a ha, limited in his emotive range." As Jaeger stepped into the light from the window, his mottled skin and wispy white hair came into better focus. Sharp brown eyes took Kip's measure but a slight smile undercut their severity. The white robe he wore looked to be the same as Forrest's but in much better condition. "I find it tiring to leave my chambers, and most apprentices do not climb as high as the sixth floor of the Tower."

Kip stepped forward and to the side so that his tail wasn't brushing the wall. "I liked coming to meet you on the roof," he said. "It was a secret. And I never properly thanked you for your help when Farley and Adamson took Coppy, a month or so ago. Patris said you vouched for me."

"I told the truth," Jaeger said, raising one eyebrow. He hobbled back toward Blacktalon with that same jerky gait. "You acted honorably. Had you not, I would have reported that as well."

"But you judged me by what I did, not by how I look."

"My boy." Jaeger turned, one hand steadying himself on the raven's perch. "I see only the minds inside your heads, not the outer covering they walk about in. To me, you look the same as any other student."

"Thank you anyway." Kip flushed at the words, putting his ears back. To be the same as any other student felt inconceivable to him.

"You're welcome. Now, you had concerns about Forrest?"

"Yes. Is there anything we can do for him?"

Jaeger stroked a finger over Blacktalon's head, which the raven accepted with closed eyes. "Blankets, although I doubt he needs them. He can get food when he needs it. Forrest has been studying magic related to trees, and in some ways he can communicate with them. An odd branch, a ha, of spiritual magic, but a known one."

"I know," Kip said, thinking of Forrest's memory.

Jaeger looked sharply at him, and he realized his mistake. "That he can communicate with trees. I mean—he attacked me when I lit a fire. He said, he said the trees were afraid."

"Oh, yes." Jaeger gave a short laugh. "What would you expect when you light a fire in an orchard?"

"I was trying to help." Kip flattened his ears in annoyance.

"Help is only valuable in the proper context." Jaeger walked over to his shelves and began poring over them. "You would do well to remember that as you continue your magical education."

Kip glanced at the shelf nearest him, which held some books: "The Spirit," "Healing the Mind," "Understanding Thought." He touched one with a finger and came away with dust on the pad. "Yes, sir."

Jaeger looked over his shoulder. "Don't say 'yes, sir,' unless you've absorbed the lesson."

The words gave Kip a bit of a shock. Further annoyance at being lectured to faded into the feeling of someone caring about whether he learned something. "Help is dependent on context, yes, sir. I'll do better in the future."

"I am certain you will. Now, am I correct in hearing that you have been communicating with a spirit in the Tower?"

Kip froze. He'd told Windsor, to ensure his and Coppy's Selection, and the dour master must have told others. "Just—just once, sir," he said, hesitating over the lie.

"What did it say?"

Windsor hadn't asked him this. "It…it said, 'Fox.'"

"So it recognized you. Hm." The old sorcerer pulled a sheaf of papers from his shelf and carefully untied the ribbon that bound them. "When was this?"

"My first day here. When I applied."

"It hasn't spoken to you since then?"

"No, sir."

Jaeger pulled one sheet from the sheaf and rebound the pages. "Not that night in Master Splint's room?"

"Ah." Kip's throat felt dry. He avoided Jaeger's eyes for a moment and then met them bravely. "I, uh." What had he told Master Splint? He couldn't remember. "I asked for help."

"You prayed."

"Yes. And then I could reach magic again."

"Well." Jaeger released the paper he was holding and it stayed in the air. "And your first day, you also experienced a rush of magical power, is that right?" Kip nodded. "At the same time as the voice talked to you?"

"Yes." The two incidents would definitely be linked, but at least Kip's conversation with Peter could remain confidential.

The page floated toward Kip. "Take that," Jaeger said. "It is a spell I modified slightly to make it easier to learn, but King's College was not interested in my modifications."

"I'm sorry." Kip grasped the page.

"It was a long time ago. I've learned to let go of the small slights and politics that may mar a life." He pointed at the paper. "It has been helpful to a handful of sorcerers in the past, and so may it be useful to you now."

Kip read from the page: "A Spell To Liberate One From Spiritual Holds." He looked up. "Why would they not want this?"

"Ah." Jaeger tottered back to Blacktalon. "They did not favor me with a reason. Perhaps they worried that their own spiritual sorcerers would be less effective if this spell were widely known. Perhaps they did not feel that spiritual holds were common enough to warrant spending more time on this."

"What is a 'spiritual hold'?"

"It is a magic that confuses the mind, not in the usual way you think of confusion, but in such a way as to alter your view of the world and make it appear natural. It is only effective for a short time and in the presence of the sorcerer casting it, but it has sometimes made appearances in diplomatic meetings, heh heh. The best way to tell that you are in a spiritual hold is that your nearby friends will all appear to be acting irrationally."

Kip frowned. "It affects your friends?"

"No. That is the point. You can never tell from your own thoughts that you are in a hold, but the sorcerer has cast it on you to make you behave in a way you wouldn't. Anyone nearby who knows you will try to stop you, and their reasons will make no sense. That piece of knowledge, by the way, is just as valuable as the spell."

"Then why do I need the spell?"

"Oh, you can't break a hold simply by knowing or suspecting it exists. But it takes very little energy to cast this spell, and if everyone around you is behaving oddly, or if you have some other reason to suspect one has been cast on you, then you might as well just cast the counter spell to be sure, eh?" Jaeger's eyes twinkled. "Simply drill that belief into your head and memorize the spell, and you will be well served."

Kip looked again at the page. There was a paragraph explaining the concepts to keep in one's head while casting the spell, and then the spell itself, carefully laid out in syllables. "Why do you think I will need this?"

"Simple," Jaeger said. "Affecting another sorcerer's access to magic is a spiritual skill. If there is a spirit trapped in these walls, demon or otherwise, it is well versed in spiritual magic. And it has communicated with you. There is a chance that it will decide it wishes to use you for its own ends, and a spiritual hold is the best way to do that."

Would Peter use him? No. Peter was another fox; he and Kip shared a bond. And yet…Peter had been a spiritual sorcerer. "Master Jaeger? Do you think it's possible that a…a human spirit could be trapped in the Tower?"

Jaeger chuckled. "A ghost?" He waved his arms and made his robes flap. "Penfold, when the body expires, the spirit passes on to wherever our spirits go, whatever your belief may be on that score. Spiritual sorcerers have tried for centuries to trap that spirit as it leaves, and none has succeeded."

Except maybe one had, Kip thought. A Calatian, whose accomplishment might constitute a Great Feat except that it had been erased by time and perhaps the hands of the humans who'd used him. He held up the paper. "May I practice this with you, once I've learned it?"

"You may come to the roof." Jaeger turned his back and shuffle-hopped toward the far end of the room. "Blacktalon will meet you and escort you here."

"Thank you, sir." Kip looked past him to the door. "Er, may I leave through the Tower?"

Jaeger turned, his eyes sharp. "Why?"

"I, ah." Kip shook his head. "No reason. I am tired of the outdoors."

"I would prefer you leave by the window," Jaeger said. "Good day. I look forward to your next visit."

And with that he closed the inner door behind him, leaving Kip alone in his study. The fox rolled up the paper and held it in one paw as he opened the window with the other. "Fine," he muttered, and was tempted to leave the window open, but did not.

CHAPTER 6: HISTORY IN THE MAKING

Kip told his friends about his failure to explore the sixth floor hallway and about his meeting with Master Jaeger, and he shared the spell the old sorcerer had written. "Seems simple enough," Emily said after having read through it. "But who can cast a spiritual hold for us to test this?"

"I've asked if I can practice with him. Maybe the rest of us can do it as well."

"Would be useful magic to use on Farley," Malcolm mused. "Make him see himself as the rest of us see him, then maybe he'd feck off and leave us in peace."

"Don't know that it would be nice for any of us to see ourselves as others see us," Coppy said. When they turned to look at him, he gestured at Kip. "What if you could see yourself as Patris sees you? Or you," to Emily, "as some of those older sorcerers see you?"

"Yes," Malcolm said, "but we're right and they're not."

Coppy laughed, but only shortly. "It seems terrible to me, making someone believe something different or see the world differently."

"Help is dependent on context," Kip said. "If you're changing the way they see the world to get them to help more people, isn't that right?"

"Maybe." Coppy shook his head. "But that should be their decision, not one you make for them."

"You can die several lifetimes waiting for them to come to that decision," Emily said.

Later that week, as Kip was poring over the instructions of Jaeger's spell and sounding out the pronunciation, Emily came to him. "Kip," she said with excited urgency, waving a sheet of paper at him, "Master Hobstone's written me again. He says he and Mr. Adams would like to meet with you at the Founders' Rest Inn on Friday next!"

Kip had sat down cross-legged on his bedroll with the spell in front of him, while Neddy snoozed on the stone nearby. Next to him, Coppy practiced levitating a group of five small marbles; Malcolm was either studying with Master Vendis or off on his own somewhere. The fox finished reading through Jaeger's words one more time and then lifted his head. "Thank him for me. I really don't wish to."

"Kip." She put her hands on her hips. "I don't think you understand what this movement stands for. They simply want to explain their goals."

"I'm not interested in their goals." Kip folded his arms. "Mr. Adams simply asking about me last time made Patris furious."

"He knows. That's why he asked to meet at the Inn. Patris need never know." She waved the letter again. "They want you to be part of the movement. This is bigger than learning fire spells."

"It's my future!"

Coppy's marbles fell to the bedroll. The otter looked up, but Emily's focus remained on Kip. "This," she thrust the paper at him, "could be the future of our country!"

"That's all very well for those who have the freedom to be concerned about it." He didn't like the edge his voice got, so he breathed in and pushed fingers through his tail fur to calm himself.

Coppy reached over to touch his arm. "Back in London," he said, "often we had to worry foremost about our survival, but we also knew we had to think about our Isle. For who else would?"

"New Cambridge is doing fine," Kip said. "Better if I remain a student here."

"But what about the Calatians in the Bronx, or in Boston? Even the ones back in the Isle?"

Kip frowned. "You never talked about revolution before."

"Aye." Coppy drew in a breath. "Nor much in London, to be honest. I thought those who talked about founding our own country, leaving the Empire behind to create a society for us Calatians, were foolish. World's not going to change, I said. But..." He gestured toward Emily's letter. "I've been sorting it out in my head the last few days. I think here's a chance for real change."

When Kip lay his ears back, thinking, Emily leaned in again. "You think I'm not worried about my own future? You think this whole enterprise comes without risk? Everyone who dares to dream of a better future faces the prospect of being expelled or exiled or executed. We risked very little to come here and force ourselves upon the sorcerers, and look at what we gained. Now we—Calatians and women alike—have the prospect to gain so much more."

Kip nodded. "And to lose so much more."

She dropped the letter and sat next to Coppy as the otter slid over to make room. "You can't spend your whole life walking inside the boundaries. If I'd done that, I'd still be married to Thomas and probably attending some dreadful tea for the wives of all the other lawyers instead of here learning sorcery."

Kip pushed aside the spell paper. "Then go ahead and do it. Why do you need me to be part of it as well?"

"I want you to be part of it. We broke the barriers of the college together, we should be part of this together, we three and Malcolm."

He couldn't stop the corner of his mouth from curving upward. "But I have so much else to do. This kind of...crusade, it's not what I'm about. You're the one who takes on authority."

Emily rested her head in her hands and gave him a beseeching look. "They need everyone they can get, Kip. You could make such a difference. Your help might tip a balance. What one sorcerer can do..."

"Coppy seems willing to go."

The otter smiled and shook his head. "They don't want someone who can lift a few marbles. They want fire and demons."

"You know that to summon a demon, I need the blood of a calyx."

Coppy looked away and Emily bowed her head. "I know it's difficult."

"'Difficult'?"

"But there are Calatians joining the fight as well. Kip, in an independent state, think of the possibilities for Calatians and women."

A new world? A new order, with new places for his people? Maybe. He didn't want to ruin the glow in her eyes with his skepticism, so he remained silent. Emily persisted. "We can help write the rules. We can make sure that women and Calatians can own property, can vote, maybe even one day serve in government. Why shouldn't we? We live here too."

"I'd like to believe it's that easy," he said, unable to help himself. "I've seen what humans think when we live next to them. They resent even the things they themselves gave us."

She sighed. "Kip, please just go talk to them. It doesn't oblige you to anything."

He couldn't stop thinking about the danger. If Patris found out about it, he could lose everything he'd fought so hard for here. Then he'd have nothing except the independence sorcerers, and who knew what they could teach him?

Coppy cleared his throat. "It's worth just talking to them," he said. "How else will you know what they're about? Didn't you once tell me you'd rather know as much as possible before making a choice?"

Kip looked from one to the other. "All right, all right," he said. "If you're both so set on it."

"Thank you!" Emily got to her feet. "I'll write back and accept."

Coppy just smiled, and in that smile told Kip that he knew whose words had made the most difference.

Emily accompanied him down to the Founders' Rest Inn that Sunday afternoon, on a day when clouds preserved what little warmth the sun provided and then spitefully added a cold drizzle. They'd decided to keep the party as small as possible, so Coppy had stayed behind, and Kip thought often of the otter in the warm, dry basement as he and Emily made their way through the cold damp down the quiet hill. The drizzle and mist were thick enough to conceal the Inn and the church spire behind it until they'd walked more than halfway down the path.

Kip hadn't attended church in weeks, not since his family had left. He really should come back down, if only to see the Cartwrights and his betrothed, Alice. But if he approached them, they might tell him that they wanted to break off the engagement. There were no other female foxes of the appropriate age here, so Kip would then have to look to Boston, New York, or perhaps London to start a family. That would be difficult, and besides, he liked Alice and wanted to get to know her better. As long as he hadn't heard anything from her father, everything was still fine and he had no wish to disturb that fragile peace.

That same sort of worry gnawed at him as he approached the Inn; while he knew nothing of the independence movement, it was easy to spurn it. What if Mr. Adams possessed the eloquence of his father and made a case Kip could not in good conscience refuse?

At the Inn, Old John greeted him. "Some gentlemen here to see the fox sorcerer," he said. "I told 'em your name. Seems as how they ought to know it."

"Thank you," Kip said. "Where are they?"

The innkeeper hooked a crooked thumb toward the back of the inn. "By the rear fire. Five of 'em."

Five? He peered back to where five men indeed sat around a table with a sixth space open at the end nearest Kip. Behind them, a fire cast light onto the faces of the three facing it, while the other two remained in shadow. Four of the five were leaning in to hear the words of the fifth, a man in his forties with well-manicured thinning hair and a high, sloping forehead. When Kip perked his ears in that direction, he heard the man's precise, educated voice concluding a joke: "…after thinking on it a moment replied, 'A little more.'"

Emily took Kip's arm and guided him toward the table as it burst into short, genuine laughter. The man who'd told the joke was the first to see them, and he got to his feet, after which the others followed. "Miss Carswell, I presume," the first man said, and then, "And there is no mistaking Mister Penfold. Thank you so much for granting us your time." He extended a hand. "I am John Quincy Adams. May I present Samuel Bayard, Master Hobstone, Master Kolis, and Alexander Lawrence."

Emily embraced Master Hobstone warmly, and Kip shook the hand of each man in turn. They smelled of scented powders, but below the powders lay the smells of the men themselves, sweating with apprehension. Over meeting him, or over discussing treason in the open? Kip took the empty seat as Mr. Lawrence, seated across from him, rose to offer his seat to Emily.

Adams cleared his throat and kept his voice low. "I am here to represent Boston; Mr. Lawrence represents New York, and Mr. Bayard represents Philadelphia. Master Hobstone and Master Kolis hail from Boston but have friends in both New York and Philadelphia as well as Richmond and Raleigh. I tell you this so that you will do away with any supposition you may have that we are a group of malcontent Bostonians. Our cause is felt throughout the colonies, and each colony has agreed in principle to an American Congress wherein we may address the issue of independence."

"Wasn't, er," Kip felt very young, almost as though he should be standing next to Mr. Lawrence. "Wasn't the first Continental Congress hanged?"

Adams laughed. "You should drive my father into a rage if you said that in his presence. No, the Empire spread that rumour to instill fear in the populace lest they attempt to organize such a Congress again. We keep our heads and voices low for the moment less out of fear of the Empire than of our fellow colonists."

"I'm sorry."

"No need to be. The rumours were spread in order that people would believe them, and until now you've had nobody with direct knowledge to contradict them." Adams tapped the table. "The Continental Congress negotiated with the King and Parliament, using the threat of war to reach a compromise that benefited the colonies. But many of the compromises have fallen away in the forty years since then. Indeed, the only concession remaining is that the American colonies have a representative in Parliament—a member of the House of Commons without the right to vote, who reports back to us that the best days he has are the ones when he is merely ignored by his so-called peers. Britain quarters soldiers by fiat, taxes us more heavily now than she did in 1775, and," he gestured toward the college at the top of the hill, "has been proven unable to defend us against the most terrible threats."

"Napoléon was a threat to the world," Kip argued. "We had to defeat him. Had he beaten England, his colonies would have taken over our own, and then we would be living under an emperor with no Parliament to check him. We would be a conquest."

"Of course," Adams agreed. "But what need was there to impose His Majesty's soldiers on the colonies, when some would have given them quarter gladly? Why, except to remind the colonies that they are the property of the Empire?"

"I don't—" Kip looked around the table, up at the young Mr. Lawrence, who nevertheless had the advantage of him by at least a decade. But he had stood up for himself against Patris, against Windsor, and these men wanted his help. "I don't know how wars are fought."

"Do you know who bore the greatest burden? Not here in New Cambridge, not near the sorcerers, but in Boston, New York, Philadelphia, and Richmond?" Adams leaned forward. "The Calatians."

Kip's ears flattened. "What do you mean?"

"Soldiers come to a town with royal decrees that they must be boarded. Very well, the mayor says, we have many households with room. The officers, of course, are boarded with the well-off, those who can afford it. But the other soldiers, the rank and file? Those are housed with the poor, the ones who can't afford to say no. Many of them are imposed on the Calatians, who in those larger cities can barely afford to feed themselves. They were required to feed the soldiers first."

Kip's ears flushed. Nobody in New Cambridge talked about it, nor had the few visitors they had from those cities. And now this lawyer from Boston, albeit a very smart man and the son of someone Kip respected greatly, knew more about the plight of the Calatians than Kip himself did. "I didn't know about that," he said.

"You have the advantage of living in a very sheltered life in New Cambridge. I'm sure your life is not free of the greater prejudices against Calatians, but with the protection of the sorcerers, you have escaped many of the small indignities that your fellows suffer."

"Is that why you are agitating for independence?" Kip curled his paws into fists. "On behalf of my people?"

"On behalf of all of our people, Penfold." Adams leaned forward. "All the people of this continent who want freedom to shape their own destinies. Including Calatians."

Kip's ears perked forward. He didn't say anything, but Adams perceived the gesture and smiled. "In an independent government of the colonies, the Calatians will have a voice in the government."

"The right to vote on government matters?" Kip's words tumbled out. "To vote for a mayor?"

"Or a governor or a president, perhaps. Yes."

The others around the table kept their expressions carefully neutral. Kip scanned them and then turned back to Emily, who returned a heartened smile. "And women?"

"Of course."

He wanted to push farther. Adams' recital of the Calatians' grievances still rankled, as if he'd been accusing Kip of not caring for Calatians as much as he did. And Kip's worry about his own inexperience and youth had faded with the courtesy and respect he'd been shown. So he pushed Adams. "Indians? Negroes?"

The man next to Adams, Master Kolis, grimaced. Kip couldn't see how Master Hobstone reacted, but Samuel Bayard remained impassive while Mr. Lawrence's eyebrows rose, his face coming to life.

Adams answered the question with a practiced air. "Those are questions that we are certainly considering but have not yet come to a resolution on."

"So you have come to a resolution on the others?" Emily said.

"Are you all," Kip gestured at them before Adams could answer Emily's question, "the leaders, the ones who resolve these issues?"

At that they did glance at one another, and the neutral expression on even Bayard's face cracked into a smile. "We represent the leaders," Adams said.

"Penfold." Bayard leaned forward. His breath smelled of meat and ale. "Adams has laid out the case for you to join independence; let me tell you briefly why you should leave the Empire."

Kip nodded in his direction. Bayard, a man with a thin face and hooked nose, continued on. "Because we hold the home ground. We have fought on this land and we fight for our freedom. If we gain our independence without war…" Here Mr. Lawrence and Master Kolis both snickered. "Then those who supported the Empire will have cause for regret."

"We will not force anyone to leave this country," Adams put in. "The benefits of our campaign will be available to all, even those who do not recognize their necessity."

"But the positions of leadership," Bayard persisted, "will go to those who have supported independence. And if it does come to war…" He closed his fist and set it on the table, and his eyes when they met Kip's were hard and cold. "We will win."

The crackling of the fire sounded very loud in the silence that followed this declaration. Kip's self-assurance weakened, but against the certainty and authority of these men, he reminded himself, he should set all the masters of the College as well as the might of the Empire. Next to such institutions, the crusade to overturn them took on a quixotic air.

"These are weighty questions we have put before you, Penfold," Adams said with a slight smile. "We meet you face to face to show you our dedication to our cause and to convince you that you would be well respected should you choose our side. We do not ask for a decision now, only to advise you that the moment when you must decide is closer than you might think it is."

"If you want to decide now," again Bayard leaned in, "it would assist us immeasurably in our planning."

The respect and courtesy now felt oppressive. Kip shifted in his seat. "I'm just one sorcerer," he said. "Not even fully trained. I can't translocate like Emily, I can't do most alchemical magic…"

"You know fire." Master Hobstone gestured to Emily. "So Miss Carswell tells us. That affinity is rare indeed. In warfare, there are few skills more prized. A master of fire can end a battle. Paired with a translocational sorcerer, he can end several battles in a day."

"Rarely are battles fought in the same day," Adams said. "But you take our point, Penfold. You may not have many talents as a full sorcerer, but the ones you do have are extremely valuable, and as a single battle may win or lose a war, the side you choose might well decide the fate of our movement."

"And there will be sorcerers on our side to continue your instruction in other disciplines," Master Hobstone continued. "I am skilled in alchemical magic and Kolis here is a translocational specialist."

Kolis's sour expression had deepened into bitterness at the mention of Kip's fire affinity, but now returned to mere displeasure at the prospect of instructing a Calatian sorcerer. Nonetheless, he nodded curtly and did not scowl as much as he had when Kip had mentioned Negroes and Indians.

Despite their patient words, clearly they wanted Kip to commit to their cause immediately. But Kip still imagined the weight of the Empire and how small and foolish this group of men looked beside all of that might. When he'd asked if they were the leaders, their answer had unexpectedly revealed to him how small their movement was. If all the men at this table were arrested, would the independence movement crumble? How much damage would they be able to do to the Empire? The prospect of improvements in the lives of Calatians was appealing, but if it were nothing more than the imaginary pot of gold at the end of a very dangerous rainbow, then he risked his own life for a fool's errand.

So he said, "I thank you all for the trouble you've taken to come here. I will think long and hard about what you've presented to me, and when the time comes, I am sure I will be able to make the right decision."

Adams didn't allow any disappointment onto his face, but Bayard leaned over, hiding his mouth, and said, "I told you," softly enough that he probably assumed Kip couldn't hear. Adams didn't react to that either, simply rose and extended his hand.

Kip also stood and shook it. "I hope you will remember the lives that hang in the balance of your decision," Adams said.

"You have made that very clear," Kip responded.

He shook hands with each of the other men as they rose in turn, and then, as they seemed inclined to stay, he and Emily took their leave.

They had not even made it outside the Inn before Emily said, "I don't understand what's holding you back."

"What," Kip said, one paw on the door handle, "you're ready to…" He almost said, "betray your country," but stopped himself in time. "Just…agree to everything?"

"Miss Carswell," a familiar dry voice called from behind them, "I would advise you to refrain from answering at the present time."

Emily's face reflected the cold that gripped Kip's stomach and chest. They both turned to see the stern, thin-lipped Master Windsor behind them. "Come," he said, "let us walk outside. The weather is so much kinder there."

They stepped out into a cold drizzle driven into their faces by the breeze. "Master," Emily said, regaining some of her composure and color—or perhaps the flush in her cheeks was merely from the cold. "We were simply having a discussion with some friends of—of my old teacher of sorcery in Boston."

"I know well with whom you were conversing," Windsor said.

"You won't tell Master Patris, will you?" Kip burst out. "You always said we have potential, and we didn't agree to anything, I promise you, but he's so afraid we might…"

Windsor held up a hand, and Kip's words lost steam. "Penfold, Miss Carswell. I have no knowledge of your conversation, nor do I wish to acquire any. I am observing history."

"How did you happen to be at the Inn?" Emily asked.

"And," he continued as though she hadn't spoken, pausing to rest with one hand against the trunk of a tree, "I do not believe that Patris need be informed of your every movement. Should you at some point decide to embrace the cause of independence, I have no doubt that that decision will be well visible to all at the College. Until that day, your thought processes deserve the privacy that all of ours enjoy. And Penfold, contrary to Patris's fears, I believe that your heritage is more inclined to pull you to support of the Empire."

"I am. I mean, it is."

Windsor fixed him with a withering glare. "I have already told you, I have no wish to be privy to your personal deliberations. Apart from being potentially compromising to my own neutral position, I am fantastically uninterested in the long and tedious process through which you come to decisions. Therefore I would be most pleased if you would do me the favor of keeping your thoughts on the matter to yourself."

Emily and Kip exchanged looks. "If you'd rather go on up by yourself," Emily said, "we can let you go."

"I would think you would prefer to keep my company. Patris is less likely to ask questions if we all return together. No, I will remain with you, and you will remain quiet for the blessedly short journey. I trust that is not an undue burden."

So they let him lead the way up the hill, to the gates, and back to the college. And when they reached the Tower, he left them without a word, striding across the Great Hall to the stairs and up to his quarters.

"Has he gotten stranger?" Emily asked. "Or is it just that we haven't seen him much outside of class for the last month?"

"We could ask Coppy." Kip stopped to greet the fireplace elementals while Emily stood a few steps ahead, impatient. "All right, I'm coming. Sorry, fellows."

They chorused their pardons as he walked on and followed Emily down the stairs, back to the dank door and the smell of old paper and phosphorus and a little bit of the scent of otter. Malcolm wasn't there, but Coppy got up to greet them. "How did it go?"

"They really want Kip to join them," Emily said before Kip could answer. "Mr. Adams was very eloquent and still Kip is being stubborn."

"They said I don't have to decide now," Kip said. He crossed past Coppy and leaned against the bookshelf that shielded their bedrolls from the rest of the basement. "They have nothing but a list of people who want independence and a few sorcerers without any affiliation."

"Is it the College that makes sorcerers great, then?"

"The greatest sorcerers study here!" Kip waved to the ceiling. "If the sorcerers aren't here, or in London, then what are they doing? What are they studying?"

Emily folded her arms. "Thomas held that school is all well and good, but there's a time when one must seek experience in the real world. That's what you can learn outside the college."

"Thomas, the husband you left because you disliked him so much?"

"He knew about law." She brushed her hair back from her face and returned her arms to their folded position.

"Sorcery isn't law. I can't just go muddle my way through casting a spell." Kip's tail lashed. "And what if it had been Patris rather than Windsor down there? What if Windsor goes and tells him anyway? He's told—" He stopped; they didn't know about Peter. "When I talked to him before Selection I told him some things in confidence, and Master Jaeger knew about them. I don't trust him to keep this secret."

"For Heaven's sake. If he meant to tell Patris, he would've told us." But even Emily's sharp words held a quaver of uncertainty.

"I think he'll keep the secret, for what that's worth," Coppy said.

"And if I get expelled," Kip said, "where will I go? I can't go to London. If only I could, though, I could study sorcery without Patris looking over my shoulder the whole time..." An idea occurred to him. He paced away from Coppy and Emily for a moment, staring down at Neddy. The phosphorus elemental was curled, just like a real lizard two and a half feet long, in a blackened patch of stone. And the stone reminded Kip of Peter, bound to the stone to guard the Tower. He had summoned Neddy; he had spoken to Peter, all on his own. He had made his own decisions there and he could make his own decisions here.

"This is more important than Patris," Emily said, and was about to go on, but Kip interrupted her.

"If I go to London." Kip's tail lashed back and forth. "Of my own accord. If I study with Master Cott. I've already got the things we discovered in the ruins. Then I'll be out from under Patris's eye and what's more, I'll be in London. He can't claim I'm conspiring against the Empire there."

"London?" Coppy said faintly. His whiskers twitched and he pressed his paws together.

"Are you serious?" Emily stood staring at Kip as though he'd suggested setting the basement on fire. "You can't leave New Cambridge."

"Not for forever," Kip said. "Just until I learn—"

"What?" Emily demanded.

"Enough to be taken seriously as a sorcerer."

She threw up her hands. "I'm sorry, was it another Calatian sorcerer sitting across from me while five important men as good as begged him to join their cause? How much more seriously do you want to be taken?"

Kip curled his tail to his side and looked down at his paws. "They have no idea of my abilities. I'm not good enough yet. I'd be no use in a war."

"There might not be a war," Coppy said faintly. Emily put an arm over his shoulder, hugging him.

"Of course there will be a war." Kip matched Emily's glare. "They all knew it. They paid lip service to the peaceful option, but they knew there would be a war. Everyone at that table did."

"Which is why it's so important that you help them." Emily released Coppy and strode toward Kip, knocking papers out of the way.

"And what if we lose? If a Calatian sorcerer helps a rebellion, if all Patris's fears come true, then what? What are the chances that another Calatian will ever be admitted again?"

"But if we don't help," Coppy said, "we might be missing the chance to write history. Kip, you already stepped out of line once to come up here. Why—why run away to England?"

"Because the risk is greater this time." Emily stopped just a foot from

Kip's muzzle, her eyes bright. "Because his father isn't here to support him and tell him it's okay for him to do it."

"I don't need my father," Kip snapped, and that brought back a whole wave of thoughts about being a calyx. "And I'm not running away. Not exactly."

"But Kip." Coppy came to his side. "Think of it. A new country! It could be so exciting."

The fox pointed up at the ceiling. "Think about making this institution accept us, about forging a place in a society that's been around for hundreds of years. Isn't that more worthwhile?"

"It seems longer odds than winning a war, if you ask me," Emily said.

"If we simply tear down structures every time we're tired of them, where does that leave us?"

Emily's face flushed. She took a step back and made a visible effort to control her voice, with the result that it came out rather cold. "You sound less and less like your precious Mr. Adams every day. I had hoped that the words of his own son would convince you, but if not even that will work then go ahead, go to London, be part of an empire that will always view you—and me—as less than full people."

And with that, she disappeared into her room. The door would not close, but there was a thunk as she slammed a book to the floor.

Kip and Coppy both stared after her, and then Kip turned to the otter. "There's nothing stopping you from joining their movement," he said. "I want to stay with you, but this is bigger than the two of us."

"I don't want to end up fighting you," Coppy said quietly.

"We wouldn't have to." But the prospect frightened Kip as well. He imagined himself on one side of a battlefield calling up fire, and watching as rocks flew at him from the other side, knowing that an otter was hurling them. What would he do in that case? "We'd refuse."

"Better to be on the same side." The otter's whiskers rose as he smiled. "Anyway, they don't want me. They want the fire fox."

"They can want all they like," Kip said with a look back at Emily's room. And then, remembering the conversation they'd had coming back, he said, "By the way, how has Windsor been?'

The otter's smile vanished. "What do you mean?"

So Kip told him some of the things Windsor had said. "And we don't know how he knew we would be there. Was it just coincidence?"

"If you're asking if I told him anything..." Coppy bristled.

"We know you wouldn't," Kip hurried to reassure him. "But has he said anything about the independence movement? Or about us? He seemed... even more sour than usual today."

"Not that I recall exactly." Coppy looked down at the floor. "We don't talk about anything in particular at the lessons."

Kip reached out to the otter. "The lessons are going well, aren't they?"

"I suppose they are."

"You don't get intimidated by him anymore, it sounds like."

"No, but..." Coppy scratched his cheek. "I sorta have the opposite problem."

"Opposite?"

"Well, I do some spells with him, but...when I practice them on my own, I never seem quite as good at them as I was in the lessons with him."

Kip frowned. "That's good, though. Maybe you're feeling the pressure and rising to the occasion." He smiled. "If you need one of us to yell at you from time to time, let us know. I'm sure we can help."

"No, no." But the otter's smile returned. "I'm sure it will all be fine. But Kip...do you really mean to go to London?"

"Coppy..." Kip sighed. He sat down, and Coppy sat beside him. "Emily won't stop with the independence movement. Already Windsor knows something that could get me expelled. What if it's Sharpe next time? Or Patris himself? They're already afraid of a," he spread his paws and indicated his body, "Calatian with powerful fire sorcery even when I'm on their side. Any excuse and Patris will expel me. In London I can learn from the only other fire sorcerer in the colleges, and I'll be out from under Patris's nose."

"That's true." Coppy sighed. "But Kip...do you think this is a just cause, this independence?"

"What does 'just' mean?" Kip asked after a pause. "The way Farley attacked Calatian cubs, was that 'just'? My parents being punished for my attendance here at the school, was that 'just'? The question isn't about what's just. It's about who has the power to do as they please. I'm lucky; I have a talent that people want. That gives me some power. The more I develop it, the more I'll be able to right the wrongs of the world. Some of them, anyway."

"I can see why you think that way." The otter rested a paw on his knee. "But if all you're after is power, you'll be no better than Farley."

Kip stared, and Coppy withdrew his paw. "I—I didn't mean it like that. Of course you'll be better than Farley. I meant that if—if you want power so you can do what you want—that's—that's just what they're doing. Can't you think about what's right?"

"It doesn't matter what I think is right until I can do something about it." Kip smoothed his fur down and stared ahead at the phosphorus elemental. "Look, I pulled Neddy from his world to come here and heat our basement. Was that right? It was necessary."

"You can do something about it now. You're valuable enough that it matters what side you choose."

"Not until I can study in London. And anyway..." He exhaled. "That's part of the problem."

"What?"

Kip looked beyond Neddy, seeing again the five men at the Inn. "They don't want me. They want my abilities. I'm no more than a weapon to them. They offered me the prize of dignity and respect and equal status for Calatians in their new country, but how can they promise that? They are half a dozen men. Our town couldn't even agree that it was a good thing for me to come here and study."

"But if Bryce Morgan had told them it was, I reckon they'd have got behind it," Coppy said quietly. "That's what leaders are meant to do."

"All right." Kip looked the otter full in the face. Coppy returned his look with earnest interest. "Do you think that all the humans in the Colonies will let Calatians own property and vote if Mr. John Quincy Adams says so? Is it that easy?"

Coppy exhaled. "It's better than nobody saying so, isn't it?"

Was it? Probably. But was it better than the alternative, building himself into someone who'd succeeded within the system, someone they couldn't say no to? Better to depend on these men or to depend on himself? Nobody apart from Coppy had proven reliable in his life; even his father had kept secrets from him and then been forced to move to Georgia.

"All right," he said. "You're from London. Do you think the Colonies should be independent?"

"I'm not the one being asked," Coppy said, whiskers lifting with a smile. "But I think if they want to be, they should. As long as they're happy being part of Britain, that's all well and good, but there's a long way between here and there and it's already different over here. I feel like I'm in a new country. So maybe it should be."

"That makes sense, I suppose." Kip rested his chin on his knee and exhaled. "Coppy, if I go with them, I have to leave the college. I can't."

"They came to talk to Patris, too. Maybe he's thinking of joining the movement as well."

"Hah." Kip snorted. "That will be the day Farley declares his love for all Calatians."

"Odden at least is invested in you," Coppy said. "Why not see what he says?"

"Maybe I will." Kip exhaled. "Thanks. It really does help to talk to someone about it, and I can't talk to Emily."

"She'll come around." Coppy smiled. "We're all friends, right?"

Again Kip saw himself on one side of a battlefield, but this time arrayed against him on the other side stood not only Coppy, but also Emily and Malcolm. He would never be able to fight that battle. Maybe that would be the deciding factor, in the end.

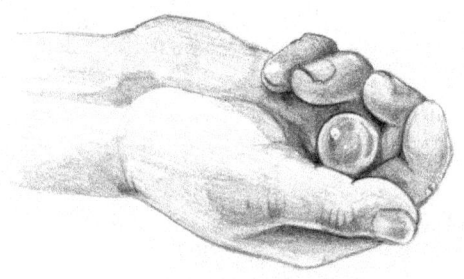

CHAPTER 7: LOYALTY

Master Odden rolled the small glass bead around in his fingers. "Extraordinary," he murmured. "You say it has a resonance with fire?"

Kip sat across from the master in his study, paws clasped in his lap. "Yes."

"How does this resonance manifest?"

The fox shook his head. "When I smell it, I catch part of what I get with fire. And the demon said…"

"Oh, demons." Odden scoffed.

"But Nikolon seemed genuinely afraid of it. She said that it was a part of her home world that had manifested in this one. Something like that." He wanted badly to tell the sorcerer about Forrest's memory, about the vision he'd sent Kip, but Peter's warning and the light at the top of the Tower bound his tongue. Of course he knew that Odden's office was here on the second floor, but what if there were a spare room, an empty laboratory?

"Hm." The sorcerer's bushy eyebrows rose and he looked at Kip from under them. "I have rarely seen demons afraid or worried. But we already suspected that the attack was the work of a demon. Now we know it was one with great association with fire, and one that leaves glass beads in the place of people. This may help in our research."

The way Odden handled the bead as though it was some kind of token and not the actual remains of a person made Kip slightly queasy. But he sat up straight and said, "Would it be useful for Master Cott to look at it?"

"Oh, indeed it would." Odden's eyebrows lowered, though his eyes continued to hold Kip's. "And I suppose you would like to be present to meet him."

A shiver ran down Kip's tail. "If you'd allow it."

"Of course I will. But there's another matter." And now the eyebrows lowered further and the brow creased below his dark black hair. "The question of whether you will be continuing your correspondence with Mr. Adams."

A rush of anger pushed Kip forward in his seat, but he restrained himself before he'd gone too far. "How—" Of course. "Windsor said he wouldn't tell anyone," he said through clenched teeth, heart racing.

"*Master* Windsor suggested, and I agree, that Headmaster Patris need know nothing about this, but as your master, he felt it important that I be informed." Odden clasped his hands together and leaned forward. "I understand why you chose to keep this meeting private, and I hope you will trust that I shall not betray it to Patris. However, at the same time I am forced to acknowledge that Patris's concerns about your loyalty to the Empire may have found some basis in fact. Should you continue your correspondence—"

"I haven't corresponded with him at all," Kip said. "That was Emily." He shouldn't have said her name, he realized, but he was still angry at Odden and Patris and at Emily, and giving her name was spiteful revenge. "I only went to the Inn to meet at his request, and I listened to him for fifteen, maybe twenty minutes, and then I walked back. Nothing more has transpired between us."

"Do not interrupt me again." Odden's frown deepened.

"I'm sorry, sir," Kip said.

"You are passionate. That is admirable. But do I have your assurance that you will have no further contact with Mr. Adams or any of his associates?"

Even though Kip had already been leaning in that direction, the prohibition from his master gave him hesitation. "Mr. Adams visited this college," he said. "Others here are no doubt in contact with him."

"Yes?"

"Why should I be singled out? Until I've made a decision—like everyone else here—about which side to be on, I'm loyal to the Empire."

"You can hardly be loyal if you feel that there will be a decision to be made in the future. And the decision, if there is one, shall be made by the Headmaster of the College. The rest of us will follow his decree or leave the College. And," he added, leaning forward, "whatever my decision, you will abide by that if you wish to continue our association."

"Yes, sir," Kip said, keeping his ears upright though he wanted to flatten them.

"So?"

The decision weighed on him. Of course he would be able to change his mind later, but Kip didn't want to be the kind of person who went back on his word. And here, as he opened his mouth to agree to Master Odden's condition, he was struck with a question: what if Adams and his men did succeed? They weren't stupid; they were all older than he was and more experienced, and Adams's father, at least, had been through one independence movement before. Wouldn't they know if the time was right?

But then, Coppy had asked him, "what is right?" The indignities and suffering of Calatians was terrible, but promises were easy to make when negotiating for a weapon—and that was what Kip was to these people: a weapon. They weren't interested in Coppy and were only somewhat interested in Emily, and that perhaps only because she was their way to get Kip.

Whereas here, Windsor had invoked Kip's heritage; Odden had talked about gaining his trust. That was not something you asked of a weapon.

So Kip looked Odden back in the eye and said, "Would it satisfy you if I were able to study in London, with Master Cott?"

Surprise flitted over his master's face, followed a moment later by amusement. "You feel you have already learned all I have to teach you?"

Kip's tail flicked back and forth. He ticked off reasons on his paw for Odden. "You're as uncomfortable with Pat—Headmaster Patris's dislike of me as I am."

"Perhaps not quite as much."

"It's not easy for you." Kip held up a second finger. "It would prove my loyalty to the Empire to be studying in the capital." A third finger joined the other two. "You yourself have said that Master Cott is the preeminent fire sorcerer in the Empire. Where better for me to learn my craft?"

Master Odden's amusement faded as he absorbed Kip's points. "Counter to your logic, if Patris does not trust you, he may not think much of accelerating your study in such a powerfully destructive magic. And yet, mastering your gift for fire magic is of paramount importance, and Cott does live in the heart of London, where I imagine the independence movement would have a harder time reaching. Hum hum."

Kip's tail twitched faster as Odden pondered his proposal. Finally the sorcerer nodded, his beard bobbing up and down. "I will ask Master Cott, first. I do not believe he is currently teaching an apprentice. If he agrees, I will wait for the right time to approach the headmaster. In the correct mood, I do think your logic will prevail. If this is something you truly wish."

"Yes," Kip said. "I very much appreciate your instruction, but the situation here…Master Patris seems to dislike me more than he does Coppy, and Master Windsor is keeping Coppy away from him. I'm a target. We'll both be safer if I'm elsewhere. Just for a little while. Until Christmas, perhaps. I do wish to remain your apprentice."

"If you undertake this course of study, you may not be able to dictate the time of your return." Odden's eyebrows lowered.

"But I may come back to visit?"

"Most likely." The sorcerer chuckled. "More likely if Miss Carswell's studies progress as rapidly as yours."

No sorcerer would be bothered to ferry a Calatian back and forth, Kip understood. He nodded once more, decisively. "I want to go to London."

Two days later, when Master Odden told Kip he would be going to London, Kip thought he would be happy, but mostly his chest was flooded with relief. The idea that he could study fire without looking over his shoulder every moment, to be free of Farley and Patris…he didn't know how much it had been weighing on him until the prospect of escaping it became real.

His friends, predictably, were not as excited. Coppy lowered his head and remained quiet, while Emily, and to a lesser extent Malcolm, tried to talk him out of it. Kip kept an ear to their conversation while he gathered his few things and set them on his bedroll.

"You know it's night in London when it's day here," Emily said.

"Not all the time." Malcolm took a piece of paper and called over to the phosphorus elemental. "Neddy, make us a charcoal, there's a good lad."

"You don't have to teach us a lesson," Emily said. "I've had enough of that for one day."

"I believe you," Kip said to Malcolm as the phosphorus lizard crunched up some paper and worked his jaw before spitting out a compressed blackened lump.

"But it's one of the few things I know." The Irishman smiled and picked up the charcoal anyway, but didn't try to write anything with it.

"Kip," Emily said. "You don't have to go to London."

He looked up from the bedroll. "Are you going to stop trying to impress me into the independence movement?" She blinked at him and didn't answer. "Then I have to go to London."

"Kip Penfold." Her voice grew so cold that even Neddy stopped and looked up at her. "I am not driving you away."

"If we hadn't had that meeting at the Founders Rest—"

"This is not about that." She folded her arms. "This is about you being so accustomed to having a master that you can't imagine life without one."

He'd bent to tie up his bedroll and now straightened again. "Who's going to teach us magic, if not masters?"

"I'm not talking about sorcerers."

Kip suppressed a growl, though his tail lashed quickly back and forth. "All right, then. Do you know what you're asking me to risk?" She opened her mouth but he talked over her. "How many of your lady friends have been attacked?"

"Nearly all of them. Some by their own husbands."

"How many vanished with no explanation? How many turned up dead?" She fell silent. "If a few thousand women were killed," he pressed on, "would the entire race of women in the world end?"

"That won't happen. Nobody would destroy the Calatians."

"But they might destroy all the foxes. How many wolf-Calatians do you know? I've never met one. They might all be dead by now."

"And what if by taking a risk, you could guarantee their safety?"

"It's too great a risk." He finished tying up his bedroll, and when he stood up again, Emily's eyes were fixed on the back wall several feet behind him.

"Fine," she said. "Have a lovely trip." And she left the basement, stomping up the stairs.

Neither Malcolm nor Coppy spoke as Kip slid his bedroll into the rough canvas bag he'd bought from the Inn. "Sorry about that," he said finally into the silence.

Malcolm nodded. "Ah, she's a passionate one, but once the emotions cool she'll understand what you're about and she'll miss you like the rest of us will. Though it is a trifle unfair to blame her wholly for your troubles. As I recall, you were the one went chasing after Mr. Adams."

"But not once I knew he was here for independence," Kip pointed out.

"Aye, aye." The Irishman put his hands up. "I'm simply saying that when your emotions cool, try to see her side as well. This cause means a great deal to her, like her divorce writ large."

"I know." Kip clasped his paws together. "But she doesn't know…"

He turned to Coppy, who nodded reluctantly. "Kip's right," he said. "We're maybe in for much worse if we join this fight and lose."

Malcolm draped his arm over Coppy's shoulder. "I understand," he said. "And besides, this," he gestured around to include Kip, "this will survive any political movement. What we've been through together, why, it's like a war."

"It is, rather," Coppy said. "Complete with battles."

Kip turned to the otter. "You understand, right? To become a sorcerer…"

"I know you're doing what's important to you." Coppy sighed and put a paw to his forehead. "Malcolm's right. I know we'll still be friends."

"Of course we will. Why would we not? Because I'm leaving to study in London? I'll be back." He gestured toward the bag. "I'm not even taking all my things with me."

"Probably should take more than that, though," Malcolm chimed in.

"It's not about that." Coppy's tail slid across some papers on the floor. "Everyone's busy and I don't know about Master Windsor…"

"You're doing better with him. You said so."

"Yes, but…what if things go bad again?"

Kip put a paw on Coppy's shoulder. "Then you'll have Emily send me a note and I'll come back."

"She'll have to come visit you to find out where to send it."

Malcolm patted the otter's shoulder. "I told you, don't worry. She'll come around. At worst she'll come visit the fox to keep on with the argument."

"Well, that's true." Kip laughed, and that felt good, but Coppy still didn't. So he said, "Look, do you want me to bring anything to your family? Maybe you can come with Emily when she visits. Tell her you want to see London and that she's the only way you can get back."

"I'll give you a letter to take to my family," Coppy said. "But I don't know if Windsor will let me go to London."

"Come on Sunday. He can't tell you what to do on Sunday."

"Patris and Odden tell you what to do in your spare time." Coppy slid out from Malcolm's arm and walked over to his bedroll, where he took out a piece of paper and a pen.

Kip appealed to Malcolm. "You understand why I'm going to London, right?"

"Of course." The Irishman beamed and patted Kip's arm. "You go become a big fire sorcerer and come back here and burn off Patris's wig until he lets you run the college."

It was nice to have someone who could make you smile like that, especially when everyone else was turning their back on you. Briefly Kip wondered if he were under a sorcerous hold, if he was convinced of some reality that nobody else could see, but at least Malcolm understood what he was doing, what he had to do.

That reminded him that he should go see Master Jaeger to ask him if there were sorcerers in London who could help him practice breaking spiritual holds, but he had to meet the translocational sorcerer from London in just under an hour, so he didn't know if he would have time. Away from the Tower, it wouldn't be as pressing an issue, but now that he knew about it, Kip wanted to learn as much as he could. He thought he was doing well with the spell, but without practicing under a real spiritual hold it was hard to tell.

"Here," Coppy stood and held out the piece of paper to him, folded over with an address written on the outside. "It's got the street on it. Just ask for the Lutris family and you'll find them."

"I'll find them." Kip tucked the letter into his bag. "I wish I could take you with me, but I won't be gone for very long. Come on, this isn't good-bye."

"It's good-bye for a little bit." Coppy reached out and embraced Kip, his eyes squeezed shut.

Kip hugged back, guilt choking his throat. But Coppy could handle it here, and besides, Coppy had protected Kip through the last year. Now it was Kip's turn to help him. Farley hated Calatians but he particularly hated

Kip, and Patris hadn't attended a single one of Coppy's lessons to threaten him with expulsion. Without Kip, hopefully Coppy could have a quieter time here. "You watch out for Emily and Malcolm, okay?"

"Of course."

Coppy looked as though he wanted to say more, and Kip worried that if the guilt got any stronger, he wouldn't be able to go through with leaving. And then his eye fell on Peter's journal, and gratefully he reached down and took the red leather-bound book in his paw.

The magic worked. Coppy looked around, puzzled, and then wandered back to his own bedroll, where he sat down and took out a spell book. Malcolm said, "Coppy, I'm going to find Emily, eh?"

"Cheers," Coppy said. "I'm working on my precision in this physical spell."

"Come along." Malcolm beckoned the otter. "It's a nice enough day out that we can work in the practice tent."

And Malcolm walked out the door and Coppy buried his nose in his book. Kip walked over to Neddy's space, looking for bare stone he could touch to speak to Peter in relative privacy.

The glowing lizard looked up as Kip came by. "Sounds like you're leaving," he said. "Goin' back to the Flower?"

Kip stopped. He looked from the book in his paw to Neddy. "You can see me?"

"Course." The elemental tilted his head. "Should I not be able to?"

"No, no." Kip crouched down. "Yes, I'll be going for a while. You'll still be bound here, never fear, and Coppy will tell me if you get too cold and need to go back. Shouldn't be for a month or more yet."

He could release Neddy now, let Emily find her own way to heat the basement. But that would be petty, beneath him, and deep down he knew that they'd find agreement again. So he smiled at Neddy's bright eyes and set a paw to the stone to say a quick *Good-bye* to Peter.

There was no response. He hadn't expected any. So he replaced the journal, hefted his bag, and walked upstairs to go to London.

CHAPTER 8: MASTER COTT

When Master MacDougal, the British sorcerer with the thin face and scraggly red hair, gripped his shoulder with a strong bony hand, Kip wasn't sure what to expect. There was a moment's disorientation and then the air was warmer, more humid, and smelling strongly of water and refuse. "Come," the sorcerer said with a noticeable northern burr. "I'll take you to Master Cott."

Clouds filled the sky overhead, but of a smoother, flatter texture than the puffy, rolling clouds Kip saw so often back in Massachusetts Bay. He and Master MacDougal stood on a wide stone rooftop surrounded by a parapet very like the roof of the White Tower. This one, though, showed signs of hundreds more years of age: lichen on the stone and dirt in the larger crevices where some hardy moss still struggled to survive. And unlike the roof of the Tower, there were four other towers around them, one ancient one within the walls that connected the other four. To Kip's right was a lighter, newer tower; to his left, a taller one that flew the Union Jack. Before him sloped a green hill down to the great murky snake of the River Thames, but he had only a moment to look at it and across at the thick mass of settlement before MacDougal called sharply to him.

Also unlike the White Tower's roof, this roof had stairs leading down. MacDougal led Kip down to a thick wooden door which he opened by placing his hand against it approximately where a lock would be. There was a grinding sound and then the door swung away from them.

"Is that a spell?" Kip asked, and MacDougal grunted. "Will I be taught it?"

"D'you expect to go to the roof often by yourself?"

The curt response set Kip's ears back. He hefted his bag onto his shoulder and said, "I don't know," even though MacDougal didn't seem interested in his reply and in fact did not pursue the conversation further.

They walked down the gently spiraling stair past two landings before MacDougal stopped and opened another door in the same fashion, striding forward into a narrow hallway barely wide enough for two to walk abreast. Sconces in the walls held some kind of magical light, which Kip paused to sniff and investigate, but the light had no odor, and in the time it took him to sniff, MacDougal had walked on another five feet without stopping, so Kip hurried to catch up.

They passed eight doors, four in each side of the wall, before MacDougal stopped and rapped on one, adorned only with a bronze plaque in the center that read, "COTT." When he got no response, he yelled through the door. "Cott! Got your Colonial Calatian here."

Some scuffling came from behind the door, getting closer. MacDougal gathered his lungs and yelled, "Cott!"

"He's coming," Kip said.

MacDougal ignored him, but didn't call out again, even though it took another fifteen long seconds for Cott to come to the door, during which Kip became very aware of the smell of fried meat and body odor that hung around MacDougal, both from his breath and from his robes, which had been much less obvious out in the open air.

And then the door opened and Kip had to look down to look into the face of Master Cott, barely five feet tall if that, a man who filled out his robes amply and wore a cheerful smile on a round face framed by an untidy mop of bright blond hair. "So it is," he said, "so it is. Come inside, Mister Penfold, and let us get acquainted."

He took Kip's paw with a strong grip and pulled him into the room. Behind Kip, MacDougal said sourly, "Oh, it's all right, it's no trouble at all, glad to be of service."

"Oh, Ian, thank you!" Cott turned to wave, but MacDougal had already turned his back. "Well." Cott let go of Kip to close the door. "That's Ian. He's like the weather around here: either cloudy or about to be. Heh heh! Now, let's get you seated and talk about your time here in London. I have the letter from your Master Odden, and a somewhat shorter one from your Headmaster. Please, this way."

Kip followed the diminutive master through a room smaller than Odden's study, barely more than a narrow hallway from the door to the closed window that looked out over bare trees and another stone tower. Bookshelves lined the walls, and as in Master Jaeger's office, many of the shelves were laden not with books but with sheafs of paper bound with twine or ribbons, although Cott had a full two shelves of books as well. Kip saw no cabinet where a knife and goblet might be kept. Perhaps Cott felt no need to summon demons or work large magics.

Beneath the window stood a wooden desk that fit so squarely against the wall that it might have been built into the room. Only one chair sat pushed into the desk, so Kip wondered whether he would remain standing. But the sorcerer opened a door set into the wall before the desk and gestured for Kip to precede him. "Let's go talk in here," he said. "The study is fine for research, but when I have company I prefer the workroom."

The workroom, it transpired, was a space the size of the entire basement of the Tower, with three windows across one wall and stone benches here and there along the interior walls. The otherwise bare space also contained three stone tables, two of which had been set on their side with the tops facing the center of the room, and the third of which stood in the far corner and bore upon it a small wooden chest reinforced with bronze that, Kip realized, would be just the right size for a goblet and a knife. Ash dusted the large bare space in the center of the room, and soot streaks marred the ceiling.

Cott closed the door behind them. "I inherited this space from Master Belladon, who mostly works with plants. He's happier with his garden anyway. He's over in that tower." He pointed out the window. "We can visit him if you like. He's very nice. But this space is far more suited to working with fire. There's the tables we can use for shields, there's windows to open if the room gets stuffy, or smoky, or dangerous, heh heh, although if you're any good, there won't be much danger." His eyes sparkled. "Let's see."

With a theatrical wave, he conjured a fire in between them, close enough for Kip to feel its heat on his muzzle, let alone his feet. He jumped back and dropped his bag. "Go on," Cott said, "put it out."

Kip reached for the fire and felt around its edges the force keeping it alive. *Come away for later*, he told it, drew its power away and into himself.

The fire and the heat vanished, and Cott's smile grew larger. "Now try this one."

This time he vocalized a spell, but Kip couldn't see any difference in the fire—until he reached out to pull it away. This fire stayed despite his initial coaxing. He met Cott's eyes over the flames. "Should I keep trying?"

"Until you run out of ideas."

It reminded him of the fire he'd lit in the Great Hall, the one only Odden had been able to extinguish, and Odden had mentioned a binding of sorts. He could speak a banishment spell, but would that even work on inanimate flames? Cott was taking his measure, not only of what he'd learned but of his ability to work with fire itself. So he reached out again, this time breathing in his surroundings. This fire was part of England, of London, of Master Cott, and it had been called into life here and Kip was here to take it back. This was the end, but no fire ever really dies; it would be born again, and soon, to judge by the look of the room. He could hold it until then. He understood it.

The fire bowed gracefully and died.

Cott clapped his hands together. "Splendid! I did not hear you unmake the binding, so I presume you simply spoke to the fire?"

"Yes." The space where the fire had been was still warm. Kip touched the floor with a toe. "Was that what I should have done?"

"Yes, of course. Undoing magical bindings is something Master Odden will take you through in some months." Cott bustled over to the table under the window, the one with the chest on it. "Now come over here for a moment. Tell me what you've most recently learned."

Kip walked over, staring at the chest. Cott wasn't going to cut him and take his blood, was he? "I've learned the summoning of demons," he said. "And their banishment."

For the first time, Cott's smile flickered. "Ah," he said. "So you have witnessed the ritual of the calyx."

"Yes."

"It must have been very difficult." The man's hand rested on the wooden chest and caressed it. "None of that here. You should have no need to summon a demon; in fact, as a general rule we avoid the summoning of demons here at King's. We have enough human servants to do for the chores, so I believe the Master of Students has a demon, you know, to supervise the use of magic, and of course for particular jobs they are needed, but…in any case, all the work we do with fire will come from within you, so I hope to avoid such difficult situations. Now, if you wish to work with fire on a greater scale, it will be a necessary unpleasantness. It's one we've all grown used to, although of course I can see why it would be more difficult for you. But rest assured, we all understand and appreciate the sacrifice your people make. There may be some who do not express, ah, but," here he looked away from Kip and out the window, "I have always supported your people and I am very pleased to see that one of you is developing your talent, that is, ah…"

Kip didn't know what to say as Cott trailed off, other than, "Thank you," so he said that, and that acknowledgment revived the man's spirits.

"Oh, you know, I do my best. But that you should be a fire sorcerer, of all things, it's quite, well, I think it's wonderful."

This last was said with a stubborn firmness of tone, as though Kip might protest that he'd really rather not specialize in fire, if it was all the same to Cott. He didn't want to say "thank you" again, so he said, "I'm pleased to be working with you."

"Yes, yes, and you had something to show me."

Now Cott's eyes shone eagerly as Kip reached into his bag and brought out the first glass bead he'd found. Saul's was still in the perfume bottle wrapped safely in one of his tunics; Odden had given him a small wooden box to hold the other, and that was what he now passed over to Master Cott.

The sorcerer took the box to the window and prised the lid from it carefully. Without touching the bead, he held the box up to the light and examined it from all angles, his expression turning intent, almost hungry as he watched the bead roll around, casting small reflections around the sides of the box.

Cott reached in with his other hand, then stopped and peered over the box at Kip. "It is safe to touch?" At Kip's nod, he gently lifted the bead out between two fingers.

"Ah," he said. "Yes. I feel it." He closed his eyes and then opened them to meet Kip's. "You felt it too, the spirit of fire left within?"

"I didn't know what it was, but it smelled like fire, and when I felt it, it reminded me of the feeling of fire." He shook his head. "I don't know how better to say it."

"Glass is fused by fire and remembers the fire that made it. If you put your hand—your paw to this window, you may feel the echo of the fire. But in this window it is very weak. The memory of fire is stronger in the bead; there is more going on here." He replaced the bead in the box and fitted the lid back onto it. "I will of course be pleased to instruct you in fire sorcery while we investigate this."

"Thank you." Kip reached out to take the box back, but Cott lifted the lid of the chest and dropped the box into it. It was open for only a second, but that was long enough for Kip to see the gleam of the top of the silver goblet in it.

That dampened his enthusiasm slightly, taking the curl from his tail so it dragged on the floor. "Will we be having lessons now or should I take my bag to my quarters?"

"Quarters? Oh. Ah, yes, I thought it best that you stay here in the workspace." Cott pointed to one of the tables lying on its side. "I know there isn't much privacy, but the alternative is for you to stay with the other apprentices, three floors down, and it would be in a bunk in a common space. Not much privacy there, either, and no guarantee as to the behavior of the other apprentices, hah."

Kip looked around the bare room. "I, uh. I won't be in the way of your fire spells?"

"Oh, if we're casting anything like that I'll remove your things to my office." Cott's cheerful manner returned. "And you may come through my office to leave anytime you like. I'm rarely doing anything private in there."

"I could leave through the windows, too?" This had never been an option in his basement, but Master Jaeger hadn't seemed to mind.

"Ah, maybe." Cott shot a look at the windows. "At night, perhaps. There might be a slight problem if you're seen levitating."

"Is that against the custom here?"

"Somewhat? We do levitate down to the Isle, but—I meant more that people might not be used to seeing you."

Ah, it was because a Calatian flying about would be unsettling, maybe raise questions. "I see. People do know I'm here, don't they?"

"Of course, of course. Myself and Master MacDougal do for sure, heh." Cott's laugh died quickly when Kip didn't join in. "Headmaster Cross knows and all the other masters have at least been told. I can't be as sure about the apprentices but their masters should have told them. Oh, speaking of that, Master Martinet and Master Farmer and perhaps Master Albright would like to meet you. I've suggested a dinner down at the Clock and Pull. That's a Greenwich pub. They do a very nice steak and kidney pie."

"Very well," Kip said. "And I would also like to visit the Isle of Dogs."

Cott's face fell. "If you insist, I suppose, although I would recommend against it."

"I have a letter to deliver."

"Ah, yes, in that case…I will accompany you there when you need to go. Yes, that should be best."

Coppy had told him enough stories that Kip was sure he could find it—start from King's College and look down across the river until you saw a town of Calatians—but he'd never had a sorcerer escort him on an errand and the prospect quite startled him, so he nodded and thanked Master Cott again. "Now," the sorcerer said, "go down to Miss Hathway and she will provide you with a bedroll to bring up. Oh, never mind, I see you have your own. She'll have linens, in that case, and will show you where the necessary is for apprentices. You, ah, do you bathe?"

"On occasion," Kip said. "About as often as normal." He stopped himself from saying, "And more often than MacDougal, from the smell of him," because it was his first day in London. But he was sorely tempted.

Masters Martinet and Farmer greeted Kip and Master Cott at the base of their tower and set off to walk to the nearby village. Martinet took Kip's appearance in stride, but Farmer, a tall, raven-haired man with a dry voice and manner, barked a short laugh. "So it's true," he said. "Is he staying with the other apprentices? No? I suppose that's prudent. Good job you don't keep chickens, eh, Cott?" Martinet, a brown-haired sorcerer who matched Cott's height and build, gave a cursory laugh to the joke, but Cott either affected not to understand or honestly didn't, and Kip remained quiet. Fortunately, that was the extent of the commentary on his nature for the duration of their walk.

The Clock and Pull was probably a light, breezy pub in the summer time, but by the time Kip and the three sorcerers arrived, darkness had been well established outside and all the pub's windows were shut to keep in the warmth and the smoke from the many oil lamps. Kip had never been in such a crowded public space with so thick a smell of smoke and oil, and it took him a good while to adjust, but even so his eyes watered all through dinner and he kept a napkin over his nose as much as possible.

The rich crust was the best part of the steak and kidney pie, though the stewy mess of chewy beef and soft organ meats inside was at least not over-seasoned to Kip's palate, as so often happened in Massachusetts Bay. Additionally, his portion was brought out steaming but was cold by the time he finished it, as he was the subject of conversation and scarcely had he taken a bite before another one of the masters directed a question at him: When did he first evince an affinity to magic? What would he have done if the College hadn't been desperate for students? Had any sorcerer helped him before his admission? How did he learn spells, and was it any different from how humans did?

On this last point Kip did have a little to say; though he was not human and couldn't tell how humans learned spells, he had noted that he put a stronger reliance on smell than humans did and thereby had learned several spells more quickly than his counterparts.

"Although," he said, "Master Jaeger at the college did give me a spiritual spell to learn and I am having some trouble with it because I don't have a scent to associate with spiritual magic."

"I will take you to Master Gugin," Cott said. "He'll help you with spiritual magic."

"Hm." Master Farmer shook his head. "You're quick to volunteer Gugin's services."

"He'll help." Cott didn't catch the warning in Farmer's tone, but Kip did.

"Is Master Gugin very busy?" he asked.

Farmer nodded, and turned to Martinet, who had made short work of his pie and already had ordered seconds. "What do you think?"

"The question is more whether Penfold can tolerate him than the inverse." Martinet covered his mouth and belched. "Spiritualists."

Cott rolled his eyes. "You know, Penfold, that spiritual magic is said to take a toll on one's sanity. Spend years cleaning coal scuttles and the dust never quite comes out of your skin. But your master Jaeger sounds perfectly fine."

Fine, Kip supposed, for someone who stayed in his rooms and talked to people through his raven. And then there was Forrest, too, and Peter, neither of whom seemed completely sane. "I'm willing to try. Master Jaeger thought it very important that I learn this spell."

"Yes, why is that?" Farmer asked.

"Because—" Kip stopped. Could he tell them about the spirit in the Tower? And if not then what other reason could there be? "Because he feared that as a fire sorcerer, untrained, I could be convinced to wreak great harm."

"Hum." Martinet nodded. "Surprisingly rational for a spiritualist. I don't know as I would've thought of that."

"Put it that way to Gugin and he'll more likely help," Farmer said, pointing his fork at Kip. "So tell me, have any other Calatians shown an affinity for magic?"

So Kip told them about Coppy, who hadn't until he'd enrolled, and then he told them about the reaction in his town when he'd enrolled, how half of them hadn't approved. The masters made sympathetic noises but little else, and in the ensuing lull, Kip finally finished his dinner. They got up and left without paying, and Kip noticed the barkeep giving them a dirty look. "Er," he said. "Did you already pay?"

"Oh." Martinet shook his head carelessly. "We pay sometimes if we have the money, but the businesses around here are quite happy to have our custom."

"You should make sure to pay if we aren't here with you," Farmer said, and he didn't have to explain why.

CHAPTER 9: THE ISLE OF DOGS

Miss Hathway grudgingly provided bed linens and asked several times why Kip wasn't bedding down with the other apprentices and whether she'd be asked to look after his sleeping area, and even after the third reassurance that she would not, she told him to keep it clean or she'd take it out of his hide. And then she gave him a red, white, and blue scarf to keep his neck warm when he went outside, or to put over his ears, and when he thanked her, she said, "Ah, dear, I have a whole stack of them. I knit when I'm bored, and since my daughter went off to work in Blackheath, I'm bored all the time I'm not working."

There was no moldering paper in the workshop, but Kip found the smell of phosphorus from the other room comforting, and the chill didn't bother him. He did, however, lie awake on his bed staring at the ceiling for quite a while, his mind returning to Coppy's expression when he'd left. Why had he used Peter's journal to make Coppy forget him? At the time it had seemed a kindness to both of them, but now he wished there'd been a proper good-bye. He couldn't even send Coppy a letter to say he was sorry. There had to be some way letters were transported from here to the Colonies, but he only knew where Cott's office, the roof, and the dining hall were. Maybe Cott would help him post a letter. But first, he would have to deliver

Coppy's letter to the Isle; then he would have actual news to tell Coppy and he wouldn't simply be writing to say he was sorry.

He supposed that if he didn't want to give the letter to anyone else, he could summon Nikolon to take the letter to Coppy. How long would it take the demon to go to the Colonies? Could she translocate or would she transport it physically? That last could take…weeks? Did demons fly faster or slower than boats?

The thoughts ran around and around in his mind like the mice in his attic. After a time, they frustrated him enough that he got out of his bedroll with its freshly-scented linens to cast fires and practice his focus for two more hours until he felt tired enough to sleep.

The morning came far too early, and when Master Cott opened the door to the workroom, he carried a piece of bread and a small cup of tea. "So sorry," he said, "I forgot to tell you where to go for your breakfast in the morning."

"It's all right." The bread and tea helped shake the sleepiness out of his head, and then he and Master Cott continued to examine the bead. Cott tried engulfing it in fire, and Kip tried talking to it as though it were a fire; Cott brought out a spell to make otherwise non-flammable objects burn, and cast it with very precise focus on the bead, assuring Kip that it would only burn one edge of it.

But that spell did not work either, and Master Cott set the bead back with the same cheerful demeanor. "We must think of other things to try. You can read, yes? Of course you can, what am I saying. I will give you a stack of books and papers related to fire and if you come across anything useful, we may try it tomorrow, or the next day."

"Yes, sir." Kip was about to ask if he would have further lessons, and then reflected that reading about fire magic would in fact count as a lesson. "Will I have some time this afternoon to go down to the Isle?"

Master Cott's smile remained fixed. "I would prefer it if you began the reading immediately."

"I would very much like to deliver this message while it's light. It won't take long," Kip promised. "I'll be back within the hour."

The sorcerer sighed. "Very well, very well. But," he wagged a finger, "one hour. And you will begin the reading immediately after. You've promised."

"Yes, of course."

"And." Cott pulled on Kip's tunic as he headed for the office. "Do use the window. It'll be faster. And Master Albright would like to have dinner with you tonight. Just him." He laughed shortly. "Don't worry, he's very nice. He treats his calyxes very well."

"I'm pleased to hear it." Kip changed direction and headed for the window, calling magic to him as he reached for the latch. He wanted to escape before Cott remembered that he'd promised Kip the great courtesy of an escort to the Isle.

"It will be down at the Clock and Pull again, most likely. I'll describe him for you when you get back."

"Thank you, sir," Kip said, pulling the window open. The cold, humid air washed briskly over his nose and ears, perking them up.

"Now, to get to the Isle, go to the roof and face north, across the river. Directly across from King's College is a little peninsula separated from the riverbank by a wall. This is the Isle of Dogs." He stopped and took a breath. "Now, once you're there, to find someone, you'll want to locate Mr. Geoffries. He's a rabbit, and he's by way of being the unofficial mayor of the Isle. Just ask him."

"All right. Thank you, sir." Kip waited with his paw on the window.

"Oh, and you should wear a robe. You are a sorcerer, after all."

"The College in New Cambridge is having some made," Kip said, but Cott had already disappeared into his office.

Kip twitched his tail and then controlled it, staring out the window at the fields and the pretty little cottages below, wondering what he would find in the Isle. If he was ever actually allowed to leave.

Cott returned with a black robe draped over his arm. "Apprentices are meant to wear purple robes as a rule, but some wear black until their purple ones are ready. Now, this may not fit you exactly, but it should do until yours arrive, and…" As he held it out, he stopped. "Well, perhaps it would be more politick for you not to wear the robes. I mean, if there are some who have not heard of you, it would be a surprise to see a Calatian in a sorcerer's robes."

"Whatever you think best."

Cott draped the robe back over his arm and looked away, then made a quick dismissive gesture. "The sooner you go, the sooner you're back. Oh! I should come with you."

He dropped the robe to the floor of the workshop and made to begin casting a spell. Kip cleared his throat, thinking quickly. "Actually, sir, I…I wouldn't want to take so much time out of your afternoon. This errand is simply to deliver a letter to the family of a friend. It won't be very interesting at all."

The sorcerer frowned. "Are you afraid the Calatians will respect you less if you arrive with a sorcerer? I assure you, all of our calyxes live on the Isle and they have the greatest respect for us."

"I'm certain of it." Kip flicked his tail. "If you really wish to come walk around the streets of the Isle and look for my friend's family for an hour, then of course you may come along."

He tried to look properly eager as Cott considered that. "I suppose…I needn't go, if…you'll just go and come right back?"

"One hour," Kip said, and cast the spell as he stepped out of the window.

From afar, the Isle looked idyllic, bounded on three sides by the River Thames and on the fourth by a stone wall. The houses were small and cramped and did not gleam, but then, not many places in London did, and anyway clouds blocked the sun.

Kip descended from the college roof but did not touch down on the ground. He levitated himself to the river and over it, and only when he was halfway across, the icy wind making him wish for Mrs. Hathway's scarf, did it occur to him that perhaps flying across the water to come up on the bank might not be the best way to introduce himself to the Calatian community here. If they didn't know he was a sorcerer, they might be suspicious of a fox flying across the water. Better to land elsewhere and walk up to the Isle.

So he altered his course and made for a dock a hundred feet or so downriver from the Isle. Despite his best efforts, he attracted a good deal of attention from the longshoremen—all human save for one otter—unloading boxes from a ship moored at the dock, as well as three sailors on the boat itself. How did the sorcerers cross the river, he wondered? Go all the way down to the London Bridge, which wasn't even visible? Take a ferry across? He hadn't seen a ferry station; then again, he hadn't actually looked.

As he drew closer to the dock, the men stopped working, all except the otter, and stood to stare at him. His nose was full of the smell of the river and the trash in it, and to his eye the men all looked very similar, dressed in simple shirts and trousers, stained with water and darker fluids. All had rough, ruddy complexions and facial hair of varying lengths, and hard stares that tracked him from the river up to the edge of the dock where he landed. Wary, he kept his spell active as he walked past the first of the men.

The first few did not speak, but when he reached one who wore a flat cap on his head over a dark scowl, the man reached out and grasped Kip's arm. "What business the sorcerers send you down for here?"

"What?"

"Seen you flyin' cross the water," the man said, as though they hadn't all been staring at Kip for the last ten minutes. "Don't see your sorcerer though. Whyn't he send you to the Isle straight off?"

"I—he—" What could he say to them? That he was a sorcerer himself? The man's grip on his arm was iron, and if Kip tried to fly off now, the man would surely come with him. "You're not to harm me."

"Now who spoke of harm?" The man's mouth twisted into an ugly smile, showing two cracked teeth. "You come onto our docks and we're asking you why. Seems simple enough."

The otter walked back to the ship and up the gangplank without looking once at Kip. At this distance, he looked enough like Coppy that Kip felt a sharp sense of betrayal even though he knew the otter wasn't Coppy and owed him nothing. "My business is none of your concern," he said. "I simply want to pass through the docks. I'm headed to the Isle."

"Then why did your master send you to our dock?" The man held out his free arm to his companions. "Isle's right over there. What's so special about our dock?"

"I don't know," Kip said. If he needed to escape, he could lift the man away and fly over the river in case the man fell. But he would prefer not to do that. "Maybe he didn't want to alarm the Calatians."

"Ha ha!" Without letting go, the man turned to the otter, who'd just reappeared carrying a crate. "Y'hear that, Dollo? Sorcerer don't want to fly him to the Isle. Fraid he'll alarm the poor Callies."

The otter paused, then gave a quick nod and kept on walking. The man returned his attention to Kip. "I've half a mind to shove you off the dock and make you swim to the Isle."

"My master—my master wouldn't like that."

"Rog," one of the other men said. "Remember how that sorcerer gave Charley the pox?"

"Charley got the pox from your wife," Rog retorted, but his grip on Kip's arm lightened. "All right. All right. Then we'll bring you to Mr. Gibbet and see what you have to say to him."

Kip would not have minded so much being pushed down into the water, but now his best hope was that Mr. Gibbet was more reasonable than his name. Holding the spell was occupying some of his concentration, so with some regret he let it lapse. "It is important that I reach the Isle of Dogs," he tried one more time. "My—my master's business is secret."

"Aye, well, Mr. Gibbet keeps plenty of secrets." Rog pulled Kip away from the dock.

The men laughed behind him, and the otter returned from the warehouse to fetch another crate, still not even sparing one glance for Kip.

During the short walk from the dock to the low, flat wooden building adjacent to the warehouse, Kip tried to think of some legitimate reason for him to have flown to the dock. "Because I didn't want to scare the Calatians" felt completely inadequate, and "because I didn't know any better," though also accurate, was no better. Even if he were to reveal that he had flown under his own power and not been levitated by his master, that would not explain why he'd alit on a dock full of humans. Calatians, he now felt, would have been much easier to explain his motivations to. At least he could tell them he had a letter for Coppy's family.

Mr. Gibbet, a man whose thinning hair was kept close to his scalp by an oil whose perfume wrinkled Kip's nose from ten feet away, looked up with sharp blue eyes as Rog pulled Kip in by the arm. "Ah, Roger," he said in a dry, quiet tone that brooked no nonsense, "I was wondering what could possibly be of such importance as to distract nearly every one of your men from their job."

"Yes, sir. Only it's this Calatian, sir."

"I see that." Mr. Gibbet glanced at the ornate clock on his desk. "And do you see this?"

"Er, yes." Rog's puffed-up manner had almost completely evaporated.

"If you could read a clock, you would see that there are only forty minutes left before the customs inspector arrives to check those crates you are supposed to be unloading. Do you think you and your men can finish the job in forty minutes?"

"Yes, sir. If we put sole to stone."

"Then I would advise you to do so."

"Yes, sir." But Rog, clearly trying to regain at least a little of his swagger, thrust Kip forward. "He come right over the water, like a sorcerer, but without a sorcerer. Says he was sent here for a secret. I think he's spyin'."

"A spy. Indeed. Come to determine the exact number of fish sent to us from Calais, was he?"

"Maybe." Rog's brow lowered. "Never know what them sorcerers want, do we?"

"No, we do not. Very well, I will interrogate him. You may leave him to me, as I am leaving the unloading of the *Cliffside* to you."

These last words were enunciated precisely, and Rog took the meaning of the tone. "Yes, sir," he said, and slipped back out the door.

Kip felt that Mr. Gibbet, demonstrating more education, would at least be more receptive to his story. "I'm so sorry for the disruption," he said. "I was only trying to—"

"I beg your pardon," Mr. Gibbet said, pleasantly enough save for the look in his eyes, "but have I addressed you yet?"

"No," Kip said, "but—"

"Dear me, if there is one thing I have always admired Calatians for, it is their impeccable manners. And yet! There is always an exception to the rule."

Baffled by this, Kip flattened his ears and stared. Mr. Gibbet stared back with a fixed, serene expression. "Now," he said after a moment, "who is your master?"

"Master Cott." Kip said. "He knows I'm here, but he didn't order me to come to the dock."

"Tch!" Mr. Gibbet's brow lowered. He reached down to one side and brought up a thick truncheon, which he rested on the desk. "I find that the lesson of waiting until one is addressed before speaking is easily learned with the aid of this instructor." His fingers caressed the club in long strokes. "I am certain your master will not mind the re-application of such a lesson."

"H—" Kip got only part of one word out before Mr. Gibbet's bony fingers closed over the handle of the club. The fox snapped his mouth shut.

He hated that he was complying, but Mr. Gibbet's confidence told him that there was only one way to escape this situation unharmed, and here in London he did not know the healer.

"Sometimes the instructor has only to make an appearance." Mr. Gibbet smiled, and his fingers resumed their stroking. "Now, why did Master Cott send you to the dock?"

Hadn't he just told the man that Cott hadn't sent him? It was not worth protesting again; if he was assumed to be nothing more than a servant to be beaten on a whim, he would demonstrate a servant's knowledge. "I don't know."

"Come, come, what did he send you down here to do?"

"To take a message to the Isle of Dogs."

"And?"

"That's all," Kip said flatly.

"And yet he sent you to this dock rather than to the Isle. Perhaps…" Mr. Gibbet rubbed his chin. "No, I cannot imagine he sent you to examine the contents of the *Cliffside*. Have you recently been disobedient to him in some way?"

"No." Kip shook his head.

Mr. Gibbet leaned in more closely. "Do you live on the Isle?"

"No."

"I am a human," Mr. Gibbet said, "and you will address me as 'sir.'"

"With all due respect," Kip replied, eyeing the truncheon, "my master has told me to call only him by that title."

It was a small rebellion, but by putting the responsibility on his supposed master, he hoped to get away with it. Mr. Gibbet's eyes did narrow, but he did not grip the truncheon. "And where do you reside?"

"At the college, presently."

"A servant of the school? But your speech rings almost like someone from the north, and yet different. Where were you born?"

"Massachusetts Bay."

"A colonist. Of course that explains it." Mr. Gibbet's hand lifted from the truncheon. "In that case, I will simply ask you to remain here until I can receive a reply from your Master Cott verifying your purpose."

"I'm to return in one hour." Kip clasped his paws together.

"I'm afraid that will be impossible," Mr. Gibbet said. "But if you are not on the Isle in an hour, your master may come looking for you and that will speed the process. Take heart in that. Now, you'll stay in the small supply room here—"

"That won't work. I need to leave now to complete my errand."

Now those fingers curled around the handle of the club and lifted it. "You interrupted a human. Perhaps a lesson is in order after all."

Mr. Gibbet stood from his desk and walked slowly around it. Kip took a step back, ears plastered flat to his head, working out whether he could get to the door and run faster than the middle-aged man. And then he had an idea, and without time to decide whether it was a good one, he acted on it. "I'm talking to Master Cott in my head now! He is not pleased that you have detained me. He says, he says to let me go now or he will set this building on fire."

As Kip spoke, he gathered magic. At the sight of the purple flickering around his paws, Mr. Gibbet stopped. "What is that?"

"That is what happens when he talks in my head." The fire spell was waiting in Kip's mind, begging to be used. Having thought of it, he now found it difficult to battle the hunger and need of the fire, especially when he himself was so on edge, desperate. *I can help you*, the fire said, *only let me out, let me out...*

"Then Master Cott," Mr. Gibbet called, "if you are listening, give me a reason I should not beat your fox."

It was going to have to be fire. Kip muttered the spell, hoping Mr. Gibbet was too far to hear properly.

The wooden floor between them erupted in flame.

Mr. Gibbet jumped back with a cry. Kip found the sight and feel of the fire soothing, and working on keeping it focused in its small area calmed him. "I told you."

But Mr. Gibbet didn't hear him. "Fire! Fire!" he yelled, and ran for the door. Kip extinguished the fire and only then thought that this was his chance to escape. By the time he reached the door, though, three of the longshoremen were already running toward it, two with buckets and one with a straw broom.

They pushed past Kip and into the office. "Where is it?" one shouted while the other two looked around wildly.

Mr. Gibbet rushed in behind them. "Is it out?" he cried. "Is it—good job, men."

"We ain't done nothing," the man with the broom said, turning. "Wasn't no fire."

"No fire? It was right there!" Mr. Gibbet pointed at the bare patch of hardwood.

The two men with buckets set them down, slopping water onto the floor. The man with the broom stepped forward, sniffing the air. "Smells a bit like fire, but no smoke, no burning on the wood." He looked up at Gibbet's desk and Kip saw his eyes light on a brown bottle sitting on the edge. "Ah, whatever it was, it ain't here now, sir."

Mr. Gibbet had also noticed the motion. "I am not drunk," he said with forceful enunciation. "This Calatian said that his sorcerer sent fire down. He must have taken it away." His face had grown redder, but his gestures were calmer and much more restrained.

"Course, sir." The man with the broom turned and gestured to the others, who picked up the buckets of water with rather more visible effort than when they'd carried them in.

Mr. Gibbet watched them leave, gripping his desk with one hand, and when they'd gone, he drew close to Kip in two quick steps and grasped the fox's wrist. "I don't know what tricks your masters have taught you," he hissed, "but you'll learn not to bedevil good Christian humans with them."

He pulled Kip toward one of the doors in the side of the room. "But," Kip protested, "my master is a fire sorcerer—"

Mr. Gibbet stopped cold a foot from the door and then with a quick motion threw Kip against the wall. He did not let go of Kip's wrist, and so the torque sent painful cracks through the bones there and up his arm even as Kip hit the wall. It wasn't as forcefully as Farley had thrown him into the Tower, but it was enough to stun him. "What," Mr. Gibbet said tightly as he opened the door, "did I tell you about speaking when spoken to?"

And without waiting for an answer, he shoved Kip into the open door and closed it after him, leaving the fox in mostly-darkness in the smell of paper and mice.

In a matter of seconds, Kip's eyes adjusted enough for him to take stock of his temporary prison. Stacks of paper surrounded him, all smelling more recent than the paper back in his basement. No trap door in the floor or ceiling, no improbable door at the back of the closet. The only way out was the way he'd been thrown in.

He dropped to the ground, sitting with arms and tail around his knees, paw holding his injured wrist. The ache was bearable if he held it still and applied pressure around it. He didn't think it was a serious injury, but when he rotated his wrist, a low grinding noise accompanied sharp stabs of pain.

Not even one full week in London and he'd already gotten into trouble. Cott would be disappointed, maybe even to the point of sending him back. And for all the power Kip had acquired, he was imprisoned here with several ways of getting out of the room but no ways of getting out of the trouble he'd caused. He could summon Nikolon, but without extra power, he wasn't sure he could bind the demon sufficiently (would his own blood suffice, and if so, how much of it?). Besides, if he really had trespassed, as Mr. Gibbet's manner suggested, breaking out with magic would only make things worse.

Thinking about Mr. Gibbet stoked a fire in his chest. Speak only when spoken to? What year was this? Calatians were free citizens with the right to speak when they chose. And yet this human had threatened him, broken his wrist, bruised his ear against the wall, and locked him in a closet, and Kip's only recourse was to wait for another human to come and set him free.

Again fire called to him, and this time restraint was a greater effort. Burning down the warehouse office, as satisfying as it would be, would certainly get him sent back to Massachusetts Bay, if not expelled outright.

Coppy would tell him to be patient; Emily would tell him to stand up for his rights; Malcolm would tell him to fight back. But he couldn't do the first very well, and the second two were impossible in this situation. The best he could hope for was that Master Cott would see to it that Mr. Gibbet was punished for the way he'd treated Kip. And since Master Cott had not wanted Kip to come down to the Isle of Dogs in the first place, that was not terribly likely.

Because he had nothing better to do, he recited all the spells he knew, practicing them in his head until the syllables became rote. The hardest was Master Jaeger's, so Kip focused on that one. The exercise calmed him, but at the same time reminded him of sitting in the basement of the White Tower practicing spells with his friends. Loneliness seized his chest and constricted his throat so that he had to stop reciting for a moment. Coppy would want him to stay calm and protect himself, he repeated, and though he missed the otter terribly, imagining Coppy's presence next to him soothed him enough to allow him to resume his memorization.

He must have dozed off at some point, because he was leaning against one shelf when the door opened and the small frame of Master Cott stood silhouetted in it. Kip recognized the scent before the face, and scrambled to his feet.

"Good God, have you locked him in there?" Master Cott asked Mr. Gibbet, whose form resolved out of the oil-lamp light in the office. "Penfold, are you all right?"

"My wrist is broken," Kip said.

"We'll get you to a healer. Come along. And you," Cott extended a furious finger at Mr. Gibbet. "I'll see you charged for this."

The man looked genuinely puzzled. "Charged? For what?"

"Assaulting a British citizen."

"He's a Calatian. And a colonial." Mr. Gibbet pointed back. "And he started a fire in my office, or caused a fire to be started."

"Regardless, that does not give you the right to imprison him in a closet." Cott propelled Kip gently to the door. Outside, darkness had fallen and the half-moon limned the clouds in silver.

"What time is it?" Kip asked. His stomach growled, though he still felt nauseated and wasn't sure he could eat.

Mr. Gibbet said something about what this world was coming to, and then, loud and petulant, "He started a fire!"

Kip had a paw on the door frame, his ears swept back to listen to the exchange between the two men. The sorcerer, still pressing gently on Kip's shoulder, called back, "I'll start a fire if you'd like to see a fire."

"You get out and take that insolent creature with you," Mr. Gibbet called, apparently gaining some bravery at seeing the back of the sorcerer.

As Kip made it through the door, the pressure of the sorcerer's hand disappeared from his shoulder, so he turned to see why Cott had stopped. The man's face, dark in the silvery moonlight, stared out past Kip into the night. Without looking back, he said in a low voice, "I did warn you."

With that, he pushed Kip one more step out just as flames engulfed the inside of the warehouse. Mr. Gibbet shrieked, but Master Cott slammed the door behind him and though it rattled, the man inside was unable to budge it.

"Please, please," Mr. Gibbet cried, and then his words crumbled into sobs that Kip could hear perfectly well through the wall. Nobody but he and Master Cott stood outside the building; the ship had gone and the longshoremen returned home for the night. Only the moon's half-lidded eye gazed down on them.

Any satisfaction Kip felt was fleeting, because as terrible as Mr. Gibbet's treatment of him had been, Cott was now doing worse to the man. Kip wanted Mr. Gibbet punished, but not tortured, not killed; he should be punished according to the law.

Cott shouted at the door. "How's that for insolent? How's that, you miserable creature?"

"Sir," Kip said. "You can't let him burn."

The sorcerer looked uncertain, then shook his head. "He's not going to burn. He can feel the fire, but it won't consume him or his precious office. Something you can learn to do."

At least his new master wasn't a cold-blooded—or hot-blooded—murderer, but that didn't make this any better. "You're terrifying him. And if he feels the fire, doesn't it hurt?"

"Yes. As ye sow, so shall ye reap. It's in that Christian book he's got on his desk." Cott scowled, and shouted again at the door. "You'd best read some Thomas Aquinas! Prudence, temperance, justice! And charity!"

Mr. Gibbet's sobs were barely audible now below the crackling and snapping of the flames. Kip could no longer stand it, so he reached out and called the fire back. Cott had created only a simple fire, one Kip was able to quench with a thought.

Silence from inside, and then hysterical laughter and bubbling words. "I'm not—I'm safe—oh, thank you good sir!"

"Thank the Calatian," Cott called out with a look at Kip. "He's the one who put out your fire. And remember that next time you feel inclined to break the bones of a weaker fellow."

In the silence that answered that remark, the sorcerer reached out to Kip and said, "Come on."

At the edge of the dock, Kip was lifted into the air alongside Cott. He still disliked the sensation, but not enough to protest, not after he'd directly defied his master. But Cott did not seem angry; rather, he looked pensively up at the moon, and when they were directly over the river, he spoke. "My colleagues have often called me quick to temper," he said. "Any sorcerer may be affected by his work, and fire, as I am sure you know, is a difficult lure to resist. It hungers, and the fire sorcerer longs to give in to that hunger."

"I've felt it," Kip said.

"I know you have." Cott's eyes, full of moonlight, met Kip's with a comradely understanding. "Had you broken one of my spells under other circumstances, I would be unhappy with you. I am still a little. But in looking back, my anger got the better of me. So thank you for being my conscience." He sighed. "I suppose I will get another letter from Headmaster Cross."

"I'm sorry," Kip said.

"Oh, one of the nice things about being a fire sorcerer is that you're indispensable and people expect you to be a little crazy, setting fires everywhere, so play up to that. It is always a benefit to appear at least a little crazier than you actually are." He laughed. "So Cross will send his letter and will inform the aggrieved scoundrel that the nasty fire sorcerer has been reprimanded and all will be quiet again."

Kip absorbed all that as they drew nearer King's College. Cott guided them toward the tower farthest back from the river, which Kip felt wasn't quite right, but he didn't want to raise an objection. "And Mr. Gibbet?" he said instead. "You said you'd see him charged...?"

"Oh. That was to scare him." Cott shook his head. "The police wouldn't have anything to do with that."

"But..." Kip lifted his arm, sending stabbing pains through his wrist.

"I know. He broke your wrist. And if you were a human, you could go have him arrested for that, and perhaps he'd be beaten, or perhaps simply spend the night in jail."

"There aren't laws against assaulting Calatians?"

"There are." They alit on the roof. Only now, up close, could Kip see the rough patches of lichen and cracks in the stone; this was definitely not the tower he'd departed from. Cott straightened his robes and ended the spell. "But any Calatian who makes a complaint may regret it afterwards. Or his friends may. Often the humans who object to Calatians being treated as equals are unable to distinguish between them. Come along."

Instead, Kip walked to the other edge of the roof and stared down across the river at the Isle of Dogs. Master Cott spoke evenly and had no reason to try to alarm Kip. And yet what he'd said seemed horribly wrong.

But there was nothing Kip could do about it. So he turned and followed his master down the stairs and into the tower. Cott brought him to the rooms of an obese sorcerer named Turner, who healed Kip's arm with a careless gesture and a muttered spell, far different from the solicitous care of Master Splint.

While he worked, Cott stood at the window and peered out through a crack of an inch. "Close that thing," Turner growled at him.

"It's dark," Cott said. "We'll go out this way."

"Then do it, and quick." Turner waved and turned his head back to the flagon from which Kip could detect the sharp smell of wine even at the door.

"Come on, Penfold." Cott pushed the window open, and a moment before Kip was to ask if he should cast his own spell, the sorcerer's magic gripped him again.

As they flew, Cott asked, "What were you doing at that dock?"

"Ah." Kip flattened his ears. "I didn't want to alarm the Calatians by flying directly to them."

"Whyever not? Never mind, never mind, but why that dock? Why not the empty riverbank?"

Well, Kip thought, anyone might be at a riverbank. "The dock looked like a place for people to arrive."

"On ships, yes." Master Cott opened the window to his workroom and flew both of them in. "But do remember what I said earlier about appearing normal. And for God's sake don't venture outside of this college again." He latched the window firmly.

"I still have a letter to deliver to the Isle."

Cott threw up his hands. "You will do what you must, then. Take the ferry next time. Good night." And with that he crossed to his narrow office. A moment later, the door to the hallway creaked open and shut.

Until then, Kip hadn't realized that Cott didn't sleep in his office. The man's smell permeated everything just as it would a bedroom, and Master Odden did for certain sleep in his office. So there were bedrooms for the sorcerers elsewhere, and for the apprentices. It was entirely possible that Kip was the only living being left on this floor of the tower.

In Cott's office, sure enough, a phosphorus elemental slumbering in the brazier was the only sign of life. Kip's desire for conversation wasn't strong enough to wake it, so he returned to the workshop. Though it was dark out, he did not feel at all like sleeping. At first he paced back and forth, but his footsteps echoed in the large space and after a little while the clicks of his claws in the silence drove him to the windows to stand still. He wondered how Coppy and Emily and Malcolm were getting along, whether Farley had left them alone or had stepped up his attacks now that Kip was gone. Had they continued to investigate the mystery of the attack on the College? None of them knew Forrest; none of them had the glass beads.

In that moment he would gladly have traded all his affinity for fire for a simple translocational spell, or even a spell that would let him talk to his friends, hear their voices. A raven, perhaps, though he doubted ravens could fly across an ocean (did Cott have a raven?). He contemplated flying up to the roof again just to get outside the workshop. But he'd gotten into enough trouble for one day, so he sat next to the stack of papers Cott had given him, called up a fire, and began to read.

The title of the first paper was "Effectes of Magickal Fire Upon Fleisch," and began with the off-putting sentence, "It has longe been wondered wheather magickal fire might consume the fleisch faster than non-magickal fire." It did not get much better from there, as Kip read through three pages of clinically described burning (of cadavers, though the cadavers had to be recently deceased for the flesh to be similar to living, and the method of procuring recently deceased bodies was not mentioned), but he did at least understand why Cott wanted him to read this: if the glass beads were the remains of humans who had been burned by magical fire, then any previous experience of the effect of magical fire on humans would be valuable to understand.

What was more, Kip was intrigued that a fire could be set to consume a building but not touch the people within. He only knew the fire's hunger, but the possibility that he could direct and control that hunger fascinated him. He thought that might be what Odden had been expecting when he'd set Kip the challenge of holding a flame in his paw for ten seconds, although it was very advanced to ask of an untrained apprentice. So he read on. Not all the papers dealt with fire consuming flesh, but enough did that he felt he might not need to eat again for a while.

He woke to movement in the workshop, sunlight, and the uncomfortable feeling of old paper underneath him and near to his nose. His fire had either gone out or been extinguished. Slowly he pushed himself to a sitting position, causing the papers to slide around.

"Good morning," Cott called cheerfully.

Kip stretched and stood. Cott was sitting on the stone table by the far window with a book in his lap. "Morning."

"I've been up for hours, so I just thought I would sit and wait for you to get up. You must have been up late reading." The sorcerer set his book aside and hopped down from the table. "I've done that many a night myself. Fascinating, isn't it?"

"Yes." Kip rubbed sleep from his eyes. He still felt tired.

"Do you need breakfast? It's over, I'm afraid, but sometimes if you go to the kitchen they have leftover bread they'll give you. Oh, but maybe not you. I mean, they don't know you. I could go if you want something."

"I'm fine, thank you, sir." Kip's stomach protested, but he still felt queasy from the previous night's activities and reading.

"Good, good." Cott paced back and forth. "So tell me what you think of what you read. Did you get through it all?"

"Most of it, I think." Kip tried to organize his thoughts. "Mainly that… the hunger of the fire can be directed by the sorcerer."

"Yes, good. Anything that might relate to our little glass bead?"

There was nothing Kip could think of, but Cott wasn't disappointed. He promised to have another stack for the fox to read that night, and then began with lessons immediately, asking Kip to cast a fire that would burn paper but not wood. The task proved enough to occupy them for hours, until Kip really was hungry and Cott took him to get lunch.

CHAPTER 10: MASTER ALBRIGHT

Each tower, Cott told him on their way down, had its own kitchen and lunchroom, staffed by workers from the nearby village.

"I don't actually know who prepares our food," Kip said with some shame. "Back at the College. Prince George's, I mean. The students and apprentices eat outside while the masters eat upstairs in the Tower."

"Mm-hmm. On holidays," Cott went on, "we have special meals and puddings. You will be here for Christmas, won't you? The Christmas feast is delightful."

That was three weeks away. "I don't know," Kip said honestly. "I would like to celebrate with my family."

"Of course you would, but look, see how lovely it is here."

They had entered the dining area, a large room with tapestries hung around the walls and a dozen or more long wooden tables around which clustered people in black and purple robes with various colors of trim around the sleeves and collars, filled with the smells of bread, roasted fowl, boiled vegetables, and tonic water. The oldest people sat at a table removed from the others to Kip's left; he assumed those were the masters. White-shirted students sat in pockets here and there but did not seem to be separated from the purple-robed apprentices. To one side, ravens perched on a long stick six feet off the ground, near the windows and away from the main eating area.

Every single one of the people at the tables was human. Not all of them matched Cott's pale complexion; that predominated, but there were shades from his pasty white through ruddy brown to a deep black.

Kip stopped for a moment but Cott pulled him forward, still talking about their Christmas feast and how the hall would be decorated for it. Around them, heads turned and conversations stopped as Kip walked by, keeping his tail tightly curled against his body. As they passed, his ears caught mutters from behind, swiveling automatically to focus on the words until he consciously pointed them forward again. "…bringing his new calyx down…" "…never know what he'll do next…"

"Come on." Cott pointed toward a table whose end was empty. "Just sit and they'll bring you lunch."

The woman who came to serve them dropped a plate of food in front of each of them and walked off without reacting to Kip's presence at all. As Cott talked cheerfully, Kip watched the rest of the hall over the sorcerer's shoulder. Nobody sat through the whole meal; apprentices and masters walked up to each other, or stood to greet someone sitting to eat. Nobody fought, even in jest. The whole gathering felt very collegial in a way that his dining tent never had. He wished Coppy, Emily, and Malcolm could be here to share it with him.

Despite all the activity, nobody walked up to Cott, not for the entire duration of the meal. As they got up, Kip asked, "Is Master, ah, Gogin? Is he here?"

"Gugin? Oh, yes, the spiritual work." Cott peered at the farthest table. "No, but I can take you by his quarters. Oh, Master Albright is here. Master Albright!"

He called across the hall, and from the far table one of the masters lifted his head and then rose to meet them as Cott pulled Kip across the room. As they drew closer Kip made out a face that reminded him of Patris's, with silvery hair in a large mane, but Albright also had a beard somewhat shorter than Odden's and a more pensive expression on his olive complexion, where Patris always looked nervously angry.

"Penfold, is it?" His voice felt like it emerged from the bottom of a gravel quarry.

"Yes, sir."

"Albright. Pleasure to meet you. Thank you for bringing him over, Cott."

"Of course, of course." Cott beamed.

"I hope you might be free for a meal tonight, Penfold. I have one or two matters I would like to discuss that you may be able to shed some light upon."

This was something of a surprise; Kip had expected another "how does a

Calatian learn magic" dinner. "I, er, I had hoped to run an errand—"

Cott spoke loudly over him. "But that errand can wait until another day. It was an errand for me. Penfold, you may dine with Albright tonight."

"I, er...yes, sir." Kip squared his shoulders. The Isle of Dogs and Coppy's family would still be there tomorrow, and the day after.

"Excellent." Cott beamed.

"Meet me at sunset at the base of Lord Winter's Tower, the side facing the village." And then Albright spoke in a very low growl in the back of his throat, a sound that Kip's ears picked up but that Cott, standing two feet away, did not appear to hear at all. "*Cott will try to come,*" Albright's whisper-growl said, "*but you must not allow him.*" And then in his regular voice he added, "Do you understand my instructions?"

"Yes, sir," Kip said, his ears sweeping back.

"Very well. I will see you then." And Albright turned and strode back to his meal.

"I did explain about you being indisposed last night," Cott said as they left the dining room. "But he's not angry. He always sounds like that."

"Yes, sir."

They walked in silence until they had climbed three flights of stairs, and then Cott spoke again in the empty stairwell. "Albright is very important. Well connected. It wouldn't do to make him wait. You can deliver your message tomorrow, or in another day or week. If you make only one friend at King's, you could do much worse than Albright."

"And you, sir."

Cott paused and then turned with a delighted smile. "Yes. And me."

That afternoon they brought the glass bead out again and examined it. Cott showed it to the phosphorus elemental in his office, but Chas (that was her name) could make nothing of it and grew bored quickly. The bead's warmth when placed near fire, they discovered, was not from the heat of the fire but from something within the bead. Cott used a spell to increase his sensitivity to fire which he had Kip repeat and memorize. "You may practice this on your own time," he said. "It's quite harmless."

Cott delighted in these researches, so much that Kip wondered if he would be sad when the puzzle of the bead was finally solved. "It's a remarkable material," he said, holding it close to the light of the sun as it dipped toward the horizon. "Glass, but it retains some property that recognizes fire. Glass always remembers fire, of course, but does not ordinarily react to it in this way."

"If it's human remains," Kip felt the need to stress this point every now and again, because Cott often lost sight of it, "then could it be something to do with the spirit of the person who was killed?"

"That's something you must ask Master Gugin." Cott waved the bead before Kip. "Or we should ask him together. We could go immediately if you like."

"I would be delighted, but…" Kip pointed outside to the sunset. "I'm to meet Master Albright shortly."

"So you are, so you are. And you know, Master Albright might have some insight as well." Cott replaced the bead in the wooden box and then closed it with a slow ponderousness that Kip already recognized as reflecting thoughts going on inside his head. "You know," he said, "I know that Master Albright wishes to speak with you privately, but it can't hurt if I come to dinner. I promise I will leave the two of you to have whatever discussion he wishes, and then I can rejoin you and we can have a pleasant meal. What do you think? I don't suppose he'll mind."

"I, er." Kip shook his head. "He did say it was to be only me."

"But what does that matter? He can't possibly have an entire meal's worth of private conversation. No, no, I shall come along. It promises to be a terribly boring evening otherwise."

"I thought," Kip said quickly, with no idea how he was going to finish the sentence, knowing only that he had to keep Master Cott here. "I thought you could use the time this evening to…to…"

Cott tilted his head. "To?"

"I would like to…" Think, think, what would be obvious that Cott wouldn't have in his own office? "To look through some of the lists of powerful demons here."

"Here?" Cott blinked. "Surely you don't believe a British sorcerer attacked our own college."

"No, of course not. But Master Odden believed that if we knew the names and powers of some of the most powerful demons we know, that that might serve as a clue to the demon that was actually called." Cott didn't look convinced. "And there's sure to be some demons the Spanish also know about, aren't there?"

"Perhaps…" Cott rubbed his cheek. "But then you should come with me."

Kip gestured down at his tunic and at the fur on his arms. "I don't know that the keepers of the names will have much trust in a colonial and a Calatian. And Master Albright was very insistent that I attend dinner alone."

Cott's brow lowered and his expression took on such distaste that Kip worried for a moment that Cott would engulf the workshop in flames. But all the sorcerer did was mutter, "Of course, of course, he would say that. Stuck up old twat." He looked up, trying to force a smile onto his face. "I suppose you should run along then, and have a pleasant dinner."

"Thank you." Kip reached for the window, and in the time it took him to unlatch and open it, Cott had retreated to his office and closed the door.

He realized upon exiting the tower on a draft of cold air that he had no idea which tower was Lord Winter's. So he dropped to the ground and walked over cold, frozen dirt around the base of each tower until at the third, the newest of the five towers, he found Master Albright waiting for him, a raven on his shoulder.

"It's fifteen minutes past sunset," the old sorcerer growled. "Were you accustomed to making your superiors wait thus at George's?"

It took Kip a moment to recognize that Albright was talking about the New Cambridge college. But he was already making the proper response: "No, sir. I did not know which tower was Lord Winter's, and I can't see very far."

"I thought your eyes were supposed to be better than ours."

Kip shook his head. "At night I can see by less light, but beyond a hundred yards I lose a great amount of detail."

"Oh well, you should be fitted for glasses." Albright barked a laugh. "Come along, come along. Henry, you may return to my office." The raven took flight as the sorcerer strode toward the village and the pub.

But Albright did not lead Kip to the Clock and Pull, nor anywhere in Greenwich proper. He left the gaslit town and turned down a lane of houses, each with faint lamplight flickering from it. "There," he said, stopping at one house and pointing to the gate that let onto it from the road. "Can you read that?"

"The Darby," Kip read, though the thick aroma of lamb and vegetable stew making his mouth water told him more surely that this was their destination.

"Better than I can do in this light. Yes, this is the place, come on." Albright strode up the walk to the door and rapped. After five or six seconds he rapped again. "Is everyone in the world determined to keep me waiting?" he snapped.

As he lifted his fist a third time, the door opened to reveal a short woman in a blue skirt and a white cotton shirt stained down one side. "All right, all right, the world keeps turning even though you're knocking," she said, staring up at him.

"Bridget, I've brought another for dinner."

"So you have." Her gaze flicked to Kip, though her face didn't move. "Does he eat lamb? I've got roasted chicken from last night, but it's cold."

"I've no idea." Albright swept into the room, and Kip followed, making sure to swing his tail clear before he closed the door.

"I do eat lamb," he said. "It smells delicious."

Bridget beamed and spun on her heels. "At least he's more manners than most of your guests, and more than you, which is inevitable. Come in, young fox, and take whatever seat His Nibs doesn't want."

The front room of the small cottage held a round table with three chairs around it, one of which Albright had already pulled out to sit down in. To Kip's left, a cold stove in the parlor squatted between one threadbare sofa and another wooden chair as plain and unadorned as the three around the table. A narrow cabinet held bone-white china with light blue patterns dancing around the edges, and none of that china set had been laid on the table. Instead, two pewter mugs and matching bowls and spoons rested around a bright oil lamp. A doorway behind the table let onto another room from which the smell of lamb and smoke drifted on warm currents to Kip's nose.

He took the seat closest to the other mug and bowl—the mug proved to be filled with ale already—and Bridget hurried past him into the kitchen, returning a moment later with a large tureen. She set it down between them and ladled stew thick with chunks of lamb and potato into Kip's bowl first. Albright muttered something under his breath, and she shot him a look before turning to fill his bowl as well.

The stew contained peas and spices, and was delicious. Albright had his spoon in the bowl almost before she'd finished filling it, and through his first mouthful said, "Where's the bread?"

"It's coming, it's coming." She dropped the ladle back into the tureen and swept back into the kitchen, returning a moment later with large chunks of thick black bread that she dropped next to each bowl. The sour smell tickled Kip's nose; he tore off a piece and chewed it. Indeed, it was so thick and sour that if he'd not heard it labeled, he might not have thought to call it bread.

Albright didn't make conversation but gulped down his food as though he'd been starved for days, alternating between spoonfuls and sopping up the stew with the bread. Kip followed suit, glad of the time to enjoy the meal. Bridget did not reappear, though he could hear her humming in the kitchen, and he felt here the collegial atmosphere he'd been envious of in the dining hall. Here he was included, at ease in a way he'd never really felt with Cott.

When his bowl had been cleaned, Albright helped himself to another serving, maintaining his silence throughout. Kip limited himself to one bowl, though he didn't eat as fast as the sorcerer, so by the time he'd finished, he only had to wait a few minutes in blissful contentment for Albright to finish as well.

"Now," the sorcerer said, pushing the bowl away from him. He stopped before the next word and held up a hand, then let out a belch that made Kip's nose wrinkle. "Now," he repeated, "tell me how a Calatian comes to sorcery."

Kip was growing practiced at his story and recounted it more smoothly for not having to feed himself during the telling. Albright nodded, asking no questions even where the other sorcerers had. "Most unusual," he said.

"How fortunate for the Empire that your father has the courage to follow his instincts."

"For the Empire?"

"Yes. Another fire sorcerer will be a great service in the next war with Spain."

"The next...?"

"There will be another." Albright exhaled. "In five years or ten or twenty. The Spanish are too ambitious to share the world amicably."

"Do you think Spain destroyed the College? Philip's, I mean, and George's?"

The sorcerer eyed him. "What do you think?"

"I don't think it was Spain." Kip spoke confidently, pleased that his opinion was being considered. "They would have followed that attack with another."

"Unless they were confounded by the survival of the White Tower."

Kip inclined his head. "Still, we were weak then—the weakest we would be. Every day since then we grow stronger." Albright nodded to him to go on. "I suspect it might have been the revolutionaries, working in concert with someone inside the Tower itself."

"Inside the Tower? So it would be one of the surviving Masters?"

"Most likely."

Albright showed little surprise, his expression remaining calm. "Do you have an idea which it might have been?"

"No," Kip said honestly.

"It might not have been someone else?"

"No, I was told—" At the last minute, he remembered that he should protect Peter. Even as much as it was a relief to trust Albright as someone outside the sphere of suspicion, Peter depended on him and Kip could not break that trust. "Shown, rather," and he recounted what Forrest had shown him.

"Indeed. That is most interesting." Albright stroked his beard. "The sharing of memories is not a trivial spiritual spell."

"You won't tell any of the masters there?" Kip asked.

Foolish to ask so late, but Master Albright nodded gravely. "Of course not. If corruption is at work in the College, we must work in secret to ferret it out."

"We've been trying to do that. I'm trying to discover the name of the demon that caused the destruction. Then we might see who knew the name."

"Excellent point." Albright steepled his fingers. "Have you examined the ledger of demon names here?"

"Not yet. I asked Master Cott to examine them. He's getting some names tonight for us to look through, names and descriptions."

The sorcerer nodded. "We have spies among the Spanish sorcerers and intelligence from the French, from the Napoleonic war. Those demon names may be kept separately. What do you know of it?"

Kip shook his head. "Not very much. It's powerful and it turns people to glass somehow."

"Glass?" Albright raised his eyebrows.

So Kip told him about the glass beads. "Come by the workshop," he said. "Master Cott and I will show you one. He thought you might have some interest."

"I wouldn't be useful at all. I don't know fire even as well as you do." Albright smiled. "Not that I haven't wished for that betimes."

"What is your specialization, sir?" Kip asked.

"Translocation. It is useful enough."

"My friend is doing that too. Have you developed any new techniques?"

"I am currently studying a way to generate a door of sorts that would allow anyone to move between two places."

"That would remain for the duration of the spell?" Kip's eyes widened. "That's like a Great Feat."

"But one that would end, and which others could also cast." Albright smiled. "I may dub it a 'Lesser Feat.'"

He laughed, and Kip laughed with him. "I'm a long way from learning even basic translocation," the fox said. "But I hope to one day, of course."

"You may, if you apply yourself." Albright folded his hands across his stomach. "Cott never did. It still rankles him sometimes."

"Really?"

The sorcerer shook his mane of hair. "Indeed. And on that subject, thank you for following my request. I am sure it was difficult. But if Cott were here, we would not be able to speak as openly and frankly as we have been."

"No, that makes sense." Kip sighed. "Is he...all right?"

"What do you mean by that?"

Albright's expression remained placid, his tone merely curious. Kip tilted his head. "I don't know. Nobody talks to him. When we went to the dining hall, everyone was talking behind his back. And he doesn't want me to go down to the Isle of Dogs."

"Hm." Albright raised a finger. "On that matter I believe I can provide some clarity. All of our calyxes come from the Isle. I do know that Cott was particularly pleased that you had come from a sorcerer's college and most likely fears that you will get caught up," he waved a meaty hand in the air, "in the grimy life of the Calatians on the Isle."

Grimy? Kip let that pass and shook his head. "What about the rest of it?"

Albright settled both hands across his stomach. "Yes, well. Is Cott odd because he's a fire sorcerer? Or did being a fire sorcerer make him odd? One thing you will come to understand is that the power in you will have a strong effect on other people."

"Really?" Kip flicked his ears out to the sides of his head. "Sorcerers fear fire more than spiritual magic? Alchemical magic?"

"Heh." Albright smiled. "Sorcerers are people. We understand the hidden workings of magic. But fire is chaos, bright and loud, uncontrollable. Fire sorcery is rare enough that sorcerers have trouble understanding it. An alchemical sorcerer may start a fire by transmuting a rock to phosphorus, for example, which ignites on contact with air, but he cannot control the fire in the way you can."

Kip considered that. He wondered whether Malcolm or Emily would start to fear him if he did much more work with fire. Coppy, he was sure, would always trust him. "Is that why you didn't want Master Cott to join us?"

"Because of the fire?" Master Albright shook his head. "Hah, no. Despite what he lets on, he can control it well enough. No, no, I wanted to take your measure myself, get to know you better, and it's hard to do that when, well… Cott likes to make himself part of every conversation."

"I've noticed." Kip shook his head. "Honestly, this is the most relaxed I've felt since I've been here. I appreciate that you've taken the trouble."

"It's common courtesy," the bearded sorcerer said.

"Nobody else has bothered."

"You've been here all of three days." Master Albright tapped the table and lowered his voice. "Though I daresay you'll not get a better meal. And if you tell Bridget I said that, I'll drop you into the Thames."

Kip leaned forward and smiled. "I wouldn't," he said conspiratorially.

"Now," Master Albright said. "It is near time we made our way back to the College. But I would like you to feel free to call upon me should you need another break from the relentless friendship of Master Cott."

"Thank you," Kip said.

Master Albright called for Bridget and got up, leaving the plates and tankards and gesturing Kip to the door. "Thank you for another very satisfactory meal," he said.

"Oh, you with your flattery," Bridget said, but Kip noted her cheeks were pink.

On their way back to the College, Master Albright did ask Kip about life in the Colonies, but only very general ones, nothing about his experience as a Calatian or how a Calatian could have learned magic. It was a refreshing change from the interrogation of the dinner of two nights ago.

Master Albright let him into his tower, which he called the War Tower, and bid him good night without making any arrangements for a future meeting. Kip realized upon entering the ground floor that he only knew Cott's workshop was on one of the upper floors, three down from the roof. But he found the stairs easily enough and walked up them, passing two startled apprentices on the lower floors (where he could smell the dormitory quite strongly) and one sleepy sorcerer on the upper floors. He committed to memory the floors of the tower, finding the level where he and Cott had eaten easily enough, but he had to go up to the roof and then down three floors to be certain of which level was Cott's. From there it was easy enough to find the workshop: he walked slowly down the hall until he smelled charcoal and Master Cott's scent, and made sure by the nameplate on the door.

When he opened the door to the narrow hallway, Cott looked up from his desk. "Oh, there you are," he said. "I hope dinner was pleasant."

"It was…" Kip replied automatically and then stopped. Cott's tone belied his words, and he felt the need to reassure his London master. He cleared his throat. "Rather dull, actually. I often wished I were back here looking up demon names with you."

"Yes, well. I suppose the food was good at least. Albright does insist on having good food."

"It was, er." Cott still wasn't quite mollified. "A bit too rich, to be honest. I feel my stomach a touch unsettled."

"Hm. Indeed." That finally brought a small smile to the master's face. He turned to his desk and picked up a slender leather-bound volume. "This will have to go back tomorrow morning, but copy out any names you feel might be relevant."

"Tomorrow morning?" Kip walked forward to get the book.

"It's not meant to leave the archives at all, but," Cott handed the book to him and then waved his arms about. "Nobody wishes to anger the great and terrible Fire Sorcerer. Especially in a library full of paper."

He smiled, but Kip heard for the first time the loneliness in that statement. Perhaps it was merely the residue of being left out of Kip's dinner with Albright, but there was a sense of isolation that called to the same feeling within Kip. "I hope I haven't angered you, sir," he said. "I think you're the only person sympathetic to me here in London."

"Oh, surely that cannot be true." Cott relaxed.

"I'm a Calatian and a Colonial studying to be a Fire Sorcerer," Kip said. "Who else has anything in common with me?"

"Well, one needn't have common ground to have respect for one another, to understand what one is going through. There are a few here…" Cott's brow lowered and he stared at the wall for a moment before turning back to his desk. He opened a drawer, then reached in and pulled out some blank paper. "That's of no importance. Here's paper for copying. I'm going to retire."

Kip accepted the paper and stood back as Master Cott walked briskly past him. The door closed, leaving the fox standing in half-darkness and silence.

Of course Cott was difficult from time to time, but Kip hadn't lived in close proximity to any master before, even for a few days, and certainly none of the masters at the college were models of civility or stability. Argent seemed the most normal, but he was also the youngest, and even so he had his weaknesses. Here, Albright had been the one Kip felt closest to, but that was based on one dinner, and he'd only been here three days. As Albright had said: patience.

As Kip settled down with the book and the sheets of paper, a strange thought entered his mind. He hadn't seen Master Albright pay for his dinner, but he'd been sure at the time that the sorcerer had some kind of account with Bridget, that the meal wasn't simply taken as due because he was a sorcerer, as Martinet and Farmer had done. But Albright hadn't said anything of the sort, nor had Bridget. How had Kip been so sure that Albright was a good and honest person?

His fur prickled. Was that what a spiritual hold felt like? Had he been ensorcelled to believe that Albright was trustworthy? Was that the real reason Albright hadn't wanted to dine with Martinet and Farmer, and had told Kip not to let Master Cott come along?

If he were back in New Cambridge, he could talk to Coppy and Emily and Malcolm and they could work out a plan to find out what had happened. But he'd barely even told them about spiritual holds at all, and here he was an ocean apart from them. When it came down to it, he knew a few spells, but was alone in a whole college full of unknown sorcerers who might want to take advantage of him.

To reassure and warm himself, he conjured a fire. Fires were simple, fires were understandable. When his tail had stopped twitching with anxiety, he set down to copying demon names.

CHAPTER 11: THE CALATIANS

Cott's pique over Kip's private dinner didn't manifest in his attitude the next day; he returned cheerful in the morning, startling Kip out of a short nap at one of the workroom tables. "Well, well," he said, rubbing his hands together. "I must return that book now. Have you gotten through all the names?"

Kip rubbed his eyes and gestured to the book, sitting halfway open. "The writing is so small and cramped. I copied out any demon that mentions fire and is fourth order, but it takes a long time to decipher."

"They're all fourth order." Cott frowned and looked down at the book. "Some of them may not specify that. Any likely names?"

"No," Kip said, and then stared at the two sheets of paper he'd filled. "At least, nothing that mentions glass beads." Halfway through the night, with only one page filled, he'd decided to try to read through the book and scan for any mention of glass, but each section's different handwriting forced him to stop and grow accustomed to the way one sorcerer had formed his 'm's, another the over-elaborate curled 's's. "Why is this not neatly printed like the spell books?"

Cott bent to examine the writing. "You don't want demon names entrusted to a printer. Nor even a water elemental, for that matter. Your penmanship is much neater. Perhaps we should commission you to recopy the book, ha ha."

"Please, no."

"I'm joking." Cott frowned. "There are more valuable things for you to do. Well, the book must go back this morning, but perhaps we can finish it quickly between us."

"How—" Kip slid to one side and swung his tail out of the way as Cott sat beside him on the bench and reached for his sheets and the quill.

"Go ahead and read off names and any descriptions that have to do with fire. I'll make a note of them here. There's no need to copy out the whole description."

Kip had tried to summarize, especially since many of the demon descriptions were flowery old speech, like "appeared in a cloud of the scent of horse dung and with the appearance of a large swarthy man entirely black of skin enfolded in bright red cloth, spoke Greek but not Latin with an accent as of a spice trader, evinced a strong affinity for setting fires but did not appear to take any enjoyment from the destruction and loss of life on the battlefield. Fought the binding constantly, such that it became dangerous to hold him for more than about five minutes." He knew not all of that was essential, but he couldn't decide which part to leave out. The description? But that might provide a valuable clue to whether they had summoned the demon correctly. The emotional state? Not essential but helpful; a demon that didn't enjoy destruction might be less likely to be compelled to destroy two colleges. And one that could not be bound for longer than a minute or two would not be able to complete the destruction in so short a time. In addition, sometimes there were two or even three entries under the name, if the demon had been summoned multiple times. Sometimes there was no description, but none of those made Kip's list because they did not mention fire (though at one point in the night he stared at the book and realized that if someone had summoned one of those demons to destroy the Colleges, of course they would not have written that experience down).

But Cott didn't seem bothered by any of that. Kip read a name and description, Cott jotted down a few words and then said crisply, "Next."

Kip, caught by surprise, took a moment to find the next time the word "fire" had been written, and Cott repeated, "Next," more insistently. From then on, the fox read quickly ahead and was ready when the sorcerer finished his short notes.

They got to the end of the book in an hour and a half, and Cott gathered it up to take it back. "Look over that list," he said, indicating Kip's two sheets and his one, and walked across the workroom. At the door to his office, he turned back. "Oh," he said, "it goes without saying that I haven't told anyone that I shared this book with you. Technically apprentices aren't allowed, you know. So don't mention it to anyone, there's a good lad."

He was gone before Kip had a chance to say anything. A moment later the outer door opened and closed, and Kip settled in to look at the list of names, shaking his head. Before going back to read through the list, he tore off a scrap of the paper and wrote down three names of demons without descriptions that had lodged in his memory. If apprentices weren't normally allowed to view the ledgers of demons, who knew when those might come in handy?

And of course, he had a list of demons associated with fire. He sighed and made his way down the list, although he'd thought about them extensively while writing them and none of them matched the memory he'd gotten from Forrest. Then again, it was likely that none of the sorcerers had asked the same kind of wholesale destruction of their demons. Most of the notations came from battlefields, either in the Seven Years' War or the Spanish War (and one entry from the English Revolution), and fully the last half from the Napoleonic War.

Kip intended to read through the list, but his head drooped lower and lower, and the next thing he knew, Cott was shaking him awake and the light in the workroom had shifted. "List of names a trifle tedious for you?" the sorcerer asked, though he was smiling.

"I'm sorry," Kip said. "I was awake the whole night."

"Perfectly understandable. Did any of the descriptions strike a chord with you?"

Kip shook his head. "There's no mention of glass beads. Some of them were asked to incinerate whole armies, so there were remains, but..." His paw trailed over the paper. "Nobody mentions the state of the remains."

Only then did he notice the plate the sorcerer was carrying, with a good portion of bread and cheese on it. "Lunch," Cott said, "if your appetite's not gone off from reading about incinerating people."

"Oh, thank you." Kip's stomach rumbled. "No, I haven't eaten since last night."

"Yes." Cott set the plate down on the stone bench with a sharp crack. "Eat up. If you are tired, perhaps it's not a good idea to pursue lessons today. I've business down in London anyway."

Kip picked up a piece of bread. "In that case...might I go down to the Isle of Dogs today? I would very much like to deliver my message."

"Ah." Cott opened and closed his mouth, clearly wanting to deny Kip permission but having lost all valid reason to. "Be back before sunset, then. And don't fly down to a ship dock. Go directly to the Isle. Use the ferry, preferably."

"Yes, sir." Kip sighed, wondering how long the ferry would take. "Er... if you have a raven, might I bring it along to—"

"I haven't a raven anymore." Whether it was pique at Kip leaving or an unpleasant memory of how he'd lost his raven, Cott turned on his heel and left the workshop and, a moment later, the office.

Kip had asked partly out of curiosity; most sorcerers in New Cambridge had ravens, and he'd seen a few wheeling about in the sky, but Cott had never mentioned one and there was no smell of raven in his office nor workshop. So there was that question answered.

The fox wrapped Mrs. Hathway's scarf around his neck and left the tower on foot, descending the stairs to the exit and passing more apprentices on the way. No; apprentices wore purple robes, and these people were in simple tunics and trousers. Servants then, perhaps.

He found the small dock at the base of the hill after several minutes spent searching among the unkempt grass and weeds along the riverbank. At least the smell of the grass was pleasant enough, and though the overcast sky was depressingly familiar, at least today there was no rain nor even mist.

There was also no indication of when the ferry might arrive. Kip scanned the river but could not pick out a ferry from the mix of barges and smaller boats dodging between them. So he sat on the grass and waited, and it wasn't long before he heard footsteps behind him and the scent of fox wafted to his nose. He scrambled to his feet as a light voice called behind him, "How long have you been waiting?"

The voice belonged to a fox about his height, dressed in a white tunic and short pants, walking barefoot down the hill toward him. The fox stopped when Kip turned. "I don't know you."

"Kip Penfold." Kip extended a paw. "I'm from New Cambridge, in the Massachusetts Bay Colony."

"Oh, a Colonial." The fox closed the distance between them and took Kip's paw. "Abelard Ruber. Abel to my Calatian friends."

"Pleasure." As they shook, they brought their muzzles close to sniff each other's scent. Abel smelled lightly of blood (of course, he must have just come from a calyx ritual) but more strongly of his natural scent, earthy and musky, very vulpine but not like any family Kip had ever met.

Abel gestured to Kip's black robe, and his ears splayed to the side. "What brings you to the Isle? And why did your sorcerer dress you in his robes?"

"Mine aren't ready yet. Oh." Kip looked away, his own ears flattening. "I'm—I'm not a calyx." He didn't know why he felt ashamed of this. "I'm an apprentice. To become a sorcerer."

To Kip's mild surprise, Abel's expression didn't change, even the slight smile. "There were rumors," he said. "I didn't quite believe them. A Calatian training to become a sorcerer? We have discussed it, of course, but the wisest among us thought it would be a hundred years or more. But it's true you've no <leffiksmed> about you."

The scent-word for "gloom" put him at ease, the more so because Abel himself had very little of that scent, so it had clearly been meant as a dark joke. Still, Kip didn't quite know what to say. The idea that a group of people an ocean away from him would be talking about him and discussing his future sent currents of unease through his stomach. "No," he said. "It's true. I'm here to receive training in—" He paused. Perhaps mentioning his affinity for fire wouldn't be the most prudent thing. "More advanced sorcery. Might say I'm <bit>."

"Oh, so you can already do magic?" The other fox smiled at the scent-word for "sharp," then lowered his voice. "Could you fly us across the river?"

"I—yes, but—" Kip looked out across the Thames. "There's a ferry."

"It'll be the better part of an hour before it arrives, if you haven't called it." Abel pointed down to the dock, where Kip only now saw a white flag stuck in the ground, and the tall post a would-be passenger would raise it onto, where it would be visible from the other bank. "You could fly us over in five minutes."

"I'm supposed to take the ferry. I tried to fly across once before." But this time he would be flying directly to the Isle in the company of one of its residents who could vouch for him. It wouldn't be so bad, would it?

"What happened? Did you fall in?"

"No, I—" Kip shook his head. "It didn't go well. I didn't know where I was going."

"Oh, well, I'll guide you." Abel took Kip's elbow and turned to face him, golden slit-pupiled eyes staring into Kip's.

It would be easy enough to say that he wasn't allowed, but Kip didn't want to appear so powerless when this fox was accepting his station as sorcerer. And he wanted to impress Abel, too. "All right," he said. "But it can be disorienting, having someone else fly you through the air. Are you sure—what?"

Abel was laughing. "The sorcerers have flown me many times. It's only when they'd prefer not to be bothered that they send us down to the ferry. I'm ready."

The confusion of boats on the Thames had cleared somewhat, allowing a clear path to the far bank. So Kip closed his eyes and gathered magic. "Strewth!" Abel exclaimed. His nostrils flared. "What's happened to your paws?"

"Magic makes an aura around your paws, or hands, if you're a student or apprentice. You've never seen this?" Abel shook his head. "Masters don't do it. It's something you can learn later. To suppress it, I mean."

"Expect you'll learn," Abel said.

Despite his protests that he was ready, the other fox did startle when Kip lifted them off the ground. "All right?" Kip asked.

"Fine, fine. Lovely."

Only then did Kip notice that Abel had nothing but a stump for a tail, less than a foot long. He kept his eyes on the other fox's face, trying not to betray that he'd seen or that the sight upset him. Coppy had told him that many Calatians in London lost their tails to human raiders, but the reality was disquieting. So he smiled as he moved them over the riverbank and said, "You don't have to hold on to my arm so tightly. I've got you with magic even if you let go."

"Right." The fox's grip loosened but he didn't let go, casting a glance down at the water barely six feet below them. "I know that. Usually we fly higher."

"I'd prefer not to call attention to myself." The air was warmer down here near the water, though not much. Kip moved them quickly enough that both foxes flattened their ears and narrowed their eyes against the wind.

Abel didn't comment on that, but a moment later pointed to Kip's left. "That way," he said.

Kip shifted course and a moment later the Isle resolved out of the low haze of wooden structures. Kip searched for Mr. Gibbet's dock to his right, but couldn't pick it out of the four or five that lined the river. "This feels better than when the sorcerers fly me," Abel said.

"How so? Because we're lower?"

The other fox shook his head. "Better, that's all."

Kip thought that perhaps sorcerers didn't allow their calyxes to grip their arms, which made him smile and then reminded him that Abel was a calyx. "Do you know the Lutris family?" he asked.

"Otters? Aye. They live to that side of the Isle." Abel gestured to the right. "You've business with them?"

"A letter to deliver." Kip patted the small pouch at his belt.

Abel squinted at the sun. "I believe Ella should be at home. Marro won't be back until sundown."

Kip focused on the low wooden buildings growing larger before them. "I think my letter is addressed to Dotta?"

"Oh! Ella's mum. Yes, she'll be home too."

"There are a lot of Lutrises on the Isle?"

Abel chuckled, but the chuckle had a bitter edge. "There are a lot of everyone. You'll see."

And indeed, on the shore of the approaching Isle, a multitude of figures moved around. Even at this distance he could distinguish rabbits, otters, foxes, from the tail and ears and the way they moved. At the same time, some of them stopped, clearly looking out at the river, and pointed at the two flying foxes.

Kip pushed on despite the flutter of trepidation. These were Calatians, his people. They wouldn't hurt him. And yet he shouldn't even be worried about that. If not for the reaction of New Cambridge's Calatians, the Cartwrights making him go and plead with them not to break off their daughter's engagement to him, the silent shunning of his father's store... He should have felt safe coming to this community of his own people, and yet he was worried.

When they were close enough to land on the dock, some otters and rabbits did draw back from Kip with their eyes firmly on him, and for a moment it seemed no-one would dare approach. He ended the spell after placing himself and Abel carefully down on the damp, chilly wood. They and the crowd faced each other without speaking for several heartbeats. But then two young foxes ran forward to Abel, crying, "Daddy!" and Abel bent to hug them both.

"Aran, Arabella, this is Mister Kip Penfold." He spoke loudly enough to be heard by the crowd, though his muzzle and eyes were aimed at his cubs. "He's studying to become a sorcerer but he's one of us. It's very exciting."

Kip couldn't tell which cub was which; the tunics that hung down below their knees differed only in the size and color of the patches of dirt and tears all over them. But the one who spoke to him had a higher voice, so he guessed that was Arabella. "Does that mean I may become a sorcerer too?"

"If you know magic," Kip said when Abel deferred to him. "But it's very difficult and takes a lot of work."

Arabella hung back still, until Abel put a gentle paw on her back. "You may go greet Mister Penfold," he said. "You shan't catch fleas from him." His eyes met Kip's, and Kip knew that the reassurance had been meant more for him.

He extended a paw to Arabella, and Aran came up to be greeted as well. "It's very nice to meet you both," he said, clasping each paw in turn.

"Run on home," Abel said to the cubs as two rabbits came forward. "I'll be there presently. Kip, this is Charles Cotton, and his brother Callo." While Kip was shaking their paws, Abel continued introducing him to some of the other Calatians on the Isle. Gradually the crowd thinned, though Abel remained at Kip's side, which was a comfort. The rabbits did not speak much out of (Kip thought) suspicion, but a dormouse, Thomas Trewel, chattered merrily when he learned Kip was a Colonial.

"I've heard the weather is more temperate in the Colonies. Is that true?"

"Not this time of year," Kip said.

"And the greenery! I've heard it puts our English countrysides to shame."

"I've never seen the English countryside."

"Oh, you should. It's delightful. I hear."

Abel cleared his throat. "Kip, Dotta Lutris lives down this way. May I show you?"

Everyone except the dormouse remained on the docks as Abel led Kip and Thomas into the thick of the town. The little streets of the Isle of Dogs wound like a tangle of string, and without Abel's guidance, Kip would have been lost after the first turn. Abel tried to cut off Thomas's chatter to little avail, so Kip answered questions about the colonies as he navigated his way through the narrow streets choked with Calatians.

He'd never in his life been surrounded by so many of his people, but the feeling wasn't reassuring. Coppy had told him that New Cambridge's cleanliness was one of the things he loved about it, the "clear air," and Kip had assumed he'd been talking only about London's smoke. There was smoke for sure, but it was also clear that many of the Isle's residents did not bathe and might not even have proper outhouses. In New Cambridge, any Calatian family that allowed their odor to emanate too far from their home was visited by the mayor or a deputy. Here, that was clearly not the case, or else there was someone doing it from sunup to sundown every day. <Monesmek> was the word for many scents combined, but Kip wanted a stronger word to describe the Isle.

Abel wore a simple, clean tunic, but many of the clothes Kip saw around him bespoke poverty: dirty, patched, and torn. Many more stubby tails crossed his path, and even when he stopped looking for them, he couldn't help but see them. Some Calatians met his eyes and smiled, as his neighbors in New Cambridge might, but many saw his robes and looked away, and still others kept their heads down and might never have noticed him at all.

If the crowds and smell were new and unsettling to Kip, the variety of Calatians was familiar to him from New Cambridge; there were no types here he didn't recognize. There were just so many more of them. Back in New Cambridge Kip had known all the foxes: four families, fifteen total people. Even not counting Abel, he saw more than fifteen foxes on the short walk to the Lutris house, along with otters, dormice, red squirrels, badgers, moles, and rabbits. And then, as Abel said, "It's just that house there, with the otter cubs playing out front," and pointed, Kip looked beyond the house to a large figure in the road, like a fox but greyer, thicker, and taller.

He stopped dead, staring, and as Abel turned to see what was the matter, said, "Is that...a wolf?"

Abel tilted his head and then broke into a smile, nodding. "Ah, you don't have wolves in the Colonies?"

"Not in New Cambridge, at any rate," Kip said. "Nor Boston. Perhaps New York."

"They're few here, too. Ho!" Before Kip could stop him, the other fox raised a paw. "Grinda!"

The wolf perked her ears and looked in their direction. "You don't have to," Kip said.

Abel waved him quiet. "She's a friend. And a good woman, if a bit <chesbit>. You'd have met her after regardless."

"Why?" Kip asked, but Grinda had reached them and Abel introduced Kip as a sorcerer from the Colonies, ignoring the question.

Grinda had a soft, low voice with a persistent growl to it that set Kip's fur on edge at first, and a powerful scent that he marked as "wolf." "Pleased," she said, and gripped Kip's paw with a huge, soft one as she turned to Abel. "And don't think I don't know your scent words. 'Sour,' is it?"

Abel widened his eyes innocently as though he'd no idea what she was talking about, and with a huff, Grinda returned her attention to Kip. "Calatian sorcerer? It's true?"

"I'm an apprentice, really," he said. "Not a sorcerer yet."

"He can do sorcery, though. Kip's got a letter to deliver to the Lutrises," Abel said, "but I thought we might invite him to tea after, eh?"

Grinda's eyes, piercing blue in the soft grey of her muzzle, studied Kip. "You reckon he's trustworthy?"

"Far as I've been able to judge." Abel smiled at Kip. "He didn't drop me into the Thames."

"Low bar to clear," Grinda rumbled.

The older fox's smile brightened. "He's a Calatian learning sorcery."

"He's a sorcerer who happens to be a Calatian," Grinda replied.

Kip took the letter out of his pouch. "He's a messenger with a letter."

"Right, right." Abel held a paw up to the wolf. "We can have this conversation in a few minutes, when our friend has completed his mission."

The fox left behind the rest of their little group, pushing his way to the small house he'd pointed out to Kip. "Here we are," he said, reaching out to the simple curtain that hung in the doorway. He pulled it aside and gestured Kip in.

"Don't we knock, or…" Kip stepped forward past the curtain into the thick smell of otter and fish. It took his eyes a moment to adjust to the dimness, but in that moment he sorted out five individual otter scents, and turned toward the female one that reminded him most of Coppy. "Dotta?"

A stocky shape with a broad tail resolved out of the shadow, rising from a chair. "That's me. And who are you?"

"Ah, Kip Penfold." He held out a paw, forgetting he was holding the letter in it, then switched the letter to his left and held the paw out again. "I'm a friend of your son. Coppy?"

Dotta's fingers didn't have much grip to them, but the feel and the webbing was very familiar to Kip, and her eyes lit up at the name. "My boy Coppy," she said, half-wonderingly. "How is he?"

"He's doing very well." Kip realized in that moment how much he missed his friend, how much he wanted Coppy to be here with him in the house where he'd grown up. "He sends you this letter."

"He's mentioned you. It's a real pleasure to meet you at last." She took the folded paper from him and opened it, holding it up to the window. While she read, other otters crowded up around Kip.

"I'm Ella, his sister."

"I'm Tokka, his sister too!"

"I'm his brother Widdin."

They ranged from close to Kip's age—Ella, with an infant in her arms—down to Widdin, who was maybe thirteen, and they all wanted to shake Kip's paw and welcome him. He grasped each of the small otter paws, and Abel, clearly a friend of the family, clapped Tokka on the back and asked her how the salvage had been that day. Kip didn't understand what that meant, but Tokka started talking about pieces of old furniture and some clothing, and then Dotta put the letter down and said, "Thank you for bringing this."

Kip focused on her again. "You're very welcome. Coppy's become my best friend and I'm so pleased to meet his family."

"But this says he's…learning sorcery." She met Kip's eyes. "Is this possible?"

Before Kip could answer, Abel said, "More than possible. Meet the first Calatian sorcerer. He flew me across the Thames so we wouldn't have to wait for Dillington and his terrible rolling disaster of a boat." He turned to Kip. "It's a true miracle how on a completely smooth day the boat can pitch and roll as if it were in the typhoon of the South Seas."

His humor passed unnoticed by the otters, all staring with wide gleaming eyes at Kip. "Can you do magic?" Ella whispered.

"Aye." Kip smiled. "I'm not supposed to when it's not necessary, but I hope you'll take Abel's witness."

"As I live and breathe, he flew me over." Abel made grand gestures with his paws.

"Even given Abel's reputation, I believe we can take that as truth," Dotta said. She smiled and set the letter aside. "What else can you tell me of Coppy?"

Kip told her about Emily and Malcolm, that Coppy had other friends in the school and was doing well with his studies, that he was under the tutelage of one of the most respected sorcerers there. He left out Coppy's difficulties and Master Windsor's demeanor; those would only cause her to worry. He didn't think himself a good storyteller, but Dotta and the children looked on raptly, and Abel asked helpful questions to prod Kip into telling more interesting details. "He talks often of wanting to come back here and use his sorcery to help. I had wanted to stay in New Cambridge, myself, but now that I've seen his home and met his family, I think I would be happy to join him here."

Dotta smiled. "You've been a capital friend to him and now you do us the service of bringing us his letter in person. We're so grateful. It's been two months with no letters. He had sent back money every month, but we hadn't heard from him since October. Right around Halloween the last letter arrived, and we have been wondering why there wasn't another one."

Of course Coppy had been sending money home. Kip knew that; the otter had mentioned it early on, but not in the last several months and not since they'd been studying magic. When, of course, his father hadn't been paying Coppy a salary from the store. Letters could take two months to travel from the colonies to England, so Coppy's last letter, before they'd enrolled at the College, would have been the one Dotta spoke of.

Kip had never thought that going to school would deprive Coppy's family of income. Coppy had never mentioned it. He'd just joined up with Kip, being a good friend, knowing Kip needed someone to protect him from Farley. "No," he said. "Students don't get paid. And he decided very suddenly. I was joining and he was kind of…he helped me out a lot. There was a bully who tormented Calatians in New Cambridge."

"Just one?" Abel said.

"Ah, well, no, uh." The room had fallen silent. And Kip, looking around, felt the implications of the question beyond the simple two words. "There, we live together with humans. Well, not 'together,' but we don't have our own town, our own neighborhood."

The otters all looked at each other and again silence fell in the cabin. "You live out on farms? We hear there's a lot of farms out in the Colonies."

"Some do, but no, my father has a shop."

"Yes, the one Coppy worked at." Dotta smiled. "It sounds so wonderful. You know, three of our friends took passage to the New World after reading his letters."

"And don't forget Hannibal Black, who walked the Road." Ella sounded wistful. "I know it takes longer but it must be so interesting, walking along the ocean like that. And you could drop in for a swim whenever you wanted."

"The salt water's not good for your fur," Dotta said.

"I'm not going to bathe in it," Ella said. "And anyway I know that I can't go along the Road."

"That's right."

"Not until I marry Byron Merrick and we emigrate together." The young otter tossed her head.

Dotta patted her. "And have you discussed walking the Road with Byron or would he work passage on a ship and be there in a third the time, like a sensible otter?"

Abel took Kip's arm again. "If you'll excuse me, I would like to steal our guest away. There are a few others who would like to meet him."

He left to a profusion of embraces and whiskered muzzles against his own, cries of, "Come back soon!" and many, many thanks. When Dotta clasped his paws, she said, "You are welcome anytime. Do tell our Coppy how much we miss him."

"If he comes to visit me, I'll be sure to bring him over." Kip held her warm paws in return. "He can bring himself over, come to that."

He left the cabin with her bright smile etched in his mind and Abel's arm on his paw. "I have to be back by sundown," Kip said as they emerged into the street.

"No worries," the other fox assured him. "We won't keep you very long. Sunset won't be for a couple hours still, and it would mean a lot to these people to meet you."

The wolf and dormouse rejoined them as Abel took Kip down the winding street to an intersection with a larger one. "One question," Abel said casually. "Your fire sorcerer, he isn't listening to you or anything right now, is he?"

"No, not to my knowledge." This sounded vaguely ominous. "He's not a spiritual sorcerer." And if he were listening, he would have known that Kip had gotten trapped in Mr. Gibbet's closet far sooner than he had.

"All right." The other fox's tone remained light. "There's nothing serious going on, just a few calyxes talking about calyx things, and sometimes the sorcerers don't like us to share them. But it's nothing we don't already know. I just want to be sure I'm not getting anyone in trouble." He scanned the skies. "On occasion we are summoned by raven, but I see none of those sorcerer puppets about now."

"No, of course not," Kip said. "I won't tell them."

Grinda growled something unintelligible. "Course you won't," Thomas said. "You're one of us, just more talented in the magic department."

They walked out along the larger street past Calatians hurrying in the other direction, many carrying small parcels that gave out a food odor when they came close to Kip. He looked up to where everyone was rushing in from, and pointed ahead. "Are we going to that gate?"

"Ha," Abel said.

Thomas came up along the other side of Kip. "That way's London proper. We only go out there when we've work to do."

"Or shopping," Abel reminded him. "The merchants on Darrow Street will take our custom."

"Aye," Thomas said. "But beyond Darrow Street, best not to be out in the city unless you have a work order. Sometimes even with."

Kip imagined a city full of Farleys and forced himself not to look at Abel's stub of a tail. "I'm sorry."

"You didn't know." Abel tapped his elbow. "This way."

They turned down a small side street, the least crowded one they'd yet walked down. Every house they passed had only a curtained doorway, and at some of them the curtains were drawn aside so that the breeze brought Kip the scents of the people inside. This was something he was not familiar with from New Cambridge, where the Calatians followed the human tradition of closed-up houses. As he walked down the street, his nose told him who was at home, or would have if he could identify the three to five scents that drifted out of each house. It felt oppressive to him, but Abel called out greetings as he passed, so the openness served a purpose as well.

"Here," Abel said, coming around another corner to a small pub, where the smell of ale and cooking meat—but not good meat, not any meat Kip could identify—filled the street over the scent of the people milling about in it. The sign outside the pub, crudely made compared to the others Kip had seen in London this week, had only a picture of a goose on it. "Welcome to The Goose's Tayle."

Inside, the smoke of cooking fires obscured both the detail of the old scarred furniture and the scents of the patrons seated thereupon. Kip followed Abel, disoriented in the dim haze, through tables of various sizes and shapes to the back left corner of the small pub. There, in a corner partially walled off from the rest of the bar, the two rabbits Kip had met at the dock sat along with an otter and a polecat. Abel gestured for Kip to take the remaining chair, and he, the dormouse, and the wolf all crowded around behind it. Three mugs sat on the table, which listed toward the rabbits so that everyone had to keep a paw on their mug lest it slide to the floor.

"Ho, all," Abel said cheerfully, and took the otter's mug. "What are you drinking, Pierce?"

"Ah," the otter said with equal cheer. "I've asked the barkeep for some of her private reserve, crafted by the finest brewmasters in Germany and carried up here to our doorstep for the pleasure of our most refined palates."

Abel took a swig and made a show of swishing it around in his muzzle. "Most excellent," he said. Upon putting it back down, he caught Kip's look of polite interest, and hid a cough behind his paw. "Er, no. Until you've had much more practice with your imagination, I wouldn't recommend sampling anything here, not if you're used to the fare they serve up in the College."

"Oh," one of the rabbits said, "now you've done it, Pierce. He's going to go on about the time he was treated to a meal by Master Sweatlodge."

"His proper name is Sweat*podge*." Abel leaned against the wall behind Kip and mimed a pot belly. "Do have some respect, Callo."

Callo was the rabbit on the left, so the one on the right must be... Kip searched his memory. Charles. And he knew Grinda and Thomas, so the only ones he hadn't been introduced to were the otter and the polecat. "Pierce?" he said, extending a paw to the otter. "Kip Penfold."

"Oh aye." The otter shook his paw. "Been told about you already by the Cottons here. And this is Barnard."

The polecat, the youngest of the seven, also was missing most of his tail. As Kip shook his paw, he said, "Is it true you can do magic?"

"It's true," Abel said. "He's not going to demonstrate here in the Tayle, though, is he?"

"Just a small trick?" The otter scraped his mug across the table. "Set the table right?"

Kip shook his head. "I shouldn't." Part of him wanted to show off, but after the situation with Mr. Gibbet, he couldn't afford to risk any kind of problem on this trip if he wanted Master Cott to approve any more travel down here. "You can come watch when I fly back, if you like."

"That'd do just fine, thank you," the otter said.

"He's said that no sorcerer's listening in," Abel told the group.

He was going to go on, but Grinda cut him off. "There's one," she said, staring pointedly at Kip.

"Yes, well." Abel rested a paw on Grinda's. "I thought it might be nice to introduce him to some of the calyxes with experience of the College to let him know what to expect. Now, both Cotton brothers there assisted materially in the defeat of Napoleon."

"Helped summon six demons," Callo said, raising a paw. "Charles there summoned ten." Charles kept his eyes down toward his tankard, from which he drank rather more frequently than the others did from theirs.

"We all helped some," Grinda growled. "Including Deveren."

The table fell silent. "Aye," Abel said. "We lost Deveren over the war."

"Lost him?" Grinda gripped the back of Kip's chair. "Those sorcerers bled him dry. They killed him."

Kip didn't feel it was his place to speak up, so was glad when Callo did. "Many died during the war. On the whole—"

"On the whole." Grinda spat his words back at him. She glared down at Kip. "Deveren died from carelessness. Many of us survived. If managed properly, our servitude needn't be fatal, only a lifetime of humiliation and violation. They've rules, you know, because they can't tell when one of us is too weakened to provide blood. Only so many times in so many days. Have you ever drunk Calatian blood?"

"Grinda." Abel's tone sharpened, but didn't distract Kip or Grinda, eyes locked.

If he said yes, what would happen? Would he lose the friendship of the other Calatians and be forever consigned to the ranks of sorcerers? After all, it didn't matter that he'd been forced to for the first two weeks of his instruction. He'd found an alternative; he'd summoned a demon without the use of Calatian blood. And what he'd done once, he could do again. If he might never need to use Calatian blood in his rituals, was it a lie to claim he never had? "I've summoned a demon without doing so," Kip said, "so I don't suppose I shall need to."

"You didn't answer the question, fox," Grinda said.

"That's enough." Abel, still speaking sharply, stepped in. "We're not here to divide ourselves."

"It seems very pertinent to understand what side your new friend is on before we start airing grievances," Grinda growled.

"I'm one of you," Kip said.

"You aren't dressed as we are." Charles's low voice, huskier than his brother's, echoed lightly from the tankard he spoke into.

Kip lifted a fold of the black robe. "I can take this off if it would set you more at ease."

Abel set a paw on his shoulder, cheery again. "Now don't go giving away for free what Miss Bertram charges two pennies for," he said, and the table laughed, all but Grinda. "No, Kip, we simply wanted you to meet some of the calyxes under different circumstances than you might up at the College."

Grinda muttered something too low for Kip to hear all of, but which seemed to include the word, "knife." He ignored her as the rest of the table was doing, and asked his more pressing question to Abel. "You've been planning this? You'd heard of me?"

"Only since we arrived a short bit ago." Abel gave a toothy smile. "I talked to the Cottons and they gathered the rest for us. Some met us along the way." He gestured to Grinda. "And others preferred to wait with a tankard."

Pierce lifted his mug. "Why walk around the streets when you can be sitting comfortably here?"

"Comfortably?" Callo squirmed around in his seat. "Has Talla laid in new chairs for you?"

Kip's wooden chair was not terribly comfortable either, but he refrained from comment. "I'm very pleased to meet all of you. Truthfully, living among humans is difficult. I'm very glad to be among my own kind again. If it weren't for Coppy, the past few months would have been so much harder."

And then he had to tell them about Coppy, and most of them remembered him as "the oldest Lutris boy," though only Pierce knew he'd gone to America; the others thought he'd taken work elsewhere in London or in the north, where there were rumored to be jobs on farms for Calatians. "And some go," Pierce said, "but life on a farm is much as you've described life in the College: among humans all the time. Most of us would prefer to be here among our own kind."

"Cheers," Kip said, because at that moment a tall marten came over with four tankards and set them down, waiting to let them go until four paws steadied them on the slanted table.

"Got them all?" she asked. "Right, whose coin am I taking?"

Abel reached for a pouch at his side, but Kip said, "I'll pay." He had a few coins for sundries, and he pulled out a shilling. "Will this suffice?"

"Aye." The marten took it, examined it, then slipped it into the pouch of her apron, where it clinked. She withdrew a half-shilling and two pennies, but Kip took only the half-shilling. "Ah, thank you, sir," she said, and executed a clumsy half-curtsy before going back to the bar.

"Reckon it's the first time she's seen a shilling?" Pierce asked.

"Now, now," Abel said. "Kip, you'll drink with us?"

The ale smelled bad, but not intolerable. For a moment he was tempted and then he remembered his training. "I'm not supposed to drink, as an apprentice. If I should impair my judgment, it might be, ah, bad."

As he said that, the memory of Mr. Gibbet's workshop erupting in flames returned to him, and he wondered whether he would ever feel comfortable drinking. If a fire sorcerer lost control, the result could be worse than simply "bad." But Abel didn't take his refusal poorly. "More for us," the other fox declared.

Pierce extended his other paw to hold Kip's mug. "More for me, you mean to say." He drained his own mug and set it on the floor. "Cheers, Kip."

"Cheers," Kip replied as the rest of them drank.

He sat with them through that round of ales, and then the Cottons declared that they should be going home. Barnard, the polecat, left with them, and Grinda and Thomas soon after. Pierce stayed for one more tankard, mostly because Abel hadn't finished his by the time the otter had downed all of Kip's. They told Kip stories of the Isle, mostly half-finished as they had a tendency to distract each other halfway through and launch into a new story while the previous one foundered, forgotten well shy of its destination.

Finally Abel offered to walk Kip back to the dock, and the two of them took their leave of Pierce. The streets of the Isle were less crowded now, with the light reddening, and it was easier for the two of them to walk side by side and talk in low voices only audible to their fox ears. "Thank you for introducing me to everyone," Kip said as they rounded the first corner.

"Thank you for your patience in indulging me." Abel smiled and flicked his ears back. "I have a way of seizing the reins of things and driving them to my own ends."

"May I ask, then, what were those ends here?" Kip asked.

The other fox nodded. "I thought it would be good for you to meet some of the calyxes you may encounter at the College, as I said. And I thought it might be lonely for a Calatian in the College."

"Yes. Thank you." Kip paused at a corner, preparing to turn right toward what he thought were the docks. Abel kept going forward, though, and Kip hurried to catch up. "I must be disoriented."

"Not at all. That road does go to the docks. But I want to take you to one more place before you go. It will be short, I promise."

Kip nodded and followed, calculating time in his head. Though the sun lay fat and red on the horizon, he had an hour before dark, and as long as he got back before then, he would not incur Cott's wrath.

So he followed Abel another two streets down, to a corner where a stone column stood with a carved plaque at its base. Unlike the rest of the Isle, this little area remained clear of Calatians; Abel and Kip stood just beside the column, and the other fox spoke soberly. "This is the site of the Blackstone Bakery fire."

"Oh." Chills lifted Kip's hackles. He bent to examine the plaque, whose inscription read: "ON THIS SITE IN 1608 THE BLACKSTONE

BAKERY BURNED." The stone was cool to the touch, the column simple and unadorned. "There's no mention of the Calatians?"

"We all know the story," Abel said quietly. "The Calatians trapped inside, ten or fifteen or twenty of them, all of them burned to death while the humans stood and watched."

Kip nodded, staring down at the simple plaque and the ground around it. "And from that fire came the rights we have today. All this <haylet>." He gestured around, meaning the word for "healthy life" to encompass the Isle.

"Ah." Abel took a step to come up next to him. "The fire brought some support to the movement, but it was the sorcerers who gave us our rights. Because they wanted to use us. And we remain <lefet>."

Lefet: living but sick. The sense of community he'd gained from the plaque faltered. "I'm only an apprentice," he said. "And I'm one person. I don't have the power to change anything."

"One person has one person's power," Abel said. He touched the column. "Sometimes one person, the right person in the right place at the right time, can wield great power indeed. You know of Archimedes?"

Kip's eyebrows rose. "Aye," he said.

"'Give me a lever and a place to stand and I will move the Earth.'" Abel smiled. "We have schoolbooks and teachers on the Isle, too."

"Of course." Kip nodded.

"So. Perhaps one day you will need a place to stand."

Kip took in the plaque again, and then looked up at the column, a simple stone monument. He breathed in and felt the weight of it; it almost seemed to anchor the whole Isle. "I'll remember that."

The stub of Abel's tail made a wagging motion, and he patted Kip on the shoulder. "Now let's get you back to the dock."

The other fox started on down the street, and Kip fell in beside him. "Ah, but Pierce won't be there to see it."

"No," Abel said. "But perhaps next time."

CHAPTER 12: SPIRITUAL SORCERY

The visit to the Isle prompted Kip to write a letter back to Coppy in which he described all his adventures over the past week, with most attention paid to the Isle and all the otter's family. He left his meeting in the pub deliberately vague, thinking he would explain it to Coppy in person, because he was going to have to find a translocation sorcerer to send this to Prince George's school who might very well read it before transporting it. Abel's caution about sorcerers listening made Kip wary about giving away any information.

The only sorcerer he knew at King's with translocation ability was Master Albright, so for a day Kip held the letter hoping to find someone else. Over the course of two nights, though, he couldn't help but imagine what his friends would advise him if he could talk to them. If Albright had put a spiritual hold on him, they would say, he had the countermeasure. He just had to remember to use it, and if it worked, he would be sure that Albright was working against him. Best to be sure, Emily would tell him. Actually, perhaps Emily would tell him he was foolish to trust any master at all. Coppy would tell Kip to be careful no matter what he did. Malcolm, of course, would not want him to run from Albright. So he resolved to approach Albright, and a not inconsiderable part of that decision was his desire to have someone to talk to other than Cott.

Whether it was lingering resentment over Albright excluding him from dinner or something else, Cott did not bring Kip down to the dining hall anymore. He took his meals in the workshop with Kip and never gave the fox a reason to leave other than to use the necessary at the end of the hall. Not that Kip was ever forbidden from leaving; when he asked about taking a walk on the grounds, Cott would say, "Why do you want to do that? It's cold outside." Kip did insist once, and though he enjoyed the freedom the walk provided, the grey and dreary evening and the damp air drove him quickly back to the workshop to dry himself in front of a fire.

On the brighter side, Cott was teaching him finer control over fire, not only the spread but how to dictate what it would and would not consume, and it was during the lessons that he found Cott's company most pleasant. The master was not only willing but delighted to talk on any aspect of fire that Kip wanted to explore, and late in his second week, brought out powders that could turn the fire different colors. "Here's copper, that's for blue, and lithium, that will give you red. Sodium will burn yellow and barium green. Just a pinch will do. Eventually you may use alchemy to infuse your fire with those elements, but that is, hah, that is rather advanced." And to show off, Cott conjured a blue flame in his hand.

Again Kip wondered about holding the flame in his paw. He'd tried holding the fire while telling it not to burn his fur, and while it didn't leave him with burns as it previously had, the heat remained intense enough that he could not stand it past seven seconds. This frustrated him, but less than he would have thought; four to five hours a day learning fire magic from Cott were worth a full week with Master Odden. Who, though still his master, had not sent any communication to check on Kip's progress nor to ask when he would return.

It was easy to remain in the small world between Cott's office and workshop, and there was plenty to do: poring over the list of demons, searching Cott's book for spells to use on the glass bead, practicing his control of fire until bright golden glows danced before his eyes even when they were closed. But after a week of this, and after Cott had put off his inquiries about reaching Master Albright several times with vague promises of finding him later, those pleasant tasks grew repetitive and Kip felt there might as well be bars on the window. Even back at Prince George's, though the basement was smellier and full of dust and insects both living and dead, he'd been able to leave, had had more exposure to fresh air than a two-foot square opening.

From the workshop's window, all he could see were the green fields outside and a few scattered houses. People walked from those houses to the College in the morning and back at night, all dressed in plain tunics, so he surmised that they worked at the College. Most likely they lived in the small village where stood the Clock and Pull pub and The Darby, though the village itself lay out of of Kip's line of sight. As he watched from his window, the thought of the village gave him an idea on how to contact Albright.

The days shortened as Christmas approached, and Cott retired early some evenings that second week. Taking the opportunity afforded by his absence, Kip pulled the black robe around himself (the College still had not provided a purple apprentice's robe for him) and lifted himself out the window and gently to the ground. He kept his fingers to the College wall, here nothing more than stone that reminded him of Peter when he touched it, and walked around the wall until he caught the smells of the pub. Then he headed along the path to the village and found The Darby easily.

Bridget remembered him, which was a comfort in this new world Kip was adjusting to, and pressed food upon him. He insisted on paying her, though she protested and would only take a pittance for the meal. It made for a worthwhile evening anyway, and Cott made no mention of it the following day, to Kip's relief. He surely would have said something if he'd heard from another master that his apprentice was seen dining in the village.

He slipped out twice more that week when Cott left him alone, and on his third excursion to The Darby, Kip opened the door to find Master Albright sitting at one of the tables. His ears perked as he hurried in, smiling widely.

The silver-bearded master looked up from his dinner and after a moment's confusion, his brow lifted and he smiled. "Ah. Penfold. Yes, Bridget tells me you've become a frequent patron of hers."

"Yes," Kip said. "The dinners are far superior to what's served at the college."

Bridget, who had just come back with a mug of ale for Master Albright, said, "Oh, go on, you. Where will you be sitting today?"

There was the table Master Albright occupied alone; there were two tables in the other room, one of which held two other dinner guests. Kip hesitated. "If you wouldn't mind, sir?"

"Of course, of course." Albright gestured to the place across from him.

"Thank you, sir." Kip took the seat as Bridget swept away, no doubt to fetch him tea and a plate of the roast pork that Albright had in front of him.

"Now," Albright said around a mouthful of meat, "Is this merely a coincidence built around a mutual appreciation for Bridget's kitchen or have you been seeking me out?"

Kip fidgeted, his ears lowering. "I have been seeking you out, sir."

"And to what purpose?"

"Well, er." Kip did not have an impulse to tell Albright everything about his life. Perhaps he'd been mistaken about the spiritual hold, or Albright was simply not casting one now. "You see, I bore a letter from my friend to his family here in London, and I would like to let him know that it's been delivered. But I have no way to get the letter to America."

"I see."

"And you did mention that translocation is your specialty, sir."

"So I did." Albright swallowed a mouthful and followed it with another. "I will of course be pleased to help. I have never been to Prince George's, though, so I will need your help to direct the letter."

"Of course." Kip's tail swished once before he calmed it.

"And…I would like to ask a favor of you in return."

Kip perked his ears. "Yes, sir?"

"Mmm." Albright finished his mouthful and his dark eyes met Kip's. "Cott is often very close-mouthed about his researches. Has funny ideas about who does and doesn't like him rather than who needs to know such things."

Bridget returned with Kip's tea and dinner, and he took a drink but refrained from eating, though the smell of the roast made his mouth water. Was Albright going to ask him to spy on Cott? "I see?"

Albright indicated Kip's dinner. "Eat. Afterwards we will walk and talk."

Afterwards. That would be the time to try Master Jaeger's spell. Trying to control the flicking of his tail, Kip ate his pork while Albright polished off another mug of ale, with none of the conversation they'd had the other night. Kip didn't want to talk while eating, and Albright was lost in his own thoughts. Finally, when Kip was done, he left a shilling on the table for Bridget and rose with Master Albright, who again left nothing.

Once they had passed through Greenwich, Master Albright's steps slowed. The cloud cover hid the moon and stars, but Kip could see well enough the empty path and the low scrub to either side of it. The scents of dinner and ale drifted to him on the breeze, as well as the stink of the people who lived in town.

Kip stayed a step behind Albright. He didn't think there was a spiritual hold on him, but could he be sure? He clasped his paws behind his back and gathered magic, then quickly cast Jaeger's spell under his breath.

The sorcerer turned. "Did you say something, Penfold?"

"A spell that Master Cott has been teaching me," Kip said. "I have been having trouble remembering it so I thought to use this time to imprint it further on my memory."

"Admirable." Albright looked up at the towers of King's College, still some ten minutes' walk away. Apparently this location was satisfactory to have their conversation, so he turned back to Kip, keeping his voice discreet. "This research you're doing with Cott into the demon that attacked Prince George's. It's of great interest and importance to the Empire, of course. And yet I fear that Cott may try to keep it to himself or use it to curry favor with certain officials in the government. That information may mean the survival or death of any number of British sorcerers. Especially in Prince George's college."

Kip nodded. He studied his feelings. Nothing seemed to have changed; he did not feel less inclined to help Albright. So either he had not cast the spell properly or there hadn't been a spiritual hold on him. "Of course I want to help those at the College—Prince George's."

"Then all I ask is that as you and Cott narrow your search down to a few demon names, you inform me."

"If we even get that far," Kip said. "We've been going through them for a week now and we've only eliminated a few. The problem is that we can't summon them to find out more about them. I mean…we can, but not until it gets to a smaller list."

"Cott is not experienced enough to bind a fourth-order demon," Albright intoned. "Not for more than a few seconds, at least. Few are."

"Who might be?" It hadn't occurred to Kip that simply investigating who could bind a fourth-order demon would be a way to narrow his search.

"Oh, perhaps ten in King's College," Albright said. "Though there are many more who are strong enough should they put their mind to it. More in the military, of course, that being their stock in trade. And perhaps one or two in Prince George's, another handful in India and Gibraltar and other overseas territories. And who knows about Spain?"

In Prince George's… "Who in Prince George's?" Kip asked, trying to keep his tone casual. Of course, a sorcerer in his college could be working with a more powerful military sorcerer, but now he wanted to know.

"The Headmaster, of course, what's his name?"

"Patris." Kip's throat was dry despite the mug of tea he'd hurriedly drained before leaving.

"Yes. I'm afraid I can't recall the names of all those who died. We were given a list, you know, but the names have faded. Is Master Thornton still there?"

Kip shook his head. Master Albright took another step. "Pity. He was a good one, Thornton was. Let's see, there was Strong, but I know he died. Who was the other one…" He mused. "Oh. Odden."

The taste of tea in Kip's muzzle soured. He couldn't see any way that Patris would have destroyed the College. Of all the bad things he thought about Patris (and if he'd started listing them when he arrived in London he would probably still be going), a willingness to destroy his College was not one of them. So that left Odden. And if Odden were the one who'd called the demon, of course he would not have suggested to Kip that they look at the sorcerers who could bind fourth order demons.

But, Kip reminded himself, Odden didn't know what he knew, about the culprit being inside the Tower, possibly a Master at the College. So he wouldn't necessarily have taken that tack anyway. "What about Master

Argent?" Kip asked. "He's young, but I believe he is quite adept with demons."

Albright rubbed his beard, looking down the path toward the college. "Generally those capable of controlling powerful demons are taken to the military unless they display other attributes. I don't know this Argent, but are demons his specialty?"

Kip shook his head. "Alchemy, as far as I know."

"Then it's possible. If the College needed him more for his alchemical research, yes, certainly. That was the case with Odden, as I recall. He was the closest thing the Colonies had to a fire sorcerer." He inclined his head. "Until a certain Calatian."

"I hope I may serve the Empire as well in that capacity."

"As well?" Here Albright turned his piercing gaze on Kip. In the night his eyes appeared black. "You would prefer to be in the College than in the military?"

"I've been accepted to the College," Kip said. "I don't know how well I would fare in the military."

"The Colleges do have the reputation of being more progressive, particularly the Colonial ones. Well. One. Though I don't suppose anyone here has given you any trouble here."

"Not yet." Kip let his tail swing free. "Cott keeps me busy in his workroom, so I have very little time to interact outside of it."

"Indeed." Albright stroked his beard. "But you said you'd delivered a letter."

"To the Isle of Dogs." He gestured down the hill toward the scent and sound of the Thames.

"And how did you like it there?"

Albright peered keenly at him. Kip searched his feelings to see whether he felt compelled to tell Albright about the council of the calyxes, but no such urge drove his words. He could attempt Jaeger's spell anyway, but it would be difficult with Albright staring right at him. He cleared his throat and repeated the answer he'd given Cott. "It was nice to be among my people again, and to meet my best friend's family."

The sorcerer turned his gaze down the hill, and then back to the College. "Have you the letter with you?"

"Yes." Kip reached into a pocket of his robe. He had taken to carrying it on his person only because he didn't trust Cott when the sorcerer was working with him in the workshop; Cott had a habit of picking up whatever Kip was looking at and reading it. There was nothing in it that would alarm any sorcerer, but Kip jealously guarded any scrap of privacy he had.

Albright took the letter without opening it. "I suppose that if you don't want to use Master Woodholm's daily translocation of mail, you would prefer it not be sent to the usual place for letters?"

"I didn't know about Master Woodholm," Kip confessed. "You're the only one I know who can translocate."

"No matter." Albright held the letter. "Visualize the location where you want it to appear and make it as real as you can."

Kip closed his eyes and focused on the smell of the basement, the way Coppy's bedroll looked in the light of Neddy's fire, and then his mind wandered: was Neddy still there? Binding spells were supposed to last without concentration, but he truly hadn't thought about Neddy in days. Kip pushed that thought away and built up the image of the location in his mind. A moment later he felt the pull of magic against his senses.

"My goodness," Albright said a moment later. "Did you live there?"

"Yes."

"Tch." Kip had no idea what that noise meant. Another pulse of magic near him. "It's done."

He opened his eyes to see the black-robed sorcerer holding out both empty hands. His letter was now in Coppy's paws, or at least on Coppy's bedroll, and the feeling of reconnecting rushed through him. "Thank you very much," Kip pushed past the emotion clogging his throat.

Albright's silver eyebrows rose, and Kip thought again of how much he looked like Patris, only with a beard and sympathy. "Perhaps we can arrange for a visit. But that would have to be with Cott's permission. And knowledge," the sorcerer added, looking up at the College.

Kip laid his ears back. "I don't see why Cott should have power over my comings and goings. I'm Master Odden's apprentice, not his."

"While you are here in London, I doubt the distinction will mean much to Cott. However, a summons from Odden might be one way to persuade Cott to allow you to leave. I presume you have arranged to return for Christmas, at least?"

"Not specifically." Kip folded his arms, still fighting the emotion of his letter reaching Coppy. "He told me to come here to consult with Cott on... the demon work, and to learn more control of fire."

"And the glass beads."

"Uh, yes." He'd forgotten that he'd told Albright about the beads. "But there wasn't any mention of when I'd return. I would like to celebrate Christmas with my family, but they've moved to Georgia. I don't even know if I would be allowed to go down there."

"For Christmas? Certainly you should be allowed. If there is a problem, I may speak to Master Odden on your behalf."

Kip had no idea whether Master Albright had any kind of rank over Master Odden, but he suspected that Patris would not welcome interference from London with respect to his least favorite apprentice. Still, the fact that Master Albright had offered was kind. "Thank you, but I don't believe that will be necessary. Besides, we do celebrate Christmas, but it's the Feast of

Calatus that's most important to us."

"I see. It was simply an offer." Albright gestured toward the five towers of the College. "Shall we return?"

When Kip returned to the workshop and summoned a fire, he reflected on the evening. There had been the secret of the calyxes that he had not felt the slightest need to tell, not like when he'd almost revealed the existence of Peter that first evening with Albright. And Jaeger's spell had had, as far as he could tell, no effect. Perhaps Albright hadn't cast a spiritual hold this time. Perhaps he hadn't cast one the previous time either, and Kip had simply been so grateful to be talking to someone who valued him that he had wanted badly to please him. Or he had cast one, and perhaps he cast that kind of hold every time he met a new person to make sure it was a pleasant meeting. Maybe he'd just been nervous about meeting a Calatian sorcerer. That still made him the sort of person Kip should be wary of, although Albright had helped him tonight and had offered him further help that he stood to gain no benefit from.

He sighed and lay on his bedroll, staring at the ceiling. Every day he missed his friends more and more. He would even have been grateful for one of Emily's lectures.

As it happened, Kip did not have to wait until Christmas to hear word from his friends. One week later, as he was poring over one of Cott's fire books by the light of a fire he was maintaining, a fluttering caught his ear, and he turned just in time to catch a piece of parchment as it fell toward his fire. Even before he unfolded it, he recognized Emily's scent, and he sat up straighter, holding it close to the fire so he could read:

Dear Kip,

Coppy wanted to tell you that he received your letter, and we have all wanted to tell you that we miss you. I am learning with Master Argent to send objects to people I know, and if this goes well I may soon send myself. "Soon" means in a few months, of course, as I've only just started translocating myself, but Argent says we will be focusing on translocation at the cost of the rest of my sorceric education, so who knows? It may be sooner. Coppy expects we will see you for Christmas anyway. Perhaps "hopes" is a better word than "expects"; he misses you most of any of us, though he would never say it. He spends a great deal of time with Neddy, who may not understand everything in our world but is an excellent listener nonetheless. I trust you are learning some world-changing sorcery there in London and having a high old time, and we're all anxious to hear about your adventures when you return.

If you receive this letter, please do send a reply by the same means and at least then we will know that we have a reliable way to communicate. If you could learn a translocation spell yourself, things would be easier still, but I suspect you are more focused on burning things, as Coppy is on marbles and Malcolm is on shutting doors.

All the best from your classmates here and from Neddy.

Emily

He read through the letter twice. There was nothing in it about John Quincy Adams; but then, he wouldn't expect there to be, not in a letter that might end up anywhere. The only hint was "world-changing" sorcery, which might easily be read as a remark on a Calatian learning sorcery, but which Kip felt had a double meaning. Nor was there a mention of Farley or Victor, and that was either because they weren't interfering with Kip's friends—unlikely—or because Emily didn't want to worry Kip.

Whatever the reason, the letter seemed to be an olive branch to Kip after their political disagreement, though he couldn't imagine the argument wouldn't resume when they met in person. His time in London wasn't going to improve her opinion of him, even though nobody here even seemed aware that there was talk of rebellion in the Colonies.

Abel, though…there was more going on there than he'd felt comfortable talking to Kip about. Kip was going to have to seek out the other fox and explore that further. Seeing the reality of the Isle of Dogs had brought him closer to rebellion than anything else, but of course the problem was that the Isle was located in the heart of London, and it was hard to tell how free and independent American colonies would help the plight of the London Calatians.

After some thought, he pulled out a sheet of parchment and wrote a note back to Emily letting her know that he'd received her letter, that he was learning quite a bit about fire sorcery, and that he missed them all, Coppy especially. He wrote that he hoped to be home for Christmas but did not know whether there were any plans to send him home. He thought about writing that Cott would happily keep him here for months, for the company if nothing else, but that seemed unwise to put into a public letter, so he left it out.

The next day, as they were taking out books in preparation for the day's lesson, he asked Cott where he might find Master Woodholm. "What, you want to send a letter?" Cott asked. "Give it to me, I can send it."

"I'd prefer it to go through the regular post," Kip said, ignoring Cott's outstretched hand.

"But why? I can do it for you."

"I'd like to meet Master Woodholm and find out how the post works between colleges. I'd hate to have to bother you every time I wish to send a message."

"It's no bother." Cott retracted his hand and smoothed down his blond hair. "Unless you're going to be sending messages every day. You're not, are you?" He peered at Kip.

Kip shook his head. "But why shouldn't I use the same methods as everyone else?"

"I'm simply trying to make things easier for you. What do you think Woodholm will do if a Calatian comes and asks him to post a letter to the Colonies?"

Kip's ears flattened. "Send it?"

"Oh, most likely, I suppose, but there will be talk. Why is a Calatian posting letters? He'll read it, you know."

Kip was by this point certain that Cott would, too. "I haven't written anything that I'm ashamed of. I'm only saying hello to my friends."

Cott took a step back, looking down at the table and the spell books. "All right, since you're so set on it. Go to Master Woodholm. You'll find him in the Red Tower on the bottom floor just as you enter."

He walked back toward his office, and Kip said, "Sir, I can go after our lesson."

"No," Cott called over his shoulder. "You're set on going to Master Woodholm, so go." And with that, he left the workshop.

Kip stared after him and shook his head. The balance between the sorcery he was learning and the oppressive nature of Cott's friendship still tilted in favor of the sorcery, but his resolve on that score was wavering.

Rather than fly out the window and then have to come in the main entrance to the College, he left via the door—Cott, sitting at the desk, ignored him—and found his way back to the stairs. Things were busier at this time of day than when he'd come in at night: servants and apprentices and the occasional sorcerer making their ways up and down the stairs. The narrow corridors forced people together when passing, and a few people flinched away from Kip or made an effort not to touch him; after he'd passed, whispers filled the air, but nobody stopped him.

Still, by the time he emerged into the cloudy daylight at the base of the tower, he was starting to wonder whether he shouldn't have left the mailing of his letter to Cott. The courtyard bustled with activity, ravens wheeling up in the sky over robes of purple and tunics of white running back and forth. A lot of servants, Kip thought, but then noticed the cleanliness of many of the tunics and the pleasant smells—no grime, no smoke, no body odor—and the youth of those cleaner tunic-dressed men. Students, then. They tended to move in groups of three to six, much as his own class had, and though some of them were startled to see him, others took little notice, whereas nearly every apprentice he passed had given him a strange or angry look.

The students talked amongst themselves, too, discussing nuances of a spell, what would be served for lunch, and one group planning to go down to the village to meet some women for activities they only discussed in euphemisms accompanied by overly-loud laughter. The normality of their concerns eased his own enough to make him smile as he surveyed the wide courtyard and the other towers.

Each tower flew a Union Jack over its entrance as well as another flag: just over Kip's head was a banner featuring crossed swords. Directly before him, the widest of the towers flew a flag with the crown of England on it, so that must be King's Tower. To his left, the oldest and smallest of the towers flew a solid red banner next to the Union Jack, and Kip made his way to that one.

A row of marble slabs, distinctive in the slate of the courtyard, formed a path between the Red Tower and the King's Tower, and beyond that rose the gleaming white Lord Winter's Tower, with a flag featuring a coat of arms. But none of these, at least in Kip's eyes, had the majesty of the White Tower in Massachusetts Bay, though at least three of them predated it. Existing alone, he thought, gave the White Tower more distinction and authority. He did wonder whether any of these older towers had spirits bound in their walls, but unless one of them was a Calatian, there might be no way to figure it out.

The doors of the Red Tower stood open, and enough light pushed in from the courtyard to allow Kip to find his way to the sign that read "Sorcerer Post" over a simple wooden door. He knocked, and when a crisp "Enter" responded, opened the door.

Inside he found a small office and the strong tingle of peppermint. It had been a while since he'd been in the presence of a demon. It must be invisible, because likely it was not the thin sorcerer sitting behind the desk, the first Moorish sorcerer Kip had met. He glanced up over his gold-rimmed glasses as Kip entered. "Picking up or posting?"

"Posting," Kip said.

A long dark finger indicated the left hand wall, where a number of neatly labeled cubbyholes held rolls of parchment and folded messages. It took him a moment to find the one labeled "Prince George's, New Cambridge, Massachusetts Bay," which was currently empty. "Ah, excuse me," he said. "Which master does the post go to?"

The sorcerer looked up, and Kip pointed to the box. "At Prince George's."

Master Woodholm frowned. "I believe Headmaster Patris takes the post."

Kip held his letter, imagining Patris receiving it and feeding it to his fire. "Is there a way to get a message to a particular person at the College?"

The sorcerer adjusted his glasses. "Has your master reason not to trust the headmaster? If messages have not been delivered, this is a serious matter."

"No, it's not that, it's—well, I'm actually an apprentice at Prince George's and my master is Master Odden there, but I'm sending this to Emily Carswell."

Woodholm's brow lowered. "Personal messages are not generally permitted by Sorcerer Post."

"Oh, it's—I'm helping her with her studies. She's learning translocation and she sent me a letter, so I need to tell her that it reached me."

"Hum." The sorcerer stroked his beard, black streaked with grey. "And you believe that Master Patris would not relay this message to her?"

"He doesn't like me." Kip took a chance. "He doesn't like the idea of someone different like myself becoming a sorcerer."

Woodholm looked him up and down. "Indeed. Why not address the message to your Master Odden and then ask him to pass it on to its intended recipient. Do you trust him?"

"Yes," Kip said, and then had an idea. "Or I could address it to Emily's master, and he would certainly pass it on to her. Thank you, sir."

Woodholm nodded and bent back to whatever he was writing. Kip cleared his throat. "May I, er. Borrow your pen?"

The sorcerer did not seem to have heard at first, but just as Kip was about to repeat his request, Woodholm half-rose and extended his pen to Kip. "Ink is there. Be quick about it."

"Yes, sir." Kip took the pen, dipped it in ink, and wrote Master Argent's name on the outside of the folded paper, then a quick note inside to ask him to pass it to Emily, and then he had to rewrite the name on the outside because it hadn't blotted properly while he was writing the inside.

Master Woodholm set about straightening the already tidy office while Kip did that, and in watching him, Kip noticed a second set of cubbyholes labeled with names. When he had placed his letter in the Prince George's box, he returned the pen to Woodholm and then walked to the other cubbyholes.

He recognized some of the names—there was Albright, there was Cott. He stayed there long enough to draw Woodholm's attention. "If you're looking to take Cott's mail back to him, I haven't sorted it yet. It will be ready this afternoon."

"No, no," Kip said quickly. He had just spotted the box marked "Gugin," and he rested a finger on it. "If I leave a message for Master Gugin here, he'll get it?"

"Hah." Woodholm's face broke into a broad smile. "Aye, he will, but faster to go to the roof of the Astronomy Tower and think his name."

"What?"

"Oh, you haven't heard the stories about him? Heh heh heh." Woodholm's smile remained fixed. "He lives at the top of the Astronomy Tower to be away from all the minds below, but if you come into his space, he will hear whatever you think."

"That's...creepy," Kip said.

"Not known many spiritualists, have you?" Woodholm's smile vanished. "But you may as easily place a message into that space. He only checks once a fortnight, though. Nobody writes to him, you see."

"That's sad."

"Spiritual sorcerers," Woodholm said, as though that explained everything.

So that evening, when Cott left him, Kip opened the window and levitated himself out into the cold winter night. The Astronomy Tower was easy to spot; it was the tallest of the towers, and its roof the smallest, barely five strides across.

It was deserted, though from its height Kip could look down on the other four towers and the courtyard, where a few people hurried from shelter to shelter. None, so far as he could tell, looked up his way, so he walked to the north side of the tower and looked down on the Thames and London and the Isle of Dogs.

Far from the smell and the crowds, the town looked peaceful, even cozy, with its small fires and smoky haze, clearer than in the rest of London. From here the Thames didn't look like a filthy dumping ground for refuse, but a calm, powerful river.

Master Gugin, he thought, feeling somewhat foolish. The feeling lasted all of fifteen seconds; before he could think the name a second time, a raven alit beside him with a flutter of its wings. He met its shiny black eye. "Master Gugin?"

The raven nodded and its beak parted. "Penfold. Why do you seek me?"

"Er." Was it a common practice for spiritual sorcerers to interact preferentially through their ravens? "I was given a spell to break spiritual holds by Master Jaeger and I wish to know whether I am casting it correctly."

"Master Jaeger, eh? You know he and I studied together?"

"I didn't know that."

"Oh aye, down at Prince Philip's. Terrible thing about that school. Do you know whether Miss Porter survived?"

"I don't, I'm afraid."

The raven clacked its beak, fidgeting even as it rambled on in its master's voice. "She made the most lovely peach pies. We get peaches very rarely here and they are almost always off by the time they arrive. Only when one of my friends translocates can I get a truly fresh one. But now nobody goes to Peachtree anymore. Such a pity. Oh yes, Scar, I know how cold it is. The fox doesn't complain, and neither should you."

Kip looked around, but Scar was evidently the raven's name, because it fluffed up its feathers and looked away indignantly even as it kept talking. "I suppose you should come in, then, if you want help with one of Master Jaeger's spells. The window is on the south side, first one you meet. You could follow Scar, but I suspect he will fly back to the fire quickly."

And indeed, the raven dropped over the side of the tower as soon as the word "quickly" emerged from its beak. Kip hurried to look over the side, but the raven had disappeared into the shadows.

So he called magic and levitated himself again. It took him half a revolution around the tower to find the window, shutters open. Inside he found a dark room furnished with only a wooden chair and a nightstand upon which sat an old, dusty book. "Close the shutters," called a muffled voice from below through a spiral stair.

Kip did so and then descended the stairs into warmer air, meeting a thick velvet drape at the next landing down. When he pushed his way through, he found that the drapes surrounded the entire circular room, only a little smaller than the roof of the tower. A balding middle-aged man, portly, lay back in a comfortable velvet chair next to a tall shelf with some books, though not as many as Kip had seen in most other offices. He did have more empty glasses and a stronger smell of ale than Kip had noticed elsewhere, but his eyes when they met Kip's were sharp and attentive. "Penfold," he said.

"Master Gugin." He stood awkwardly, but Gugin didn't rise to meet him.

"To what do I owe the pleasure at this hour? You have perhaps forty-five minutes of my time until I would be accustomed to retire."

"This early?" Kip shook his head and moved on, not wanting to question a sorcerer's habits. "As I said, Master Jaeger gave me this spell—"

"I know about the spell, you told me that. Why the hour?"

"Oh. I'm working with Master Cott on fire sorcery and that keeps me busy for most of the daylight hours."

"I see. So Master Cott is more important than your spiritual health?"

"I." Kip swallowed. "I didn't think...I mean, Master Cott is the reason I'm here."

Gugin waved a hand and looked over at Scar, who had perched on the top of his bookshelf and was preening. "Yes, well, you're here now, so let's hear the spell."

Kip took a breath and recited the words. Gugin didn't seem to be paying close attention, but when Kip finished, he nodded. "Aye, all that sounds right. But does it work?"

"I don't know," Kip said.

"Obviously. The question was rhetorical. Very well, I will place you in a spiritual hold and you will see if the spell breaks you out of it."

"All right." Kip braced himself. "When—"

And then he was gripped by the certainty that the tower was going to fall over with him inside it and land in the Thames. He ran to the stairs but the velvet curtains threatened to smother him. Stumbling back into the room, he couldn't believe Gugin was remaining so calm.

"When you seem to be acting at odds with how you should, or how others are acting, suspect a spiritual hold." Gugin's voice came with the bored flatness of a lecture delivered many times.

"Right," Kip gasped, but he couldn't summon the words.

The fear vanished. His heart was racing but without cause. "That was terrible," Master Gugin said.

The sensation of being consumed by fear and having it vanish just as suddenly weakened Kip's knees to the point that he sat down on the carpet, breathing heavily to regain his composure. "I've never done this before."

"Clearly. Perhaps I should not have started with such a drastic one. Let's try again."

"No," Kip said, and then wondered why he'd said no. Gugin only had his best interests at heart. "I mean, sorry, of course, whatever you like."

"Excellent. If I were to suggest that you run down to the Clock and Pull and fetch me a pint—no, no, Penfold, it was only a hypothetical."

Kip stopped with his paw on the velvet curtains. "No, no, I like going to the village," he said.

"Oh Lord, you're even mirroring me. All right, how about you try that spell Master Jaeger taught you?"

"Yes, definitely." He called magic to himself, recited the spell, and then waited. "How was that?"

"Hm." Gugin levered himself up off the chair and tottered across the floor. He stood a few inches shorter than Kip, but Kip didn't have the feeling of looking down that he did with Cott. "Here is the easiest way to think about it. The spell is you. It is the truth inside you that nobody else can know. Grasp at it, hold it tight, and the spell will work."

"I understand," Kip said.

"Good." Gugin waved a meaty hand. "Try it again."

Kip took a breath. Find his truth, his inner truth. As he spoke the words of the spell, he thought about his father, about Coppy, about the Isle and about the leaping joy whenever he reached out to fire. Those were the things that lay at the core of him.

He finished the spell, and looked around the room. "I don't think it worked," he said. "I don't feel any different."

"Really?" Gugin dropped back into his chair. "Fetch me an ale from the village. I'm parched."

"Right now?" Kip asked, and then stopped. "I don't want to go to the village now. Why did I then—oh."

"Yes. I had thought that the fear would be more recognizable as a hold. The more complicated the hold, the longer it takes to prepare. I took only a matter of seconds because those holds were very very simple. 'Your life is in danger,' and 'you love me unconditionally.' I didn't even specify what danger it was. What did you think was happening?"

"I thought the tower was going to fall."

"Interesting. We could make something of that perhaps."

"What do you mean?" Kip was still trying to remember how it had felt to cast the spell, and asking himself: if the spell hadn't worked when he'd cast it with Albright, what did that mean?

"Just that it can be worth delving into the causes of your fears. But not tonight, obviously."

"I thought that spiritual holds would be more complicated. Like would make me believe I was French or something."

Gugin shook his head. "The best ones are very intricate and are cast with a specific goal in mind, so they differ from reality in very small measure. Of course in any diplomatic setting there is always the danger of a spiritual hold. They can't be maintained out of the presence of the sorcerer—at least, binding spells seem not to have the effect one might think on the spell. Current theory—my theory—is that all spiritual holds revolve around the sorcerer in some way and that therefore the sorcerer must be present."

"Thank you," Kip said.

"Now you know what it feels like, and now you know the spell works. Anything else you need?"

"I—could I practice more?"

Gugin squinted up at him from the chair. "I can spend half an hour with you any night you bring me an ale from the village."

Kip laughed, but the sorcerer's expression remained serious. "Oh, I see," Kip said. "Well—yes, all right. Any night?"

"Come to the Astronomy Tower and Scar will let you know whether I am receiving company. But I will tell you, I do not receive company most nights, so you may be confident in your approaches."

Kip nodded. "If I may ask, sir, why not?"

"Oh." Gugin exhaled and looked toward Scar. "Do people fear spiritual sorcerers because they worry over the privacy of their thoughts, and do I read that fear and isolate myself so that I needn't feel it over and over? Or, having heard it once, do I find it lurking in every cautious thought? Does the constant exposure to the chaotic miasma that is the human mind take its toll over time so that I see the bad in sharp relief while the good fades away? Because, Penfold, here is the paradox of the human mind: the good in people outweighs the bad by a considerable amount. Yet it takes only a small amount of bad to create great harm for many. Have I the responsibility to prevent that bad whenever I see it, knowing that most of it is idle fantasy and will come to nothing? How can I judge someone's intentions to action?"

Kip struggled to digest the onslaught of words. "I—don't know, sir."

Gugin heaved a sigh. "Should you ever come to learn the answer, I will teach you for the rest of your life in exchange for it."

CHAPTER 13: CHRISTMAS

And so Kip's life became studies with Master Cott during the day and studies with Master Gugin on alternate evenings. The barmaid at the Clock and Pull prepared bottles for him and he brought back the empty ones on his following visit.

This caused a problem with Master Cott one day when he found an empty bottle in the workshop. "Penfold," he said, brow lowering, "you know that alcohol is forbidden."

"It's not for me, sir." And Kip explained about Master Gugin's drink. "You know that I had wanted to speak to him. He has been kind enough to help me with Master Jaeger's spell. Just as you had recommended." He caught himself; on their second session, Master Gugin had advised that Kip tell no-one of their work, because if any parties desired to place him under spiritual holds and knew he was learning to break them, they would become more cunning in their execution.

But Cott showed no interest either way in Kip's evening activity, and in fact seemed to have forgotten that he had recommended Master Gugin. "Ah. Quite good. Keep up that work. But no more bottles in the workshop."

Where was he supposed to store them, then? Kip settled on the roof of the Astronomy Tower as few people seemed to venture there, and indeed the bottles remained undisturbed. Perhaps in summer, the rooftops were more social places, but with the chill winds and rain more often than not, the residents of King's College mostly hurried to the roof to depart from there, or hurried inside after arriving.

Apart from Cott and Gugin and the occasional conversation with Master Albright, the only other person Kip spoke to regularly was Emily, through her letters. Those remained unsatisfying; they were both aware that the letters might be read by any of the sorcerers who handled them, so they didn't talk about any of the things they wanted to. At least he was confident now that Master Argent would pass along messages to Emily, and she learned that she should not send him letters before her lunchtime, lest they appear while he was studying with Cott.

As for his studies and his confidence in mastering fire, they progressed along quite well. Not so the mystery of the glass beads, at least until four days before Christmas.

Kip had received a note from Master Odden instructing him to return to the College on December 24th and that he would be returning to King's College after Twelfth Night, on January 6th. "Patris is quite pleased with your London instruction," he wrote, "so it would be best for all that it continue indefinitely, if Master Cott is amenable."

Cott would certainly be amenable, Kip thought, but why was he not to be consulted on his own apprenticeship? Did Odden want to be rid of him? What of searching the ruins? And least important to his master, of course, but most important to Kip, what about his friends? In terms of education, he was learning a great deal about fire and spiritual holds, if not very much more about demons, and he felt confident that he would in the course of another month be an effective military sorcerer (if he wasn't already), but the power he was gaining didn't make him miss Emily, Malcolm, and Coppy any less. It was hardest in the dark hours between dinner and sleep, when the workshop was silent and Kip was left alone to re-read Emily's letters with only his thoughts and the ever more elaborate fantasies of his imagination filling in what was left unsaid.

Would Emily entice Coppy to the cause of the revolutionaries? Would Master Windsor drive Coppy mad? Would Peter, having lost Kip, turn to Coppy as his confidant? He tried to hold their scents and their voices in his head, and more than once he woke in the morning reaching out for the comforting solid bulk of the otter only to find a cold stone floor. On those mornings he comforted himself with a fire, losing himself in its depth until Cott arrived to begin his lessons.

He did take dinner at the Darby several more times, but only twice encountered Albright. Each time, they had a pleasant meal during which Albright asked whether he and Cott had made any progress (they had not, Kip reported), and then the sorcerer excused himself, again without giving Kip cause or occasion to attempt his spell to escape a spiritual hold. Kip's fur still prickled to think about their first meeting, but Albright did not seek him out, so there was little for him to investigate.

He visited the Isle of Dogs once more in December, striding through the streets where the residents were putting up candles for a Christmas holiday. He found Coppy's family easily and spent an hour talking to them about their son, and that gave him great comfort. Toward the end of the hour, he looked up and there was Abel in the doorway, leaning there and listening, and when Kip met his eyes, the other fox smiled.

Afterwards, they walked back to the docks together. Kip asked Abel whether the calyxes met regularly, and the other fox said, "Not all of them," but wouldn't elaborate beyond that. He did, however, invite Kip back to dinner in January, which Kip gratefully accepted.

On December 21, Kip visited Master Gugin for what was to be his last lesson before leaving, and Gugin praised him on his progress. "If you are as quick a study in fire as you are in spiritual holds, Cott may have some competition in a few years," the sorcerer chuckled. "He will hate that."

"I'm doing well enough," Kip said. "But the whole reason I came here, we haven't touched that in a week or more."

"What was that?" Gugin asked, and when Kip hesitated, the sorcerer said, "You may as well tell me what the glass beads mean. I can see them in your thoughts plain as the nose on your face."

"Why not just read what they are, then?"

Gugin shook his head. "Would mean delving deeper into your mind and like as not learning a great deal too much. Rather you tell me what's pertinent."

"Then why look into my thoughts at all?" Kip asked.

"How else," Gugin said in all seriousness, "would I know if you planned to kill me?"

Kip had no rejoinder for this. So he explained the glass beads as succinctly as he could. Gugin listened attentively, and when Kip was done, he rubbed his cheek, looking up at his raven. "Something familiar about that, eh, Scar? Glass beads, turning people…it was from a long while ago, but let me ponder it."

Even though there was nothing substantial, Kip returned to Cott's workshop excited, cursing himself for being so careful. Why had he not told Gugin as he'd told Albright? The more people who knew, the more might be able to solve the mystery.

And, he reminded himself in the cold, lonely darkness, Albright had tricked him into telling him—perhaps, probably—and thus set Kip on his guard. Besides, the more people he told, the more chance they might alert someone who'd helped plan the attack. If someone at the College had carried it out, it was not inconceivable that someone at King's had assisted. The thought discomfited Kip enough that he started a fire just to have some company, and it was at that moment that a sheet of paper popped into being in the air and fluttered to the ground.

He read the note from Emily with a smile. In large part, it read: "I know this note is not necessary as we will see you in three days, but we are all very excited to see you and besides, Master Argent says the more practice I get, the better."

As he put the paper aside, however, the thought struck him that Emily might use his return home to pressure him into meeting with the revolutionaries again. Patris had been furious last time, and Kip didn't feel strongly enough about revolution to risk the Headmaster's wrath again. But he would worry about that problem when he faced it, he supposed. Perhaps independence too observed the Christmas holiday.

A rattle of wings drew his attention to the window, where a black shape alit. Scar opened his beak and said in Master Gugin's voice, "I have assembled as much of the memory as I can. May I share it with you?"

"Er. What do you need—"

"I can cast the spell quickly if you return to my chambers now."

Kip got to his feet. "I haven't any more ale."

The raven's beak opened in a laugh, but the sorcerer's voice that issued from it remained as serious as usual. "As this is a request from me, you needn't bring any. But you should always have some on hand. It's salutatory."

Kip chuckled as he followed the raven through the air and over to the Astronomy Tower, this time going directly to Master Gugin's office. When he set his feet on the carpet and pulled his tail over the windowsill, Master Gugin, already on his feet, stepped forward.

"You permit me to share this memory?" He asked the question in the same tone he used to ask permission to cast a spiritual hold, which he had every single time after the first night.

Familiar with the protocol, Kip said, "Aye."

Gugin lifted his hands, murmuring under his breath. Kip braced himself, but what happened was nothing like what he'd become used to in a spiritual hold. The world didn't change. None of his thoughts were different. But Gugin lowered his arms and said, "There."

"I don't feel any different."

"But now if I ask you about glass beads, what do you think of?"

The bead safe in his perfume vial. The work he and Cott had done. Finding the beads with Nikolon. Coming across a mention of glass beads in an ancient book lying on a thick oak table with the musty smell of books all around him, weaker than he was accustomed to in libraries.

"Wait," he said, and Gugin smiled. "That memory isn't mine."

"Easier than trying to tell you all I remember." Gugin grunted and sat back on his couch.

"That's amazing." Kip relived the memory again. "I didn't even notice anything. I feel like it was me there in the library."

"Some differences, I imagine." Gugin looked as pleased as Kip had seen him.

"Scent, mostly."

"Ah well, someday you'll have to allow me one of your memories so I can know what it's like to have a nose as long as your head."

Kip bowed. "Of course, sir."

"Right. Now, go make what you will of that."

It was clearly a dismissal, so Kip turned back to the window and stepped out, then flew back to Cott's workshop.

There he sat, summoned a fire to help him think, and examined the memory more closely. A book in a library, some mention of glass beads in cribbed, foreign text. Enemies being imprisoned in glass beads by fire, something like that. It was just the thing Kip and Cott had been looking for. Which library was it, then? Which book? He scoured the memory for details. Normally he would rely on scent to pinpoint his location, but the scent wasn't strong or familiar enough in the memory.

Or was it? The two places he knew Master Gugin had been were Prince Philip's in Georgia and here. If this were in Prince Philip's, then the library, the book, everything was destroyed. That wouldn't help him. But the library in his memory was old, austere. The book under his gloved fingertips (his human fingertips; he ignored that detail) was ancient parchment that he had to handle with great care. That pointed to London, King's College, hopefully. So he had to gain access to the library and then figure out which of the thousands of books Master Gugin had read as a student several decades ago.

Kip sighed and stared forward into the fire. If solving mysteries was easy, he supposed, they wouldn't be mysteries.

MacDougal appeared, as taciturn as ever, to bring Kip home. Having deposited the fox in Master Odden's office, he turned just as Kip started to say, "Thank you," and was gone before Kip had finished the first word.

"How did you find Master Cott?" Odden asked.

Kip breathed in Odden's scent and the specific musty smell of his books and scrolls under the phosphorus of his elemental, slumbering in the brazier. The fox's tail wagged as the familiarity of the setting sank in, and with it the knowledge that Coppy and Emily and Malcolm were here in this building and he would be seeing them in moments. He composed himself as best he could and answered his master's question. "Challenging," he said, his enthusiasm at being back lowering his caution, and then flattened his ears. "I'm sorry. He's quite brilliant as regards fire. He seemed to be very afraid that some of the other people in the college would not like a Calatian apprentice among them."

"He may not be wrong." Odden rested his elbows on his wide desk and leaned forward. "But I would like to see what he has taught you."

So Kip called up a fire and then three more, precisely placed in a square. Then he took one of the practice branches Odden still had—by the look of it, one that Kip had gathered before he left. He set paper among the branches and conjured a fire that burned the paper but left the branches intact, then burned specific branches, fed the fire so the wood fell to ash in minutes, then put all the fires out.

"Exceptional," Odden said. "How have you worked with larger fires?"

"I put out one very large one." Kip did not feel like recounting the circumstances around the warehouse fire. "And we worked with larger fires in Cott's workshop because he had more space there."

"Have you burned non-flammable materials yet?"

Kip shook his head. "He spoke of attempting earth and stone, but not for several months."

"Do you feel you could attempt that?"

"I suppose it wouldn't hurt."

Odden held up a hand as Kip raised his paws. "Not here in the Tower."

"Right. I'm sorry." Forrest's reaction to the fire near his orchard was likely nothing to how Peter would feel if Kip tried to burn the stone he was living in, not to mention how furious Patris had been when he'd only thought Kip had set fire to his tower. "But you think I could do it?"

"I think you will be able to eventually, yes. And who knows when 'eventually' may be?"

"Thank you." Kip told Odden about the colored fire effects and the other work he'd done, and then about the slim lead he had on the glass beads.

Odden stroked his beard. "I'd be very interested to see what you find in the library. Should you need more assistance, I can vouch for you."

"That might help. Thank you."

A knock came at the door of the office, and when Odden said, "Come," Master Vendis walked in.

Surprised, Kip stood straighter. "Good morning, sir."

"Good morning, Kip. Ready?"

"For what?" Kip asked.

"He's ready," Master Odden said. "He is making excellent progress in the study of fire."

"All right." Master Vendis came forward and took Kip's arm.

"Wait," Kip said. "Where are—"

"—we going?" He spoke the last two words in a breeze smelling of old leaves and swamp, his paws in a brittle stand of grass.

"Welcome to Prince Philip's," Master Vendis said.

They stood in a wide meadow where the grass was still green, the air cooled rather than froze Kip's ears, and stands of trees rose around them, some with unfamiliar glossy green leaves though it was the middle of winter. Closer than the trees, one near and two far, sat three mounds of rubble that Kip did recognize. Up at Prince George's, they were covered in canvas, but he knew immediately that they were the remains of three college buildings.

"The town's down this way." Master Vendis began to walk.

Kip remained standing. "I wanted to see Emily and Coppy and Malcolm," he said, but not loudly.

Master Vendis stopped and turned. "What was that?"

There was a moment when Kip felt the urge to set his feet in place, to refuse to move until Master Vendis took him back to Massachusetts. He had endured all of Cott's obsessive behavior and the warehouse and the sadness of the Isle, the isolation in the workshop and the anxiety over Albright, his patience worn down to the skin. Coming home, he'd hoped to be able to relax and regain some control over his life. And yet here was Master Vendis, whom he'd known for years, treating him just as everyone else had.

In the next moment, he remembered that his father was waiting, and his feet carried him forward to follow Vendis down the path.

If there had ever been gates as in New Cambridge, they had been dismantled and little trace remained of them. Kip thought they might have passed a large gatehouse-sized patch of clear ground, but he could also have been mistaken. "Where are they building the new college?" he asked as he caught up to Vendis.

"Just on the other side of the town." The sorcerer pointed as they came through a small copse to reveal the buildings of Peachtree.

Whereas in New Cambridge the college overlooked the town from Founders Hill, here the path from the college wound down a gentle slope, and within fifty feet they were passing shops, their large front windows bustling with humans and Calatians alike. Both the shops and streets sprawled across wide spaces, so that even though the street was busy, it didn't feel crowded. Farther down, a small church nestled among a cluster of homes, each with a small plot, and beyond those, a river burbled, its scent strong on the breeze. Kip tried to see where on the other side of the town there might be construction, but beyond the stream everything faded to indistinct shapes.

He turned his attention back to the sorcerer striding just in front of him. "Master Vendis, might I be able to see my friends in New Cambridge before returning to London?"

Vendis gave a sharp nod. "I don't see why not. I'm to come and fetch you back after Twelfth Night. If you don't mind waking early, you should have a few hours before MacDougal returns to take you to King's."

"Thank you. I haven't seen them in ages. And is there a sorcerer's post from here to there?"

"Not yet, I'm afraid." Master Vendis sighed. "Your Emily is the best candidate to take over that post, but she won't be ready until next year. I come down every few days to collect news, and if you have correspondence, I can carry it back."

They had reached the houses, and here the crowds thinned, though the scents remained of many different Calatian species in addition to all the humans around. Kip was about to ask whether this was a purely Calatian neighborhood when one of the scents set his ears straight up and his tail wagging. No longer needing Vendis's guide, he ran to one of the small houses and knocked excitedly on the door.

When his mother opened it, Kip fell into her arms. A moment later his father joined the embrace. "Happy Christmas," Max said.

"Happy Christmas." Kip let go, keeping one paw on his mother's arm. "It's so good to see you again."

"You didn't bring Coppy?" Max asked.

Master Vendis, just arriving, shook his head. "Odden only asked me to bring Kip. I believe Master Windsor wanted to keep Coppy for work over the holiday."

"Even on Christmas Day?" Kip asked.

Master Vendis sighed. "I will inquire."

"Thank you so much," Max said. He draped an arm over Kip's shoulder. "You understand that he is as much a part of our family as our son."

Vendis's expression softened. "Yes, I see that. Max, a word before I return?"

The two of them stepped out of the house as Ada escorted Kip into it. "You see," she said as Max closed the front door, "we have only been here a month, but already it feels like home."

"You're not coming back to New Cambridge, then?"

"Oh...no." She flattened her ears. "We bought this house from the sale of the shop license."

They'd sold the shop. The place where Kip had spent so much of his childhood, gone. "I see. Dad didn't tell me."

"It's all been very busy." Ada took Kip's paw. "We had an offer and your father thought it best to take it. It allowed us to buy this house rather than renting at the Inn."

"That's good." Kip let his paw lie in his mother's. "I'm glad. The house looks wonderful."

If he put his feelings about the shop aside, that wasn't even a lie. With its large windows open, a pleasant breeze came through, and the earth out front had been turned for a garden. A large one, too, like the kind his mom had always talked about wanting one day.

"The weather is so temperate here," she said. "Of course, the air is moist and my fur looks terrible." (It didn't.) "But the town is a little smaller and everyone is quite friendly."

"That's wonderful." Kip clung to that one word, unable to come up with any other positive ones but wanting very much to be happy for his parents.

Max and Vendis returned from the living room—Kip assumed, having only been in the parlour thus far—and clasped hand to paw. Vendis then raised a paw to Kip and said, "Happy Christmas, everyone. I'll return in a fortnight."

"Unless you—"

Vendis was already gone. "Bring Coppy." Kip's shoulders sunk.

Max took a seat in the parlour. "You'll at least see Coppy in January. I wish he could be here too, but if he's working with Master Windsor…"

"I know, I know." Kip put on a smile. "And I really am happy to see you. I have so much to tell you."

He spent a good two hours telling them about Master Cott and about Abel. It wasn't until he brought up the calyx that he remembered his anger that his father hadn't told him. His narrative faltered and his gaze crept to his father's exposed arm, but no scars were visible there. Max folded his ears down as he caught his son's look, but if Ada noticed, she didn't let on at all. So Kip moved on to talking about Coppy's family and how delightful they were.

But later, while Ada was preparing dinner, Max took Kip aside in the parlor. "You know what it means to be a calyx now," he said.

Kip nodded. "Master Odden had me summon a demon. I had to undergo the ritual."

"You had to—" Max set his ears back, eyes widening. "He took blood from you? No—ah, I see." He rested a paw on Kip's shoulder. "It must have been a shock."

Kip didn't move to acknowledge the gesture. "Why didn't you tell me?"

Max sighed and paced to the large front window, where flickering lamplight lined the street. "When you've kept a secret for so long, it can be hard to know when to let it go. I don't have any other excuse than that. It is impressed on us from the moment we enter the sorcerer's presence that this is a private, special moment. We are performing a service, in exchange for which they protect our community. And how would our community see it if they knew? Would they understand?"

"I was becoming a sorcerer. I had to understand."

Max's tail swished. He leaned against the window frame, still looking outside. "There wasn't a good time to tell you. Please don't be <chesbit> about it."

Kip sat back in the wooden chair he'd sat in and played on all his life. It felt strange for it to be here, in this different house with the thicker air and strange scents. "So you've been bleeding for them for twenty years."

His father exhaled. "When they needed me. Us. We helped win the war against Napoleon, and the tribes before that. We helped explore this new land."

"I know about all that," Kip said. "Who told you about it?"

"Jeremiah Stave."

Kip shook his head. "I don't remember him."

"He was a polecat. He left New Cambridge after his sorcerer passed away, shortly after I began with Master Vendis."

"Does every calyx only bleed for one sorcerer?"

His father's ears stayed down. "Generally. I have visited two other sorcerers when their calyxes were indisposed. Kip, you knew that we served the sorcerers. Why does the manner of our service matter?"

"Because it's—" Kip stopped. He didn't want to say that it was disgusting, that it was intimate, that it was a violation. It was all of those things, the Calatians literally exchanging blood for security.

"Disgusting?" His father eyed him. "Does it bother you that we must do it, or that you will have to do it as a sorcerer?"

"You could have prepared me." Kip flushed, recalling the ritual when he'd summoned the demon. It had felt wrong, but he'd put it out of his head, only now it all came flooding back to him. He licked his lips against the memory of the taste in his mouth. "Master Odden made me drink it on the spot, no time to understand what was happening."

"I'm sorry you weren't prepared," Max said. "If you'd been anticipating it for days, would it have been any easier?"

Kip sank back against the chair. "Probably not." His father didn't say anything, and after a moment, Kip said, "But that doesn't mean you shouldn't have told me."

"Maybe you're right." Max's tail lashed against the wall. "But Kip...you are not a calyx. You're a sorcerer. Our bargains are not yours, and maybe... maybe I didn't want you to be bound by them. To have preconceptions."

"You knew that I would have to..." He didn't want to say "use," so he changed what he was going to say. "That I'd meet calyxes. That I'd find out. And besides, didn't you tell me that even if I'm a sorcerer, I'm still a Calatian?"

"Yes." Max turned slowly to the window, looking outside. "Maybe that's why I didn't tell you."

Kip thought about that conversation a great deal over the Christmas holiday, even as he was occupied with helping his mother prepare a few holiday dishes. The secret of the calyxes was a distasteful one, to be sure. But the more Kip thought about it, the more it felt to him that it would be worse for the sorcerers if it became known. The Calatians were offering of themselves to help the nation; the sorcerers were drinking blood. That wouldn't be received well by the population. This, he grew certain, was the real reason the sorcerers talked about how "private and special" their ritual was. They didn't want to be seen as a bunch of blood-drinkers. And the

Calatians were too dependent on their protection to let their secret slip out.

He couldn't confront his father about that, though, and besides, Max was hardly where the practice had begun or ended. So Kip stayed quiet, thinking about calyxes and his friends and the look on the face of Jacob the dormouse as he sat in front of Kip and Odden during Kip's demon lesson. And he thought about Peter granting him power without him having to drink any blood.

After all, Kip reasoned, he had Calatian blood in him already. Why would he need to drink more to gain power? Could he just drink his own? That was disgusting too, but it was far better than drinking someone else's.

He met many more residents of the town during his stay, including their distant relatives the Shantons and one other fox family, who had a teenaged daughter. They were very interested in Kip, even after he told them about his engagement to Alice Cartwright, which puzzled him until he found out he'd been mistaken about the reason for their interest. They were looking out not for their daughter, but for their grandchildren. "You and Alice should come live down here with your parents," they said. "The more fox families, the better."

Kip said that he would consider it, but that his job would likely dictate where he was allowed to live, and there was some talk of the rebuilt college. But as the conversation flowed on around him, he thought about the crowded Isle of Dogs and how many families could come live in Peachtree in comfort—if they wanted to. Only Coppy come from London to New Cambridge in the last few years, but certainly some London Calatians had settled in New York, where the Road ended, or Boston or Philadelphia. Travel was difficult if you weren't a sorcerer, and there were already communities in those large cities ready to welcome immigrants, so there was little incentive to venture further south. Maybe when Emily was more trained, he could prevail upon her to bring some of the Isle's residents around for a visit.

To be calyxes here instead of in London. That thought sobered him, and every time his spirits rose and he thought of Coppy's family, for example, or Abel and his family coming to Peachtree, he ran up against that reality again.

On Christmas Day, the town gathered for a quiet celebration at the church, and then a communal supper afterwards to which everyone brought their favorite dishes. They tended to congregate in like groups, the humans on one side and the Calatians separated by species on the other, not because of friendships or enmities, but because each group made food tailored to their tastes. As the gathering went on, the groups mixed, and there was considerable laughter as humans tried some of the foxes' dishes and thought them bland, where the foxes couldn't eat more than a bite of the pudding the dormice had made for the sharp burn of rum in it.

His father had told him there were two London sorcerers supervising the rebuilding, but they did not join the festivities. Kip left his robes behind in his parents' house, but they had already bragged about him to their friends, so during the Christmas feast he was pressed to demonstrate a magic spell, and he obliged with the simple physical magic of carrying all the tables to the side of the large town square to leave more room for the post-feast gathering. His father asked why he chose not to create fire, and he repeated Cott's words about how fire could scare people.

Late at night, every night, he did conjure fires for himself. They comforted him, and he was confident enough that even on his parents' wood floor the fire did not leave so much as a trace. He tried again to hold a fire in his paw, but still could not overcome the pain in the leather of his pads. Even when he told the fire not to consume his flesh, even when he knew he wasn't burning, he could not hold it longer than six seconds.

But on Christmas night, with his thoughts spinning around calyxes and sorcerers and rituals, he gazed into his fire and thought about Coppy, Emily, and Malcolm. He wanted to be practicing with them and talking with them and hearing how they were doing. He wanted them to laugh at Cott's behavior, appreciate his progress with Gugin, commiserate over the plight of the Calatians. He wanted to give Coppy news of home and hear Malcolm's stories of his family and even argue politics with Emily.

And it was amid those thoughts that he recalled the nearby ruins, remembered searching the New Cambridge ruins, and made a connection that he felt stupid for not having made previously. If he summoned Nikolon again, he could order the demon to go to Emily and Coppy, to relay what they said to him and to speak back to them. He could probably even order Nikolon to assume his shape. No, that might be too strange.

The idea excited him enough that the fire flared to reflect his mood. He knew the spell, could hear the words in his head and feel the magic around him. He could cast it, he knew. Or could he, without either Peter's help or a calyx's blood? It was the binding that was the hard part, Master Odden had said. Which meant that Kip might summon Nikolon only to be unable to bind it.

But he'd summoned and bound Nikolon without blood before, with only Peter's help. Cott had been teaching him techniques to gather more power into himself, to control fire better and extend his range. He knew what that power felt like, and he could draw it into himself—at least enough to control a first-order demon, he thought.

So he seated himself and gathered magic. His paws flickered, then glowed, and he kept going, focusing his thoughts on his connection to the earth. The power rose in him, built, and then he felt the itch to cast a spell. At first easily ignorable, it grew with the power in him until it was all he could do to resist it.

He spoke the spell quickly, and finished the binding spell as Nikolon appeared before him, again in the guise of a naked vixen. "Make no move save on my order; speak no word save on my order; exert no power save on my order," Kip said quickly.

The vixen straightened, then tilted her head. Kip should have dismissed her immediately at that. Instead he tested the binding spell with his mind. Normally he would be able to feel the aura of power between himself and the demon and recognize the spell. Now, though the power was there, something felt a little different.

He started the dismissal spell, but Nikolon raised a paw before he could get it all the way out. His throat dried up in a moment and the words choked off. Kip forced himself to keep going. A moment later the power vanished with the vixen in front of him.

That had been close. He rose and went to get a glass of water for his throat, scratching at his neck. By the time he got to the kitchen, the itch had spread to his chest and back, and it was all he could do to keep his tunic on as he worked his paws under it to relieve the sensation.

Nikolon had done this, obviously, and Kip had no idea how to undo it, so he would have to call the demon again. But this time he would do it by the book. He fetched one of his mother's knives, the long one for carving small fowl. Returning to the room he'd been given, he held the knife in the fire to sterilize it, then extinguished the fire so there would be nothing drawing on his concentration. Quickly, before he could change his mind, he pressed the hot tip of the knife into his left arm.

Pain flared and then subsided. He pressed fingers around the wound until blood appeared, staining the fur, and then he put his mouth to it. There wouldn't be a half goblet this time, nothing like, but the taste came strongly into his muzzle, coppery pressure on his sinuses. Again he gathered magic, and fancied it peaked more strongly this time. Still scratching his fur, he cast the summoning and then the binding.

Nikolon stood before him. Kip gave the order, and this time the vixen remained completely stationary. "All right," Kip said. "First off, lift this curse or whatever it is you've done that's making me itch."

The demon didn't move, but the itching stopped, leaving in its place sore skin where Kip's claws had dragged. "Thank you," Kip sighed, and exhaled. "Now, I want you to go to Prince George's College of Sorcery in New Cambridge, where we searched ruins. Go to the basement of the White Tower and talk to Coppy the otter. Relay to me everything you see and hear, and relay my responses back to them. You may use that form when appearing to them. Do you have any questions?"

"Yes." Nikolon remained perfectly still. "Am I to be punished?"

Kip tested the binding spell again, but it was secure this time. "Why would you be punished?"

"For inflicting Aberine's Crawling Skin upon you."

The fox's eyebrows rose. "I knew the risks of the binding. It's in your nature to test it and take advantage if I haven't cast it properly. The fault is at least partly mine. Though," he said, thinking it over, "you didn't have to do anything. But I suppose you could have done worse as well."

"Very well." Nikolon's words betrayed no emotion, but her expression, to Kip's eye, was uncertain.

"Is there confusion over my order?" Kip asked.

"No."

"Then depart."

"Yes, sir." And the demon was gone.

Kip focused, and a moment later saw great stone walls in his mind's eye. The outside of the Tower through the iron bars of the gate, the great stones streaked with rain and moonlight. And then he saw himself sitting in a small room in his parents' house in Georgia, and he opened his eyes to the vixen standing before him. "Why did you not enter the Tower?" he said.

"I was forbidden. When summoned inside the grounds of the college, I may come, and I may leave. But when summoned outside, I may not enter."

"What prevents you?"

"There are wards I am bound not to pass."

Was it Peter? Kip didn't know how to ask that without revealing the presence of Peter to the demon, and who knew what mischief that might create? "All right," Kip said, letting his shoulders slump. "Thank you, Nikolon." And he spoke the words of the dismissal.

He'd hoped he would be able to talk to Coppy tonight, but it seemed that would have to wait another twelve days, an eternity during which he would have nothing to do but talk to his parents and the townspeople. He extinguished his fire and crawled into bed. Sleep would bring the next day sooner, and with it his return to New Cambridge.

CHAPTER 14: MAKING PLANS

The days passed more quickly than Kip had expected. In his spare time, he practiced with fire and searched Master Gugin's memory for any other details he might have missed. Otherwise he spoke to his parents about the new construction in Peachtree, their hopes for a store, and about the revolutionaries.

His father was as cautious as Kip himself, but his mother, to his surprise, took up the cause of independence. "Why shouldn't we hope for better circumstances?" she said over candlelight late one night.

They were seated around the dinner table with mugs of peach nectar, diluted to be less overpowering to the foxes' palates, and Kip had just taken a drink when Ada spoke those words. He put his mug down quickly. "You didn't want me to become a sorcerer," he said. "But revolution is all right?"

"The system as it is does not favor us," she said. "To try to thwart it as you are doing is dangerous. If you're to incur danger, why not replace the entire system?"

He knew in that moment who had been behind the move to Georgia and making it permanent. "The risk is so much greater."

"Not to you." She looked over her muzzle at him, and he thought how much she'd changed in just a few months. Her eyes had always been a haven, warm and safe. The warmth remained, but the fur around them was tinged with grey and her gaze was distant. "If you join the revolution and it fails, you'll be hanged as a traitor. But if you anger the wrong sorcerer, you'll be disgraced, thrown out without reason, maybe lose your magic—your father won't tell me if that's possible."

"I don't know," Max said mildly.

"And in the worst case, killed. Or you'll just disappear and I'll never know. So the risk isn't so much greater, and at least if you join the revolution you'll be working towards something worthwhile. You'll be standing with others."

"And vulnerable to their mistakes as well," Kip pointed out. "I'm making friends among the sorcerers."

"Friends." Ada shook her head. "Friends like the ones we had in New Cambridge? Friends who turn their back on you when you need them most?"

Kip shook his head, but he had no answer for that, and Ada went on. "These friends, have they been tested? Because testing is when you will know your friends."

Whom, he thought, would he trust by his side? Coppy, of course. Emily. Malcolm. None of the sorcerers, that was certain. Master Odden had sent him to London and left him there; Master Vendis wouldn't even choose him as an apprentice. The sorcerers at Prince George's who were friendly to him were friendly because it was not inconvenient to be.

London was no better. Master Cott wanted to keep him under lock and key in his workshop. Master Albright's motivations remained cloudy. Master Gugin would barely get off his couch without the incentive of ale. And Abel shared a bond of species, but Kip had only talked with him twice.

"As long as I play by the rules," he said.

"They made the rules, Kip. They can change them whenever they like."

He looked to his father for help, but Max's ears were perked up and he showed no inclination to speak. "I took an oath to defend the Crown," Kip said. "I can't break that to fight against it."

His mother looked away and said, "That's very honorable of you."

"You want me to go join the revolutionaries?" he asked.

"No," she said. "I want you to come home."

They didn't have another serious talk his whole visit, and when he left the house on January 6th to return to the school, his mother embraced him and said, "Come visit when you learn how to appear in places by sorcery."

"I'm not being taught translocation," Kip said, "but I'll work on it."

He and Max walked to the site of the old school under a cloudy sky, the air warm and moist. They didn't speak until they arrived at the wide meadow, and then Max hugged Kip. "I trust in your judgment," he said. "Choose whatever path you deem wisest."

"Thank you," Kip said. "And good luck here in Georgia. It looks lovely."

And then Master Vendis was there to take him back to college. He held up a paw to his father as Master Vendis took his arm and the warm damp air was replaced with the cold dry winter air of New Cambridge, the snow-dusted grass and bare-branched trees with close stone walls.

"Do you see my father often?" Kip asked as he disengaged his arm.

"Once a fortnight or so." Master Vendis swept the hem of his robe around his feet, brushing the floor.

'If I send letters to Emily, might you bring them to him?"

A flicker of annoyance passed over Vendis's face, but it cleared quickly. "Of course," he said. "One of our tasks is to reopen the Sorcerer's Post in Peachtree."

"And I'll use that as soon as possible," Kip said. "But in the meantime…"

"Yes, yes." Master Vendis shooed him away. "Now, your friends have been told of your return and I believe they are awaiting you in the basement."

Kip needed no further permission to hurry out and down the stairs. The familiar smells of the White Tower, more than his parents' transplanted furnishings, called "home" to him. He pelted down the stairs to the Great Hall, empty of desks, and called out a quick hello to the elementals crowded in the fireplace, their bemused replies following him down the stairs to the basement door.

He found it fastened shut, and rapped against it twice. "Hey!" he said. "It's me!"

A moment later, the door opened to reveal Malcolm's short-cropped black hair and wide smile. He threw out his arms and hugged Kip. "You've cut your hair," the fox said when they stepped apart.

"Ma did, over Christmas." Malcolm grinned. "Said, 'Clothes make the man, but hair makes the face, and you might as soon be a wild man peering out from a forest with those locks.' And she was holding a scissors, so I wasn't of a mind to gainsay her."

"Welcome back." Emily stepped forward, and Kip hugged her as well. "It's marvelous to see you. We've all missed you."

And behind her was Coppy, and Kip gave him the warmest hug of all. "How have you been?" he asked.

"Surviving," Coppy said with a smile. "Master Windsor's tried me on translocation spells the last week. He figures I should try a little of everything."

"So he's not being horrible to you?"

"Oh, he is." Coppy's smile didn't falter. "Only now I'm used to it. And I'm doing better in the lessons. Sometimes I do better with him around than without him, if you can believe that."

"You told me that," Kip said, a touch uneasy. "Can you do translocation?"

The otter looked around. "I been practicing with papers, so…" He bent and picked up a dusty page, laid it down flat on his paw, and gathered magic. Turquoise flickered around his paws and then the paper vanished, to reappear over Neddy. The phosphorus elemental didn't notice until the paper settled on him, then he raised his head as it caught fire and spun until it fell off him, leaping at it to devour it.

"Hi, Neddy." Kip crouched by the edge of the boundary. "How have you been?"

"Feelin' a mite cold, if I'm perfectly honest," the elemental said. "Been missin' the Flower, I have."

Kip straightened. "It's been two months. Would you like to go back?"

"Oh aye!" Neddy brightened.

"All right. Easy enough to do." And Kip gathered magic as well, feeling the stable binding around Neddy and working to dismiss the elemental as the others chorused good-byes. In a moment, the fiery lizard had vanished, leaving his heat behind. With a short rest, Kip gathered magic again and reached into the world of the phosphorus elementals. He hadn't been back since summoning Neddy, but he slipped into it easily: a world of fire that rotated around a purer, brighter fire that the elementals called "The Flower." Around it he perceived the spirits that were phosphorus elementals, and with his finer control, he selected one and reached out to it. It came to him willingly, and a moment later, with a pop of acrid smoke, a new lizard, glowing bright, sat in the space Neddy had just vacated.

"Hallo," Kip said, crouching down. "I'm Kip. What's your name?"

This lizard had a higher voice. "You can call me Betty if you like."

"Well, Betty," Kip said, "we hope you'll feel welcome here. Coppy and Emily will feed you paper, and if you start to feel cold, we'll send you right back."

Betty spun around in a circle and then looked around at all four of them. "It's right refreshing, it is," she said.

"Good." Kip stood and faced his friends. "So tell me what else has been happening here. Do you always lock the door now?"

"Aye." Malcolm answered, and the smile left his eyes, if not quite his lips. "One can never tell when Farley's going to test out a new spell on us. Since you left, Adamson seems uninterested in talking to any of us, and we're fighting every day."

"Not every day," Emily said, "but close to it."

Coppy didn't speak, but his brave expression struck Kip more than either of the others' words. "I'm sorry about that," he said. "I thought when I left, they'd stop."

"Oh, he just says, 'got rid of one, now to do for the rest of you,'" Emily said.

"Only without so much elocution and dropping consonants left and right," Malcolm added. "And he's still pursuing Emily in his own charmless manner, but so are half the school."

Emily waved Malcolm's words aside. "There's nothing to it. It becomes a noise like the ocean after a while, and like the ocean it won't harm me if I don't wade into it."

Kip forced a smile, hating the image that brought up. "Have they done anything serious?"

"Farley keeps threatening to summon a demon, but they keep the names well locked up, and even Patris seems disinclined to let him at them," Emily said.

"Good God." Kip shook his head, imagining Farley with a demon at his disposal.

"Quite." She shook her head. "I fancy it's just talk. All we've seen him learn are more and more physical spells. Not even basic alchemy or translocation."

"But he got a bug up his bum when you got to summon a demon," Malcolm put in. "An' he hasn't let that go."

"Never mind us," Coppy said. "We're managing well enough. I want to hear about London."

So Kip told them about his time in London, about Cott and Gugin (though not about spiritual holds, still reticent to mention that even in this safe place). He told them about Abel and the Isle of Dogs, and told Coppy all the stories he could remember about his family. The otter leaned against him and smiled. "Tell them I miss them," he said.

When Kip told them about Cott burning Mr. Gibbet's office, he had to work back and tell them about his mistreatment there. Emily sucked in her breath, and even Coppy clacked his tongue. "Say what you will about Patris, he hasn't locked us in a closet yet."

"Don't think the idea hasn't passed his mind," Malcolm chimed in. "Only the closets here are all old and we'd easily break out."

"I'm glad you're all healthy," Kip said. "I've been worried about you. I wish we had a better way to communicate than letters. I tried to send a demon here, but if they're not summoned in the College, they can't get past the wards on the grounds."

"Demon'd be right useful." Coppy stroked his whiskers. "What if we went down to the Inn every other night or so?"

Kip's ears perked up. "That might be too public, but any place outside the gates would work, aye."

"Too cold to be outdoors," Malcolm said. "The Inn's public room would be fine enough. Just tell the demon to appear as a human and he'll attract no attention."

"Won't Patris wonder why you're leaving the College every other night?"

"True," Emily said. "And going to the Inn wouldn't be good, with alcohol forbidden."

"The church, then?" Kip suggested.

"Just outside the church," Coppy said. "Rather not bring demons inside. I mean, you never know. They might be struck down."

"Just as cold outside the church as anywhere else," Malcolm pointed out.

"Pity Kip's not here to make a fire," Emily said with a twinkle in her eye.

Kip sighed and shook his head. "Rather than set a schedule, why don't you have Emily send me a note whenever you're going to be free, and I'll send a demon if I can?"

"That's fine," Malcolm said. "More than fair."

It wasn't too long after that that a demon appeared in their basement, a tall, slender taciturn woman with obsidian snake scales for skin. She told Kip that Master Vendis required his presence, and then vanished. "What happened to Burkle?" Kip asked as he stood.

Malcolm shrugged. "We weren't meant to meet him in any case. I suspect they dismissed him and summoned this new one."

"Burkle at least got outraged at us," Coppy said. "We don't even know this one's name. She barely talks."

Kip said his good-byes, hugged everyone and promised to stay in touch, and then ran up the stairs to Master Vendis's office. He expected to find Master MacDougal there, but to his surprise, Master Albright's rotund form and wide smile greeted him. "I haven't been to Prince George's in an age," the London master said. "Thought it worth a visit."

"It's rather cold at the moment," Kip said, his guard up.

Master Albright drew his cloak around his shoulders. "I can bear the chill for a short time. Will you show me your college before we return to London?"

Kip glanced at Master Vendis, who gave a short nod. "Of course, sir," he said.

So he led Master Albright down the stairs, into the library, where Florian greeted them with a dry "hello," and through the Great Hall, pointing out the fireplace and the elementals. "There isn't much more to the Tower," Kip said. "Unless you'd like to see the basement, where I live."

"I've seen it, when I sent your letter. Tell me again why you stay there?"

Kip reached up to scratch his ear. "That's where they housed us as students. When we became apprentices, we wanted to stay together. The apprentices here lodge with their masters; there isn't a dormitory room like at King's."

"I see." Albright gestured toward the great doors. "Shall we take a short walk outside?"

Here, perhaps, was Kip's chance to test his theory again. So the fox pushed open the great doors into the stiff wind of a New England winter, flattening his ears and narrowing his eyes. He held the door for Master Albright before pulling his robes around himself more tightly. "It's a brisk one today," he said.

The London master didn't immediately reply, not for the first few steps out onto the slick stone path. To either side, the shapes of grass were still visible under a light coating of snow, which gleamed white even though the sun had not broken through the thick cloud cover. Kip inhaled the sharp, cold scent of snow, waiting for Albright to say something, and after a moment the sorcerer said, "So I see. Those tents, those are where the buildings stood before the attack?"

"Aye." Kip nodded. "The near one is the dining tent, the far one a tent we use to practice magic. We did as students, that is. Master Patris forbad us to use sorcery unsupervised in the Tower, so we had to go outside."

"Curious," Master Albright said. "The Tower has withstood nearly two hundred years of students practicing sorcery in it. But I suppose Master Patris is justifiably cautious in that regard. Still, it seems a burden to place on the students when the weather can be this inclement."

If Master Albright had been headmaster, Kip was sure, they wouldn't have had to practice outside. Master Albright would have taken far better care of all his students, women, Calatians, and Irishmen alike. "For most of the students it was fine," he said. "They lived near the sorcerers. But we didn't have a sorcerer near us. It wasn't that bad, though. The weather was bearable, and I was learning fire, so it kept us warm."

Albright nodded. "And under there is where you found those glass beads?"

"Yes." Kip patted the pockets of his robe for the small vial, eager to help. "I can show you…"

His fingers closed around the vial and he realized that the adoring feeling he had for Master Albright was familiar, and not only from their first dinner together. Since then, Master Gugin had put him into many similar holds and had warned Kip that these were the most insidious. It was possible to take actions counter to it once you realized what was going on, unless the caster made a direct request.

With a struggle, Kip forced himself to change the sentence he'd been about to say. "A place where the wreckage is more visible. If you'd like to go around that corner?"

If Albright asked him to show the glass bead, he'd do it. He almost wanted to anyway. And it was silly to think that Albright was casting spiritual holds on him for some nefarious purpose. If he were, he probably had a very good reason for it. Still, Kip thought, best to cast the counter spell anyway. But how to gather magic without the sorcerer noticing? If Albright saw that Kip didn't trust him, he'd be so disappointed, and Kip didn't want that.

Last time he'd tried…he walked at Albright's side, falling maybe a half-step behind him, and clasped his paws behind his back as though casually strolling. This was how he'd done it before, and nothing had changed. Surely nothing would now.

"I understand you've also consulted Master Gugin about the beads."

"Yes, sir." Kip gathered magic as quickly as he dared.

"Has he been of any help at all?"

He started to tell Albright about the memory, and though he knew he shouldn't, it was hard to remember why. Truthfully, he told himself, Gugin's information hadn't led to anything yet. "He had a vague memory of having seen something." Kip gritted his teeth against saying anything more, and instead turned his head slightly so he was speaking away from Albright, hoping the wind would cover the soft sound of the spell he was reciting.

Master Albright rounded the corner with him, scanning the snow-powdered lawn. "The orchard is over there?"

The bright surface made it hard for Kip to focus on the rigid black silhouettes of the trees, but Albright was pointing in the right direction and his human eyes were better. "Aye, sir."

As they approached the tent, Albright's eyes fixed on the debris visible under the tent flap, even below a thin layer of snow: bricks and boards below the wooden floor of the tent. "You visited him often, Gugin? Why was that?"

Kip completed the spell, finding the heart of himself easier to find as he'd just come from talking to Coppy and Emily and Malcolm, and waited. A breeze ruffled his fur. Was he still worried about disappointing Master Albright? No; now he wanted to tell the man nothing. He wanted to go back to his basement and tell his friends about Albright. There seemed little doubt he'd been under a spiritual hold.

The sorcerer turned from the wreckage to stare at Kip, and the fox's heart jumped. Had Albright detected the dissolution of his hold? "Penfold?"

"Sorry," Kip said, trying to behave slavishly as though the hold were still in effect, which was nearly as difficult as fighting it. "I went to see him because of a spell I'd found, and he was very lonely. I don't have many other people to talk to in London; Master Cott doesn't let me out much during the day. So it was a nice evening ritual. He liked me to bring him ale, and we talked about sorcery and the college.'

"I see." Albright returned his attention to the tent. "And did he teach you any spells?"

"No, sir," Kip said truthfully. "We only discussed spells a couple times, because I think his specialty was spiritual magic and he said that even in the normal course of things, I wouldn't begin learning that for a few years, and because I was being taught only fire spells, he wasn't sure I would even get to spiritual magic in my life."

It was hard to pretend to be affectionate and garrulous, especially when Kip was aware that any slip might alert Albright to the failure of his spell. But fortunately, Albright's attention was partly taken by the tent and the debris below it, and so he merely nodded. "Gugin is an odd fellow," he said after a moment. "I shouldn't visit him for a little while if I were you. I can arrange for more appropriate companionship in the evenings, if you feel lonely."

"Would you, sir?" Kip feigned delight. "That would be very kind of you."

"Not at all, not at all." Albright rubbed his arms and then set one hand on Kip's shoulder. "Now, let us get out of this cold."

The moment he finished speaking the sentence, they were atop the War Tower, the cold afternoon wind replaced by chilly rain in the dark London sky. "Is it night?" Kip asked stupidly.

"Indeed," Master Albright said. "Have you not been taught basic science and understand the progression of daylight around the world?"

"Yes, of course." Kip tried to recover his poise. Malcolm had told him, but all his trips had either been early in the day or at night. "I hadn't noticed it so dramatically illustrated before."

"Ah, yes." Albright straightened. "It can be masked if you jump during one of the long nights, or early in their morning. At any rate, now you have seen it, and here I will take my leave of you." He wagged a finger at Kip. "Remember what I said about Master Gugin."

"Yes, sir," Kip said. "And thank you for looking after my evenings."

With that, Albright blinked out of existence. Kip searched the other towers and thought he saw a blur of motion on Lord Winter's Tower, but it was the farthest from him, and even with his night vision, seeing at a distance was difficult. "I should have a demon around all the time," he thought as he found the stair and descended. "Better than spectacles."

CHAPTER 15: MASTER GUGIN

Master Cott, at least, greeted Kip with unfeigned delight. "I've found three more spells for you to work on," he said, and pushed two large books at Kip.

Two of the spells in question were about creating fire at a distance: one allowed the sorcerer to send fire to a particular substance, so for example you could make the rifle stocks of an entire company combust if you had an example of what they were made of; the other used a simple translocational spell to send one of Cott's colored powders to a spot and then ignite it, so you could create variously colored signal flares. The third spell would allow the sorcerer to create a fire underwater. "Normally," Cott said, reading over Kip's shoulder as he perused that last one, "this is the one that would give you the most trouble, as it did me and my master both. But with your lack of schooling in translocation, you might find that second one more challenging until you master at least the basics of that discipline."

"Who will teach me that?" Kip asked.

"Albright, perhaps," Cott said. "You seem to get on well with him."

"Er…" Kip folded his ears back. It was nice to be able to allow his ears and tail to express his emotions in front of Cott, who either didn't care or didn't know what those movements signaled. "Why do you say that?"

"He fetched you today from Prince George's, didn't he? MacDougal came and told me about it. Thought I asked for him to be replaced. I told him I wouldn't care one way or another who fetched you as long as they brought you over alive. Why would I care if MacDougal or Albright went?"

"So who did ask?" Kip was pretty sure he knew, but he wondered if Cott knew.

The master did not, and what's more, was as uninterested in that question as in anything that didn't involve fire. He didn't even ask Kip about the glass beads, and when Kip brought it up, he said, "I haven't had time to think on that," which to Kip meant that he hadn't had any motivation to think about it. It didn't surprise him.

"I'll start the spells," Kip said, but thinking about the glass beads had given him an idea. "Where is the library, and do you think I might visit it sometime? I would greatly like to read more about the way these spells have been used."

"I can fetch books for you," Cott said.

"I wouldn't want to trouble you to go looking for more books." Kip smiled as ingratiatingly as he could. He wondered briefly if Master Gugin could teach him how to cast a simple spiritual hold to make Cott allow him a little freedom. Of course that would be unethical and wrong, but it was a pleasant fantasy. "If you have research to do, perhaps I could go along?"

Cott thought about that while Kip pretended to read through the spell. "Aye," he said, "We can go down tomorrow."

"Thank you," Kip said, and bent to study the first spell.

True to his word, Cott took Kip to the library the following day. It was in the King's Tower, so they had to descend to the base of the War Tower, cross the courtyard, and enter the largest and most ornate of the College's towers. Crowds of students flocked around them, but unlike the other day, paid Kip almost no attention. In the train of a sorcerer, a Calatian nearly vanished in the sight of the average student.

Cott led him to a large room with the doors wide open and a bored-looking student leaning against them. Here Kip caught the peppermint tingle of a nearby demon and looked about for one only to have his attention caught by the student. The young man lifted his head when Cott approached, his eyes flicking to Kip, and only then did Kip see that his eyes were bright green and slit-pupiled like a fox's. "Who's the Calatian?" the demon asked in a stilted voice with a dry, brittle timbre.

"My apprentice," Cott replied. "He is allowed to enter."

This satisfied the demon, and he went back to watching people walk back and forth in the hallway as Kip and Cott strode past him.

This wasn't the right library. The ceiling beams were set against stone rather than wood, and though the smell was similar, it wasn't as thick with musty paper, the wood smelled different, and the windows were narrower.

But Kip followed Cott and spent the afternoon looking through history books anyway. Mostly he studied records of battles, looking for places where fire had been used.

All the incidents were sadly unimaginative. Fire set in an enemy battalion, fire set on an enemy warship. Fire inside a besieged keep. There were no underwater fires, no distant fires, and only two instances where signal fires had been used. But some of the tactics used were of interest, so Kip read through to find accounts of how the fires had caused the most confusion. He doubted he would ever have to use that information, but the words of the revolutionaries kept echoing in his mind. There was at least the possibility that there would be a war soon, and whatever side he was on—the Empire's, he was…well, mostly sure—he would be of most use if he knew how best to use his power.

There were also defenses against fire magic, he read. Several of the spells the fire sorcerers had tried were blocked by wards or the fires were suffocated by air elementals. Often the fire sorcerers themselves were the targets of assassination, he noted, and had sorcerers attending to them at all times. He wondered whether Malcolm had learned to set wards yet.

In the remaining time before Cott gathered his books, Kip looked up wards. Defensive magic was difficult because it was reactive rather than active, because you could never know the nature of the spell that was coming against you. The books of defensive magic contained complicated paragraphs which Kip thought he understood when he read them, but couldn't have explained to anyone else, let alone put into practice.

As they left the library, Kip asked, "What other libraries are available to sorcerers? Master Gugin recommended I look up some histories to find out more about the glass beads."

"Oh, I'm sure I don't know." Cott waved a hand. "I've always found whatever I needed here. I suppose you could consult the Royal Archives if you wished, but we will have to send for a special dispensation. It might take weeks."

"What if you told them it was about the attack on Prince George's?" Kip asked. "Could it come in faster then?" When Cott demurred, Kip said, "I think we both should go, of course."

"Yes, yes, very interesting." They crossed the courtyard as Cott pondered that. "I will ask Master Albright."

Kip's ears went up. "Master Albright? Why?"

"Oh, he knows you, and he's quite well connected. He's had an audience with the King, I believe. At least, that's what Martinet says. Albright won't talk about it, and I suppose that's proper. But I hear he does procure the odd favor when asked."

"I would—that is," Kip said, "please don't trouble him. Not yet. I'll see if I might find another way. Is there an official way to request access?"

"That's ridiculous." Cott strode up the stairs of the War Tower. "Whyever not avail yourself of his help?"

It took Kip three flights to think of a proper answer, but he had to come up with something. He couldn't tell Cott that he did not trust a respected sorcerer who had—to all appearances—only been generous to him, that he was sure that generosity masked a more sinister motive. "I don't feel I've earned a favor from him yet. I very much want to make my own way where I can. Perhaps—perhaps if I'm not able on my own, I will go ask him."

"Ha." Cott preceded Kip to his office door, opened it, and strode inside. "I suppose I can understand that. Very well, as you wish. I won't mention it to him. You may go to the Royal Archives and submit a request yourself."

"Thank you," Kip said, though he had no idea when he would have the time to do that.

Master Albright, true to his word, sent two apprentices to take Kip out that evening, a short straw-haired boy with a northern accent, and a tall boy with a narrow face who had grown up in London (in a neighborhood called Kensington). This latter talked in disparaging tones about the businesses in the village, how they were perfectly fine for students, but the shops and pubs in Kensington were much better, and when he'd learned to translocate he would go there more often. Both apprentices were studying under a Master Pembroke, and told Kip it had been common for a master to take two or even three apprentices until several sorcerers returned from the military after the defeat of Napoleon. They had been apprenticed for nearly four years now, and expected to take their examinations to become Masters in another three. The shorter one hoped to be sent to Gibraltar for the climate; the other wanted to remain at King's College.

In a polite, formulaic way, they asked Kip about his own life and studies in tones that indicated near-complete disinterest. So he kept his answers short and followed them up with more questions about their studies. There were aspects to physical magic he hadn't considered, like causing objects to spin, moving small particles very quickly so as to heat up an area, and using a delicate touch to assist engine-driven machines to help them conserve fuel. The apprentices hinted at other sorcery they were studying, but didn't wish to talk about.

On the whole, they were pleasant company. Kip enjoyed listening to their stories and learning about their world, and though they didn't want to hear about his life specifically, they were interested in life in the Massachusetts Bay colony. They had heard about the movement to revolution from many years ago and asked Kip if people still spoke of Samuel Adams, Thomas Payne, and other traitors. Kip acknowledged that they did, but did not mention John Quincy Adams nor even John Adams to his companions.

They took him out two nights, and begged off on the third so they might attend a dinner being given for the apprentices. They invited Kip, but the fox felt that the invitation should be issued from the college. As none was forthcoming, he remained in Cott's workshop.

The solitude was pleasant for a short time, but after an hour with a cup of tea and a warm fire, Kip's thoughts turned to Master Gugin. He really should visit the sorcerer, if only to explain to him why he hadn't come to see him since his return.

So he flew over to the Astronomy Tower. The chill in the air made flying uncomfortable, even over the short distance between two adjacent towers. As he landed, Kip wondered how hard it would be to learn to translocate to such a familiar location. He thought, *Master Gugin,* and scanned the parapets for Scar, but the raven was nowhere to be found.

The shutters at the raven's window were closed and locked. He descended to the window that let onto Gugin's chamber, the one the old sorcerer never wanted open, and found them similarly secured. Shivering, he raised a paw and rapped on them. "Master Gugin?" he called.

No answer. Kip's fur prickled from more than the wind. Of course it was possible that Master Gugin had simply left on a trip. He owed no explanation of his time to someone else's apprentice. Kip hesitated, but curiosity overcame him and he pressed his eye to the gap between the shutters.

There wasn't enough light inside for Kip's eyes to make out any details. He gripped the stone windowsill, just in case, and called on fire to burn the inside of the shutters. Very small fires, barely enough to consume anything, just enough to cast some light on the inside of the room.

The familiar room took shape before his eyes. He couldn't see the couch, but he could see the bookshelves, the door, and the carpet. Everything in the room looked quiet and normal. But his hackles stayed up and he peered through, looking more closely.

A shadow on the carpet, deep black, drew his eye. It might just have been the shadow from the couch, but it wasn't quite the right shape. And then he realized what was wrong with it: part of it was a wing, black and still as night.

His breath caught. He pressed his eye to the shutter, convinced that he'd only caught Scar in a moment of rest, that in one more second the raven would get up and fly to the window, despite the fact that he'd never seen a raven lie with its wing outstretched on the ground. But the seconds passed and the shadow remained still, and so Kip extinguished his fires and lifted himself to the top of the tower, where he sat against the wall. What was he to do in this case? Cott was asleep somewhere, and he had no idea where the Headmaster of King's College was, nor had he ever been introduced to him.

He should go back to the workshop. The wind was only cold on his nose and ears, really, but it hissed past him and brought smells of the Thames and made it harder to think. If he could only—

A tingle in his nose made him look up and around, wildly. He hadn't detected many demons here at King's College, but the sharpness was unmistakable. The roof of the tower appeared to be empty, but that meant only that the demon wasn't visible. So—what if Kip summoned Nikolon? The demon could enter Master Gugin's chamber, tell Kip what it saw there, and possibly even find the Headmaster's office.

But he'd need a knife, or at least some way to cut himself. He could bite his tongue, but hard enough to draw blood? No, back at Cott's workshop he had a knife. He hated to leave the Astronomy Tower, but if Gugin had been brought to harm—

What if he weren't dead? What if he were merely injured, dying slowly? The same certainty he'd felt looking at the raven's wing returned to him.

He gathered magic again and hovered beside the shutters, pulling them apart with magic and then opening the window with cold, shaking paws. When he got the iron-bound glass to swing aside, the puff of air that greeted him left no doubt as to the state of the inhabitants: the sickly smell of <storf>, dead person's flesh, made him gag. He held his breath, clambering into the window and closing it behind him, and conjured a fire in his paw long enough to identify a place on the windowsill where he could set it to burn and provide light.

Master Gugin lay on the couch, his face a mottled purple, mouth open and eyes staring at the ceiling. Scar lay with wings outstretched on the carpet in front of him. Kip backed away from them, and as he did his legs weakened and he had to sit down. He couldn't look away from Gugin's face, and though their relationship had been short and largely formal, his chest tightened and he had to focus on steadying his breathing. Master Gugin had been one of the few masters in London to treat him as a worthy pupil. And what could strike him down?

The gleam of silver in a nearby cabinet drew Kip's eye. He waited a moment to gather his strength and then walked over to take the short knife, its metal cold in his paw.

Nikolon appeared again as the vixen when he summoned her, but he ordered her to take on a human form and go seek out the Headmaster of King's College. Before he completed the order, another thought crossed his mind. "Wait," he said. "Is there another demon nearby now?"

The human, a golden-haired dark-skinned woman in a golden robe, cocked her head and then shook it. "How nearby, master?"

Kip judged the distance to the roof. "Fifty feet."

"No."

"Has there been in the last fifteen minutes?"

"There has been none since I was summoned," she said. "Beyond that I have no way of knowing. I do not command Time."

"Very well," he said. "Go fetch Headmaster Cross."

He lit the lamps in the room with a simple fire spell, then sat and waited. At worst, he thought, the head would be something like Patris, but he hoped for someone reasonable. Patris, if he found Kip in a room with a dead sorcerer, would likely attempt to hang him on the spot. Albright at least would give him the benefit of the doubt; Kip was sure of that even if he didn't trust Albright anymore. And why was he thinking of him in connection with Patris? An echo of that last spiritual hold. Kip growled and paced the room until Nikolon returned.

The demon appeared as the vixen when she did, her fur glossy in the lamplight. "Headmaster Cross is on his way. He has asked your permission to send me to alert two other sorcerers to join him here."

"Yes," Kip said, heartened by the request for permission. "You may alert the other sorcerers he specified. Did he say anything? Should I do anything?"

"He did not specify, but when I told him how you entered, he said," and here her voice took on a low rasp, "'Then I shall fly up myself in a moment.'"

"Thank you," Kip said. "You may go alert the other sorcerers. But use the human form. Wait." He tilted his head. "Why did you return as the vixen?"

Back in human form, Nikolon inclined her head. "You specified that I should seek out Headmaster Cross in human form. Once he was sought out and I had left his presence, there were no restrictions on what form I should take."

"Very well." Kip gave a quick nod. "Go about the headmaster's errand. When you return to me, do so invisibly."

A moment after Nikolon vanished, Kip's ears perked to noise at the shutters. The window flew open, and in stepped an old man in a thick wine-red cloak with a white dressing-gown under it. His bald head and round clean-shaven face gave him a casual, friendly air as he was making his way inside, but when he straightened up and closed the window with a gesture, his authority and piercing stare brought Kip to his feet.

First the Headmaster stared at the dead Gugin, then at Scar, and finally his eyes alit on Kip. "Did you light the lamps?"

"Yes, sir."

"So you are Cott's Calatian apprentice," he said. "I asked him several times to bring you around to meet me, but stopped short of ordering him."

"He never told me, sir," Kip said.

"I'm Master Cross." The old man extended a hand, and Kip shook it. "And you are Kip Penfold. So tell me now how you came to discover poor Master Gugin, with every detail. I don't suppose you can show me? Ah well, then, words will suffice."

So Kip spoke as quickly and clearly as he could. The Headmaster nodded, his eyes remaining on Kip. "And the outer door there is locked?"

"I don't know," Kip said. "I haven't tried."

"Silas and Burton will be coming that way, so let us see." Cross gestured to the door beyond the velvet drapes, and a moment later a series of heavy thunks came from the lock. "There. Now, another question: how have you such experience to summon a demon in your first year of apprenticeship?"

"It isn't so uncommon in Prince George's College," Kip said. "I summoned an elemental months ago, and I had to summon Nikolon to search the ruins under the tents—I'm sorry?"

He stopped as Headmaster Cross held up a hand. "Do not name your demon in front of others."

Before Kip could ask why, the peppermint tingle returned to his nose and Nikolon said in his mind, *My task is complete.* A moment later, the door opened. The first sorcerer to push aside the heavy velvet drapes had salt-and-pepper hair and a matching mustache and goatee, along with a pale complexion and a slight squint that darkened his eyes. The second was Master Albright.

Kip stared, and then Albright met his eyes and he averted his own quickly, stepping back to be out of the way as the salt-and-pepper sorcerer stepped up to Gugin's body without any trace of surprise. He moved his lips, but either he was making no sound or he was talking so quietly that even Kip's ears couldn't catch the words.

Master?

Wait, Kip ordered. *Stay near me.*

Master Albright came to stand beside Kip. Very quietly, in the same voice he'd used to tell Kip to warn Master Cott off their dinner, he said, *I warned you to stay away.*

Kip swallowed. Neither Master Cross nor the other sorcerer turned or gave any indication they had heard. He fox-whispered back, *What do you know about this?*

The salt-and-pepper sorcerer straightened. "Choked," he said. "Hard to tell when. One to three days ago." His eyes lit on Kip. "What was the Calatian doing here?"

Kip's mouth was dry. Now all three sorcerers were staring at him. "Master Gugin was kind of a friend," he said. "I'd visited him…he said he was lonely. So I came by to see what he was…I thought he might be lonely."

They continued to stare. Headmaster Cross said, "And then?"

"It was quiet. And dark." Kip swallowed again. "I looked in at the shutters. I saw Scar's wing, and I didn't know if Master Gugin might need help, so I broke in."

"And why summon a demon?" the salt-and-pepper sorcerer said. "Rather than come get the Headmaster yourself?"

"I didn't know where his office was. My demon could search more quickly."

The sorcerer raised his eyebrows and then fixed Headmaster Cross with a sarcastic smile. "Really. An apprentice has been studying in this college and never introduced to the Head?"

"He came directly from the Colonies," Master Albright said. "He's apprenticed to Cott."

The salt-and-pepper sorcerer's squint relaxed. "Ah, well, in that case… but how does he know how to summon a demon?"

"It's more commonly taught at Prince George's, I'm told," Headmaster Cross said. "The Church does not keep as close an eye on them out there in New Cambridge as here in London. Penfold was using that ability in the investigation of the attack there."

"Couldn't get any proper sorcerers to do it, I suppose." The sorcerer straightened. "It is odd that he wasn't able to remove the obstruction himself, but that happens sometimes. Can't breathe, panic, and if they're not a physical sorcerer, it's hard to focus on objects in your throat. Might've torn his throat out."

"But what happened to Scar?" Kip asked.

"If a raven is very old," Cross said, "it's only the will of the sorcerer keeping it alive. Once the sorcerer dies…" He gestured to the small prone form.

Kip found it very sad that Scar had died. To the extent that familiar ravens had personalities, Scar had always seemed young and energetic. He stepped forward and knelt next to the small feathered body.

"I see no reason to hold the Calatian," the salt-and-pepper sorcerer said. "It looks like an accident. There's the food he was eating." He pointed to a half-eaten chicken that clearly had been next to Gugin for more than a day. "He choked, his raven died, nobody noticed because nobody comes to see him." He waved a hand. "I've told you, sir, that we need to check in on all our residents daily."

"Many of the residents don't want that," Cross said equably. "Gugin himself told me he did not want anyone 'poking around his body,' in his words."

"He was paranoid," Kip put in.

"Spiritual sorcerers often are," Master Albright said. "Seeing the depths of human minds is not always a pleasant experience."

"That's what he said." Kip didn't want to look back at Gugin's body and staring eyes, but remembering the man's words made it hard not to.

Master Albright put a hand on Kip's shoulder. "Headmaster, if I might have a moment with Penfold here? It must be hard on him, being one of Gugin's only friends."

"Aye, of course," Cross said. "And Penfold, you're staying with the apprentices?"

"I'm staying in Cott's workshop," Kip said. "There's more space and I don't disturb anyone when I study at night."

"Hmmm." Salt-and-pepper left the room, but Cross studied Kip for a moment longer. "Come by my office tomorrow, Penfold. Tell Cott I insist."

"Yes, sir," Kip said. His heart sped up, but his nose and mind told him it was unlikely that Cross meant any harm. Being left with Albright, on the other hand, made him very nervous indeed. But he couldn't think of any way to get out of it.

When the Headmaster had left, Albright beckoned Kip to the door as well. "We needn't stay here."

Kip nodded and followed the plump master out. Albright closed the door behind them and beckoned Kip down the tight spiral stair. "There's a vacant office just below that we can use. Don't worry, I won't keep you for long."

In the close quarters, Kip was very aware of the sorcerer's rank scent. He was sweating even in this chilly air, and perhaps that could be explained away by the exertion of having climbed nearly to the top of the tallest tower in the College. But it had a different character to it, not quite <leffikfar> (fear), but not entirely <leffiksot> (exertion) either. It was also reasonable to be afraid when finding one of your number dead, but Kip thought there might be more to it. *Nikolon*, he said in his mind, reaching out to the demon. *Follow us and if Albright takes any action against me, silence him immediately.*

Yes, master.

"Here we are." Albright cracked a door open at the next landing, cautiously peered in, and then opened it wide. "I thought I remembered that Gugin—poor Gugin—enjoyed the buffer of an empty room between him and the rest of the College."

Kip followed into a mostly-dark room, but after the dark stair his eyes had adjusted enough to make out a table and two chairs, one lying on its side on the floor. Albright shut the door behind them, and Kip's first reaction was to go to the window and check the latch on it. He had Nikolon, but the memory of Albright speaking inaudibly stuck in his head; he couldn't discount the possibility that Albright also had a demon around. Kip could detect the presence of demons, but not to a fine enough degree to distinguish one from many.

"Would you mind providing the fire?" Albright's voice came from behind him, steady despite the odor lingering in Kip's nose. "To my poor old eyes, it's quite dark in here."

"Of course," Kip said, and slid the window latch open. It made noise, but Albright didn't comment. So Kip turned and drew fire into life on the floor, consuming the dust that lay there.

The light was plenty for him to make out Albright's troubled expression. The sorcerer put his hands behind his back and drew in a breath. "Please leave the window shut, Penfold. In addition to keeping out the chill, I have taken measures to ensure that we cannot be heard here, which will be slightly less effective with an open window."

"I was just checking the latch."

"Indeed." Albright paced over to the table, looked down at it, then paced back to the door. "I must confess, Penfold, that I have not been entirely truthful with you. The sensitive nature of my work means that I cannot place my trust without a good deal of investigation, and even then only to a select few."

Kip's ears perked. "I understand," he said, though he didn't quite, yet.

"You are investigating the attacks on your school. So am I. I am working under the direct order of Lord Castlereagh—the Foreign Secretary. We had been working under the assumption that it was the work of a foreign power, but recently have uncovered some evidence that the attack may have been planned in part in the colony of Massachusetts Bay itself. You are aware, I believe, that there are factions there promoting revolution?"

"I have heard of such." Kip stayed alert for any trace of a spiritual hold, but did not feel any untoward shift in his emotions. "But why would the revolutionaries weaken the sorcery of the colonies?"

"Indeed. I will point out that the military sorcerers remained unharmed, so perhaps they felt the loyalty of the Colleges was closer to England than that of the military."

"That seems backwards."

"Does it?" Albright looked across the room at him. "The sorcerers at the College remain in near-isolation, while the military sorcerers work with soldiers and the people of the Colonies. If there is revolutionary sentiment stirring, the military will be more likely in the thick of it than the sorcerers at the College. When the failed revolution happened forty years ago, the only sorcerer to take the rebels' side was a Royal Army sorcerer."

"I didn't know that," Kip said. But he thought about John Quincy Adams and his mission to plead his case to the College. That did not feel like a group that had given up on the loyalty of the College. But it was also possible that there were factions within the revolutionaries. Mr. Adams might not know anything about the plot to destroy the college. And it could have been a rogue sorcerer who'd summoned a demon, one trained in London and expelled from this college, or sent to America for some other reason, who'd fallen in with the revolutionary cause.

"So that's where my suspicions are trained. I'm sorry if I misled you in certain respects, but coming from the Colonies, you understand why I couldn't trust you immediately. Cott vouched for you, and after you spent a month here without pursuing any revolutionary ends that I could see, I had already made up my mind that you are not part of the revolutionary movement. I had not intended to reveal myself so soon to you, but this death has rather forced my hand."

"Gugin's death?" Kip sucked in a breath. "You think it's suspicious too?"

Albright inclined his head. "Master Clover will have more to say on that than I will. The cause of death—well, anyone may choke, I suppose, and a hermit is less likely than most to be in the company of someone who might render assistance. But it is strange to me that this should happen so soon after you spoke to him." He glanced upward. "It may be coincidence, of course, but I have learned to be suspicious of coincidences."

"You think what he was going to talk to me about was important?" Kip asked.

"If his death wasn't accidental, then someone thought so." Albright rubbed his beard. "Can you think of anything else he might have told you that you haven't mentioned to me?"

Kip wanted very much to believe him, but he couldn't get the <leffikfar> smell out of his nose, and Albright still hadn't confessed to using the spiritual holds on him. That could just be a way he gathered information, but until he did so, he hadn't been completely honest with Kip, and Kip wasn't going to be completely honest with him. "No," he said. "I told you, we only visited a little bit. I told him about the Colonies. He'd studied over there, you know, but hasn't—hadn't been back in a while."

"I did know that." Albright gave a quick nod. "All right, Penfold. Do contact me if you think of anything else. I'm on the fourth floor of Lord Winter's Tower; you may visit me yourself or send your demon. And," he said, holding up a finger, "do exercise care with the use of your demon. They are not as common here and must not be detected outside the College save in extraordinary circumstances."

"Yes, sir," Kip said.

Albright turned to leave, and Kip remembered Cott's words. "Sir," he called, and the sorcerer turned. "Master Cott said you might have access to the Royal Archives?"

"Yes," Albright said slowly.

"He thinks that perhaps some research there might be beneficial, only he doesn't want to bestir himself to go. Would it be possible for me to look through the materials there?"

Albright looked keenly at him. "It could be done," he said slowly. "Do you expect to be here another fortnight?"

Kip nodded. "I don't know when I'm to go back to Prince George's, sir. I believe Headmaster Patris is happy to keep me far away."

"Very well." Albright put a hand on the door. "I will make an enquiry on your behalf tomorrow. I may reach you via Master Cott, as usual?"

"Or you could translocate a letter to me," Kip said. "That works for my friends in the Colonies."

The sorcerer smiled. "Indeed. Good night, Penfold."

When he'd gone, Kip sagged back against the wall. He turned his eyes upward, toward the ceiling beyond which Master Gugin lay. They hadn't been friends, not exactly, but he'd felt sorry for the old half-crazy sorcerer, living far away from everyone else, separated not only by distance but by history and his abilities. Kip had liked that they'd gotten along, and he'd fancied that Master Gugin enjoyed his company. And now he'd choked to death, an undignified end. He deserved better.

CHAPTER 16: IGNITION

He wanted badly to tell his friends about Gugin's death, but no letter had appeared from Emily since the day he'd returned, when she'd sent one telling him how good it had been to visit with him. She hadn't named a time when they might talk via demon, but promised to name one in her next letter. And yet it had been a week, and no letter came.

Kip told Master Cott of the death the next day, and Cott showed little surprise. "He lived alone, much as I do. I expect to die alone as well."

"But it's sad. And a surprise."

"I lost friends in the War," Cott said with abrupt sharpness. "I know what's sad. It is a waste that he died in such a way, but he was wasting what was left of his life anyway. He fought in those wars, you know."

"Gugin did?"

"Not 'fought,' I suppose, not like I did." They had been working on the underwater fires, and Cott now turned from the large glass bowl to Kip. "I was at Albuera, you know. Napoleon had a fire sorcerer as well. We went back and forth, burning rifles and tents and ground and putting out each other's fires until we were both exhausted. I noticed that certain fires were put out faster than others and guessed where he was located, and Master Twine raised the dirt all around that area in a great storm. While he was occupied, I sent fire to devour the ground beneath their feet so they could not find a footing."

"Can't you just burn their clothes?" Kip asked. "Or the soldiers themselves?"

Cott reacted more strongly than he had to the news of Gugin's death. "God's blood, boy, we're not savages. That's what the barbarians did when they sacked Rome: burned people, performed alchemy right on their bodies. They didn't have demons, nor some of the spells we have now, but still, it was horrible. No, we've risen above that."

Kip pictured the glass beads and thought, *Not all of us.* Aloud, he said, "So what did Master Gugin do?"

"Ah. He was present at the talks, so I heard. Great work in monitoring the moods of the other heads of state to put together the coalition to fight Napoleon. Everyone brings their own spiritual sorcerers, you know, all probing at each other." He mimed this with his hands. "To see if they can influence a bit here, a bit there. To gauge the moods of the leaders as the talks progress and report back. I know Gugin was offered a post with Lord Castlereagh but he turned it down."

That was the second time in as many days that Kip had heard that name. "The Foreign Secretary?"

"Aye. Don't know why he turned it down. Quite the sinecure when there's no war on."

Was there some other connection between Gugin and Albright? Kip stored the question away. "He seemed to have a very comfortable life."

Cott nodded. "I'm certain he did. He brought a good payment into the College, as I did from the war. The College funds him as it funds me."

"Funded him," Kip said.

"Eh?"

The fox shook his head. "Can you show me the underwater fire again?"

The lack of interest in Gugin's death, as far as Kip could see, bothered him both that day and the next. To his surprise, the two apprentices Albright had sent to keep him company (whose names failed to stick in his head, especially as he rarely had to address them) continued to take him out. He didn't see that they were enjoying his company, but they did appear to enjoy the evenings, and in the week following Gugin's death they tried to engage him more, now with talk of the Colonies and the revolutionary movement there.

"I just don't understand what they think they'll gain," one of them said.

"Why not be part of the greatest Empire in the world?" The other took up the argument. "If we split in two, we're that much easier for Spain to conquer."

"Not splitting in two," the first said with a great deal of scorn. "More like shaving a small piece off a great whole. But the question remains."

"I don't know," Kip said. "I haven't really talked to any of them nor read any material."

That didn't stem the flow of the conversation, but it allowed Kip to sit back from it while the two apprentices talked about how foolish the revolutionaries were. Neither of them mentioned Master Gugin until Kip brought him up, and then they made the usual disinterested platitudes about what a tragedy it was, and one of them said that it wasn't a great surprise that he'd choked to death. They exchanged looks and smiles while Kip clamped his muzzle shut.

So the following day, when Cott had announced he would not be working, Kip took advantage to seek out the only person he could be sure would listen to his thoughts without judgment, with whom he could have a private conversation. He summoned Nikolon and asked her to look for a fox named Abel, either on the Isle of Dogs or somewhere in the College. "And if you leave the College," he said, remembering Master Albright's warning, "on no account become visible or allow anyone to perceive you."

The demon returned in a matter of minutes, reporting that a fox with a stub for a tail was in the King's Tower of the College, but that two more were on the Isle, and she had waited to see them both being addressed to discover that one of those was Abel. "He weaves rope on the dock," she told Kip.

He dismissed Nikolon, put on a plain tunic without his black robe, and flew down to the Isle, careful to be as discreet as possible in his movements. When he approached the dock of the Isle, again a crowd grew, but this time some people recognized him and raised paws, or called out, "Ho, Sorcerer-Calatian!"

Thomas the dormouse was the first to approach him that Kip recognized. "Penfold?"

"Kip," Kip said, shaking the proffered paw.

The dormouse flicked his ears with a broad smile and looked around as if to make sure everyone had seen that. "What brings you to our Isle?"

"Ah, I hoped to talk to Abel," Kip said, and spotted the large warehouse from which strands of rope extended away from him. Along the path, several rabbits ran back and forth carrying strands to the large wheels at either end. Other Calatians walked up and down

Thomas grinned. "Aye, I see." He followed Kip's gaze and pointed. "He works the ropewalk today, but for a visit from you he might persuade another to take his place. Shall we walk down and greet him?"

"I don't want to take him away from work," Kip said.

"Nonsense." Thomas waved a paw. "Look at all these fellows loafing about."

The crowd around them certainly seemed busy to Kip, carrying boxes or sorting through piles of what smelled like rubbish, but there were some sitting with their legs hanging over the edge of the dock. Here where the people hadn't seen Kip fly up, they paid him little mind in his plain tunic, which eased the tightness in his chest. His tail swished more freely as Thomas walked with him along the edge of the river, chattering about how the chilly weather was lovely for the Calatians. "With our fur, we don't mind being outside so much while the humans all stay inside. We don't get much sun to enjoy, but the weather's lovely, just lovely. How is winter in the Colonies?"

"Sunnier," Kip said, "but also colder. There's snow on the ground for much of it."

"I'd love to see snow more often," Thomas said wistfully. "When I was a kit we had a week of snow and the Thames mostly froze over! We skated on it and had such fun."

"My father said they had a hard winter when he was a kit, too. I wonder if it was the same year."

"It was harder to get food, but it's always hard to get food." Thomas pointed inside the building as they came up alongside it. "There's Abel."

The ropewalk house didn't have walls as such; it was more of a few wooden beams supporting a roof over the large mechanisms inside, three great wheels that turned by cranks manned by Abel and two other Calatians. One was a wolf that Kip thought might be Grinda, but he couldn't tell at this distance by sight, and the breeze blowing from the Thames past him into the ropewalk house made it impossible to identify her that way either.

The wheels squeaked and the Calatians around them chattered enough to make a decent racket, especially beneath the bare wooden roof. Kip didn't want to disturb Abel at his job, but Thomas strode into the building and called loudly, "Ho, Abel!"

The fox turned, ears canted at a quizzical angle, and then he looked past Thomas and saw Kip. He sniffed the air and his ears perked. "Ho, Kip!" he called. "I'll just be a moment."

"No hurry," Kip called back, because some of the other rope-makers had turned to look from him to Abel.

The rope-spinner, a cunning device Kip hadn't seen before, consisted of a large wheel with three smaller wheels set into it. As far as Kip could tell, strands of twine or yarn were run along the rope walk by the rabbits and spun into thicker strands on the smaller wheels. Then the larger wheel turned while a rope-maker ran along the tightening rope with a wooden tool that perhaps guided the ropes properly? Kip couldn't tell exactly. But both the beginning product, the skeins of spun yarn, and the end result, a tightly bound rope, lay in the warehouse in piles he could sniff. They smelled oddly like people.

He turned to find Thomas watching him. "Are these ropes made from fur?" he asked.

"Shed fur, aye." The dormouse beamed. "And some of the dogbane around here. We collect it and make our own ropes out of it. We're likely just close to the end of our store of it now, and in the late winter and spring we'll hire out to people who want cheap rope made, or if we have money we'll buy the material to make more of our own and sell it. We use a good bit of it for building, for the few ships we have."

Kip's parents had collected his shed fur and disposed of it. Nobody had ever wanted it, nor needed it.

Thomas chattered on about the rope and had Kip pull on a length to see how strong it was, and generally made himself good company until Abel walked over, rubbing his paws together. "Hallo, Kip. Happy Christmas and Twelfth Night."

"Happy Christmas," Kip said, and extended his paw.

Abel took it and shook gently and quickly. "Apologies," he said. "The wheel is hard on my paws."

"No need to apologize." The presence of the other fox perked his spirits up, whether it was the familiar fox-scent or Abel's easy smile.

"Let's go somewhere quieter." Abel gestured, and Kip and Thomas followed him outside. "What brings you back to the Isle, Kip?"

"I wondered if you might mind a walk over to that plaque again." Kip lifted his head to the air from the river and turned to the haze of the Isle. The column wasn't visible over the houses, but he knew about where it was, almost as though it were a fire whose energy he was attuned to. "I have been thinking about death and what we leave behind."

Abel lowered his ears. "Ponderous subject, though I suppose the dead of winter is the time for it. What brought it on?"

Kip's chest tightened at the memory, the purple face, the sprawled raven. "I...lost a friend recently."

The other fox nodded, and then looked around Kip toward the dormouse. "Thomas, would you give us a moment, please?"

"Ah, of course, of course." The dormouse's grin widened as he brushed a paw along his whiskers, bowed, and stepped off to the side, looking out over the Thames.

The rest of the dock remained crowded, but Abel spoke in a low fox-whisper, enough to carry over the breeze. "A particular death?"

"A sorcerer," Kip said in the same pitch. "One I was friendly with. He choked to death and it might have been an accident. Probably it was." He took in a breath. "I can't see any reason for someone to kill him except that he was helping me research the attack on the college. But who knew that? Only a few people. Unless someone was listening with a demon." But he hadn't detected any demons when he'd spoken to Gugin.

"So it must be one of the people you told."

"Or he told someone." Kip shook his head. "Do you know a Lord Castlereagh?"

Abel laughed. "He wasn't at the last high tea I was invited to."

"I'm sorry," Kip said, but the other fox put a paw up.

"No, no, I shouldn't make fun. I've heard of him, I believe. Doesn't he hold some position in government? Had something to do with Napoleon's defeat?"

"Aye." They had turned down a narrower street and now had to weave to avoid people. Fortunately, there were no vehicles on the street as there were in New Cambridge; everyone walked on the Isle of Dogs. Kip kept his pitch low. "He's the Foreign Secretary. The sorcerer had worked with him and refused a post."

Talking these things out with Abel was nice. Kip would've preferred to talk to Coppy about them, or Emily, but he still hadn't heard from either of them, and especially here among all the Calatians he missed Coppy and it was difficult to think of him. Though he'd only known Abel for a day—less than that—he felt more comfortable with the fox than with anyone else he knew in London.

"I don't see why it couldn't be an accident," Abel said. "Coincidental, of course, but still possible."

"There's someone else investigating it who thinks it might be suspicious," Kip said. "Of course, I don't trust him completely either."

"I was going to ask why you're talking to me rather than him." The other fox smiled.

Kip exhaled. "I just want someone else to know that something's going on, and I can't reach my friends in the Colonies."

"Did you really want to see the plaque?" Abel asked as they approached a corner Kip remembered.

"Yes." A paper fluttered past Kip's sleeve to the ground.

He glanced at it, but Abel picked it up just as Kip realized what it was. "This yours?"

He held it out, and Kip took it. "I think so." Unfolding it, he recognized Emily's writing. *Tonight*, it read. *An hour past sundown, the Founders Rest. Urgent.*

Urgent? He looked up at the sun. A good portion of the day remained here, and even more back where Emily was. How could she write "Urgent" on a paper when there were hours and hours before he could talk to her? And what could be so urgent? Had something happened to Coppy? To Malcolm?

"Kip?"

He looked down into Abel's eyes. "My apologies. Message from a friend of mine."

"Something wrong?"

"I think so. But I won't know until…" He looked up again. "Well after sundown."

"Hope it's not too bad." Abel smiled. "So, the plaque then?"

The column stood between buildings with nowhere to sit nearby, but

Kip didn't mind standing. He and Abel leaned against a wall as they gazed at the plaque, and Kip thought about the Calatians who'd stood on that spot, who'd burned in the fire, not knowing that their deaths would be meaningful. They only knew pain and fire, and then nothing. But people had remembered their deaths and made them meaningful, and from them had come laws and the Council of Birk, and better living conditions for most. All these things that the people had never seen, could never know, stemming from that one tragedy. Was Master Gugin's death going to result in anything? Did most people's deaths?

"Do you think," Abel asked quietly, "that this sorcerer's death was part of a war?"

That was the question, wasn't it? Kip scratched at the base of his ear. "I don't know. I think so. I think some people want me to think it is and some people want me to think it isn't."

"That many people are interested in what you think?"

Kip nodded slowly. He weighed his next words, but they weren't anything Abel couldn't find out by asking some sorcerers—perhaps already had. "I'm a fire sorcerer. It's a rare ability."

Abel took that in. "In a war, then, you'd be valuable to whichever side you choose."

"I serve the Empire," Kip said.

"As do we all," Abel responded quickly. "And some of us wonder whether the way we are currently serving it is the best way."

"Maybe sometimes the best way to serve it is by dying." Kip clasped his fingers together and stared down.

Abel put a paw on his shoulder. "That's not true of you for sure, nor for me or any of my friends, we think. War or no war."

It took Kip a moment to remember that Abel had mentioned calyxes who'd died in the Napoleonic War. Was the fox saying that those sacrifices had been in vain? Could have been avoided? He heard Grinda's growl again, and as when he'd looked at the rope made of shed fur, wondered whether his assumptions born in New Cambridge might bear further challenging. "I think," he said, feeling comfortable speaking aloud to Abel, "that London has much to learn from the Colonies, more than they think they do. In New Cambridge, we look to London for guidance, but it is not always the case that London looks to New Cambridge for insight."

"So the practices in New Cambridge are different?" Abel tilted his head.

"Somewhat." Kip sighed. "The Calatians are part of the town, not segregated. Well...not entirely. And even during the war, none of us died. From the war, I mean. In the regular course of things, Calatians are sometimes beaten up, kidnapped, killed—"

"By humans?"

Kip nodded. "There's always one or two who resent us, think they should be able to do what they want. Especially—well, the one I knew was my age, and big. He was a bully, but one who knew if he was smart about it he could injure Calatians and nobody would punish him for it."

Abel nodded. "Human children often throw stones when we go out into London proper. The police are rarely around, and don't stop them even if they are."

"In New Cambridge, there was at least one 'accident' most years I can remember. Sometimes the people were only injured, a few times they disappeared, but once or twice they'd be found at the bottom of a quarry, or trampled by a horse. Nobody could prove they'd been killed, but there was talk." Kip sighed. "In my eighteen years, I lost five classmates. Three disappeared, one was found dead, one died after being hit on the head."

"Calatians disappear from here, too," Abel said quietly. "Once or twice, one turns up floating in the Thames. Last year, someone brought Richard White's body back to the gate, a knife wound in his chest, and said he 'tripped and fell.'" He sighed. "At least the calyxes, whatever Grinda says, died for a cause."

Kip winced. "The one calyx we lost disappeared the night of the attack on the College, not even during the war at all."

Abel nodded. "He must have been at the college during the attack?"

"I don't—" Kip paused. Abraham Lapelli had been mourned by the town, but nobody in the College had mentioned him, nor which sorcerer he'd been bound to. Kip and his father had talked about it, but none of the Calatians knew his fate either. Abraham had previously been the calyx to a sorcerer who'd died, and he was called up occasionally for other duties but had not been formally or informally bound to another sorcerer. His wife hadn't even known he'd been called away that night, not until she was woken by the noise of the attack and found her bed empty. "I don't know. He just disappeared. It might have been a coincidence."

Abel rubbed his whiskers. "You don't believe that."

I have learned to be suspicious of coincidences. Master Albright's words echoed in Kip's head as he brought his ears up. "No. I hope to solve the mystery of the attack, but I don't know where he fits in. His wife saw him before they went to bed. She didn't wake up when he left. Nobody else heard anything." And there was no plaque commemorating his death, no more than any plaque commemorated Saul's death or the deaths of the other students and sorcerers at either College. They were gone, buried, turned to glass beads under bricks and timber and soon would be forgotten. Had one of the glass beads been Abraham, Kip wondered? Would a Calatian turned to glass be noticeably different from a human?

The other fox took in the crowds around them and lowered his voice again. "Last-minute summonses without explanation are not uncommon here. Definitely not during the war, but few sorcerers give any warning to their calyxes about when they will be needed next, and only perhaps half of them go to the trouble of keeping the same calyx over months or years."

"They said they don't summon demons often," Kip said. "What do they use calyxes for, then? I thought it was mostly demon summoning."

Abel raised his eyebrows. "They rarely confide in us, but I know that they use calyxes for any spell they think will take a large amount of energy."

Perhaps they summoned demons for use far away, for communication with territories or exploration or other purposes. "Did Master Gugin have a calyx in years past?" Kip asked.

"The name isn't familiar, but I can ask around." Abel's body shifted, and it took a moment for Kip to realize that he was moving his stub of a tail. Slowly, not wagging, but relaxedly. "It feels like the way of doing things in New Cambridge is worth thinking about. We have been arguing about how to talk about change here, but it will be easier if there is a real town to take lessons from."

"I wish you could come see it," Kip said. He envisioned Abel and Coppy's family coming to New Cambridge, and then returning with new ideas about how Calatians should live. In a flash, he understood what the response to those ideas here in London would be from people like Mr. Gibbet. And for the first time he thought that the independence movement might not be about pushing away the old, but about protecting the new.

"One day, perhaps." Abel smiled. "For now, it's enough that I know it's there. It proves that this is not the only way we have to live, and lights a path to a better future."

"Let me tell you about Peachtree," Kip said. Standing there against the wall, as he told Abel about the Georgia town, he really believed that there could be a better future.

He begged off dinner with the two apprentices in the evening, not sure what time sunset would be happening in New Cambridge. Finally, he summoned Nikolon, who this time appeared as a robed male human, and ordered her—him—them?—to report to New Cambridge and let him see through their eyes. Nikolon perched atop the church steeple (it took Kip a moment to realize that) and showed him his home in the dim wet light of a steady rain. An intense longing to be there washed over him, but he recovered himself, aware of the effect of strong emotions on the demon binding.

The sun had not set yet, but it looked close. So he directed Nikolon to the Founders Rest ("you may wait in the fire if you find it more comfortable," but they chose to lie atop one of the rafters), and instructed them to wake him when Emily appeared, if he were asleep.

The double vision of the Founders Rest and Cott's workshop was more tolerable when the workshop was dark, but then it was cold, and so Kip lit a fire and closed his eyes to focus on the scene below him. Familiar people came and went as he watched, but he couldn't focus Nikolon's ears to catch any individual conversations, having to sort instead through the cacophony below. This frustrated him at first, but later allowed him to relax.

Master.

He snapped awake. Focused in Nikolon's gaze were Malcolm, Emily, and Coppy, sitting at a table below him. *These are the people you wish me to pass your words to?*

"Yes," he said, speaking aloud as he rubbed tiredness from his eyes.

His viewpoint drifted down until he felt as though he were seated at the table. Coppy sat to his left, Malcolm across, and Emily to his right. They talked in low voices and took no notice of him. All three looked as well as they had when he'd seen them the previous week, except that Emily's hair was disheveled and Malcolm kept running his hand through his own. Coppy talked in a low voice about someone having or not having come to harm. Again the homesickness overwhelmed him, and again he fought it back to remain in control of himself and the demon.

When you speak, they will hear your words, Nikolon said.

Kip cleared his throat. "Hi," he said. "What's happened?"

All three of his friends jumped and stared toward the invisible demon. "Kip?" Coppy said, and put his paw out.

"I'm talking to you through a demon," Kip said. Coppy withdrew his paw hurriedly.

"We know." Emily kept staring through him. "I wish you would hurry up and learn to translocate."

"I've had a hard enough time learning the things I'm assigned to learn," Kip said. "What's happened?"

Emily and Malcolm both looked at Coppy, and the otter stared down at the table. "Sheriff Winters came looking for you yesterday. He said Alice Cartwright didn't come home from school."

Didn't come home from school. The words were always followed, as they were now, by a pause as everyone digested the name and mentally catalogued them with the list of other Calatians injured, missing, or killed, with a small hopeful notation that there was still time, they might turn up.

"There's more," Emily said tightly. "Farley wasn't at lunch or dinner today."

"Oh, no," Kip said. "No, no."

"Adamson was at lunch." Malcolm rested both elbows on the table, his rough hands clasped together. "But not at dinner."

"We think he went looking for Farley." Coppy still wouldn't look toward the place at the table where Nikolon approximately sat.

"All right," Kip said. "Nikolon, how quickly can you search through the town?"

"Who's Nikolon?" Emily asked.

As quickly as we searched the ruins, master.

"Don't repeat what I say when I address you," Kip said.

"We're not." Malcolm leaned forward. "Listen, Kip, don't you worry about this. We're going to find her."

"No," Kip said. "I mean, thank you, but I have a demon here. I'll find her." Then he said, silently, *Nikolon, let's go.*

In a moment, they'd left the confines of the Inn's public room. If any of his friends had a parting word for him, Kip did not hear it. He described Alice and Farley for Nikolon, enough that the demon would be able to differentiate them from any other human-Calatian pair that was likely to be found.

New Cambridge was not large, but Kip realized quickly that it would take hours for them to go through every room of every building. "You don't have to search houses that have no fire or lamp lit," he said after the third house whose residents were asleep. Nikolon confined their searches to houses where the residents were active, of which there were many fewer, but Kip grew frustrated with this search as well. Farley wasn't going to be in the house of Mrs. Partridge, sitting up to read a paper from Boston. He would be in his mother's house, perhaps, or out near the farm he'd used to own.

Kip directed Nikolon to Mrs. Broadside's house, but she was the only one awake in it, writing a letter by lamplight in her bedroom dressed only in a thin dressing-gown. Kip hastily directed Nikolon to leave, the fox's ears flat with shame at the intrusion.

The demon continued to search through nearby houses while Kip's mind raced, trying to speed up the search. Farley would likely have a fire of some sort, he thought, whether in a lamp or in a fireplace. If Kip were there in person, he could perhaps locate fires through his sensitivity to them, something Master Cott had referred to but had only begun to teach him.

Nikolon. Can you channel my power?

I don't know what you mean, master.

Stop for a moment. The demon obliged, just outside a house where one lamp burned in the upstairs window. Kip focused on that lamp, on the fire within it. He couldn't feel anything from it; it was as though he were trying to feel a drawing of fire in a book. He cast the spell Cott had taught him to increase his sensitivity, and then he could feel the fire, but could not reach out beyond it to find more of them. Frustrated, he told Nikolon to go on.

But in every room, whenever the demon's gaze passed over a flame, Kip reached out to it. He tried the tricks he'd learned over his few months in sorcery: remembering what the flame smelled like, feeling its hunger, losing himself in it. He even tried thinking of the Flower, but none of that worked.

Not until they appeared in the home of the Pendletons, Saul's parents. A modest house, but filled with small ceramic children, which Mrs. Pendleton loved. Mr. Pendleton spent most of his time downstairs in his leather workshop and store, but today he was hunched over a desk, staring at a piece of paper. Neither of Saul's parents had much approved of the time their son spent with Kip, and though he'd tried to visit them after Saul's death, they hadn't received him.

But he had been in their house once, when they were both downstairs in the store, when it was raining outside and Saul had dragged the fox upstairs to get out of the wet and dry his tail by the stove.

Kip pushed the memory away; there was no time for that now. What he noticed was that knowing the room, knowing where the lamp stood and where the fire in it burned, that helped him connect to it. Not enough here to do anything with it, as his knowledge of the room was not quite certain enough. But if he found a place he knew better…

He directed Nikolon to the home of the Coopers, where Tom sat working a piece of wood by lamplight while the noises from the other room suggested that Alicia and David had gone to bed without him. Kip asked Nikolon to shut out the sounds, but to linger in this room. He knew Tom's workroom, had played here when his parents went to Boston. Five years older, Tom was old enough to be a playmate but responsible enough to watch Kip around the sharp woodworking tools, and his mother, like Kip's father, was a calyx (the senior Mr. and Mrs. Cooper had retired to the small apartment in back of the main house two years ago when Tom had taken over the business).

So Kip knew this room well, and now when he tried to reach out to the fire, a faint flicker responded. *Wait*, he commanded, and Nikolon responded that they were already waiting and there was no need to issue an order twice.

Ignoring Nikolon's words, Kip stared into the flame and reached out again. *I know you. I feel you*, he said to it, and now, knowing where it was very precisely in his memory, the response came more strongly: heat and hunger no less fierce for being confined to a glass cage.

Tentatively, he searched outwards, using the Coopers' house as a base and trying to find other fires. For an agonizing several minutes, he didn't think it was going to work. And then, like the stars at twilight, another lamp appeared to him. Then another, and then a fire in a fireplace.

Can you follow my senses to those fires?

Nikolon did not answer immediately. After a moment, they said, *If you command me to follow them by looking into your mind for them, then I will be able to. I am bound by your orders and at this moment I cannot look into your mind.*

Kip took a breath. In his heightened state he knew it would be easy to slip up in his orders, and allowing a demon unfettered access to a sorcerer's mind—he didn't need Odden to tell him how dangerous that would be. But it could mean the difference between minutes and hours in finding Alice.

He thought through his command for a moment, and then reached out to Nikolon. *Follow the flames as I sense them with my mind. Do not look for any more time or matter than is necessary to locate the next flame. And if I tell you to stop, withdraw completely from my mind.*

Yes, master. And they were off toward the nearest flame in Kip's awareness. He continued reaching out to sense more of them, sparing only a moment of attention as Nikolon reached each flame to examine the room and ensure that Farley and Alice were not there.

He had lost count of the number of flames they'd jumped to when his vision opened onto a stall in an old barn, a lantern hanging on one wall. *Stop here*, he said.

I already have, Nikolon replied, and their presence withdrew from Kip's mind.

Alice Cartwright lay with her paws tied behind her back on a bale of hay. Her muzzle was unbound, but she remained quiet; this barn must be on the edge of town and far from the farmhouse that owned it. On either side of another bale of hay, Farley and Victor Adamson stood arguing, Farley holding a long knife in his right hand. Three sheets of paper and an open book lay on the bale, but Kip didn't order Nikolon to move close enough to read them. The mug next to them along with the knife told him all he needed to know.

Can you translocate Alice to her home?

No, master.

Can you paralyze both of those young men?

Not for very long, master. If they are sorcerers then they would be able to break the binding.

Of course Odden wouldn't have given him a demon with any great powers. Kip chewed his lip and thought. Alice was at the back of the stall, so she would have to run out past the two. They could go find the Watch, but how long would it take for the Watch to get to the barn?

Let me hear them.

"—know it still rankles you," Farley said.

"That has nothing to do with it." Adamson looked as furious as Kip had ever seen him. "That is an underage girl."

"It's his bitch," Farley said. "He wants to have a litter on her, he'll be back here soon enough."

"And then what? You're going to try this spell, which you've never cast before? Penfold has summoned demons."

"He won't summon nothin' without a calyx's blood. Which I've got and he ain't got." Farley brandished the knife. "You told me that."

"I told you that I heard he had successfully summoned a demon. I was not witness to it, and Patris did not specify that a calyx's blood was involved. I assumed that blood was involved because it would be extraordinary if he were able to summon a demon without it, and Patris did not treat the summoning as extraordinary."

The knife swung around, glittering in the lamplight. "An' meanwhile he's in London learning what you an' I ought, and if we wait much longer we won't have a chance to give him the skinnin' he deserves. No," Farley said. "We're doin' this now. You don't like it, there's the door."

"I don't like it," Victor said, but he didn't budge. "I've told you, apply yourself to learning magic and I will open doors for you that Penfold has no chance of passing through. This blood feud is going to end with one of you dead."

"See, I knew you was smart." Farley pointed the knife at Adamson's head. "Even if you are pigeon-livered. Bested once by an animal and now afraid of it? That's not how you deal with 'em." He swung the knife to point at Alice. "They think they bested you? You take back twice over from 'em. Show 'em their place and if they won't stay in it, shove 'em back."

"You can't 'shove them back,' as you say, forever. What you can do is keep moving your own place ahead."

"Ha." Farley gestured with the knife. "Maybe such as you can move ahead. I know those like me get left behind. My father served the Empire, died in its service—"

"You've told me."

"—and what did me and my mom get? We got dilberries."

Adamson's face twisted in distaste. "If you'd simply listen to me, you could improve your lot."

"Oh, I tried that. Nearly got meself burnt up, and you tellin' me I'd be safe. Carmichael told me the way you was lookin' at us, how you ran out the back of the tent. Now he's gone an' it's just me, and I'll be twice-damned if I'll let you push me around any more, you cock robin."

Adamson tried to step forward, but Farley spoke a few syllables quickly and raised both arms. They glowed a bright lime green. "Nah, nah, I can still do a few tricks you can't," the heavy bully jeered. "Now, you can walk out on two feet or get carried out with help, and I don't much care if you hit some walls on your way to a pile of horse shit."

Victor took a step back. "How do you suppose Penfold will even know where you are?"

"Oh, I'll tell the demon to go fetch him," Farley said.

"If the summoning even works." Victor straightened, his voice gaining cold bravado. "Simply because Burkle isn't here anymore doesn't mean he's available for anyone to summon."

"It's the only name I got!" Farley shouted, his face reddening. "What of it? If it don't work...I suppose the other animal's told him his broodmare's missing. They notice, y'know. So maybe I got to wait for him to come to me. Don't matter. I can best him once he's here, then he'll watch his bitch bleed and I'll have his tail for my wall."

"Just the tail?" Adamson kept a wary eye on the knife.

"Aye. The rest can go on the dung heap."

Nikolon. Whisper very softly in Alice's ears that she must be ready to run, and then loosen her bonds.

Alice had remained calm through this, though her nostrils flared and her breath came in quick pants. Kip's chest swelled with affection and pride. He had only known Alice as a pleasant, engaging young girl, but her bravery here in front of the men callously discussing her torture and calling her by degrading names would have done credit to anyone Kip knew. He hoped she wouldn't startle too much at the demon's voice.

Again, she comported herself well. A flick of her ear was the only indication that Nikolon had spoken to her, but around her paws and feet, hidden in the shadows from Farley and Adamson, the rope holding her loosened until it hung more like a grotesque decoration than a bond. All through this, her lips moved without sound, probably reciting a prayer.

In the meantime, Farley had threatened Victor yet again, and the blond boy now stood at the entry to the stall, apparently hesitant to leave. Farley, like Kip, thought that Adamson hoped his presence would forestall what he'd planned, so he brayed a laugh. "Watch if you want," he said, and turned toward Alice.

Bind him now!

Farley stopped cold, frozen like a statue. His face twisted into a grimace.

"Alice, run!" Kip called.

She rolled off the hay bale and struggled to get to her feet, but fell again. She tottered toward the mouth of the stall, where Adamson backed up, confusion on his face. But as Alice reached for the frame of the stall door, she too froze in place. Unbalanced, she fell to the hay and lay there motionless.

Sweat dripped from Farley's brow though the night must be cold. "Vermin!" he shouted. "Can't hold me!" His face twisted and then his limbs moved slowly. "Show yourself!"

Adamson ran. Kip cried to Nikolon, *Hold him!*

I cannot, master. He surpasses my abilities.

Farley's arm lowered toward Alice, the knife blade glittering in it. *Make him drop the knife!*

Whatever was holding Farley back gave way, and his arm shot downward, but his fingers flew apart and the knife fell to the floor inches from Alice's muzzle. Breathing hard, Farley knelt and reached out for the blade; as soon as his fingers closed around it, they flew open again. "Right," he snarled. "That's how you wish it."

He recited the syllables again and his arms glowed. Alice came free, struggled to her feet, but the knife was lifting from the floor.

Stop it, hold the knife!

Master—

It wouldn't work, he already knew it. Farley was stronger than Nikolon and the knife was already turning, hovering, following Alice as she pulled herself toward the door and through it and in a moment it would bury itself in her throat.

"No!" Kip howled, and pulled magic into himself from the earth, drew flame from the lantern where it still hung on the wall, and consumed the stall in it.

Only the walls; he did not touch Farley directly, though only with the great restraint Cott had drilled into him. But fire blanketed the walls, caught the hay and the wood, sprang up in the doorway as a barrier that Farley shrank back from. Alice stumbled away from the stall, and Farley, blind now, sent the knife through the air where it embedded itself harmlessly in the opposite wall of the barn.

Stay, Kip told the fire, stay and do not spread. Do not touch flesh, do not go to other stalls, keep him prisoner. Several minutes would suffice for Alice to get away, and—

Find Coppy or Emily or Malcolm, if they are still at the Inn. If not, find any man patrolling the streets with a rifle.

His awareness was wrenched away from the fire, speeding back to the Inn. *No! I need to stay with the fire!*

Master, I cannot occupy two places at the same time.

Kip was panting. *All right. Quickly, see if they're still at the Inn.*

They were not. So Kip directed Nikolon to return to the barn. He didn't know how well the fire would obey his orders if he wasn't in contact with it, and in fact in the few moments he'd been gone, it had spread toward the center of the stall where Farley cringed away from it. The air had grown smoky and Farley was coughing terribly.

Kip reached for the fire and coaxed it back, held it to the stall entrance. And then he heard noises, men shouting at the entrance to the barn, and he brought the rest of the fire down, soothed its hunger, put it to sleep. He waited to see two men of the watch led by Victor Adamson charging into the barn to the stall, and then the energy he'd expended took its toll all at once. He knew he should dismiss Nikolon before falling asleep, so he gathered magic and spoke the dismissal in a fog.

CHAPTER 17: REGROUPING

"Penfold!"

Kip jerked awake. Cott was shaking him by the shoulder. "Penfold."

"I'm awake, I'm—what?"

The sorcerer's sour face and breath receded from Kip's muzzle. "What did you do last night?"

"I—" Kip wiped his muzzle. Maybe it was his breath that was sour. "Let me get some water."

Then he noticed the other two shapes standing against the bright sunlit window. Master Argent's brow was lowered, his normally bright smile gone, and Emily kept twisting her hair around her finger and looking away from Kip. "Emily?" he said.

She half-turned, silhouetting her tunic and skirt against the window, and remained silent. Argent, in his sorcerer's robes, stepped forward. "Mister Penfold," he said. "Please accompany us back to Prince George's. Master Patris wishes to question you about a matter of sorcery that occurred in New Cambridge last night."

"Oh," Kip said. "No, wait. I was helping!"

"I did not say I wished to question you." Argent gestured to the floor. "Collect your things."

He tried to meet Emily's eyes, to glean something from them, but the only time she raised her head to look at him, she had the frustrated expression on her face that she got when Malcolm was being too wordy or too glib. So Kip collected his papers and the vial with Saul's glass bead in it. He rested a paw on the books he hadn't finished reading yet and his bedroll. "Am I to come back?"

Cott, too, looked interested in the answer to this question. Argent said, "I do not know."

"You'd better," Cott snapped at him, and then pointed at Argent. "He'd better."

"If it were my decision," Argent said, and left the statement hanging as he reached out a hand to Kip. "Come, Penfold. Miss Carswell, I will leave you to find your own way back as an exercise."

Kip reached out for Master Argent's hand. "What's—"

"—going on?" he finished in the Great Hall.

"I would prefer to let Master Patris explain the circumstances." But Master Argent waited, looking around the hall.

The elementals stirred in the fireplace. "Penfold?" one said.

"Who'sat?"

"It's Penfold," the first one said. "He's almost a skipper."

Two of the elementals appeared to be new, because another voice said, "Never heard of someone bein' almost a skipper. He's so cold."

"Not when you get to know him."

Emily appeared with an exhalation and a shake of her head. "I know it shouldn't feel different because it's a longer distance," she said. "But it's not even sunrise here and it's midday there and that makes it harder somehow."

"Don't worry about the position of the sun," Argent told her. "You can't appear at the wrong time. Remember, focus on the permanent qualities."

"Thank you." She nodded, still avoiding Kip's eyes, and walked to the basement.

He wanted to call out to her but Argent grasped his arm in that moment and guided him toward the stair. In silence they walked up to the fourth floor and all the way down the hallway to the last door, where Argent knocked. "Come," came Patris's voice from inside.

Argent opened the door for Kip and gestured for the fox to precede him through. The outer room of Patris's office, which in all the other sorcerers' quarters was a dormitory, had clearly been an adjunct office in which he'd added a cot that smelled of Adamson's perfume, though the young man himself was absent.

The outer chamber lacked a brazier, but the chill of that room let onto a warm, stuffy room where Patris sat flanked by two impressive shelves of books, neatly arranged and dusted. To the left stood a cabinet topped with six cubbyholes much like a smaller version of the Post at King's, and to the left of that, a small casement window that was closed, though behind it the outer window stood open. That was likely why the copper brazier holding a phosphorus elemental was placed right there, to counteract the chill outside air that seeped in. The faintly glowing elemental did not lift its head to examine the visitors.

Patris's desk sat clear of all but two pieces of paper, both of which rested under his large right hand. "Stop," he said as Kip reached the center of the room.

Kip obeyed. Beside him, Argent turned to leave, but Patris said, "Argent, stay."

The younger sorcerer stopped a pace behind Kip, who kept his eyes forward, waiting. Patris arranged the two papers in front of him and read through them again before speaking. "I have here statements from Farley Broadside and Victor Adamson, as well as a short report from James Burgher of the Watch." He paused, but Kip didn't say anything, so Patris went on. "Broadside alleges that you, Penfold, became invisible, assaulted him with physical magic, and then set fire to the barn in an attempt to kill him. He says that if the Watch had not pulled him from the barn, he would have died." He turned to the other sheet. "Adamson says that Broadside had abducted a Calatian girl and was intending to use her as a calyx. He witnessed Broadside struggling with a spell and heard a voice that he believes could have been yours, but he also admits that the situation was very stressful and he is not prepared to swear to that."

Not prepared to swear to it, but he had put it in his statement regardless. Or else he'd told Patris and Patris was acting as though it were in the statement. "Adamson also says," Patris went on, "that the fire was extinguished by the time he returned with the Watch. The Calatian had fled and they did not find her. If she indeed existed."

"She did," Kip said as calmly as he could. He could already tell which version of events Patris was inclined to listen to.

"I'm not finished." Patris said. "Don't interrupt again or I'll silence you."

Kip gritted his teeth but held his tongue as Patris went on. "The account of the Watch more or less corroborates Adamson's." He looked up at Kip. "What most interests me is whether you were present in any capacity and what spells you cast."

He waited, but Kip held his tongue until Patris, clearly annoyed, said, "You may speak now."

"Thank you, sir." Kip told Patris as factually as he could of being told of Alice's abduction, how Farley's absence suggested he was responsible, how he had commanded Nikolon to search the town. He left out the way in which he'd used fire to find Farley out of fear that Patris would be intimidated by this power, restricting himself to spells Patris would know he'd learned from the school. "He said he was setting a trap for me, that he wanted to bleed her and cut my tail off. The demon loosed Alice, and I only set the fire to protect her," Kip said. "I didn't let it harm Farley. As soon as he started coughing from the smoke, I pulled the fire back. I didn't even let it consume the wood. Much."

"The Watch noted charring on the stall," Patris said. "The owner of the barn will have to be compensated. But that is almost irrelevant. What matters…" His eyes glittered and a nasty smile spread over his face. "Is that you summoned a demon without the supervision of a master and used it to spy on people, which is expressly forbidden."

"Master Odden didn't tell me that!" Kip cried.

Patris waved a hand, and Kip's muzzle clamped shut so hard that his teeth ached. "What's more," the headmaster said, "you allowed emotion to overcome your restraint, using fire in an aggressive manner and endangering the life of another student."

Maybe Kip should have been more clear about Farley intending to kill him. But it was too late now and very likely it wouldn't matter anyway. He clenched his paws into fists and then forced them to relax. His stomach fluttered but he found he wasn't as nervous as he might have been a month ago. He'd done what was necessary to protect Alice.

"Your apprenticeship here was predicated upon your ability to control and restrain the significant potential you exhibit. Of course this situation was emotionally charged, but sorcery largely takes place outside the classroom. Of course most students must be given time to learn," and here his eyes flicked back to Argent, as if that line were specifically meant for him, "but you have been warned from the beginning of the potential danger of your actions."

Kip tried to talk, but his muzzle was still being held shut. He struggled for only a moment, flattening his ears as Patris went on.

"Therefore, I have no choice but to conclude that no amount of education at this college will be able to help you."

A chill swept through Kip, down to the tip of his tail. Was he going to be sent to King's permanently?

"You are hereby expelled from Prince George's College." Patris waved a hand, the mean smile still in place. "You may retrieve your belongings from the basement after Master Argent takes you to Master Jaeger's office."

To Master Jaeger's…Kip's eyes widened. "No," he said, and found he could talk again. "No, I can go to King's…I don't have to stay here…"

"My decision has been made," Patris said. "If you wish to apply to King's College, of course you may do so. You may even be accepted. But I will be certain to inform them in full of this incident so they are aware of what a volatile personality they are considering."

"I made sure the fire wouldn't hurt him!" Kip couldn't help the sharpness in his voice.

Patris made a threatening gesture, and Kip shut his muzzle. "My decision is final. What you choose to do now is no longer my concern, and I cannot express what a relief that is."

Master Argent took Kip by the arm and gently pulled him back. "What about Coppy?" Kip asked. "He can stay, can't he?"

Patris pushed the papers on his desk to one side and opened a drawer to take out another sheaf of them. He spread them out and examined them as though the fox hadn't spoken. Kip glared at him, but the headmaster didn't look up, and so finally Kip turned and stalked out of the room ahead of Argent, leaving the sorcerer to close the door behind them.

"I am truly sorry about this," Argent said as they walked out to the hall. "I tried to change his mind, you must believe me."

"Jaeger is going to take magic away, isn't he?" Kip asked.

"Yes." Argent pushed Kip gently up the stairs.

The fox resisted. "Can't I get my things first and do that last? Please?"

Argent exhaled a long sigh. "I don't believe there would be any harm in that."

He slowed his pace as he walked down the stairs, taking in every scent and touch on the stone of the Tower so he could fix it in his memory. The Tower was quiet, with most apprentices in with their Masters, and the Great Hall remained empty as he and Argent crossed it to the basement. Even thinking that he might never descend the dank stairs again tightened his throat and made him pause with one paw against the cold wall.

Emily had stirred up a good deal of dust pacing back and forth, and it was from a small cloud of it that she looked up when they entered and then ran to embrace Kip. He returned the hug, and then she stepped back and shoved him in the chest. "What on earth were you thinking, running off without us? We would have helped! We looked all over for you and found nothing, and Malcolm tried every detection spell he could find but you weren't anywhere around. And then you went and set a barn on fire?"

"I rescued her," Kip said. "She's safe. That's what's important." He walked back toward Coppy's bedroll, avoiding looking at Emily because he didn't want to have to say good-bye to her.

"So what happened? Fetching food for the rest of the year? Will they have you do laundry as well?"

Kip found the bag he'd brought his clothes up the hill in. Methodically he packed what little of his things remained while Emily talked, and then picked up one of his spell books.

"That belongs to the school," Argent said softly, apologetically.

Emily came over to stand by Coppy's bedroll, her face flushed. "Kip, what's happening? Why are you packing?"

His eye fell on a little red journal in the bookshelf near his bed. It was important for some reason, he thought, but it probably belonged to the school also. He shouldn't take it. "I'm being expelled," he said dully, turning to Emily.

Her eyes widened and she drew in a quick, gasping breath. "Oh, no no no," she said, and stepped forward to put a hand on his arm. "You can't. I forbid it."

He managed a smile. "You may go plead your case to Patris. I wager you'll have more luck than I did."

She whirled, fingers still closed around his forearm, and opened her mouth to talk to Master Argent, but he already had a hand up. "I have also attempted to sway the headmaster, without any success. Obviously. I would counsel you both to keep quiet and follow his orders—for now. I will talk with Masters Odden and Windsor, and together we may impress upon Patris the importance of having Penfold continue as a student of this college."

"When?" Emily asked. "In a year? Two?"

"The headmaster is stubborn, but not bereft of reason," Argent said. "In the meantime, Miss Carswell, you are free to spend your evenings visiting whomever you choose, as are Lutris and O'Brien."

She whirled back to Kip, standing awkwardly with his bag in one paw. "Where will you go?" she asked. "We'll come see you."

"I…" He shook his head. He could go to Georgia and live with his parents, or possibly he could go back to London if he wanted to attempt to get Cott's endorsement to enrol at King's. Abel might be able to put him up somewhere on the Isle. "I don't know. I'll have to arrange something."

"Tell me as soon as you do."

"I will." He stepped forward to embrace her again and breathed in her scent, fixing that, too, in his memory. She had a light sheen of sweat and dust from all the pacing and worry, which to Kip smelled like friendship and family. "Tell Coppy and Malcolm I'm sorry I didn't get to say good-bye."

"This is ridiculous." She let him go, bracing his shoulders. "Be down at the Inn tonight and we'll meet you there."

"All right," he said. Having a plan for the future, even a rendez-vous in the evening, brought some solidity to his world. He could go to the Founders Rest and wait there until sunset. He had a little money to pay for some ales, which he hadn't drunk in a while but which he felt would be entirely appropriate today.

Argent guided him up the stairs, all the way up to the sixth floor and Master Jaeger's office. It was very much as Kip remembered it, with the Persian carpet, the brazier, the shelves and shelves of scrolls, and the light scent of dust and neglect. Jaeger himself shuffled over from one of the shelves, and Kip, realizing he'd never seen him sit, wondered if perhaps the old sorcerer spent his entire life walking circles around his room. The thought reminded him that he'd rarely seen Master Gugin stand up, and then of the London sorcerer's body dead on his couch. He shuddered and tried to drive that image from his mind.

"Most unfortunate," Jaeger said. "You know, Argent, I wonder that Patris did not ask me to see the truth of the incident from Penfold's point of view."

Neither Argent nor Kip responded to this, and Jaeger gave a wheezy laugh. "I beg your pardon. The humor of an old man must not seem amusing to you at this moment. Of course I do not wonder at that, nor do either of you. And yet here we are, all bound to the orders of a man whose judgment we know to be flawed, eh? And should you wonder, Argent, young Penfold here does have death on his mind, but not that of his fellow student, nor one dealt by his hand. I had not been told of Dmitri's passing."

"I'm sorry," Kip said. "I forgot that he said he studied with you."

"I have lost many friends," Jaeger said with a cough. "Many I did not learn about for years. So consider this a very prompt conveyance of news. I wonder, though, what brought you to my friend's deathbed."

Kip said, "He—" and then thought very deliberately about his lessons with Gugin, the work on spiritual holds. "He was an acquaintance of Master Cott's. I was running an errand for Master Cott."

"Yes," Jaeger said. "I see. Thank you, Penfold. Now, let us get this unpleasantness over with."

He lifted one hand, closed his eyes, and spoke a series of syllables that were completely unfamiliar to Kip. A chill ran through the fox and then Jaeger lowered his arm. "Ah, ah," he said, catching his breath. "I do dislike performing that spell."

Kip swallowed. He didn't feel any different, but when he reached out to the earth for magic, he felt nothing. No power ran to his arms, no purple glow appeared. His fists clenched again and his tail curled up behind him; this was like when he'd woken in Splint's office, but now it would be permanent.

Memory jolted his panic away. In Splint's office—

No. Don't think of it now. He replaced the thought with the memory of the burning barn and Farley's terrified coughing, focused on it as strongly as he could.

"You may escort him out now, Argent," Jaeger said. "Penfold, I wish you the best of luck, and I hope that someday I may resume our acquaintance."

This was it, this severing of his ability from the magic world. At least, he thought, resting against a flowery relief in the hallway outside Jaeger's office, Coppy was still enrolled here, and as long as the otter was here, there could still be a Calatian sorcerer. Kip wanted desperately for it to be him, but if that were impossible, then his best friend was the next best thing. He could even smell Coppy here.

"Come, Penfold." Argent was two steps down already, but Kip brought his nose to the stone of the hallway, down at his waist level. Yes, unmistakable, there was the oily, musky smell of otter. Coppy had been in this hallway.

"Penfold," Argent said gently. "He will not reverse it, no matter your argument."

"I'm sorry, sir," Kip said, and hurried away from the stone.

Argent's mention of reversal led Kip back dangerously close to the subject he didn't want to think about. How far from Jaeger's office was far enough to safely think about things he didn't want the old sorcerer to hear? Gugin had stayed three floors above everyone else, so perhaps the third floor. But as Kip followed Argent down past the fourth floor landing, he remembered that on his previous visit, Jaeger had made reference to Kip's stay in Splint's ward. So he knew, and he hadn't told Argent nor Patris. Would Splint have told them?

Kip focused on the stone as his bare paws touched each step. *Peter? Please, I need your help.*

There was no answer. They descended another level, closer to the Great Hall and the last chance Kip would have to talk to Peter. *Please, please*, he said. *They're going to take all of this away from me if you don't help.*

One more floor. No response. They descended to the Great Hall, Kip holding his breath waiting for an answer. Still the Tower remained silent. "Please," he said to Argent, "may I have a moment to say good-bye to the elementals?"

The sorcerer nodded, so Kip walked over to the fireplace. He leaned on the stone against it and said, "Good-bye, fellows. I hope I'll someday see you again."

As the elementals chorused their questions about where he was going, he pleaded silently one last time with Peter, focusing on the stone. Still he heard no response, so he reached for magic again and again felt nothing, a blank numbness where there had been power. *Peter, I won't have another chance.*

Still there was only silence. "Penfold." Argent rested a hand on his shoulder.

"One more good-bye," he said, his mind racing. "Forrest, in the orchard. I promise I'll make it quick. It's cold out."

"That is outside the Tower," Argent said, "so you may take more time if you wish. But you must leave the Tower now."

On the way back from the orchard, Kip could contrive to touch the wall one more time. He nodded and made his way outside.

Snow covered the ground and got into his pawpads, making him hurry his steps as he ran to the orchard through a brisk, chilly but not cold morning. The trees stood in skeletal lines, frost and snow dotting their branches, shadows in the first light of dawn stretching like bony fingers across the orchard and the wood beyond. Kip reached the edge without seeing any movement amid the harsh shadows; even the birds that filled the air with their song sat fluffed and still in the crooks of branches. He called out, "Forrest?"

A bird took flight. Kip flattened his ears and lifted his nose to the wind. Forrest's distinctive scent was nowhere on the breeze. Where would he be, if not here? It was too early for the dining tent, and he wasn't in his master's office.

Kip recalled again Gugin's body on the couch, and his fur crawled. He took another breath, looked back to Argent waiting on the path, and walked slowly in a circle around the orchard. Two more birds took flight, but nothing stirred between the rows of trees. And then he caught a scent, sweat and earth together. He froze, casting about, but it vanished.

The air had brought the scent to him so he slitted his eyes and stepped forward into the breeze. Ten paces brought him to a snowdrift with an odd, lumpy shape. The scent came to him again as he approached, and when he put his paw to the snow, he already knew what he would find.

Kip waited outside the doors to the Great Hall. When he'd run back to tell Argent about Forrest's body, curled in a fetal position against a tree and frozen nearly solid, Argent had gone to see for himself and then grimly told Kip not to go back into the Tower, but that he could wait inside a tent if he wanted. Kip would not have minded getting out of the wind, but he found a place to stand with his back to the ancient stone where only an occasional breeze caught his ears and nose. He wrapped his arms around himself and looked up as a shadow passed over him. A raven had taken flight from the Tower and now soared for the orchard.

Kip.

He jumped, bringing his body away from the Tower, and then pressed back against it. *Peter?*

He was watching for me, the old one, but he is distracted now.

Warmth suffused Kip. He gasped, sagging back against the stone, and when he reached for magic, it came easily to him. *Thank you,* he breathed.

Extinguish it, Peter said, but Kip was already letting the magic seep away from him. The purple glow around his paws faded and vanished.

Thank you, thank you, Kip said again.

Keep my secret.

I promise.

And then the Great Hall doors opened, and Patris stormed out with Argent at his side. They pushed off from the ground and hovered a foot above the snow, flying out toward the orchard. Kip strained to watch them through the blinding white, but lost them until they returned, the body of Forrest floating at their side with a raven, likely Blacktalon, perched on it. Patris glared at Kip and said something to Argent as he and the frozen body floated into the Hall. Argent stopped and landed on the path near Kip. "Wait out here," he said.

Kip nodded and settled back against the stone. It was cold, but the knowledge that Peter was there and still talking to him allowed him to relax back against it.

A trio of ravens departed the Tower not long after, but no person emerged from it for a good half an hour. Then Patris came out, ignored Kip, and walked to the gates. Feeling invisible, Kip padded around the corner of the Tower and waited while Patris greeted a lanky man who resolved in Kip's eyesight into Sheriff Winters as the two returned to the Tower. "Afternoon, Penfold," Winters said, and turned to Patris. "Penfold involved in all this?"

"He found the body," Patris growled.

"Let's bring him into the Tower where it's warm and we'll conduct our investigation, what d'you say?"

Patris's cheeks grew even redder. "You may question him here," he said. "He's no longer allowed inside the Tower."

"Ah." Winters looked Kip up and down. "At least we could go into one of those tents?"

"Yes, yes. Not that one." Patris gestured at the dining tent. "Lunch will be served soon. But the one beside it, that's fine."

The practice tent still had not been repaired from Adamson's fire. "That'll do just fine," Winters said, so affably that Kip couldn't tell whether he knew about the state of the tent or not.

When they reached the practice tent, the sheriff ushered Kip inside through the burned doorway. "At least we can get a little bit out of the wind," he said, and as he followed Kip in, he went on, "Now what's this about you not being allowed in the Tower?"

"Ah." Kip rubbed his paws together and then reached up to warm his ears. "I've been expelled from the college."

Winters' eyebrows rose. "I suppose the surprise isn't that it happened, but that it took so long, given what I hear from the headmaster."

"I was useful," Kip said. "I obeyed all their rules, until Alice was kidnapped." He couldn't stop himself then, pouring out all his account of the incident to Winters, who listened impassively. "He was going to kill me, and probably her," Kip finished with a snarl. "But they don't care about that. Patris doesn't care about that. He only cared that I broke the rules, even if I had to do it to save a life."

"Well," Winters said, "Speakin' as one who has to keep the peace, we generally frown on breakin' rules as well. There wasn't nothing you could've done but set the fire?"

"I…" Kip shook his head. "I don't think so. Farley's strong at physical magic. I wouldn't have been able to hold him back that way. And I don't know much other magic yet. If I'd learned translocation I could've brought myself here and gotten Alice out easily."

"None of your friends knows that?"

"Emily does. But I didn't know where she'd gone, and Farley was getting ready to cast his spell…" He paused. Could he have called Emily to come help him? He could have. And maybe if he'd not set the fire, if he'd only told her where to go, she could have rescued Alice and he would have been reprimanded only for personal use of a demon. Or maybe not even that, if there were no reason for his presence to be revealed at all. The unfolding of the very simple means by which he could have avoided expulsion tightened his chest again. Why wasn't there a spell to go back in time and undo stupid mistakes?

"Be that as it may, I only want to ask about how you found the body."

Kip nodded, rubbing his eyes. "I wanted to delay leaving. I was saying good-bye to the elementals in the fireplace and as we went out the door I thought of Forrest in the orchard. I'd talked to him and knew him so I wanted to say good-bye to him as well. But he wasn't there. I walked around and sort of caught his scent through the snow. I put my paw into the snow and…" He shuddered. "I touched him. So I told Master Argent and he brought Patris out and they brought him back. That's all."

"Right." Winters scratched his beard. "When was the last time you saw him before today? Alive, I presume."

"Aye." Kip thought back. "It was before Christmas, probably about a month ago. I went out to bring him blankets and I set a fire to try to warm him up, but he didn't like that."

"Mm." Winters looked Kip up and down. "Like setting fires, do you?"

Kip gritted his teeth. "If you've a better way of warming someone quickly, I'm happy to hear it."

"Ah well, I find a nice hot toddy does the trick. But the College is dry, isn't it? More's the pity."

"You'd rather have drunken sorcerers?"

Winters conceded his point with a wag of his index finger. "All that said, Penfold, I won't say that I haven't seen many a sorcerer makin' a show of their magic when there's no need. So you seem to fit in right well with the sorcerers. And if you want to make a job out of lighting fires, I believe Carrier's smokehouse might have a job for you."

"They've stopped me using magic." Kip's heart sped up at the deception. "So I'd have to do it with matches and tinder, the same as everyone. I'm sure there are many in town who'll be pleased by that."

He didn't have to fake the bitterness in his voice. Winters raised his eyebrows again and then nodded slowly. "Reckon there are." He put a hand on Kip's shoulder. "Reckon you best not spare those kind much thought."

"You came up here on their request, back when I was first admitted." Winters had come up on behalf of the town to ask that Kip's matriculation to the College be revoked. Patris's pride had stopped him then from kicking Kip out, though if the headmaster could have looked into the future, the fox thought bitterly, he would have swallowed his pride.

"Aye, I'm bound to do so. Took more pleasure in returning the answer than in carrying the question."

Kip's shoulders sagged. "Thank you," he said.

"Wish you had more t'thank me for." Winters shook his head. "Ought've jailed Broadside a while ago, but his ma a widow and all, what would she have done without him to work their farm? Always held out hope he'd learn a trade and settle down. Not much to be done about it now."

Kip wanted more to be done, but he couldn't see what right at the moment. So he said his good-byes to Winters, but stayed in the practice tent. As long as the investigation was going on, perhaps Patris would forget about him.

Not five minutes later, his name sounded loudly outside, but the voice wasn't Patris's. He poked his head out of the tent, drawing the attention of Malcolm and Coppy, who were standing by the Tower calling. Malcolm, in a thick coat and bright green scarf, reached the tent before the otter did. "Strewth," he said, "we thought you'd be gone already."

"I would be if not for Forrest," Kip said.

Malcolm shook his head. "Saw the body. Everyone heard so we all came down to the Hall and saw him float it through on the way to Splint's office. Terrible thing. Not a surprise, though."

"I suppose not." Kip reached out to hug Coppy. "But why now? We've had colder days."

"A body can only take so much before it wears down, I suppose."

"I'm coming with you," Coppy said.

"What?" Kip pulled away. "No, you have to stay and learn. You're doing better, you said so! If I can't be the first Calatian sorcerer, I'll be happy for it to be you."

The otter shook his head and stifled a yawn. "Windsor's better, but I know enough already. Besides, who's going to take care of you? You've no magic now and Farley's still out there."

"If you leave, they'll take away your magic."

"Not if I go to join the road crew." The otter smiled. "You can come back to the Isle with me. Stay there while I work around London."

It was tempting. "I thought," Kip said slowly, "that if I could keep going, to figure out who attacked the college...I'm so close right now."

"Are you?" Malcolm asked.

Kip patted his bag. "I've got a glass bead here and an idea of how to find the demon that made it. We know someone cast the spell from the sixth floor, and there's the one locked room we can't get into..." He trailed off. The door that had had Coppy's scent on it. "We have so many clues, there has to be something there. I mean..." He lowered his voice and sniffed, but no tingle of demon magic came to him. "If Gugin was killed, then maybe Forrest was too. Maybe they were killed because they have information."

"If they gave you the information," Malcolm pointed out, "then why kill them? Why not kill you?"

Coppy grabbed Kip's arm. "Kip has fire."

"Not any more." He didn't want to lie to Coppy, but it was too dangerous not to, here on the grounds of the College.

"All the more reason you need me to protect you."

Kip shook his head again. "I'd rather you succeed even if it costs my life."

"Don't say that."

Kip wrapped an arm around Coppy's shoulder. "I mean it. I want to learn sorcery more than anything, but if it comes down to you or nobody, of course I want you to succeed. You'll be the sorcerer the young Calatians look up to, the one who inspires them to tell the College they can do magic and demand to be taught. And they'll ask for Master Lutris." Kip forced a smile, looking down at the otter. "Imagine that."

"I don't want to be Master Lutris," Coppy said. "Not if there's no Master Penfold."

"That's silly." Kip hugged him. "You'll be a good sorcerer. And if I can figure out the attack, there will be a Master Penfold. But whatever happens, sorcerer or no, I won't leave your side. Even if I'm powerless." With his friends, he felt the return of the energy that the expulsion had sapped from him.

"Can we have a look at that bead you mentioned?" Malcolm rubbed his hands together.

Kip nodded and rummaged in his bag for the vial. Malcolm peered in as he did. "What's that?" he asked, pointing at a scrap of paper. "List of possible suspects?"

"Demon names," Kip said. "Powerful ones. Too much for me to summon, but I thought they'd be useful."

"Aye, I can see that." Malcolm stared down as Kip brought out the little perfume vial. He took it from the fox and held it up, letting the glass bead rattle inside. "You think this is a clue?"

"It is for sure," Kip said. "It used to be a person."

Malcolm dropped the vial into Kip's bag with an exclamation, and then rubbed his hands vigorously. "Strewth, Kip, you carry around corpses in your bag?"

Coppy, too, was eyeing the bag a bit askance even as he brought a paw to his muzzle again. Kip pulled it against his side. "It's an important clue," he said. "But first, I think I have an idea about what to do about Farley. I'll need Emily, though. Can you all meet me at the Inn tonight? I don't know how much longer I'll be allowed to stay on the hill."

"Not long once Patris remembers," Malcolm said.

"Aye." Kip released Coppy and embraced Malcolm. "Thank you both. I feel much better about this."

They didn't want to leave him, but Malcolm's cheeks and ears grew more and more red and eventually Kip told them to go inside, that he was going to go down to the Inn. Having talked to Peter and gotten magic back, he felt much better about leaving the college now. Especially as the Inn was likely to have a fire on.

By the time Emily, Malcolm, and Coppy arrived at the Inn, Kip had spent a good hour listening to Old John's stories and another two hours composing a letter following the idea he'd had about Farley. Taking any kind of action, even something as uncertain as this, felt good until he could resume his investigation.

"Malcolm said you had a plan?" Emily said without preamble as she sat down.

"What did Sheriff Winters find about Forrest?" Kip asked.

"We don't know. Weren't allowed to hear the results," Malcolm sat down as Coppy did, though the otter sat down more heavily and rested his head on his elbows.

"You all right?" Kip asked, reaching out to the otter's shoulder.

"Mm. Just tired." Coppy waved a paw. "Carry on, I can hear."

Kip pushed the letter he'd written across the table to Emily. "What do you think of that?"

She read through it. "You write very neatly," she said at first, and then, "Do you think this will work?"

"Adamson sounded horrified when he was talking to Farley," Kip said.

Malcolm reached for the letter. "What is it?"

Emily slid it over to him. "Kip wrote a letter from the College informing Adamson's father of what Farley has been doing with the tuition he's been paying." She looked up at Kip. "You should add a bit about how the newspapers might be very interested in how Adamson's money is being spent. Thomas used to threaten people with that and it was very effective. There's the Independent Chronicle and the Boston Herald, those are the ones his clients read."

"Good thought." Kip took the letter back from Malcolm when he'd finished. He worked out the sentences with Emily's guidance and added them to the end. She read it through again and suggested one correction. He complied and then folded the letter and held it out to her.

"I'll need you to bring it to Boston," he said, "and deliver it. Mister Adamson won't listen to me."

"Should we take it now?"

They discussed that for a short time. Mister Adamson might still be at home, and would receive the letter, but it would be more effective if delivered to his place of business. That would mean that Emily would have to miss a lesson in the morning, but it shouldn't take her very long to deliver the letter.

"And then what will you do?" she asked.

Malcolm leaned forward. "Sounded like you had a lead with those glass beads," he said. "What's next with that?"

"A library in London. But I don't know if I can get into it now. Coppy." The otter didn't stir. Kip reached across and shook him. "Coppy."

"Mm what?" Coppy blinked.

"When did you go to the sixth floor?"

"I didn't. I don't."

"Windsor's office is on the third floor," Malcolm said.

"Yeah. Third floor," Coppy murmured. "Roses."

"You'd better get him back before he falls all the way asleep," Kip said. "And come tell me how it went in the morning."

Emily and Malcolm stood, and Emily helped Coppy to his feet. "M'fine," he said.

Kip had never seen his friend that tired. "What have you been doing? Running up and down the hill?"

"Studying hard and waking early," Malcolm said. "Pleasing a taskmaster like Windsor takes it out of a man. What you going to do now, Kip?"

Kip glanced around the Inn. "Find somewhere to sleep for the night. Get up in the morning and maybe..." He stood with his friends and took Coppy's other side from Emily. "If I can get back to London, maybe look in the library."

Emily sighed. "I'll bring you a book on translocation and you can teach yourself."

"That would be all right. But don't get in trouble."

Malcolm, behind them, said, "Kip doesn't have magic anymore. Don't taunt the fellow like that."

They reached the door and turned to maneuver Coppy's dragging steps through it. Emily sighed. "I'm sorry. Of course I'll take you to London."

"I'd take a book as well," Kip said. "I'd love to learn translocation, at least memorizing the spells so when I come back to school, I'm ready. Even if it takes me months after that."

"It might take you longer to be readmitted than to learn the spell." Emily stopped at the base of the hill. "It only took me five weeks and you're better than I am."

"Not at translocation." Kip's tail wagged to see Emily's proud smile. "But I was doing something similar with fire, last night—was it just last night?"

"Oh? Did you bring that fire in the barn from elsewhere?"

"No, but I was...talking to fire over long distances."

Her eyes flashed with sudden interest. "Do you mean you could talk through fires?"

"No, but—" Kip stopped. "Maybe? That's an interesting idea. I don't think fire perceives sound. It's all about consuming."

"Rather like Broadside himself." Malcolm came up on Kip's side. "I'll take our friend the rest of the way up."

"No." Emily took a breath and gathered magic, her arms flickering with lavender light. "I'm not carrying him up that hill. Malcolm, I'll see you tomorrow."

"Aye," the Irishman said, but before he'd raised his hand, Emily and Coppy were gone. He turned to Kip. "Palling around with sorcerers, I ask you. I wish I had a flashy talent like fire or translocation. All I can do is lock doors and stop spells, and that not well."

"That's valuable enough," Kip said. "That's the kind of thing that will save lives."

"Hopefully never need to use it for that. Rather come up with new and better spells for the people who do need it." Malcolm kept his cheerful smile on but his eyes told Kip he knew how vain his hope was. "All right, I should get up to bed m'self. Not as badly used as our otter friend, but we've been working hard all the same and I need my sleep if I've any hope of producing a decent counterspell tomorrow morning for good Master Vendis."

"Go on then," Kip said.

Malcolm put a hand on his shoulder. "Where you going to sleep?"

Kip folded his ears back. "Emily reminded me of the old barn. I thought I might go see if that's abandoned."

His friend remained quiet, but the downcast turn of his mouth and eyes told Kip what he thought of that. The fox smiled. "It's all right," he said. "It will smell bad, but at least there'll be hay."

"I suppose." Malcolm's expression didn't match his words. "I'll bring some food down from lunch if you've a mind to wander over this way."

"I could do that, aye," Kip said. "I'll be anxious to hear of Emily's progress."

He wanted to tell Malcolm not to worry, that he could light a fire to stay warm, but again he didn't quite want to give away his ability to do magic yet. So he settled for a warm good-bye and then set off in the night to find the old barn where Farley had taken Alice.

Without fires and Nikolon, it took him half an hour, even with the cloud-covered moon providing an adequate amount of light. The barn still smelled of smoke, but he found a stall where Farley's scent didn't cling, and the smoky smell reassured him, reminding him of Cott's workshop. What would the fire sorcerer be thinking now? Had he been told of Kip's dismissal? Would he think Kip had simply abandoned him? No, he'd seen Master Argent and Emily come and take Kip back, so probably he would assume Kip had been returned to Prince George's, unless he were told otherwise. And if he hadn't been told, how long could Kip study there before word got back across the ocean? Patris had to know that Kip had friends who could translocate, and in fact Argent had brought Emily over with him.

Had Argent done that on purpose, so Emily would be able to bring Kip back? The fox lay back on the straw, warming it with his body even though the air remained cold. What allies did he have in the College still? Vendis, most likely. Argent, perhaps. Odden, he hoped. There was an outside chance that Windsor remained on his side. At least Windsor remained dedicated to teaching Coppy. He wasn't sure what any of them could do, but it was important that whatever he did, Kip not alienate them.

Coppy. The otter had been so exhausted tonight. Was he like that every night? Emily and Malcolm hadn't acted as though it were peculiar at all. But Coppy had always had so much energy that if Kip hadn't been so absorbed in getting the letter to Mr. Adamson right, he would have been more concerned. And what's more, the otter had seemed scattered, doing things like repeating himself about the lessons with Windsor. Now, looking back, Kip felt guilty about letting his closest friend sleep without asking why he was so tired.

And how had Coppy gotten up to the sixth floor to get his scent on the door? The only times he wasn't with Malcolm or Emily was during his lessons with Windsor.

Kip sat up. What if Master Windsor were taking Coppy to the sixth floor, and there doing something that tired him out. But that the otter didn't remember? That implied that Windsor had spiritual magic, strong enough to make Coppy forget their sessions. What could Windsor be doing with Coppy that would take this much time, though? Obviously he needed the otter for something, and if he were the one who'd orchestrated the attack… he could be researching ways to finish the job.

And Kip had told him there was a spirit in the Tower.

Peter's words echoed in his head: *Keep my secret.* He flexed his fingers, itching with the need to go now, to somehow remedy that mistake. But there was nothing he could do right now, nothing except keeping Coppy away from Master Windsor (and how would he ever manage that?). He would have to convince Emily, then they could transport Coppy somewhere. Perhaps London, if Master Cott were amenable.

Kip did not sleep well, tossing and turning, getting hay in his nose and sneezing several times. Each time he waited, listening, but nobody walked by this barn at night unless they were being led here to investigate a crime, it seemed. Several times he thought he saw glimmers of dawn, stood up, and found he was mistaken.

Finally, after a few fitful hours of sleep, he woke to find the barn lit by the soft light of morning coming in the open front. The fox sprang to his feet, performed a basic toilet on his fur and clothes, and then hurried down to the Inn to wait for Emily.

CHAPTER 18: ALICE

The Founders Rest hadn't opened yet, so he waited against one of the maple trees at the bottom of the hill, rubbing paws up and down his arms and hopping from one foot to the other to keep his blood warm and moving. The streets of New Cambridge already bustled with people, and smoke rose from all the chimneys, dominating the other scents in the air. Only a few people came up to the Founders Rest, and none of those ventured beyond, though Elizabeth Scour, the mouse who cleaned rooms for them, waved at Kip as she walked around to the back entrance.

Old John threw the doors open as soon as the church bells tolled Matins, letting in the three people huddled outside. Kip's ears were cold enough that he considered going in to warm up, but then he would feel obliged to buy something (and what's more, his empty stomach would urge him to). His supply of money was limited and now he wasn't getting free meals at the school, so he felt very frugal at the moment.

For an hour he walked back and forth between the maple trees, looking up at the patterns their branches made and going over his revelations of the night before. In the light of day, he tested his theories. Coppy had been on the sixth floor; Kip was certain of having smelled him there. But Coppy didn't remember going to the sixth floor. He had to have gone during Master Windsor's sessions with him. He couldn't see any other way around that.

Every time he crossed between trees, he looked up at the hill where the Tower was framed between the stark, bare branches. Finally he saw a person walking down toward him in a white dress and brown skirt, and he hurried up to meet Emily. "Good morning," she said, took him by the paw, and before he had a chance to answer, they were in the basement of the Tower.

"Hallo," Betty said cheerfully, coming up to the edge of the binding circle.

Emily released Kip's paw. "I'm sorry for not asking," she said, "but this way it's not your fault, you see, it's mine. I wasn't going to stand outside and have a whole conversation in the wind and cold, and besides, Betty asks after you constantly and so here you are."

"Thank you." Kip sat as close to Betty as he dared, and she curled up at the edge of the clear area, warming him considerably. "So how did it go with Adamson?"

"Well." She brushed down her shirt and skirt, which Kip now saw were the finest ones she owned. "Better than we'd hoped, in fact. I had thought that I would most likely have to leave it with a secretary. But he wasn't busy first thing in the morning, and I think I made an impression on the men in his office." She brushed back a lock of hair from her forehead. "So he received me personally. I said that I knew his son from Prince George's College and that I bore a letter from the college regarding his son's best friend. Oh, don't look at me that way. The letter was from the college, just not the College."

"I'm not arguing with your rhetoric, simply admiring it."

The door opened abruptly. Both of them turned, staring, but it was only Malcolm. He slipped in, then turned and cast a spell on the door. "There. Won't be disturbed now."

"Where's Coppy?" Kip asked.

Malcolm brushed his hands against each other. "Still at his morning lesson, I'd wager. I told Master Vendis I felt quite unwell and he's released me, and if Coppy does the same with Windsor as we arranged, he'll knock and I'll let him in."

"With Windsor?" Kip sprang to his feet, his tail sending papers flying. Betty leapt on two that came within her reach. "We've got to go get him."

Both Emily and Malcolm stared at him. "Whyever for?" Emily said.

"Windsor's the one who planned the attack."

There was another moment of silence, and then both of them chorused, "No, no."

"How did you come up with that?" Emily said faintly. "Windsor has been horrible at times, but he Selected Coppy."

"He's using him to come up with some spell to break the Tower's defense," Kip said. He pointed at the basement door. "I smelled Coppy up on the sixth floor, but he swore he'd never been there. Windsor's making him forget."

"That's curious, to be sure." Malcolm walked around to stand beside Emily. "But what if something Coppy touched was up in that hallway. Would that smell different?"

"Yes," Kip said, but now his memory wondered. What if someone had taken one of Coppy's tunics up there and it had rubbed against the stone? "It wouldn't be as strong. I can tell the difference."

"There could be any number of reasons for that." Emily didn't sound convinced.

"Like what?"

Malcolm shrugged. "Maybe that's where he takes people for untoward activities. Doesn't want to besmirch his office, does he?"

Emily made a face. "Or Coppy could have gone up there once and Master Jaeger made him forget. It doesn't have to have been with Windsor."

Jaeger...what could Coppy have seen? The old sorcerer was temperamental, but he'd seemed very respectful of people's minds, just as Gugin had been. "I don't think Jaeger would have done that."

"Jaeger, whom you've met once? Twice? As opposed to Windsor, whom we practically lived with? You think it more likely that Master Windsor has been plotting the demise of the College for months?" Emily shook her head. "You're desperate to solve this mystery so you can come back, and you've seized on the first idea you had. Think this through, Kip."

Kip sighed. "Maybe you're right. I don't know." He paced back and forth. "Coppy was so tired last night. Is he always that tired now?"

His friends exchanged a look. "No," Emily said. "But maybe once a week or so he's exhausted all day."

"You said Coppy's with Master Windsor now, right?"

"Aye," Malcolm said.

"All right." He stood with his feet pressed to stone. *Peter? Can you see my friend?*

Silence. He asked one more time, and again got no answer. But he knew there was a way he'd thought of to go around the school unnoticed. Why couldn't he think of it now?

"I have to show you two something," he said, and as they watched, he reached into the earth and gathered magic. Purple light bathed his arms, eliciting a gasp from Emily and a curse from Malcolm.

"You're not supposed to have magic," the Irishman said.

"I know. Jaeger...didn't quite do it properly." Kip recited the spell to break a spiritual hold. It can't hurt, Jaeger had told him, and it might help if things didn't seem right.

"What are you casting?" Malcolm took a step back.

"That's why I don't think Jaeger did it," Kip said. As he finished the spell, he remembered clearly the red journal and what he could do with it. "Malcolm, open the door, and leave it open until I get back."

"You can't go out into the Tower," Emily said.

"Have you cast an invisibility spell?" Malcolm asked curiously, going over to the door and releasing the binding on it. "I thought Broadside was inventing stories to cover his own failures."

Kip walked over to Coppy's bedroll and pulled the red journal from the bookcase, breathing in the otter's scent. "Better," he said, but they were already turning toward each other and engaging in conversation about him and what they were going to do now that he'd been sent away. Kip hurried out the door, not wanting to hear too much of this discussion. Betty followed him with her eyes but didn't say anything as he eased his way through the door.

As quietly as he could, he padded up the stairs and through the Great Hall, which was fortunately empty. His nose tingled there, but he edged away from where the tingle was strongest and got to the staircase, where he stopped dead. Master Splint was descending the stairs and had almost reached Kip.

The fox stepped back to one side, and Splint walked to avoid him. "Afternoon," the red-haired sorcerer murmured.

Kip nodded and set his foot on the stair, listening. No other footsteps sounded, so he walked quickly up the first flight, then the next. At the second floor, he had to avoid Master Patris and Victor Adamson leaving the library, but the stairs were unoccupied going up to the third floor. There he crept along the hallway to Master Windsor's office, listening at each door. At the third door, he heard Master Windsor's voice, and he waited.

Finally, there was Coppy responding. The otter sounded as though he were still tired, but it was him. It was hard to make out the words, but Kip thought they were working on a translocational spell.

Holding the red journal, he sagged back against the wall. So Windsor did bring Coppy to his office, at least some of the time. He could go back now...

But he wanted to know.

Ears and nose alert, he climbed three more flights of stairs and reached the flowery relief on the sixth floor: roses with a tangle of thorny vines around them. And—he bent to the flowers again—yes, Coppy had rested his paw here, or more likely leaned his whole body against this wall.

There was Jaeger's door, and beyond it two more doors in the hallway. Kip padded past Jaeger's to the second one and sniffed it, getting a nose full of dust and a little bit of Coppy's scent. He might have gone on to the third door? But no, there Kip caught only the scent of a human he didn't know. One of the masters he hadn't met; perhaps Barrett, if the spiritual sorcerers here followed Gugin's habit of living as high and far from everyone else as possible.

He returned to the second door. The paneling was covered in dust so thick he could barely see the painting on it of a knight in silver armor atop a white horse. But when his finger dropped to the brass door handle, he found it clean.

His heart sped up. He put his ear close to the door and heard nothing, and no scents came to him through the crevices that seemed strange in any way. When he tried the door, he found it locked, of course, probably magically as well as mechanically. But when he bent to the handle, there he caught a human scent, and it was one he knew well, because its owner had visited their basement often.

Emily and Malcolm didn't notice him when he slipped back in through the basement door. Malcolm had her hand in his and was talking in a voice too low for Kip to hear if he folded his ears back, which he did as he padded over to replace the journal in the bookshelf. Then he stepped out into the open and cleared his throat.

The two of them jumped apart. "Strewth," Malcolm said. "Where did you pop up from?"

"Magic," Kip said. "Not mine. I can't explain it, but—Windsor and Coppy were both definitely on the sixth floor."

Emily glanced up and then back down at Kip. "Are they there now?"

"No. But…" He stopped as she shook her head.

"We can't go and tell anyone that you smelled a couple things on the floor. Remember all the times Farley left his odor around? And that's powerful enough that even I can smell it sometimes."

Kip's tail lashed behind him. "Yes, but—we have to. Coppy could be in danger. He is in danger. I'm sure of it."

"Look." Malcolm stepped forward and clasped Kip's forearm. "If he's survived this long, he'll survive another day or week. But Emily's right. We need to find them in that room and find out what they're doing."

Kip bared his teeth. "My friend is being used up there—"

"He's our friend too," Emily said just as heatedly. "And he's being used in a way that a lot of people are used without it endangering their lives. I'm not happy about it by any means, but if we act before we're sure, we might make things worse."

In that moment, he wanted to be as tall and imposing as Grinda, to growl his urgency to them. But the moment passed; Kip stepped back and breathed in, forcing himself to relax. He needed Emily and Malcolm's help, and as much as he wanted to rush upstairs and save Coppy now, they were right. The otter probably wasn't going to die today, and if they wanted to be sure of what they were doing… "Yes," he said. "Fine. All right. But as soon as possible."

"Of course," Malcolm said. "But measure twice, cut once, you know?"

"Aye." Kip sat tiredly and looked up at them. He remembered then that they'd been holding hands, and pushed himself back to his feet. Likely they wanted to be alone.

"You didn't let me tell you the rest of what happened with Mr. Adamson," Emily said.

Kip sat again, ears perked, and Malcolm and Emily sat across from him. "He read the letter," Emily said, "and when he got to the part about the newspaper, he got very cold. You remember him," she said to Kip. "I thought he might turn red. Thomas said they did sometimes. But he merely pursed his lips and lowered those neatly trimmed eyebrows and then he asked me if I personally had witnessed any of this. I thought it would be better to be honest, so I told him that a person I trusted greatly had witnessed it and would swear to it.

"He made me wait while he dictated a response to his secretary. I wasn't meant to hear any of it—or maybe I was." She smiled. "He wrote two letters and I was to deliver them both to his son. One was to Victor, telling him that there had been reports of his friend's behavior made and that if they were true, Victor was to give the second letter to the headmaster. If they were not, Victor was to write back immediately and Mr. Adamson would engage an investigator to determine the truth of them. He stressed that this would be a great expense which he implied Victor might be responsible for."

Kip's tail thumped a pile of papers. "It worked? I hoped, but..."

"It was a good plan."

"Your idea about the newspaper was good too. It sounded like that made a difference."

She nodded. "In any event, the second letter was to Patris and was very short, simply telling him that no more tuition would be paid for our Mr. Broadside."

Kip squeezed his paws together. "Did you give the letters to Adamson? What did he do?"

"Of course I did." She drew her knees up. "He looked uncannily like his father when reading the letter. But at the end of it, he merely nodded and didn't look me in the eye at all. He took the letter that was meant to go to Patris and said, 'Thank you.'"

"So he took it to Patris?"

"I don't know for certain, but I believe so."

Malcolm shook his head and whistled. "You two cooked up a better plan than I did."

Kip flicked his ears. "What was yours?"

"Ah." Malcolm waved a hand. "There's naught will come of it now, so it's best left back in my head where it started. Truth be told, I was thinking better of it today and wondering whether I could—aye, but if Broadside's given the boot, that'll take care of it as well or better than I could have hoped."

Emily frowned. "What did you do last night?" But Malcolm wouldn't tell her, though color rose in his cheeks and Kip wondered what he could possibly have done that would be so embarrassing he wouldn't tell the two of them.

Emily didn't want to send Kip back to the barn, but he insisted. "I can't stay in the basement," he said, though he was tempted to keep Peter's journal on him and see how long he could evade notice.

"I didn't mean that," she said. "You should go to Boston and see our friends there."

He understood what she meant, though he was amused at her sudden shift to talking obscurely after they had been discussing the possibility that a master was involved in treason, not to mention that he wasn't supposed to be on the College grounds at all. "I think I can do more good here," he said.

"I'd bring you there and then back." Her eyes brightened.

He shook his head. "I'm less convinced than before that our current friends are as good as I thought. I've talked to a lot of people and heard a lot of arguments. But I'm not ready to run to Boston yet."

"They could teach you magic. You can't stay here, and you probably can't go to King's."

He nodded. "But I don't want to make that choice just because that's the only place I can learn magic."

Emily folded her arms. "That's how you were choosing sides a month ago."

"No," he said, and then stopped. "Well, maybe yes. But—I want to talk to Abel again. I want to think about the things we're fighting for, come up with a list of concrete ideas to implement, and then talk to your Boston friends and sound them out on it."

She frowned. "You want to prepare a list of demands?"

Malcolm put a hand on Emily's shoulder. "You can lead a fox to water, but the decision to drink rests with him."

Kip snorted, and Emily glared, though she didn't remove Malcolm's hand. "So the cause is all about what they can do for you?"

"Yes." He tilted his head. "Isn't that what it's about for you?"

"No!"

"The right to own property, the right to vote? You'd support them even if they weren't advocating those things for women?"

Her lips tightened until Malcolm squeezed her shoulder. "He's got a fair point," the Irishman said. "And it's naught to be ashamed of. People might claim the noblest of causes, but often when it comes down to it, they're fighting for their own gain. And aye," he went on as she turned her glare on him, "freedom from mistreatment is a gain just as surely as the right to vote."

"All right, you two." Emily pushed Malcolm's hand off her shoulder.

"Anyway," Kip said. "I want Coppy safe before we go do anything else."

"They might help with that."

"And what if they're the ones behind it?"

Emily rolled her eyes. "Get him some food," she told Malcolm.

With a loaf of bread and a lump of cheese, Kip walked back from where Emily had left him outside the Founders Rest to the old barn, which in the daylight looked even more decrepit. Many of the timbers had rotted through, and others had been scavenged for buildings. Kip didn't know who owned this barn, though he thought the land belonged to the Oswald family, whom he knew from their occasional forays into his father's perfume shop. This was not a part of town where many Calatians lived, and the Oswalds did not hire any to work their land, as they had three families who each had multiple children. Perhaps they had once owned horses and given them up for the more lucrative farming of sheep, who did not need shelter in a barn.

The hay in the barn snapped rather than bent and smelled dusty and ancient, with a little bit of mold. But the inside roof remained surprisingly sound, so several of the stalls had not gotten wet at all this winter.

He didn't mind the hay and the dirt, not today. Farley would be expelled from the college when Patris learned there was no more tuition for him, and over the next few days they would make some plan to catch Windsor and save Coppy.

The bread and cheese tasted wonderful to his ravenous appetite, and even though he'd intended to keep some for dinner, he ended up eating all of it. There wasn't really a place he could have stored it or set it down anyway, he told himself, licking his fingers. And he would meet his friends tomorrow and hopefully they would bring him more food. He didn't like being dependent on them, but it wouldn't be for much longer.

To keep his mind busy, he worked on small, precise bits of fire magic that Cott had been teaching him: igniting dust particles (which would be good for a quick, low light and also for cleaning, if he were so inclined), and creating a small intense flame in the middle of one piece of hay. It wasn't that he was afraid of setting the barn on fire; he had never been less afraid of fire in his life. But a large fire or a large amount of smoke might attract attention if someone from New Cambridge was looking in the right direction at the right time, and Kip didn't know how long he was going to have to stay here.

The idea of going to Boston continued to occupy his mind. The treatment of Calatians on the Isle of Dogs was terrible; he had thought New Cambridge the norm and was now forced to acknowledge that it might be an exception. In that light, the promises of the revolutionaries sounded at the same time both more fanciful and more important. Their promises for Calatians had felt unattainable to New Cambridge-raised Kip; when presented to Coppy or Abel, they would seem ludicrous. And yet, they were addressing the problem, which the Empire showed no signs of doing that Kip could see. Even if all Calatians were only raised to the life that the New

Cantabrigians had, that would be a vast improvement in the world.

Likewise, the idea of starting something new appealed to Kip, who had already broken barriers, but at the same time the difficulty in taking the one large step of becoming the first—second— Calatian sorcerer made him aware of how great the challenges would be to smash the entire system and start over. He had been making progress, and all hope was not yet lost, but if the government he was impressing was done away with, what proof did he have that he could duplicate that process in a new Colonial government? One day of promises from men who desperately needed someone to set fire to opposing armies? Emily believed in the goodness of those men and had faith in their promises, but to Kip they were still merely men.

These were the thoughts he turned over in his head as he cleared his stall of dust, burned hay stalks into smaller and smaller halves, and wished he'd saved some of the food Malcolm had given him. As night fell and he had no word from his friends, he began to reconsider his decision not to go to Boston, because he felt sure that at least there he would have had a warm bed.

The sun had fully set when movement outside brought his ears perked to full alertness. He cursed the smoke and still cold air that stopped him from smelling who was approaching, but the person was small, to judge by their footsteps. Kip had magic gathered and ready when Alice Cartwright's voice called out his name.

He relaxed, sagging back into the hay, then scrambled to his feet and dispelled the magic just as she came around the corner. She was humming a tune he didn't recognize, wearing a wooden necklace of beads and a plain tunic cinched around her waist so that it almost looked like a dress. "Hallo, Kip," she said, her tail wagging.

"Hello," he said. "How did you know where I was?"

"I went to the College to look for you and the nice young man at the gate brought out a sorcerer who went and fetched Emily, and she told me." She scratched her whiskers. "I think the young man was a demon," she said. "He wasn't wearing shoes."

"What do you know about demons?" Kip asked with some surprise.

"Pearl Cooper at school told me. She said that I'm engaged to a sorcerer and that means I'll have to lie with a demon as well, and I didn't know what a demon was, so she said they're spirits brought to this world to do the bedding of sorcerers. And I said it didn't sound very logical that a sorcerer would make a demon do his bedding for him, but she said sorcerers were strange." Her bright golden eyes met Kip's. "But of course we couldn't have cubs if you did that."

"No," Kip said. "She may have meant that they do the *bidding* of sorcerers. But no, you would not have cubs from a demon, if such a thing is even possible."

"And that's the reason we were engaged. All of that 'Will of Calatus' they say at the Festival." She looked away from him, around at the stable. "This can't be very comfortable."

"It's fine." He smiled. "Thank you for coming."

"I wanted to thank you for rescuing me."

"You were very brave," he said.

She leaned against the wall, her tail still swishing. "I don't know about that. I wasn't really afraid." Now she turned his way, and his astonishment must have shown, because she smiled. "I wasn't. Not until he said he was going to try to kill you, and then I was worried for you, but I also know you're very clever, and I felt sure you wouldn't just walk into his trap. I thought at first that he was going to force himself on me, and I didn't want that, but I knew I would survive it. Pearl did."

Kip sucked in a breath and nodded. The thought of Farley forcing himself on Alice made his fists tighten. If he'd witnessed anything like that, there might well have been a murder to answer for. A moment later he took in the rest of what she said. "Pearl was…?"

"Yes. Three of my friends have been this year." Alice said it matter-of-factly. "Never by him, but it happens if we don't go around in a big group or with our parents. But I didn't come here to talk about the horrible things we have to endure. You certainly have to endure things as well."

Maybe if he'd had his tail stolen, that violation would compare. But Kip made himself return her smile. "We're hoping that in the future, we won't have to endure as much. And our children even less."

"Yes," Alice said. "I did come to tell you that Papa has called off our engagement. He's writing to Boston again. There was a fox family there."

"Ah." Kip leaned against the wall. "That's probably for the best."

"I don't think so." Alice folded her arms and kept her ears up, tail swishing behind her. "I don't think it's for the best at all. I haven't met many other foxes, but I can't imagine one who'd be a better father for my cubs than you. And what's more, I like you. You're always kind to me and I think you're very clever. I said that already. I asked Papa to change his mind, but I don't think he will. Still, I thought you should know that I would still marry you."

"Thank you," Kip said. His mind traveled to the Isle. Maybe Abel had a female relative who wouldn't mind marrying a sorcerer.

Now Alice kicked at the straw on the floor. "I thought that maybe you could come live with me and my husband, if I can't marry you. Not all the time. I know you must stay up in the Tower. But when you wanted to get out of it, like when I want to get out of my house and take a walk, you could come stay with us. Like the Coopers, or the Ashers."

"David Cooper and Carrow Asher are different species from the other Coopers and Ashers, though," Kip said. "Three foxes? People would wonder whose cubs yours were."

"I suppose you're right." She sighed. "Bloodlines and all. I do wish Papa would see that what matters is you and not his prestige or my standing or anything like that."

"What matters is our cubs. Your cubs." Kip's tail uncurled, relaxing.

"Yours, too." Alice reached a paw out to him. "You'll find someone, I know you will. Someone whose father appreciates you."

He took her paw and held it. In the cold barn, her warmth anchored Kip. He chuckled softly. "It's funny. I never really knew you. I just knew we had to have a family, because that's what we do. I pursued the engagement because it was important to my parents."

"And mine," Alice said. "Don't feel bad. I didn't know anything a year ago."

Kip smiled. "But now that we're not engaged, this is the time I discover that you're someone I would very much like to get to know better."

She squeezed his paw. "You are older than I am. You've had more time to do things."

"When I was fourteen, I wasn't half as clever as you are now." Kip shook his head. "I spent most of my wits not getting my tail cut off, or worse."

"Does that mean I'll get even more clever?" Alice's tail wagged faster.

"Hard to imagine," Kip said.

She squeezed his paw again. "I meant to ask, what were those things he said before he tried to cast a spell?"

Kip thought back. "Oh. That's a bunch of nonsense sounds that help you focus on reaching magic to start with. Most of us don't need to speak them anymore, but Farley isn't exactly full of cleverness."

"I don't know anything about how magic works." Alice looked down, scuffing her feet through hay.

"Those sounds are part of how it starts, and there are a lot of different ones. If one set doesn't work, you can try another. Coppy tried three before he found one that worked."

"And you just say them and then you can cast spells?"

"You have to find magic first, and it's...down in the earth, sort of. It takes you a while to get to the point where you can feel it, but when you learn, it becomes...like breathing, almost."

"Oh." She went back to humming, and after a moment said, "I think it's wonderful that you've worked it out. The way you made the fire appear..."

"Fire is what I have an affinity for," Kip said. "For whatever reason, I understand it."

"Mm."

They stood there, paws linked, for several more minutes. Finally, Alice interrupted her humming with a sigh. "Mama will be wondering where I am. May I come see you again some evening?"

"I don't know how long I'll be here," Kip said. "But it won't harm anything if you come by and I'm not here."

"All right, then." She reached out to hug him.

He returned the embrace. "Thank you for coming."

"Stay warm," she said. "But don't start a fire too large."

CHAPTER 19: TRUST ISSUES

Over the next few days, Kip remained mostly around the barn. Emily and Malcolm visited, bringing Coppy once, on the day that Farley was gone from the school. "Packed and left last night as far as we can tell," Malcolm said, "and if we were allowed ale I'd have God's own punishment for it this morning."

"Expelled?" Kip asked.

"Nobody knows." Coppy leaned against the fox, "and Patris isn't saying. Adamson won't say either."

"But he's already tried to be friendly with us today. Jacob Quarrel wouldn't have anything to do with him." Emily's upturned nose told Kip that Adamson hadn't fared any better with her.

"I can't believe he's gone." Kip exhaled. "And magicless."

"I know." Coppy grinned. "It's like Christmas."

The otter stayed awake and kept his head up, which made Kip happy, but he and Malcolm and Emily couldn't discuss their plans for Windsor in front of Coppy, and they all badly wanted to.

And once again, after Coppy visited, Kip wanted to take the otter away from Windsor immediately. On their next visit, Emily and Malcolm convinced him to wait. "We're watching him," Malcolm said. "Every time

I'm working with Master Vendis, I tell him I have to use the necessary and then I go to see if Coppy is in with Windsor in his third floor office."

"Isn't Master Vendis getting suspicious?" Kip asked.

Malcolm laughed. "He's told me to use the necessary before our lesson, and today he told me that I might want to visit Master Splint for a look at my nethers. But every day they've been on the third floor."

"If they're not," Emily put in, "he's to come down to where I'm working with Master Argent and make some excuse why I'm needed."

"I decided to tell Master Argent that her mother is here for a visit."

"Don't forget to tell him how much she's missed me all these months," Emily said with more than a trace of sarcasm.

"Divorce and then magic school." Malcolm shook his head. "Past redemption, you are."

"At any rate." Emily smiled. "We'll come fetch you and take you to the basement and then you can do your disappearing trick that you won't tell us about."

"If I told you, you'd just forget about it," Kip said. "It's not my magic and I don't understand how it works."

"Yes, fine."

Malcolm raised a hand. "So you see, we're all prepared, and one more untoward expedition…" He snapped his fingers. "We'll get him."

"The only question is," Emily said, "which of the masters we should bring along. We can't apprehend Windsor on our own."

"Not Patris." Kip shuddered.

"Obviously. Vendis or Argent might be best."

Kip rubbed his chin. "If we asked Master Jaeger, he might have the best chance of stopping Windsor. He can do things to people's minds."

"Any sorcerer can stop another with the element of surprise."

"But if Windsor is making Coppy forget, he has spiritual magic," Kip pointed out.

"Ah, he has the right of that."

"But what if Jaeger is the one behind it?" Emily asked.

Malcolm summed up their dilemma. "The same could be said of any master from New Cambridge." And he looked at Kip.

Kip drummed his claws against the wall. If they were to ask sorcerers from outside Prince George's, he had really only three choices with Gugin gone. Cott would likely come along, but he would also be unpredictable and mercurial in mood. Headmaster Cross might come, as he'd seemed well disposed to Kip, but also he was likely very busy and Kip would have to spend a great deal of time explaining the situation. "I could ask Master Albright," he said with some reluctance. "He's the London master who said he was investigating the attack on the school."

"He'd be perfect," Emily said. "Why didn't you think of him before?"

"Because…" Kip thought about how to express his concerns. "He was… putting spiritual holds on me."

Then he had to explain spiritual holds, because Emily knew a little bit about them but Malcolm knew nothing. "That seems dodgy," the Irishman said when Kip had finished.

"But it sounds like he had a good reason for it." Emily was trying hard not to touch anything in the stall, but as she gestured, her hand brushed a sooty wall. She tried to rub the black mark off it as she went on. "He couldn't very well come out and tell you that he was investigating the case. What if you were involved? Or unwittingly told the real culprit?"

"I know." Kip scratched his ears. They itched all the time now with the straw in the barn. "I don't know why I still don't quite trust him. It might be because of Master Gugin."

Emily winced. "I'm sorry you had to see that."

Kip closed his eyes and tried not to remember their lessons together and the discovery of the sorcerer dead on his couch, and failed. "He was a good man."

"We've got to pick someone," Malcolm said. "My da used to say, guaranteed way to lose on a bet is not to pick a side."

"That doesn't make any sense." Emily shook her head. "But we won't know any more sitting around here."

"I vote for this Albright fellow," Malcolm said. "The less association with our college the better, and he knows spiritual magic."

"If only Jaeger weren't so old." Emily laced her fingers together. "And I still don't know about him."

"You haven't spent time with him. I have."

"And he took your magic away. Or tried to."

"Y-yes." Kip shifted away from that subject. "But maybe Master Vendis? He knows some defensive magic."

"Aye," Malcolm said. "What if we asked both of them? You bring Albright and I'll bring Vendis, and that way if one of them isn't right, we've still got the other."

"I like that idea." Emily's tone indicated that the discussion was over.

"Listen," Kip said. "Tell Coppy that I'll see him again soon."

After that, the only thing left was to wait. Alice came to visit two other nights, and Kip quite enjoyed those evenings. In the back of his mind, he held out a faint hope that if he succeeded in apprehending Master Windsor (who in his mind had become definitely the architect of the attack), he would be returned to the college and celebrated so much that Thomas Cartwright could not help but renew his daughter's engagement. In soberer moments, alone, he remembered that the engagement had already been broken and re-made once, and that if they succeeded in engaging Alice to a fox from Boston, they would not soon break that commitment.

It didn't escape his mind that after this ordeal with Windsor was over, he would still have to make a decision about independence, one he felt less and less sure about. He wanted to have a long talk with Coppy about it to get the perspective of someone who'd grown up on the Isle but also seen New Cambridge. And he missed the otter's warmth of body and spirit, here in his cold ruined barn.

The Monday morning after Kip was expelled, he was awoken by a loud rapping on the outside of his stall. "Penfold?"

"Master Albright?" He scrambled to his feet, brushing dust from his clothes and tail. "How—what are you doing here?"

"Cott has been quite the nuisance." The silver-haired sorcerer looked up and around the stall. He wore his black robes and held a purple bundle in one arm. "Heavens, I know his workshop was not the most comfortable, but surely it was better than this?"

"I've been expelled," Kip said. He pointed to the blackened marks on the wood. "One of my classmates abducted my betrothed and was going to kill her. And me. So I set a fire to save her from him. Also," he reflected, "I summoned a demon to track him, which I did not realize was forbidden. Master Cross said nothing about it, nor did you." He lifted his nose in as much of a challenge as he dared.

Albright stroked his beard. "We could have asked if you had permission, but your use of your demon was eminently responsible, so the question seemed unnecessary. Unsupervised summoning is forbidden, but allowances can be made. Of course, they need not be made if expulsion was desired for other reasons as well."

"So," Kip said, "you haven't been told? By Patris—Headmaster Patris?"

"I wouldn't be told in any case," Master Albright said. "But Cott has not been told, or if he was, he did not understand the import of the information."

"How could he not understand?"

Master Albright shook his head. "Cott receives a letter saying you are no longer a student, he thinks to himself, 'oh, Penfold has gone to great lengths so he doesn't have to come back and see me,' for example."

"Did he?"

The old sorcerer held up his hand. "I provide an example. For all I know, no letter was sent. Cott came to me and said very peevishly that the only apprentice he'd ever enjoyed teaching had been taken away from him."

Kip blinked at the unexpected compliment, and Albright smiled. "Indeed. As I'd met you, he nagged me for three days until I agreed to come find you. I must confess, I did not expect you to be living in a ruined barn."

"Necessity is the mother of invention."

Albright's smile widened. "I appreciate a classical education. Nevertheless. If you have been expelled from Prince George's—"

"Sir," Kip broke in, "do you think if I were to apply to King's College, that…"

He trailed off at the fading of Albright's smile. "Unofficially, between Cott and myself you would certainly be welcome. But officially, were you to apply, almost certainly Patris would be consulted, and I imagine you know what his response would be."

"He might…he might be glad for me to be elsewhere." But Kip remembered, during the debate over admissions that he hadn't been supposed to hear, that Patris had said that a master of King's College had advised him against the admission of Kip and Coppy.

"The best I can do," Albright said, "is relay the information to Cott and make sure he understands that you would very much like to continue as his apprentice. He's not allowed to teach you outside of the College, but…" He shrugged his shoulders and shifted the purple bundle he carried to the other arm. "These were your apprentice robes, by the way. Cott sent them along. He thought they might entice you to return."

Kip eyed the robes. "They would have," he said. "I would have come back anyway, if I were allowed."

"Alas—"

"Listen." Kip held up his paws. "Listen. I think—you're investigating the attack—I think I know who did it."

What was left of Albright's smile vanished, and his face took on a wide-eyed intent stare. "How—who was responsible?"

Kip took a deep breath. "I believe it was Master Windsor."

Albright's neutral expression remained fixed. "*Master* Windsor. At Prince George's?" Kip nodded. "This is a very serious accusation."

"I know." Kip swallowed. Faced with Albright's severe visage, his evidence felt insubstantial, but he forced himself to go on. "There was a light on the sixth floor right before the attack. The office it's in is abandoned, but—but someone's been in it. And the only one it could be is Windsor."

The silver-haired sorcerer shook his head slowly back and forth. "That's not enough to take any action on."

"I know," Kip said eagerly. "We're waiting—we have a system—my friends are going to alert me when he's in the room. I was actually going to come ask you to accompany us when we go."

Albright shook his head, and Kip's heart sank, but as he was about to renew his plea, Albright said, "I find it difficult to believe that I'm agreeing to this. But any possibility—I would be remiss if I did not follow it. So yes. How will you reach me?"

"Emily knows how to get to Cott's workshop," Kip said. His heart pounded faster. "We were going to go there and find you."

"Hum. I can't think of a better way right at the moment. I will have my raven keep an eye on Cott's window so that you need only open it and signal."

Kip nodded. "Can you warn Master Cott to expect Emily as well? It might be easier for her to alert you directly without having to bring me along. She's only starting her translocational sorcery." Then he felt bad about downplaying Emily's abilities, so he added, "But she's very good at it."

"I will do that," Albright said. "If you are correct in this, Penfold…well, I can't promise anything, but you would certainly improve your case for reinstatement."

"Thank you, sir," Kip said.

And then Albright was gone. He took the purple robe with him, but left behind a greater sense of hope than Kip had had in days. Now he only had to worry about whether he was right.

CHAPTER 20: THE DEMON

The next morning, Tuesday, Kip walked out to the back of the barn to relieve himself. Something rustled behind him, probably a tree squirrel of some sort. The light morning breeze blew through the barn, bringing charcoal and no hint of what was behind him, so he cupped his ears back, and at that moment he was lifted from his feet and slammed into the wall of the barn. Stars exploded in his head. Dazed, he tried to focus on gathering magic, but a voice behind him said, "No you don't," and air rustled through his fur again—

He came to lying on his side on the ground with the sun in his eyes and a horribly familiar rank smell in his nose. Dirt stung one of his eyes, and when he tried to bring up a paw to rub it, his arm wouldn't move. Another moment and he realized that he was being held down with magic, his tongue as paralyzed as the rest of him so that while he might gather magic, he wouldn't be able to speak any spell. He couldn't even close his eyes or blink with the outer eyelids, but fortunately Farley's magic had not affected his third eyelids. Since humans didn't have them, likely Farley wouldn't have known to specify them in the immobilization. That at least provided Kip with some relief.

Farley was about, but this couldn't be him, could it? He'd been expelled and shouldn't have magic, unless…he too had made friends with Peter somehow? No, impossible.

Kip breathed in and out, willing his heart to slow. His left arm throbbed, as did the back and top of his head, but he couldn't tell whether any of them were broken or simply bruised. His trousers were still around his ankles, which might be the worst part. And though he could smell Farley, he couldn't see or hear him.

No, wait. There was the labored breathing he knew well. Kip focused. Anyone else? No, nobody he could hear. If it were only Farley, that was good and bad. Good because Kip only had to worry about one enemy (and no hostages), and bad because that enemy was Farley, and there was no Victor Adamson to talk sense into him.

That he was still paralyzed meant that Farley was somewhere paying attention to him. Maybe the waiting was part of the torture? That wasn't Farley's style, though.

Sure enough, a moment later a shadow moved across him as rustling sounded from behind. "It's awake." A scuffle and an impact in his back, the sharp pain of a kick, made worse when he couldn't twist in anticipation. "We're gonna have some fun."

Farley walked around him in a circle, aiming kicks casually, opportunistically. Kip could see trousers and a tunic, but nothing of Broadside's face. The glint of metal swung in and out of his vision. "Fun for me, that is. Lesson for you." A kick in the stomach. "See, I can do what I want. Because we *made* you." A kick to the back of Kip's head. "Made you to be servants. Work in fields, work for us." A kick aimed at his nose that scraped along his muzzle instead, sprayed dust into his other eye. "Not take our houses and take our shops." A kick to the groin that connected. Kip's stomach roiled. Another kick to the groin. "Not go learnin' magic, showin' me up. I'm better than you." A kick to the small of his back that almost rolled him over onto his stomach, but for the spell holding his arms and legs in place that kept him stationary. "An' I'm gonna show you. You can summon a demon? I got a better one. You're gonna see it and know I'm better than you. That's the last thing you'll know.

"But first I'll have my trophy." He crouched down and showed Kip the knife, holding it in front of his eyes. "Pity y'can't move. It'd be fun to see those ears go back." Farley stabbed forward and pulled the knife to one side, and a sting of pain flared at the base of Kip's ear. "But I'll take what I can get." He stood and walked around behind Kip. "Course, I can take anything now. So I'll just take what I want."

If the pain in his ear had been a sting, the pain at the base of his tail was a scream, and though Kip couldn't move his tongue, he gave voice through a guttural moan, his heart and breathing quickening. Warmth filled his head because he couldn't bring cool air over his tongue, and his vision swam. Something was pushed at the base of his tail, cold and metal, but not the knife—a mug. Farley was collecting his blood.

Then he stood and stepped over Kip. "There." A ball of russet fur dropped in front of Kip's nose. It took a moment for him to recognize his tail. "It'll do nice on my wall, wherever I'm sent, an' it'll remind me why I'm sent there. Because some shit-footed vermin told lies and got me kicked out." Farley stepped forward and knelt, and the point of the knife settled between Kip's legs. "I could take this, too," he said in a low voice, pushing the point into the skin. "Prob'ly should. But I don't want this filthy thing on my wall, and you won't have the use of it anyway in a few minutes."

Kip held his breath until the pressure vanished. The pain from his severed tail spread, but he fought against it. Must keep a clear head, he told himself as Farley stood. Wait for an opening, any opening. "Think you're so clever," Farley said. "I learned to keep one spell going while casting another. Very handy if you want to keep some animal still and quiet while you fetch the trapper to do for it. You and your demons. I got a second-level demon and it's going to eat you from the inside out." He laughed. "Or maybe something else. Adamson was right, I got not so much imagination, but I hear demons got plenty. I'll let it decide what to do."

Nikolon had only been able to cause him an itch. Could a second-level demon really kill him? It could at least stab him, and oh God the pain in his tail throbbed and threatened to consume him. He fought to keep his senses. What were his options? Kip couldn't gather magic because Farley would see it, and without magic, all he could hope for was that today was the day Windsor took Coppy to the sixth floor and Emily came looking for him.

And he had to stay alert in case Farley's control wavered while he was casting this other spell. Kip could hold a simple spell while casting another, but it was hard to keep perfect control of both. If Farley had cast a binding, he was out of luck, but he had to hope for the best.

Farley put the cup to his lips and drank, then spoke his magic-gathering words and began the summoning. Kip listened for the demon name and was surprised when he heard Farley call, "Giroloka." The name was familiar, though he couldn't remember where he'd seen it.

An explosion of the tingle of magic in Kip's nose made his eyes water as the demon took shape between them, a writhing nest of serpents of all colors and sizes that extended up past Kip's field of vision. Farley spoke the binding spell. "Giroloka, I am your master," Farley said. "I order you to destroy that creature in the most entertaining way you can."

Idiot, Kip thought, he hasn't even learned how to order demons around. But that would be small solace to Kip if he were killed along with Farley. He couldn't stop panting, the loss of blood making him even more lightheaded, but he decided that with his paws behind his back he might as well risk gathering magic now.

It was more difficult than he'd imagined to find the right state of mind. The snakes in front of him hissed and writhed, though their attention was focused on Farley rather than on him. A deep voice said, "*Are* you my master?"

"Yes!" Farley's voice wavered. "I—I summoned you. I bound you!"

"Bound?" The voice came from some ten feet above Kip's head. It shook his bones with its deep rumble. "Ah. You mean this little trifle."

No sound came, but Farley backed up five feet in the matter of a second. He recited the first syllables of the binding spell again.

The voice said, "No," simply and patiently, and Farley's words cut off.

At the same moment, Kip's muzzle flew open and his tongue lolled out onto the dirt. He sat, bringing another shock of pain, and then struggled to his feet, wiping the dirt from his eyes and mouth. The nest of snakes, he now saw, was only the lower base upon which rested a giant man's torso, naked, white tinged with blue. His hair, too, gleamed white as frost in the sunlight. He was so large that Kip could see nothing of Farley beyond him.

"Tell me, little man, where you learned my name."

"O'Brien!" Farley screamed as though the word was flesh being torn from him. "O'Brien!"

Kip backed up, still reaching for magic, and there it was, like cool water over his parched tongue, flowing up and into him. His arms glowed and his mind cleared.

"Where is this O'Brien? Ah, I see."

An unbound demon could wreak terrible havoc on the world, not to mention Malcolm in particular. Kip reached around to the wound where his tail had been and then brought his bloody fingers to his mouth. With that taste, he called for more and more magic, and the magic came.

"And now, *master*, I hope you find this entertaining."

This scream of Farley's had no words. It was followed by a mad dash into the brush and then a crash.

Kip couldn't focus on that. The words of the dismissal spell hung before him. The demon was called Giroloka. He spoke the first few syllables, building it carefully in his mind. He would not get a second chance, he was sure.

Giroloka remained facing away from Kip. There was a rush of air and then Malcolm's voice saying, "—Carswell's mother is at the—" He stopped and cried out. "Good Jesus, Mary, and Joseph, what—"

Giroloka spoke. "You should know better than to give my name to untrained idiots. There, for a start."

Malcolm cried out again, but in surprise rather than pain. Kip whined through his nose and spoke the last of the spell and then the demon's name: "Giroloka."

Now it turned toward him, and he was reminded of the pictures of Old Man Winter in children's primers, except that Giroloka's bluish-white face bore a nasty smile that made Old Man Winter look downright paternal. "Ah, another stripling," he said, struggling against the spell. Kip put both paws out toward him and gritted his teeth.

"But," Giroloka said, and cold wind swirled around Kip. Frost bit his ears and crept into his nostrils. He pushed his magic against the demon's as the cold seized his bones. But the spell was cast now, and all that remained was Kip pitting his will against the demon's.

He wavered at first. Giroloka was strong, so strong. How could he hope to subdue it? But then Malcolm's face swam into his mind. Malcolm was right here, and the demon had done something to him but not killed him yet. Kip's spell was all that stood between Malcolm and death.

Once it had finished with Malcolm, it would turn to New Cambridge. Alice and her family, all the Calatians, Saul's parents. And then the College: Emily. Coppy.

In the end, it was Malcolm, Emily, and most of all Coppy that set iron to Kip's will. He would not allow Giroloka to maim or kill them, and if he was the sole bulwark between this unbound power and their lives, he would hold or die trying. And slowly, that will gained ground, grinding the demon's presence inward. Giroloka's deep voice chilled him, filled him with its reverberation. "I've not...finished...my..."

Kip contained the demon's presence within the dismissal spell and bore down, and the presence howled in his mind, battering him, and then— vanished. The unnatural cold disappeared with him, to be replaced by the natural January cold but also the warmth of the sun. Kip staggered forward as though he'd been pushing physically against something, and someone rushed forward to catch him. Emily's scent filled his nose over the tang of blood still in his mouth. "That was incredible," she said.

"Exhausting." Kip leaned on her more than he wanted to. "That was—a fourth level demon."

"Fourth? Are you sure?" Then she looked toward the brush, and her breath caught. "Malcolm."

Kip looked up. Their friend was shuffling slowly toward them, arms outstretched, looking perfectly healthy except that where his eyes should have been, unbroken skin stretched from his forehead to his cheek. "I can hear you two," he said. "Tell me, is it as bad as it feels?"

Emily let go of Kip and ran to Malcolm, taking his arm and peering into his face. "Good Lord. Why did he do this to you?"

"Suspect it was because I gave his name to Broadside there. Well, not exactly 'gave.' Bragged loudly about how I was learning to summon powerful second level demons, dropped the paper there. Our boy took the bait, but..." His smile didn't waver, but his voice did. "Kip, I didn't think he'd catch you first. I'm sorry. I just thought he'd try to summon it and then make it go after you, and it'd get him instead."

"Mostly worked."

"I thought at the College, you know, there'd be other demons, other sorcerers—"

"But oh, Kip," Emily had turned to face him and her eye fell on the ground behind him. "Your lovely tail."

"Never mind that," he said. "We need to get Malcolm to Splint."

"And you too. He can put it back on. Maybe," Emily said.

"Did the demon take your tail?"

"Farley did." Kip pointed out into the brush. "And—he's out there too."

"Devil take him," Malcolm said. "But aye, Kip and I need attention. We can wait until next week for Windsor."

The pain in his tail along with all the various bruises was reasserting itself now that the demon had been banished, but Malcolm's words made Kip's heart pound again. "What?"

"They're on the sixth floor," Malcolm said. "You were right about that. But we can wait until next week. They'll go back again."

Kip bit his lip. "I don't want to wait." He had to save Coppy, and all the things Farley had said about him, about Calatians, made him even more determined to save his friend. He couldn't explain to Emily and Malcolm; they had been made by God.

"Kip," Emily said, "you're hardly at your best."

"Not to mention me."

It was unnerving to see Malcolm without eyes making pleasant conversation. "I'm fine, I'm good enough to go."

"No, Kip." Malcolm reached out and found the fox's shoulder. "We can wait."

"No." Kip gripped his friend's hand and looked into his sightless face. "Every time I've seen Coppy the last month or two, he's as much as begged me to leave the College. I always told him no. Grinda—I met some calyxes on the Isle who said that you can't tell when a sorcerer's drained enough blood to kill a calyx. That's how they died, the ones during the war. What if Windsor's bleeding Coppy every week? What if he's killing him?"

Malcolm lowered his head, but Emily nodded decisively. "You're right," she said. "And Coppy's our friend too, don't forget. If you feel you're up to it…"

"I fear I won't be much help," Malcolm said.

"It's all right." Emily kept one arm around him and reached out to grasp Kip's shoulder with the other. "If Kip has magic and we have Master Albright, then I think that will be enough."

"Master Albright being the important part," Kip said.

"I suppose you have the right of it." Malcolm dropped his hand. "All right, you two go on, and I'll find what's left of Master Broadbum. What did the demon do to him, anyway?"

"Don't know," Kip said. "I couldn't see." He clapped his paws over his muzzle at the thoughtless words, but the blind Irishman didn't lose his cheerful smile.

Emily gathered magic. "You get Malcolm and the other one up to Splint. I'll go fetch Albright. It'll be more sure if I'm by myself, and you need to be Malcolm's eyes."

Her eyes dropped to his tail, and he knew she had another motive for making him go to the Tower. There wasn't time to argue. "Go to Cott's room and wave out the window," Kip said. "Albright's raven should be watching."

"You talked to him?"

Kip nodded. "He came looking for me."

She opened her mouth to ask more questions and then shook her head. "All right. I'll bring him to the sixth floor landing."

"I'll be there," Kip said.

She stared one last long time at Malcolm's face and then vanished.

"Right," Malcolm said. "Good luck, and thanks." When Kip didn't respond, he said, "She's gone already, isn't she?"

"Aye." Kip reached out for his friend's hand. "God, Malcolm, I'm so sorry."

"For what? Brought this on myself, I have. Pigeons always come home to roost, my ma used to say, and she was right. It was a damn fool idea to give Broadside a demon name out of your bag, and a dishonest thing to do as a friend besides. But I've still got my voice and my wits, and you're alive and Emily's alive and it sounds like Farley's been punished, so there's hope yet."

Kip wiped his own eyes. "If I'd been faster with the dismissal…"

"Sure, Kip, and if wishes were horses we'd have no need of sorcerers. I hope you'll tell me all that happened—you said the bastard got to your tail, and I'm sorry about that." He squeezed Kip's paw. "I'm certain that tonight I'll be cursing my fate, but from what I saw of that demon, being struck blind is a fortunate outcome compared to what might've happened. And we've got a marvelous healer up at the College, so let's see what he can make of it."

What Kip knew of demon curses left him with very little hope. "And if I hadn't brought Farley's fight to the College—"

"Let's not stand here debating while you've got a tail to mend, and speaking of Farley, let's see what the demon's made of him."

Kip guided Malcolm toward the brush where he'd heard Farley stagger and fall, and the first clue he had of what had happened was the smell. It was Farley, but different, more earthy and less rank. And then Kip saw the form lying insensate in the leafless shrubs, and he gasped.

"You'll have to tell me," Malcolm murmured. "As unpleasant as it may be. And the more unpleasant, the better."

Kip swallowed. "We're standing before a large fellow, Farley's size, only…" He shook his head. "The demon's made him a Calatian. A marmot, I think, or—I'm not certain."

"A fat rat," Malcolm said. "Strange how the demon knew him so well after only a moment's acquaintance. All right, where's the great load? I suppose I'll have to touch him to lift him."

"I can lift you both."

"No, you can't. You've had your magic removed, remember?"

"Oh. Aye." Kip exhaled. "Thank you."

"Just be my eyes. Though if Broadside strikes a few trees on the way up, I won't hold it against you."

So they knelt beside the unconscious Calatian, and Kip put Malcolm's hand on Farley's leg. "Right," the Irishman breathed, keeping the other hand on Kip's arm. "I think I can do this."

His arms glowed orange and then he, Farley, and Kip rose into the air. "Don't forget your tail," Malcolm said, and Kip directed him over so he could pick it up. He'd held his tail so many times, but now that it was disconnected, it felt like someone else's. The feeling was worse than touching Farley, and he tried not to touch the tail with his bare paws, but he was obliged to as Malcolm lifted them higher in the air.

At the start of the flight, Malcolm dropped a cheerful comment here and there, but as they flew further, he grew quiet. Partly Kip thought this might be due to the cold wind, which brought a red sheen to his friend's cheeks, but he also thought that Malcolm was feeling acutely the limitations of flying in the dark now.

"Can we go over the back fence?" Kip wondered aloud.

"Is that where we are?"

The fox nodded, and then said, "Aye," feeling guilty. "Let's go around the front. Slowly ahead, slowly, now reach out, the fence is just ahead of you. There you are."

"I've got it," Malcolm said, and they followed it around to the front.

"Corimea!" Kip called. But there was no answer, no tingle in his nose. "Odd."

"They must dismiss and rebind him sometimes," Malcolm said.

"But to leave the gates unguarded." Kip rested his paw on the iron. "Can you imagine Patris agreeing to that?"

"I don't know," Malcolm said. "Shall we go over?"

Over the gates and to the main entrance, where Kip opened the doors and said, "Here's the Great Hall, careful now," as Malcolm felt the edge of the door and Farley's head hit it.

"Ah, pity that." The incident returned a little of Malcolm's good humor to him.

Kip closed the door behind him and looked down into the empty Hall. When the apprentices were in private lessons, apparently everyone stayed in their offices. "Burkle?" he called, but nobody answered that call either. No; Burkle had been dismissed and he didn't know the name of the new demon. But there was no tingle in his nose. "All right," he told Malcolm. "Stay here and I'll get Splint."

He ran up to the second floor—running was strange without his tail, his balance slightly off so that he kept feeling he was about to pitch forward— and found the red-haired master in his office. "Penfold?" Splint said, startled, and then jumped to his feet when he saw the severed tail Kip carried. "Good God, what's happened? Is that yours?"

Kip nodded quickly. "Farley summoned a demon, a big one. Malcolm dismissed it, but it got both of them. They're downstairs."

"And you?" Splint asked, then called, "Quetz. Quetz? Damn, what could be—Kikka!"

A raven flew in from the inner office and landed on Splint's desk. "Go get Master Patris and bring him to the Great Hall."

The raven croaked once and took off. "I know," Splint said to Kip, "but Patris will have to know, and the sooner the better."

"Maybe I should be gone before he arrives." They hurried to the stairs, and Kip looked up. "In fact…" He thrust his tail at Splint. "Take this. I need to go find Emily."

"But Penfold—"

"Take care of Malcolm! I'll be there soon." Kip hoped dearly that he was telling the truth.

CHAPTER 21: THE ANSWER

On the third floor landing, Kip nearly ran full tilt into Master Patris. The headmaster stopped, eyes so wide they appeared mostly white for a moment. "What are you doing here?" he growled.

"Go see Master Splint, he'll explain!" Kip ran up the stairs as fast as he could before the jarring in his tailbone and groin nauseated him. Then he slowed for a few steps to let his stomach calm and ran up again.

"You," Patris shouted behind him, "go follow him!"

That wasn't aimed at Kip, or if it was, Kip paid it no mind. At the fifth floor landing he heard voices, and when he rounded the next dogleg he saw Emily and Master Albright waiting for him on the sixth floor.

"Kip!" Emily said. "Did Master Splint heal—some of you?" She craned her neck so she could see that he was still missing his tail.

"I'm fine," he said, and took a breath. "You'll have to have magic prepared as I've been expelled and don't have any. Thank you for coming, Master Albright."

"I'm only doing my duty," Albright said mildly.

Footsteps sounded on the stairs below them. Emily looked past Kip and her expression darkened. "What's he doing here?"

"Headmaster Patris enjoined me to follow Penfold," Victor Adamson said, "most likely because Penfold is no longer permitted in the Tower. Good day, sir, I don't believe we've been introduced. My name is Victor Adamson and I am Headmaster Patris's apprentice."

"Get out of here," Emily snapped.

Kip held up a paw. "He'll be a valuable witness if we find what we think we find."

"Valuable?" Emily's voice rose. "Did you hear his account of Alice's kidnapping?"

"I related the facts as I saw them," Adamson said calmly, his hand still outstretched to Master Albright.

Albright watched this exchange with interest. He nodded to Adamson but did not extend his own hand. "I am Master Albright of King's College London," he said. "I have no material objection to Mister Adamson joining us. Another apprentice will be useful."

"He doesn't have any magical ability," Kip said.

"Those are just the facts as we see them." Emily looked daggers at Adamson.

The blond apprentice nodded. "It is true; however, I have applied myself in the area of magical study and I daresay knowledge will be as useful as magic."

"We're wasting time," Kip said.

"Right." Emily swept down the hallway and paused at the middle door. "This one, Kip?" When he nodded, she gathered magic as she tried the handle. "Locked."

"Can you force it?"

"With magic? Maybe."

"Allow me." Master Albright stepped between them and put his hand to the door. He murmured a spell, and the door's latch clicked open. "There we go."

They walked cautiously into a dusty room that contained only two old cots thick with cobwebs. The door to the main room stood ajar, and beyond it Kip could see a chair and bookshelf. Unlike most of the bookshelves he'd seen in Prince George's and King's College, this one was mostly empty save for a few books on the bottom shelf and some scrolls on the top one. Coppy's scent was thick in the air, as was Master Windsor's. "They were here," he said. "But they're not now. Windsor—Master Windsor—must have taken him somewhere."

He followed Emily into the main room, Albright and Adamson trailing him. Next to the chair was a small stand with stains on the wood, and a threadbare plain woven carpet occupied the middle of the floor. Kip examined the stains on the stand. "Blood," he said.

Emily had gone to the bookshelf and knelt to examine the titles of the books. "Hecataeus. Didn't Windsor ask us about that during our exams?"

"Aye." Kip and Adamson both replied, and exchanged a look. Kip went on. "I don't understand why he would work in this office, with spiritual sorcerers on either side."

Master Albright turned from examining the walls. "This office is strongly warded against spiritual magic. We are undetectable in here, and I would guess that the other inhabitants of the college have forgotten our existence while we're in this room."

"Fascinating," Victor said.

Emily shot Kip a wide-eyed look, and he knew she was remembering his "disappearing" trick. To distract from the subject, he asked, "Any clues where he might have gone?"

Master Albright cleared his throat. "If I may make a suggestion. Miss Carswell, your specialty is translocation, is it not? You have sent letters to Penfold in London, I believe?"

"Yes." She straightened.

"Translocating to the side of a person you know well is a difficult spell, but it may be our only chance. Can you bring us to your friend?"

Emily opened her mouth to respond and then looked at Kip. She nodded. "I'll do it. I'll try to bring all of you with me, but," here her eyes shifted to Adamson, "I'm still learning. I apologize if anyone is left behind."

"Bring him if you can," Kip said softly, stepping closer to her. "I know, but…he is Patris's representative and Patris is headmaster."

She scowled and put her mouth to his uninjured ear, lowering her voice to the softest of whispers. "We don't always have to obey the rules."

"In this case," Kip responded just as quietly.

Albright and Adamson watched as Emily stepped back, fixing both with an arch stare. "Very well," she said.

Her right hand, wreathed in lavender, closed firmly around Kip's wrist, and her other hand reached out to take Master Albright's. Adamson moved two steps closer and took Kip's free paw. "Will this work?" he asked.

Emily didn't favor him with a response. She breathed in to start the spell, but Master Albright spoke up. "We will have a moment of surprise. I will prepare an immobility spell that will prevent Master Windsor from casting anything. Then we can make an examination and get to the truth. I agree that this does not look good, but it does not mean that he engineered the attack on the college." His stern look swept the three apprentices, and all three nodded. "Very well. Proceed, Miss Carswell."

Emily took a breath, then spoke the words. "He's a long way," she said.

"Distance is irrelevant," Master Albright told her. "Use the connection. Do you feel it?"

"Yes." She nodded. "I—"

"—do." They were standing in a stuffy, warm room lit only by two oil lamps. Kip took in the most important sight right away: Coppy lying on a wooden bench, Windsor holding a wicked knife very like the one Farley had held, a small stand with a bronze goblet. Windsor turned toward them and Kip had a moment to think, *wait, an immobility spell won't work on a Master because they can speak the spells without moving their tongue.*

And then Master Windsor straightened and brushed down his robe. "Penfold, Miss Carswell. I expected your third to be O'Brien."

Kip nearly gathered magic then. "Coppy!" he called.

The otter turned toward Kip at the sound of his name, and his eyes widened. He struggled against cords that bound his arms to the bench; he opened his mouth but no sound came out. Kip's heart thumped against the inside of his chest and he hurried forward, but someone behind him grabbed his arm, jerking him to a halt.

"Lutris is not speaking at present," Master Windsor said. "You have them, Charles?"

Kip turned, but not fast enough to stop Master Albright from seizing his other arm and binding his wrists together behind his back. This pulled on several of his bruises and jarred his tail wound, but he ignored the flares of pain. "You were part of this all along," he snarled at Albright, furious at himself for not listening to his original doubts.

Beyond the sorcerer, Adamson was also struggling, arms behind his back, while Emily stood rigid, evidently the victim of the immobility spell Albright had prepared. "Of course I was," Albright said, "and now that it's obvious you've no need to speak it aloud."

"Did you kill Gugin?" Kip demanded.

Albright raised his eyebrows. "Aye. Thank you for discovering that he knew about the glass beads. That could have been disastrous for a number of reasons."

"He didn't know what they were. You didn't have to kill him."

"Ah, but he might have given you more of a clue—in fact, I have not ruled out the possibility that he already has—but to be honest, we have a history, he and I. To my mind, King's College is better for his demise." Albright smiled thinly.

"Penfold," Windsor said. "Attend to what I have to tell you. You as well, Adamson and Miss Carswell."

"Whyever for?" Kip snapped. "Are you about to tell me you have some greater purpose in killing a hundred of your colleagues?"

"Closer to two hundred," Windsor said calmly. "Do not neglect Prince Philip's. I took no joy in the act, but it was necessary for history. Had Hecatæus taken a few lives in the Ionian cities, thousands might have been spared a devastating war."

"Enough history, David," Albright said. "And Penfold, you owe him some courtesy. If not for his argument, you would not have a chance to survive this day."

"You killed Forrest!" Kip cried.

Master Windsor raised a hand. "If I am forced to silence you, I will, but I would prefer to concentrate my efforts on the spell we are about to cast. Let me explain the choice that lies before you. Prince George's College is about to cease to exist. You provided the clue that a spirit protected the Tower against the last attack; you will momentarily provide me the name of that spirit so I may cause my demon to remove it."

Kip opened his mouth to protest and then fell silent. He spared a glance back at Adamson, who shifted his gaze between Kip and Windsor, and Albright, who was watching Emily.

"If you choose to do this voluntarily, you and Miss Carswell and even Lutris here will miraculously survive the destruction of the College. With myself and Charles here, we will rebuild the Colleges in the colonies. I have assured Charles that you all understand that you are party to the act we are about to commit, and that this complicity will mean your silence. I should emphasize that you will be granted the opportunity to be full sorcerers at the new college, regardless of your sex or race." His gaze shifted between Kip and Emily. "Both of you have displayed the talent and passion required of sorcerers, and I feel confident that you would be a valuable part of the Empire's magical force."

"You're bribing us?" Kip asked bitterly.

"I am outlining one path you might choose," Windsor said. "Allow me to explain the other."

"You kill us all, basically," Kip said.

"After plucking the name from your mind, yes." Windsor gestured to Master Albright. "Charles has some amount of training in the spiritual arts."

"The otter's memories were my doing," Albright said with pride.

"But why are you doing this?" Kip asked, as much because he wanted to know as to buy himself time.

The answer came not from before him but from behind, in Victor Adamson's quiet voice. "Because they are loyal to the Empire," he said. "Because the revolutionaries were defeated by sorcery forty years ago, and now they will not move without Colonial sorcerers. There are some in the Royal Army, of course, but they are all under British command. The College, even a crippled College, could provide a rallying point for revolutionary sorcerers."

"Full marks, Adamson." Windsor turned back to Kip. "A protracted revolution, though sure to fail, could leave the Empire vulnerable to the Spanish in many places. By removing the lynchpin of the revolutionaries' hope, we forestall such a war before it could even begin."

"And in the process," Albright went on, "keep the Colonies where they belong for another half-century."

"You didn't have to do that. You don't have to do this." Kip tried to keep his voice under control. "Patris is loyal."

"Patris is loyal to the College," Windsor said. "Penfold, you know even less about the politics that go on between the sorcerers of the College than you do about translocational magic. I have heard the discussions, including many that people did not know I was privy to. At least a third of the sorcerers at the College favor revolution strongly, and that may not seem like many, but the remaining ones, present company excepted, do not feel a strong loyalty to the Empire. It would take very little to sway them, and I believe you were present for the recent visit by Mr. John Quincy Adams that was the first salvo in that battle. Despite Charles' and my entreaties, London seems content to rest on her reputation rather than send countervailing emissaries."

"Sir," Adamson said, "won't the Empire be vulnerable as well by destroying all of the sorcerers in the Colonies?"

"Somewhat," Windsor said. "But—"

Albright interrupted. "Not as much nor for as long as in the case of a revolution. Our spies report that the Spanish have not fully recovered from the Napoleon campaign and would likely not strike."

"As they did not after last May," Windsor said calmly, "though we were prepared for that eventuality."

This whole scene was hard for Kip to take in. He kept staring at Coppy, who was staring back at him. But what could he do? He'd shifted twice already but he couldn't find a position where he was certain that neither Albright nor Windsor could see his arms if he started to gather magic.

"Enough talk," Albright said.

"Patience, Charles." Windsor pointed to Kip with the knife. "We have asked Penfold to make a choice. He is entitled to a full explanation before making it."

"I'm not going to be the only one to choose," Kip said. "I can't speak for Emily, or Coppy. Or Adamson," he added, turning. Victor watched him impassively. Emily he couldn't read; she was still immobilized staring straight ahead.

"This is ridiculous."

"Not at all." Windsor held up a hand. "We have discussed this for years, and these youngsters should have a little bit of time in order to make their decision. Can you free Miss Carswell's arms? I believe she may indicate her preference with a raise of her left hand to join our cause, right hand to perish in the coming tragedy. Lutris, I assume, will go along with Penfold's decision."

"They should trust their superiors," Albright said, but a moment later Emily lifted her right hand defiantly, making a rude gesture at Windsor.

"Can you get Malcolm out?" Kip asked. "You said you were expecting him anyway."

Emily's hand dipped slightly. Albright looked disgusted. "For God's sake, David."

"Patience." Windsor had bent to the straps binding Coppy's arm to the bench with his knife, but only drew the point of the knife across them, not cutting them. The knife was also very close to Coppy's chest, and the threat as Windsor met Kip's eyes was obvious. "Remember that we have a fire sorcerer here, and one—in your own words—considerably more sensible than Cott."

"Cott can be made to be sensible," Albright growled. "And Penfold is not being very sensible right now." At Windsor's look, he subsided. "Yes, yes, I know. Yes, we can extract O'Brien. He'll know nothing of what happened here."

"And Adamson?" Kip asked. He was stalling, knowing he couldn't bring himself to condemn them all to death. He alone had led Coppy to the College, set him on the path that led to him being bound to the stone, and to reject Windsor's horrific bargain would be the final betrayal.

Ironically, he'd pledged loyalty to the Empire just a month ago, and now, when to renew that oath would save the lives of his friends, he no longer felt the same loyalty. It wasn't only that he would be making himself an accomplice to two dozen deaths. It was Mr. Gibbet, it was Abel's missing tail, it was Farley. It was Patris and Peter's master, who'd taken credit for his spell so that Peter no longer remembered that he had invented it. It was the town of New Cambridge, so afraid of change that they'd driven his parents out. It was the town of Peachtree, hoping for a bright new future in the wake of their own tragedy.

If they remained part of the Empire, he could bring about change, as he'd always believed, but now he saw how slowly that change might happen. What incentive would anyone have to listen to him? How many Calatians would be maimed or killed, how many would see their talents wasted, in the years it would take for his example to take root? Mr. Adams and his friends were human, yes, but they had reached out to Calatians as part of their revolution, and they were a chance to make a change now.

There had to be some other way he could save Coppy. If only he could wipe Peter's name from his mind, or be sure neither Albright nor Windsor would see him gathering magic…if he could pull the magic into himself, then he could bring fire to his aid again.

"Everyone here is included," Windsor said impatiently.

Kip squeezed his arms as tightly behind him as he could. Breathing, trying not to betray his action, he gathered magic, trying to go slowly. It came up easily, and from the sensation, he knew his arms were showing the first flickers of a glow.

Adamson came up to stand beside Kip. "Sir," he said, "I will happily join your cause. I have always been loyal to the Empire."

He pressed very close to Kip's left side, annoying the fox until he realized that Adamson was shielding his arms from view of the sorcerers. He turned to his right—

At that moment, Windsor drove the knife into Coppy's arm. The otter arched his back, but Windsor held the knife firmly in place. Blood spilled out around the blade into the waiting cup. "I estimate that you now have about one minute to make your decision, Penfold. When I have enough blood I will cast the spell," he said. "If you haven't given us the name by that time then Charles will take it. So, will you condemn Lutris—and yourself— to death? Or will you stand on the proper side of history and become a sorcerer of the greatest empire known to man?"

Before Kip could respond, or Windsor could finish, Coppy pushed his arm sharply up into the knife. Windsor sprang back with an oath, but the knife had already done its work. Rich red blood spurted out around it, splashing onto the goblet and the floor. Coppy shook his head at Kip and mouthed something, then lay his head back with a serene smile.

Kip lurched forward to try to help Coppy, though with his hands bound there was little he could do. Albright cursed, and Adamson kicked at the back of Kip's leg, not to unbalance, but to alert him. Kip snapped his head up and met Albright's eyes, full of dawning understanding.

He acted out of reflex, calling to fire, and it came joyfully to him in a matter of syllables. But when he sent it to Albright, the stout sorcerer was gone, and his fire flared in the space where he'd been, burning air but nothing else.

Windsor had dropped to his knees beside Coppy and now lifted the goblet of blood to his mouth, drinking from it. Emily lifted her glowing arms, freed from Albright's spell, and the goblet vanished. But Windsor was smiling with his bloody lips and in his eyes was the spell he was casting.

Adamson charged across the floor, but wouldn't get there in time. Emily spoke the first syllable of an incantation, but Windsor was already halfway through his. Kip didn't have to cast a spell. The fire he'd summoned came as quick as thought from the air to the black-robed master, eager for fuel to consume.

Windsor erupted in flame, as if he were a phosphorus elemental. His scream matched the flare of the fire, but cut off as the fire continued to sing in Kip's mind. His arms flailed ineffectually at his face, and then he staggered back a step. A moment later, his body fell back onto the stone floor, still burning, filling the air with the horrific scent of cooking flesh.

Don't burn the paper or wood, Kip told the fire as he ran to Coppy's side and knelt in the blood. Emily ran to the knife and bent to cut the otter's bonds. "Don't worry about that," Kip yelled, "bring him back to the Tower! Coppy. Coppy!"

Coppy's eyes, half-lidded, seemed to have sunk back into his head with that last effort. "Would've killed you," Coppy murmured. "Not body, but— but soul—couldn't let you betray yourself to save me—"

"Stay with us," Kip said, even as the stone floor they were on changed from the cabin to the familiar dusty floor of their basement. He slid his arm under his friend's head, heedless of the blood. He'd embraced Coppy before, but now the otter's head lay heavily against him, as though Coppy were asleep. With his other paw, he squeezed the knife wound, trying to staunch the flow of blood. "Stay with us, Coppy, c'mon."

Emily cursed. "Why did I—"

"I'll go get Splint," Adamson said, already halfway to the door.

"You and me," Coppy whispered, and Kip realized that those were the words he'd mouthed when he'd stabbed himself.

"You're going to be okay, we're getting Master Splint." He lowered his muzzle to Coppy's ear.

"I'm sorry, Kip," Emily said. "I know the basement best of all, I just came here—"

Kip's ears perked up. "Peter," he said, and then, into the stone. *Peter!* Coppy's head lolled in Kip's arms. *Peter!* Kip called again.

"What are you—"

"The spirit in the Tower," Kip said. "Maybe he can help, at least save Coppy's spirit…"

I am sorry, came Peter's voice in his head.

Your spell! Kip clutched his friend tighter. *Take his spirit out into the stone!*

Kip. Peter's voice was gentle. *The spirit must perform the spell himself. I cannot cast it on another.*

He couldn't hear the otter's breath anymore. "No, no," he moaned. "Not after that. Please, please stay." He searched his mind for any spell he knew, but the wounds in Coppy's arm bled less powerfully now, so much blood already lost. Emily knelt beside him, and Betty came up to them, uncharacteristically silent. "You and me," Kip whispered, but he was no longer certain the otter could hear him.

And a short time later, when Master Splint hurried to Coppy's side, the red-haired sorcerer rested one hand on the bloodstained tunic, closed his eyes, and lowered his head.

CHAPTER 22: RESOLUTION

There was Patris, after that, but even when Kip was first shown in to see him, he had little of his usual bluster, and at the sight of the fox's bloodstained tunic, subsided even more. Master Jaeger was also present, for which Kip was grateful; the only question he did not want to answer truthfully was when Patris asked how he was still able to use magic, and Jaeger stepped in at that point to say that he'd determined that what worked on a human did not work exactly the same on a Calatian. With some irritation, Patris asked whether that meant they could never prevent Calatians from using magic, and Jaeger said the matter would require further study. Kip thought to himself that the matter only concerned one person left in the world, and that thought made it difficult for him to talk for several seconds.

But all in all, Patris's questioning was restrained and polite, and at the end, when Kip stood up stiffly and prepared to leave, the headmaster cleared his throat. "Penfold," he said, and Kip stopped, one paw on the chair back. "Should you wish to re-enrol at Prince George's…"

Kip waited, perversely wanting Patris to finish speaking the invitation. The headmaster scowled, and Jaeger again stepped in. "You will be welcome."

Kip nodded and looked Patris in the eye. "I would like that very much. Thank you, sir."

"Hmph. You have rendered a service to this college, and while we must work on your restraint, someone of your ability…" He shook his head. "I would rather have you as an apprentice than an enemy."

All three of them waited, Kip for a dismissal, the other two for something he couldn't guess at. Finally Patris said, "And I am convinced that you place the welfare of this college above all else."

"I do, sir," Kip said. "And that of my friends."

He put a slight emphasis on the word, like poking at a fresh wound. The smell of Coppy's blood was all that was in his nose, Coppy's last words all that rang in his ears. Even during the interview with Patris, Kip replayed the scene in the remote cabin over and over. If only he'd been quicker; if only he'd had more confidence in gathering magic; if only Adamson had moved sooner; if only he'd trusted his first intuition about Albright's intentions or trusted Jaeger or taken any other sorcerer with them. He'd revisited every conversation he'd had with Albright and found every moment that should have made him more suspicious than he had been, had revisited everything he'd been told about Coppy and found every moment where he should have acted sooner.

He returned to the basement and walked numbly around the piles of paper. Betty chattered at him for a little while and he grew tired of the talk and dismissed her. It seemed more fitting for the basement to be cold anyway. He walked over to Coppy's bedroll and sat beside it, rubbing his eyes every so often.

Emily returned some time later. At the opening of the door, Kip reached up quickly and took Peter's journal down, not wanting to be disturbed. Indeed, Emily wandered around the basement, rubbing her arms, and then sat down near where Betty had last been.

Why can't people see me when I'm holding your journal? Kip asked the stone. *Who did this to you?*

Peter answered quickly, as though he'd been waiting for Kip to talk. *I did it to myself. I am bound to protect the Tower, and so the fewer people who know of my existence, the easier my job. But I was so surprised to see another fox, to feel the touch of your mind, that I forgot myself. And I wanted you to know me. So I lifted the spell for you.*

Why keep the journal around at all?

Someday I might be killed or released. I want my story to survive beyond that.

Kip lowered the journal and stared at Coppy's bedroll. Who was going to tell Coppy's story now? He wished he'd kept a journal, so he could have recorded all the moments they'd shared. Now those moments relied on Kip's memory, and he'd been careless with them, sure there would always be more to take the place of the ones he'd forgotten.

I'll make sure it does, he said, and then noticed that Emily was crying into her hands. Embarrassed, he put the journal back on the shelf and cleared his throat.

She stood, composing herself quickly, and wiped her face, leaving dust marks on it. "I didn't see you there," she said. "Were you doing your trick again? Is it like the spell on that room?"

"How did it go?" Kip stepped out from behind the shelves.

"Patris is more pleasant than I've ever seen him," she said. She wiped her cheek and sniffed. "I suppose tragedy and nearly losing your school and life will do that. How are you doing, Kip?"

"He was polite to me, too," Kip said. "Said I can be an apprentice again."

Emily took his paw. "Why don't we go up to the Great Hall, where it's warm?"

"Too much talking," he said, but he was very glad that she understood Betty's absence. He let her lead him up the stairs to the large, open space, where at least it didn't smell like otter.

Up at the front of the Hall, Adamson sat with Jacob Quarrel on two of the desk chairs; the others were scattered about in no particular formation. Master Brown and Master Warrington had been here when Kip had come down from Patris's office, but now they were gone. Emily pulled two chairs near the fireplace, but Kip shook his head. "Back here," he said, and walked to the two chairs farthest from the talkative elementals.

"All right." Emily came and sat with him. When he didn't talk, she took a breath. "Did you hear Adamson's account?" she started, glaring up at the front of the room. "He made out like he planned our moves. It's all the right facts but somehow he comes out the hero of it all. As if you or I couldn't do the things we did without him guiding us. It's insulting and I told Patris so."

"I heard. He can say what he likes."

"I told Patris my story and Jaeger confirmed it, for all the good that will do."

Kip curled his tail around into his lap. The place where Farley had sawn through it still ached, even though Master Splint said it was as good as new. His mind went to Abel and the Calatians on the Isle, who did not have a healer to reattach their tails, and thence to other wounds that could not be healed.

"Kip, I'm sorry. I'm so sorry."

He turned. Emily's eyes brimmed with tears again. "If I'd gone directly to Master Splint."

"No." He put his paw on her hand and she squeezed back. "He said…" He tried to clear his throat, unsuccessfully. "He said there was so much blood lost…probably he'd lost some for weeks…he said he can't replace blood. He can heal wounds, but…"

Emily nodded quickly. "I—please don't hate me for it."

"Hate you?" Kip saw for the first time that fear in her eyes, only now that she'd expressed it. "What—no. You did everything you could. If anything, I hate myself."

"No."

"If I'd been faster."

"Kip."

"If I hadn't trusted Albright. I forgot about this but—when he sent you that first letter, he said he'd never been to Prince George's. But he came to get me over Christmas. He was lying so often, and if I'd remembered—"

"Kip, stop."

She grabbed his paw. He met her eyes and saw the same pain there that he felt. When he spoke again, that pain leaked out into his words. "He saved me before I could save him." He didn't have to say that he meant Coppy, which was good because he thought the name might bring him to tears. "But even that's not true. I had so many chances to save him. He wanted to leave the Tower, wanted to go back to London. I kept pressuring him to stay. God, if I hadn't come here in the first place he never would have—"

"Stop." She squeezed his paw. "He made the decisions he wanted to make. While you were gone in London, he and Malcolm and I talked often about what we wanted to do. He always said he was amazed at how the world opened up to him now that he'd learned sorcery, all the things he could do, where back on the Isle he had a choice of hard labor or being a calyx, or both, or else he could leave and take a chance with no guarantee. He had possibilities, and you gave them to him." She sucked in a breath. "And Windsor took them away. Not you, not me. Failing to prevent is not the same as causing."

That last phrase sounded recited. Kip nodded, committing the words to memory. They would be helpful later, even if he could not appreciate them now. "How's Malcolm?"

Emily blinked, and then let out a half-laugh, half-sob. "Oh, that one. He's—he's Malcolm. Splint is trying some things, but…"

"I know," Kip said. "He told me too." And Kip had already known from Master Vendis that demon curses were not easily cured. Master Splint said that his skill lay in restoring the body to the shape it knew; demon curses made the body's new shape the one it wished to return to.

"But he's keeping his good humor. Did you go see him?"

"No. I should. I will." He stared down at his knees. "What about…?"

"That one was still asleep." Emily's voice turned cold.

Kip nodded. "I might go back to London," he said. "Work with Cott. Maybe see what I can find out about the glass beads."

"But we know who attacked the college now."

"Yes, but." He could see the glass bead in his mind, the thing that used to be Saul. "Albright said there were other reasons that he killed Gugin. There might be more to learn. And there might be more people involved, too."

"Have you heard anything about Albright?" Emily's voice kept its chill.

Kip shook his head. "I don't suppose he's gone back to London, but…if it's true that London planned all this, then maybe he has."

"Then maybe you shouldn't go back to London."

At the front of the room, Adamson left Quarrel and walked in their direction. Kip glanced up at the footsteps, but Emily didn't follow his gaze. "I was thinking about something else. You know how they were talking about Albright altering Coppy's memory?"

"Yes." Another thing he should have picked up on: Coppy's vague memory of his lessons with Windsor.

"Why do you think they didn't just change our memories?"

He shook his head. "I don't know."

"Nor do I." Adamson raised a hand and stopped about ten feet away. His eyes traveled down to Emily's hand around Kip's paw, then back up. "Sorry to interrupt."

"Go away," Emily said roughly without looking away from Kip. "I haven't the strength to pretend to be polite."

"I only wanted to say two things, but your remark has added a third, which is: how likely do you think it that Albright would have killed Windsor as soon as he'd destroyed the Tower?"

"They seemed very close," Kip said. But Albright had pretended to be many things.

Adamson spread his hands. "It's what I would have done in his place. The fewer witnesses, the better. And then of course he would have killed all of us as well. Perhaps sparing you, Kip, for your power."

"Say the rest of your piece and go." Emily now stared over Kip's shoulder at the far wall where the door to the basement was.

"Of course. The first thing is that I never properly thanked you, both of you, for saving my life. I don't feel we would have survived much past the destruction of the Tower, no matter what Master Windsor promised."

"You could have said that to Master Patris," Emily snapped.

"The second thing," Adamson went on, "is that I am really very sorry about the—"

"That's fine." Kip talked loudly over him. "Thank you. You can go."

Adamson's polite expression soured, but he bowed. He took a few steps back, half-turned, and then returned to Quarrel.

"I don't suppose Jacob likes him any better than we do," Emily said. "Have you ever known someone so ruthlessly determined to make sure you know just how intelligent he is?"

Kip shook his head. He held Emily's hand more tightly. "Would you come up to see Malcolm with me?"

They walked up to Master Splint's office and the room that served as the infirmary, where Kip had been bereft of magic. Malcolm lay in the cot closest to the window, while in one of the other cots a shape lay huddled with a blanket over him, only the tip of a narrow furred tail poking out. Kip ignored that cot and walked straight to Malcolm.

"Hello," Malcolm said. "Don't tell me. It's Kip, isn't it? The click of your claws sounds very unlike shoes, and I beg your pardon, but since you've not been using your perfumes, there's a certain scent that announces your presence. It's not unpleasant, mind you. I'm noticing smells more and more."

His eyeless face disturbed Kip, but the cheer was so characteristic of Malcolm that Kip almost felt the face were a mask, that Malcolm could pull it off any moment and have his dancing green eyes back, that he kept this appearance up only because it amused him. "It didn't seem worthwhile to put on perfume to live in a barn," Kip said.

"Ah!" Malcolm cried, and a smile broke over his face. "Do you know, I'll add that saying to my store."

The image of Malcolm saying to someone in the future, "My friend Kip used to say…" struck the fox, and he let out a laugh. Like Emily's earlier, it caught at the end, as any release of emotion was going to for a while yet, but it felt good all the same. "You may have it," he said.

Malcolm reached out in the generally correct direction of Kip's arm, and the fox obliged him by moving into his reach. Fingers closed around his fur. "Em's caught me up on what's happened," he said in a soft voice. "That Windsor deserves all he got and worse, and when I think of the times we had him right in our basement…" He squeezed Kip's arm and shook his head. "What I mean to say is, you and Em both were braver than you had any right to be. We're a bunch of children still, and you two faced down two experienced sorcerers and won."

Kip made a noise, and Malcolm went on. "At a cost, aye, a terrible one and one we won't forget, not ever. But you brought back yourself safe and Emily brought herself back too, and for that I will forever be grateful to you both." His other hand had found Emily's. "I believe that whatever we set out to do, the three of us can do. And by the three of us I mean mainly you two, but I'll be following right behind you and just you try to stop me."

Kip's eyes were wet again, and Emily's had a matching shine. He put a paw on Malcolm's chest. "Just try and leave," he said. "See how far you'll get."

Master Jaeger came looking for Kip not too long after and found him still in the infirmary room. "A word, Penfold."

Kip nodded to Emily and gave Malcolm's chest a pat, and padded out of the room, past the still-immobile Farley. The old master moved slowly, so it took them several minutes to gain the hallway, after which he stopped with one hand on the wall. "Master Splint tells me I must walk every so often," he said, "but I find it tiring." He nodded slightly in a rhythm as though singing a song in his head. A moment later, he rose half a foot off the floor. "Much better. Come."

At a brisker pace, Kip followed the floating wizard up to his office. Rather than a desk, Jaeger had in his outer office a wooden surface much like a draftsman's table, set at an angle with no chair in front of it. He passed that to drift to the other side of the outer office, where he seated himself upon a chaise longue covered in dusty pillows. Kip stood beside the drafting table and waited.

"I wished to talk to you up here," Jaeger said, "about the spirit in the walls. Barrett is in conference with Patris, so you may trust that our conversation will remain very private." He held up a wrinkled hand. "I understand that you feel you have been entrusted with this secret, so allow me to speak first, and you may confirm or deny what I have found, and after that we may proceed. Yes?"

Kip nodded. He didn't dare call out to Peter in the presence of a spiritual sorcerer, but he felt that the fox spirit was listening. Jaeger went on. "You told David Windsor that you believed a spirit to be bound in the walls."

This reminder of his mistake made the fox squeeze his eyes shut for a moment. "As was right and natural," Jaeger went on. "He was your tutor, and you felt the burden of your Selection rested with him. There was no way you could have known his intentions. He hid them successfully from experienced spiritual sorcerers. So. This belief made its way to me via various states of incredulity and curiosity, and while Barrett dismissed it as 'hedge-witch nonsense,' I thought it merited investigation. You will remember that I taught you how to break a spiritual hold. As it happened, I don't believe you had cause to use that spell, but caution is rarely wasted."

"I did use it," Kip said, "but it wasn't here, not the first time. Albright put spiritual holds on me."

"Ah. Even better." Jaeger nodded, his hand describing loose circles in the air as he went on. "For my part, I conducted a series of investigations here, along much the same lines, I believe, as David, though with an entirely different end. Obviously."

If only he'd trusted Jaeger.

"A bound spirit such as a demon might be able to stop another demon. A demon bound to stone—such a thing has been done, but the result is generally a cursed object sooner or later, because the original summoner either breaks the binding or dies, and then the demon is free to pursue its own desires while held to this earthly plane by the connection to stone. It usually results in a terrible mess, often a tragedy, and sorcerers must undertake to unbind the demon from the stone or destroy it, which takes much more power, but is a last resort when unbinding is not known or not effective." He coughed. "I beg your pardon. I have not taught in years, and perhaps I miss it."

"It's interesting," Kip said. And it gave his mind something to focus on besides the memory of blood and thick brown fur.

"Thank you. At any rate, I wondered if perhaps a demon could be bound and made to serve an ongoing order. Or, alternately, if the spirit of a person could be bound. We are enjoined from experimenting on human spirits, of course, but this was a new world and it is possible that an ambitious spiritual sorcerer might have made one or more essays and succeeded."

He stopped and looked at Kip, and Kip tried to figure out what to do next. Peter, if he was there, remained silent. "I believe," the fox said finally, "that your intentions toward whatever spirit I have been talking to are noble and honorable."

"They are," Jaeger said. "What's more, I believe that ultimately it would benefit the defense of this Tower and college for a living sorcerer—only one—to be entrusted with the secret. There could be a way, when our outer buildings are rebuilt, to extend the spirit's influence over them."

"And Prince Philip's school," Kip said. "If we knew how, we could possibly guard that school as well, when it's built."

"Yes." Master Jaeger looked around the room as though expecting the spirit to materialize.

Kip waited as well, but listened for an inner voice. *I trust him*, he said down into the stone, not caring whether Jaeger could hear him. *You may talk to him without telling him your name.*

In the other room, Blacktalon croaked. Both Kip and Jaeger ignored him.

And then, softly, *It has been a very long time.*

Jaeger's face lit with joy. "Hello," he said. "Spirit, I have so many questions for you."

"And company," Kip said. "You needn't be lonely any more."

"What shall I call you?" the old sorcerer asked the air.

Before Peter could answer, Kip remembered the first thing Peter had said to him, and his promise to Peter more recently. "He was the first Calatian sorcerer," he said. "Two hundred years before me. You can call him 'Fox.'"

EPILOGUE

I magine a maelstrom," Kip said, "but instead of water, it's formed of magic. And each of the eddies, the big ones and little ones and everything in between, each one of those is a demon."

"Are you reciting or are those your own words?" Malcolm sat cross-legged on the grass outside the Tower. It was the first day of spring that couldn't properly be called "cold," though it wouldn't be called "warm," either, not by most. But Kip had not sat out in grass with his tail lying through the blades in a long time, and Malcolm liked the sun on his face, so they were outside. There was another reason, too, that Kip could not bear to stay inside the White Tower for very long even now, two months later, even though Malcolm and Emily had moved upstairs to stay with their masters and nothing remained in the basement save for moldering papers and a clear semicircle of floor covered in char.

Malcolm's fingers rested lightly on Kip's arm; he didn't need the touch, but Kip knew it reassured him and helped ground him, and the first time after his curse that he'd touched Kip's fur he'd said with wonder that he'd never realized how wonderful and complicated a fox's fur was. Kip enjoyed the connection as well, for reasons he couldn't articulate.

"My words. Or, I suppose, a demon's words, whoever it was that Master Odden summoned months ago. I asked him. Her. It."

"Surely you can tell the difference." Even without eyes, Malcolm could raise eyebrows and turn the corner of his mouth up into a smile.

"Heh. They take whatever form they feel appropriate. Often it is female because they want to distract us, but becomes male for other reasons."

"Perhaps to distract those of us who might not be tempted by the female form."

"Perhaps," Kip said, thinking of lying next to Coppy. He thought of the otter every day, but in the last two weeks he was able to do so without his throat closing up. It felt like a betrayal that his grief should fade so quickly, but Emily and Malcolm both reminded him (often) that Coppy would not wish him to grieve. What helped him more was that they shared his grief and understood it. "In any case, you won't have to worry on that score."

"What if she attempts other methods of seduction?" Malcolm asked. "I'm missing my eyes, but all the rest of my body is in perfect working order."

"You've resisted Emily for months, and what demon would be the equal of her?" Kip asked.

"I'll not tell her you said that." But Malcolm laughed as he replied. "All right, I'm picturing it. What's the name I'm searching for?"

"Daravont," Kip said.

"Daravont, Daravont, where might you be?" Malcolm gathered magic, and as his arms glowed orange, he spoke the summoning spell. Kip prepared a binding in case Malcolm needed it, but this time, too, there was no need. The spell cast out like a wide net, and came back empty.

"I thought I had something that time," Malcolm said. "I was closer, I know it."

"Ready for me to summon Nikolon yet?" Kip asked.

"Not yet. It's only my second lesson, and I'm getting it already. I don't know what I'd ask a demon, after all; I've never summoned something." He breathed, arranged his legs to provide a more stable base, but did not gather magic again. "Give me a minute to think on what I did."

"Of course." Kip had gotten used to verbalizing more often when around Malcolm. He leaned back on his elbows and watched the clouds move across the blue sky. "How are Emily's meetings going?"

"Well enough. Since you were here last, Patris has shaken hands with Mr. J. Q. Adams. It was a momentous occasion. And she's brought four women from Boston this time. They'll be a majority before you know it. What do you hear from London?"

Kip shook his head. "Nothing. I still haven't heard back from the headmaster, not since I told him about what happened. Nobody else seems to know anything about Albright being gone. There was that Lord Castlereagh fellow he worked for, but that was a long time ago and I'm hesitant to go spy on the London government." Cott, of course, took very little interest in any of it except to ask whether they had found the name of the demon among

Windsor's possessions. They had not, and so he considered their task undone and insisted that they keep at it, though Kip learned quickly that that was mostly an excuse to keep teaching him fire sorcery. Kip, however, pursued the investigation on his own initiative. Coppy had died in the course of it, and he would not allow that death to be meaningless.

"You might have to before long," Malcolm said, and Kip knew what he meant without having to ask.

He'd forced himself to return to the cabin when Emily took Master Patris there, to confront the thing he'd done. Emily was the one who couldn't stand to look at Windsor's charred body; Kip smelled the blood in the room and the anger rose in him again, setting his ears back and bringing a snarl to his muzzle, and if Windsor had been magically resurrected, he would have incinerated him again, and Albright too, given the chance. Patris had regarded the body with curious dispassion, though he had given Kip a look of respect afterwards. His display of emotion came when he picked up the lone paper on the plain wooden table and scanned it. His brow darkened and he pushed the paper into a pocket of his robe, but not before both Kip and Emily had seen a large, elaborate wax seal that Emily later said bore a crown.

The cottage was in Australia, Patris had determined, a land recently discovered and home only to a small trading port fifty miles from where the cottage had been built. He would not allow anyone else to visit it, and made Kip and Emily swear to bring nobody else there.

Malcolm broke into Kip's reverie. "Mr. Adams says they will send their demands to London in the coming month. It would be best for you to return here permanently before that."

"I hate leaving the Calatians," Kip said. "Dotta wants to hear more stories of—of Coppy, and every time I have to leave it tears at me. Abel has only introduced me to a third of the Isle so far. And he was going to take me—or let me take him—up to Bath. It's supposed to be outside Bath that the Calatians were created, and nearby, Birk, is where they held the council that declared us people."

"Oh?" Malcolm leaned forward. "Do you make pilgrimages there?"

Kip took a new shoot of grass in his fingers and broke it, rubbing it between his pads. "No. We honor our past but we dedicate ourselves to our future. So they think there will be war?"

"They hope not."

"There'd be no need to call me home if they thought there would be peace."

"Sharp like a fox," Malcolm said. "Aye. Mr. Adams is an idealist, and even he says, 'If King George has a change of heart,' or 'if we can convince enough ministers,' which sounds to me like, 'if we can jump high enough we can catch those clouds,' aye?"

"Aye." Kip closed his eyes and sighed toward the future. He would be called to fight, of course; that was what fire sorcerers did. Fire was for destruction and fear. He wondered whether he would meet Cott on the battlefield one day.

"Might I remind you," Malcolm broke into his reverie, "that you promised to tell me what you found in the library after our lesson, and here it is many minutes following the lesson and you've still not told me."

Kip cracked an eye open and smiled. "You haven't summoned a demon, have you?"

The Irishman tapped Kip's arm. "The lesson is the teacher's work; the learning is the student's. I'll master it in time, sure enough, but for now I want to hear what you've found."

"I'd hoped to wait until Emily was back, but…" The fox looked toward the Tower.

"She's in her element, making plans with all those sorcerers and politicians. I don't want to wait hours for those meetings to be over."

"All right, all right." Kip smiled. With the permission of Headmaster Cross, Kip had visited the Royal Library. Five times he'd wandered with a librarian through the dusty shelves, telling the young man everything he remembered from Gugin's memory. On the fifth visit, the librarian had found a book that felt familiar, and Kip spent two hours reading through its pages until he found what he'd been looking for.

Here on the grass, nobody else was within earshot, and the tingle of demon presence did not sting his nose. So he rummaged in his bag and pulled out a piece of paper.

"I hope you're not planning to taunt me with written words," Malcolm said.

"If you'd summoned the demon, you could have it read them," Kip told him with a smile, and then went on to read. "I copied this out of the book. I don't know how much help it will be. The book is actually a transcription of a text recovered from Egypt off a scroll or something, or maybe carved on a wall and recopied, and the story is second or third-hand."

"Get on with it," Malcolm said amiably.

"All right. So. 'Then Setka perceived from his position overlooking the temple that the Phoenician sorcerer Azmelqart raised his arms and from the temple erupted great gouts of flame as though the interior had been coated in pitch and set alight with a hundred torches at once. But the flames subsided before Setka could let out his breath. And then the Phoenicians marched into the temple and emerged holding their trophies held aloft, small crystals that Azmelqart caused to be set in his helmet, saying that the glass contained the spirits of his vanquished foes. And thus did the Temple of Isis at Tarsis meet its end.'"

Malcolm waited until Kip replaced the paper in his bag. "That's all?"

"That's all about the beads. There's a little more about Azmelqart. He was killed in a shipwreck that may or may not have been an attack on him or might have just been a storm. Unless someone claimed responsibility for stuff like that, in those days, you never knew. And sometimes people claimed responsibility when they were later proven to not be responsible, so, you know."

"He sounds like the sort of person for whom drowning in a storm was getting off easy."

"Quite." Kip exhaled. "I don't know where to go from here. Obviously he knew the name of the demon, so I suppose I shall have to search for his records. If Albright was worried enough about this to kill Gugin, there must be more to it than a horrible old story. Maybe there are records somewhere else in the world. Headmaster Cross told me that Albright spent a year studying in Egypt, so perhaps I need to go there."

"Maybe Azmelqart was the demon?"

"I thought of that." The fox thought back to the hours poring over old books. "But this Setka, or whoever was telling his story, he knew the name of the sorcerer. We keep demon names so secret, why would they broadcast theirs?" He shook his head. "The Phoenicians—a lot of these old cultures— they made heroes of their sorcerers. Azmelqart isn't one of the better known ones but he fits the type."

"Become a star history student, you have."

Kip snorted. "Try spending days reading through old accounts and not learning a little something."

"Hold up." Malcolm sat up straight. "How did he summon the demon without a calyx? There were no Calatians then."

"I asked that of the librarian. He said that some cultures used to take the blood of lesser sorcerers, and others simply don't talk about it at all, so they assume they did it but were ashamed. And then in the Dark Ages, all that was lost until the Calatians came along." He had hoped that there might be an alternative to using Calatian blood, but it turned out the likely alternative was using human blood, which he doubted the sorcerers would embrace.

"Kip! Kip!"

The young female voice came from beyond the gates. Kip turned his head and saw Alice Cartwright, her slender form in a green dress, gripping the bars with her black paws. "Let me in!" she called.

The fox got to his feet. "I'll be right back," he told Malcolm, sliding his arm out from his friend's fingers.

The peppermint tingle in his nose grew stronger the closer he got to the gates. He addressed the air. "Halla. She's a guest of mine. You may open the gates."

The demon didn't appear, as Corimea usually had, but the gates swung open. "Hallo," Kip said as Alice rushed forward. "Has your father found another engagement?"

"Never mind father," she said. "I want to marry you. I'm fifteen now and you're a fox and a hero, and there's no reason we shouldn't be married. Father's gotten three responses and he's written back to them even though I've told him not to, so that's his worry."

"I'm not saying no, but we'll have to work it out with him." Alice had grown since January, it seemed; her head now came up to his chest, and as he put an arm around her shoulders, she hugged him back, but pushed away again.

"That's not why I came up here. Look!"

She said something in a sing-songy voice. It took Kip a moment to recognize Farley's magic-gathering chant, sounding as lovely as Alice made it, but when he did, his eyes widened.

Turquoise sparkles danced along Alice's paws. Her eyes shone as she looked up at Kip. "What do I do now?"

ACKNOWLEDGMENTS

This book, like the previous one, has been some seven years in the making, because it was originally conceived as a single story. Unlike the first book, *The Demon and the Fox* has changed significantly from its original conception.

Instrumental in the re-imagining of this story have been my fellow Unreliable Narrators: Ryan Campbell, David Cowan, and Watts Martin, whose advice has been helpful in most of my writing over the last decade; my fellow Comets: Alisa Alering, Don Allmon, M. Milks, Kodi Scheer, Dayna Smith, Brooke Wonders, and Becky Wright, who helped plot out what this story became; Malcolm Cross, who is always available to talk about 19th century London and the inhabitants therein; and Jim Worrad, who provided helpful comments on an early draft. The encouragement of everyone who read and appreciated *The Tower and the Fox* also helped me greatly in putting this book together.

Once again, I am delighted with Laura Garabedian's fantastic artwork both on the cover and at the head of each chapter. And Mark and Grant from Argyll again deserve thanks for their help and for believing in this series.

And of course, Mark, Jack, and Kobalt are an integral part of every book I write. Without their love and support, this would be a much harder journey.

ABOUT THE AUTHOR

Tim Susman started a novel in college and didn't finish one until almost twenty years later. In that time, he earned a degree in Zoology, worked with Jane Goodall, co-founded Sofawolf Press, and moved to California. Since finishing Common and Precious, he has attended Clarion in 2011 (arooo to my Narwolves!) and published short stories in Apex, Lightspeed, and ROAR, among others. Under the name Kyell Gold, he has published multiple novels and won several awards for his furry fiction. You can find out more about his stories at *timsusman.wordpress.com* and *www.kyellgold.com*.

ABOUT THE ARTIST

Laura is an illustrator of weird and whimsical work primarily of a fantastical bent. Her weapons of choice when assaulting her canvas include watercolors, ink, oil, or pencil, and her subject matter is as widely varied as walking trees, bleeding flowers, or dancing gryphons.

The niece of an illustrator, Laura grew up knowing that art was in her blood and took every opportunity to decorate her schoolwork, clothes, and skin with drawings, but was torn between Veterinary school or a career in the arts. Laura's current work often attempts to bridge that gap, incorporating her love of animals and anatomy into every piece that she creates.

Nestled near the Rocky Mountains, Laura draws inspiration from the inspiring vistas, her goofy noodle-dragons, Isis and Baku, the small plot of land that she is curating for vegetables, and the local wildlife.

www.ingramcontent.com/pod-product-compliance
Lightning Source LLC
Chambersburg PA
CBHW051533260626
47170CB00003B/915